We'd Know
BY THEN

First published in the United States of America April 2022 by Lake Country Press & Reviews

Cataloging-in-Publication Data is on file with the Library of Congress.

ISBN 978-1-7377679-6-1 (paperback) 978-1-7377679-7-8 (e-book)

Author website: https://www.kirstenbohling.com

Publisher website: http://www.lakecountrypress.com

Proofreading: Rachel Talavera of Yours Truly Book Services

Cover: Emily's World of Design

Formatting: Dawn Lucous of Yours Truly Book Services

Lake Country Press & Reviews

For Fay May.

Thank you for teaching me everything, but especially the love of reading.

QUOTE

"His grief he will not forget; but it will not darken his heart, it will teach him wisdom."

—J.R.R. Tolkien

PLAYLIST

Check out the music behind the book on Spotify.

Chapter 1

*F*lying was barely tolerable at the best of times. With cantankerous flight attendants, mediocre food, and a cramped feeling that was hard to shake until long after the landing gear hit the tarmac, it wasn't something many looked forward to. Everything leading up to flight 1202 to Chicago that day was worse than usual.

Brighton Evans was *late*, practically flying past every suited-up business person and unaccompanied minor. She dashed towards her gate like Macaulay Culkin on Christmas Eve, every second ticking away faster than the last.

It was late afternoon, and John F. Kennedy airport was a seething mass of humanity, filled to the brim with a mixed cacophony of sound. It echoed across the tile all around her—from the shrieks of a metal detector at the security checkpoint to the distant melody of a guitarist-for-hire noodling away for tips down the terminal.

The muffled voice of a gate attendant warbled overhead as she flew over scuffed linoleum, sliding to a breathless halt at the gate. Her red hair stuck to her face as her brown eyes roved over the LED board behind the counter.

"Delayed?"

The gate attendant gave her a tempered smile. "Our apologies. The weather in Houston delayed the departure of Flight 1202. It shouldn't be too long, ma'am. Feel free to peruse any of the shops or restaurants within the terminal while you wait."

Brighton wanted to argue but knew it was no use. She grumbled, tugging her yellow satchel over the shoulder of her bright turquoise blouse as she clenched her jaw. "Where's the nearest bar?"

If she couldn't drink herself numb on a plane, then she might as well prep accordingly and bide her time with a proper drink—one not in a miniature bottle fifty-thousand feet up in the air.

The attendant looked her up and down, customer service smile frozen upon her face. Brighton wondered if she had *The Glimpse*, thinking it was *almost* pointless dressing in bright colors when the rest of the world saw things in black and white. The overly polite woman was swathed in red and blue. Brighton could tell by looking, a designer with the sight selected the uniform.

"Down four gates to your left." She motioned over Brighton's shoulder with a two-fingered point.

"Fantastic." Brighton flashed an exasperated smile, spinning on her heel to search over the sea of passengers.

A woman on a mission, Brighton powered through the busy Friday travelers with a friendly smile here, a nod there, eager to get to the swanky-looking bar tucked behind a cool slate facade.

The designer in her was pleased by the sight, sure it was constructed to help passengers forget they were *i*nside an airport. A few small details transported them for an hour to a quiet corner of a Spanish veranda, made to ease aches and pains before setting off on their destination.

Brighton rounded the corner, holding up a single finger to show the host she was on her own as Judy Garland crooned *Over the Rainbow* from inside her bag. "Hello?"

"Where are you?" The slightly warbled voice of her best friend, Andi, came through the other end. "It sounds like you're at Wrigley."

Brighton glanced up at the sign. "Um . . . El Deseo del Corazón."

"You're not at the airport?" Andi sounded annoyed. "You're going to miss your flight."

"Am not."

"Don't argue. Timeliness and lies were never your strong suit. It's best not to try."

"I swear, I wasn't *that* late. I'm here. My flight's delayed a couple hours." Brighton smiled to herself, sliding onto a stool at the bar.

"But you *were* late, right?"

Brighton let out a titter of laughter, slipping her bag on a hook beneath the bar. The bartender caught her eye and gave her a nod to say, '*What's your poison?*'

"Mezcal Negroni, please," she whisper-shouted over Andi.

"Are you getting drunk?" Andi interjected.

"Maybe a little. I've got the time." Brighton crossed one royal blue trouser leg over the other, pressing her elbows on gleaming mahogany. Out of the corner of her eye, she spotted a man beside her and suppressed a shiver. With a swallow, she trained her gaze to the coaster in front of her. "What's up?"

"Oh, I wanted to tell you my cousin called again. I think I might finally take him up on that blind date he's been begging me to go on with his friend. Eli, I think?"

"You sound *so* optimistic about it," Brighton snickered, smiling gratefully at the bartender when he placed a coupe glass on the coaster and filled it to the brim with a fragrant, orange concoction. "Why bother going on a blind date at all? Isn't there, like, some website where people could compare soul marks and get it over with?"

Brighton practically heard Andi roll her eyes. "Okay,

designer-lady. You get right on that. You know full well there are alternatives to soulmates. Not like you're one to talk about shopping around, Bee. Besides, dating is *fun!* Just because *you* find the soulmate search scary doesn't mean the rest of us plebs can't partake."

"I don't think it's scary. Things are *fine* the way they are, thank you very much." Brighton took a sip of her drink. Her finger found the coaster, trailing around the yellow and blue lettering on the cardboard, sneaking a quick glance at the man out of the corner of her eye.

He was *broad*. Brighton wondered how he wasn't taking up all the space in the room. Tall, maybe. He certainly had a good head over her, even sitting down. There was a shadow of scruff along an impossibly square jaw and the slightest glimpse of a dimple when he smiled to himself. No, when he smiled *at her*.

"*Fuck.*" Brighton panicked, tearing her gaze back to the coaster when he turned her way.

"What is it?" Andi asked, pressing pause on the blind date talk.

"Nothing." Brighton's cheeks were blindingly hot. She wanted to blame the tequila, but with only a sip beneath her belt, she knew it had been because of him—because she got caught looking. Brighton shouldn't have been so obvious, drawing the attention of the stranger she had no intention of making much small talk with. Maybe she could stay on the phone and avoid it, entirely.

"What if he's *him*?"

"Who?" Brighton pressed her knuckles against her face. Maybe that would take away the burn.

"*My date*. What if he's *the one*?" Andi was adorably optimistic, and Brighton couldn't help but smile, even though her mind went through the statistical likelihood it'd *actually* happen.

"That'd be pretty awesome." She felt a rush of happiness for her friend. "Maybe he is, and you two will get married and have babies and, and, and . . ."

"Brighton, don't be jealous," Andi teased. "We'll get you married off to a *good* guy before you know it."

Brighton laughed, rolling the idea over in her head. It wasn't half bad and probably the only foolhardy wish she let herself hang onto, more than eager to have the same kind of happiness her parents did. For the briefest moment, Brighton let herself entertain the thought.

She imagined herself in a white gown, radiant like all brides ought to be. Her heart flipped when she conjured the image of a kiss that'd send her spinning or the curling of tiny pink fingers around hers—*true happiness.*

Her stomach gave a nauseating lurch, and the image of a perfect life she'd constructed ripped to shreds in a flash of red and blue lights. An ambulance in the driveway or a suitcase by the door—reasons and fears to hold herself back.

Brighton summoned a smile, pushing the grim thought away to humor Andi. "Oh yeah? Who am I gonna find to marry me?"

A distant buzz filtered through the background. "Shit, sorry, Bee. Takeout's here. I gotta go."

Brighton pulled the phone from her ear when the line went dead, swearing to herself with a laugh when she realized her roommate had hung up on her. "*Rude.*"

Without her excuse to avoid small talk with the stranger beside her, Brighton locked onto a scuff on the bar. Maybe, if she stared long enough, it would become a more interesting sight than the tall drink of water beside her.

It didn't stop *him* from looking, though.

Brighton felt his eyes on her, and no matter how she tried, she couldn't stare at the bar any longer. But, when dark brown met blue, she wished she kept her eyes down.

His mouth quirked up at the corner, breaking the silence

with a crisp, unmistakably British accent. "Fancy meeting you here."

Brighton held his gaze a second, maybe more. She couldn't help it, too caught up in a color somewhere more between a stormy sea and the tranquil waters of a Caribbean cay than merely *blue.*

After a slow blink and a whispered sigh that came out of nowhere, Brighton pursed her lips and looked into her coupe glass. "No."

Sure, it was a little blunt, but the stranger didn't seem put off in the slightest when his grin grew, and he leaned a little closer. Brighton lifted the bright, tangerine-colored drink to her lips, questioning if she'd said no to him . . . *or to herself.*

Taking a sip of the sweet, smokey cocktail, Brighton tried in vain to shake the want—*the need*—to meet his eye again. Though, maybe another look wouldn't hurt.

"I could give you a ring now if you'd like." His voice broke through her thoughts.

Brighton tried to keep her face passive, staring into her glass and answering with more bite than she meant. *"Excuse me?"*

His handsome face bent into an exaggerated frown. "That's not a very nice way to speak to your future husband. Here I was, thinking our love was *true.*"

If Brighton ever wondered what Mezcal felt like up her nose, the question was answered when she coughed into her drink. *That* deep voice shouldn't be talking about him and *her* like they were anything but strangers.

No, it wasn't deep. It was a grumbling rumble of thunder on the horizon, bringing with it the promise of a summer storm. One Brighton would happily stand in for hours until she was drenched from the inside out.

Jesus Christ, get ahold of yourself. He is just a man in a bar.

"I don't even know you." Brighton barely spared him a

glance, willing away the heat in her cheeks as she swallowed down another gulp of her cocktail.

"See, I disagree." His brows—strong and bold because, *of course,* they were—puckered as he gave her a crooked smile. "I can't shake this feeling like I've seen you before."

"I sincerely doubt it." Brighton turned back to her drink. His broad shoulders bounced with a silent chuckle like he knew she was running through a list in her mind.

Dark hair. Was it curly? Blue eyes. Impeccably dressed. Coordinated colors. Accent. British Superman.

An amused smile pulled at the corner of her mouth when she rolled his words over in her mind. If she'd met someone like him before, Brighton *certainly* would have remembered.

"Why's that so hard to believe?"

She gave in to her curiosity and cast him another sidelong gaze. "Do you propose marriage to all the girls you meet in airport bars?"

He laughed—a lovely, rich sound that rumbled around in his chest—and shook his head. "Just the exceptionally lovely ones who have loud telephone conversations in public places. How about you? Immune to a bit of British charm, are we?"

"Oh, you *admit it!*" Brighton couldn't help but really, genuinely smile.

"You caught me," he chuffed, holding his palms up in mock surrender. He lifted a pint of tawny beer to his lips and took a deep drink. "Drowning your sorrows for any particular reason?"

"Oh, you know." Brighton shrugged with a glance down at the suede fuchsia of her shoes before looking back at him. "It's a typical Friday afternoon. I come to the airport *just* for the Happy Hour deals. You?"

"Same, same . . ." His gaze fell to the gathering carbonation around the edge of his glass with a dramatically heavy sigh.

"No, but seriously." Brighton looked over the man sitting

beside her, impossibly intrigued as she took in the details of his navy suit.

Expertly tailored to his broad shoulders, it had incredible attention to detail Brighton hadn't often seen—complete with a crimson-trimmed pocket square and a matching tie pulled loose. The top button was undone, leaving just enough room to give a glimpse of chest hair beneath his crisp white shirt.

"You come here often?" Brighton couldn't help but laugh at the corny, stereotypical nature of her joke, but he met her with a chuckle of his own which instantly set her at ease. "I mean it as a compliment. You don't sound like you're from around here."

"I'm not." He bobbed his head with another heart-shattering smile, using two long fingers to lift the pint of beer to his lips for a quick sip. "I was in the city for a quick blip for work. You?"

"Same. Interior design."

"Ah, I see. Curtains and tile and such?"

Brighton let out an exasperated laugh. She didn't know why she cared. They'd never see each other ever again. Why did it matter if the handsome stranger knew the specifics?

"More like . . . spatial planning and compiling specification packages. Furniture, textiles, tiles . . . you name it. I'm a commercial interior designer. It's a bit more complicated than picking out throw pillows and paintings. I was sent out to a design center Downtown to find fabric selections for a large order we have coming in locally. It's important for them to be cohesive, and I . . . I've got a bit of an eye for it." Brighton smiled, unsure why she kept her colorful sight to herself. She took another drink, letting the spiciness of the Mescal coat her tongue and stoke the budding, delightful heat in her chest. "How about you?"

"I've just made my way up from Boston. Revenge for the tea

party you lot had and such." He loosed another musical chuckle.

Brighton was *sure* he had to know precisely what kind of effect he had on those around him. Still, as she watched how he fiddled with the cufflink in his sleeve or held the rim of his glass, she started to wonder if—by chance—he wasn't *too* aware of himself in the most endearing way.

Perhaps, the one affecting someone was *her* on him.

It was odd—her random encounter with a stranger at an airport bar. Usually, Brighton would try and keep to herself. Sure, she was confident enough to wear the brightest colors in her everyday life and wear them well, but she was absolute shit at small talk.

Talking with him, though . . . was *easy*.

They lingered there at the bar, shuffling through different subjects like they'd done it their whole lives. His voice was so warm. It summoned the ghost of a permanent smile that played on Brighton's lips while he moved his hands around, conducting every phrase like a maestro with his baton. And when he listened, Brighton could tell he *listened*, taking in each word with a look of quiet awe.

Silences were filled with an energy of such ease, she almost hesitated to break whatever strange spell they cast. Her oddly persistent need to take in as much information about him while she had the chance kept the silences short.

She learned he worked in sports marketing and, like her, found himself away from home frequently for work. They talked about music and discovered a shared fondness for The Smiths and Twenty One Pilots. Brighton listened intently while he went on an elegantly put soliloquy of why Taylor Swift—in his opinion—was so wonderful. Brighton laughed, and he looked so adorably cross, she found herself immediately saving *Folklore* to her list with a promise to listen to the album on her flight.

Time was cruel, catching up with them as quickly as they'd fallen into an uncomplicated cadence. The garbled voice of a gate attendant came overhead as it had done for what felt like a thousand times in the period they'd sat there, only this time—it was calling for her.

He was the first to break the spell, drawing up the sleeve of his long-discarded suit jacket with a grumble. "That's my cue."

Brighton pulled her bag from the hook by her knee, sliding from her stool as she tugged it over her shoulder. "Yeah, me too."

He held her gaze as he rose to his feet. Brighton smiled up at him, heart somersaulting when she realized how *tall* he was. Her eyes darted between his, focusing on a freckle of brown tucked into the bright blue—mesmerized when they crinkled at the edges with another one of his memorable smiles.

Brighton broke the wondrous study of his eyes to glance at his proffered hand.

"It was lovely meeting you, Colour Girl."

Colour Girl...

Brighton's heart stuttered—could he *see* her? She looked up at his handsome face, down to his hand, and back. Her fingers ached to reach out and touch him for even a single moment—all her fears forgotten. But, when she began to move, the gate attendant interrupted on the overhead speaker again.

"I—" Brighton breathed, looking over her shoulder towards her gate. "*Same*. Good luck with your travels back to Krypton, Kal El."

His smile faltered. "What?"

Brighton stepped back, cheeks burning as she motioned toward him.

"You know, 'cause you have the whole ... *super* vibe goin' on ... I ...." With each word and every inch she pulled herself away, the more she wished a fissure would open in the floor and swallow her whole. "You know what? Never-mind. It was really nice meeting you, too."

Before Brighton could come up with some ridiculous reason to linger, she offered him one last smile and headed toward her gate.

Brighton's smile had to be contagious, practically buzzing through her entire body, from her arms down to her fingertips. Nothing could bother her. All the stereotypical things she—and everyone else—hated about traveling weren't even a blip on her radar.

The gate attendant—practically star-spangled like it was the Fourth of July with the surliest face Brighton had ever seen—plucked a radio from an unseen spot behind the counter, announcing boarding was about to begin.

As usual, the mass of humanity surged forward like a gaggle of tweenagers at a Backstreet Boys convention, pushing against her back as they tried to make their way toward the front.

Brighton pulled her bag up with a chuckle, her smile a seemingly permanent fixture, regardless of the rude passengers around her—a smile that only grew when she met a familiar gaze on the other side of the gate's waiting area.

Her cheeks grew hot all over again when the mystery man's eyes drifted away before snapping back, his own brilliant grin on display. They shared a look . . . then another . . . and another before Brighton was ushered to an expectant attendant with an impatient hand waiting for the barcode on her phone—too distracted by the fact that he might be on the same flight to notice it was her turn.

Brighton's stomach fluttered as she walked down the jetway, and a sliver of hope bloomed that Chicago might be his destination, but she squashed the thought. Her analytical side ticked off a handful of reasons why a man who worked in sports marketing might travel to a city with *five* major teams.

Fate had nothing to do with it.

It didn't stop Brighton from searching for him once she was settled comfortably in Business Class with a laughably small bottle of Bombay Sapphire in her hand.

As the miles ticked away on the display in the seatback in front of her, Brighton tried to focus on her book, lucky enough to have a bit of extra legroom so she could cross one cobalt leg over the other and lean against the wall while she cracked open the worn pages of *North and South*. She tried to lose herself with Margaret Hale and Mister Thornton. Still, since the woman beside her—a sweet old bird in her sixties—kept finding brand new, less than fascinating topics to talk to her about, Brighton was repeatedly torn away.

Typically, the act would be one that bothered her, along with all the other annoyances of air travel, but Brighton found a particular head of dark hair a few rows ahead in First Class that drew away any ounce of indignation.

The flight started to tick a series of boxes, one after the other, of everything that could go wrong with any frequent traveler. Somewhere in Brighton's radius, someone took off their shoes, the seat in front of her remained reclined the entire trip, and six rows back, a baby wailed.

"Me too, kid. Me too," Brighton whispered, her heart going out for the poor mother.

Through it all—even upon her return from a horrifying smell coming from the cramped confines of the lavatory, Brighton's smile was permanently etched on her face.

Why, though? Beyond an electric conversation she initially tried to avoid, there was nothing to write home about. Still, every word exchanged lingered in her mind, etched so deeply, Brighton was sure he would remain there, forever.

Brighton's doubt seeped in. The colorful little girl of her memory, the one who was hopelessly optimistic about finding her soulmate one day, was pushed to the side as the realist Brighton poked holes in her hopes and dreams.

Her smile faded the more she thought about it. What on Earth would make her believe there would be any chance she'd see him again? Even if she did . . . what then? It didn't change anything in her life. It didn't change the pain she feared.

She'd gone her entire life without the same kind of feeling others had. Most found their soulmates in more conventional ways—walking down the sidewalk or sitting across the aisle on a Subway ride, when the grey curtain was lifted, and they found their soulmate on the other side.

Brighton didn't have any recollection of her "moment" at all. Hell, she could have met the eyes of another baby in the maternity ward or toddling around the park with a dandelion in hand and caught *The Glimpse.*

Of course, she'd been lucky enough to live her life in color, but not lucky enough to remember when or *who.*

Where in the hell would Superman fit in with all that? Even then . . . even if he did . . . *if they did* . . . it would only end in pain. It always did. The safest bet was the best bet, and hanging distant hopes and dreams on a stranger wasn't something Brighton could—or wanted to—afford.

After a few hours, the plane touched down in Chicago, jostling all the passengers like crayons being shaken around in their yellow box. Brighton pocketed her book, rolling her eyes when the *entire* cabin stood in a mass exodus from the jet when the overhead chime rang to signify their arrival at the gate.

By the time the rows began to empty out, Brighton found an empty First Class with no handsome stranger in sight. As she strode down the narrow aisle, she decided it was probably for the best.

It didn't stop the confounding, bitter taste of disappointment on her tongue, seeping in with each step of her pink stilettos.

The long, sweeping corridors of O'Hare were quieter than

the usual hustle and bustle, allowing each step of the lingering passengers to echo high above in the glass arches overhead.

Brighton smiled, thinking how it would only be a couple months before the white beams would be hung with a brilliant crimson and green garland, taking her straight back to her childhood when she'd sit curled up between her parents to watch Home Alone. The memory felt like it happened yesterday, where—desperate not to be alone—Brighton begged her mom not to ever, ever, ever leave her behind, *ever*.

She carried a solitary, involuntary tear from the corner of her eye as she passed through the security checkpoint, heading toward the escalator to take her to the baggage claim.

"You alright, Colour Girl?"

Fingers mere inches from the escalator's moving rail, Brighton stopped, the same wild flush returning to her cheeks. A smile tugged at her lips when she turned and met the same blue eyes that'd caught her attention back in New York.

"Yeah . . . better, now." Brighton tugged her bottom lip between her teeth, nodding over his shoulder toward the checkpoint. "You're on the wrong side of security to be making a connection. What, do you have business with the Cubs?"

"Actually—" He further loosened his tie and took a step forward. "I do."

"*Oh*."

Reason said it was for work. Brighton wouldn't be so lucky as to have him be so close. She was *sure*, as with his other trips, this one would be temporary, too.

The pair stepped toward the escalator as the charged silence stretched and Brighton's stomach churned.

"I'll be with them for a while . . . I mean, I'll be *here* for a while."

"Oh? The airport?" Brighton's dark eyes lifted to his with a flutter of hope. "Or like . . . in the city for a week or something?"

Her mind buzzed with all the reasons why it was too good to be true.

"Home team. I live here." He leaned toward her, his face serious as the warmth of his touch hovered near the small of her back. "Listen, this might seem really forward, but—seeing as we've already had a drink—I'd love to take you to dinner."

"I—" Brighton's lips parted with the ghost of the same, permanent smile, eager—*needing*—to say yes, even though her mind told her no.

"Brighton!" Another voice called out from the bottom of the escalator.

Her stomach dropped as she tore her gaze away from the mystery man and looked upon an equally well-dressed gentleman waiting for her with a bouquet of flowers.

Chapter 2

*G*ideon Baumgartner was, by all accounts, a catch.

On paper, Gideon was everything a girl could ever dream of. Successful. Handsome. Well dressed. He had an apartment on Lake Shore Drive and a dedicated indoor parking space.

Anyone would be lucky to have him, and *boy*, did Gideon know it.

Brighton met Gideon at a University of Chicago alumni dinner, and at first glance, he was memorable. Tall—a respectable six-foot-two—with a crisp, stylish suit, expertly coiffed blonde hair, a square jaw that could probably cut glass, and gorgeous green eyes.

Brighton's foolishly hopeful heart had leaped when she saw the way his ensemble was so wonderfully curated. Often, Brighton could spot someone without *The Glimpse* by how they dressed, but this guy . . . this guy knew his stuff. Maybe she was wrong about not being sold on the search for a soulmate.

Gideon came up to her first, rattling off some line that made Brighton laugh from the sheer audacity of it. He was nice enough, with an eye-catching smile and a great laugh. When

Gideon asked for her number at the end of the evening, Brighton couldn't find any reason to say no.

Brighton had been patient, eager to not seem, well—*over-eager*—texting Gideon the next afternoon.

Andi sat excitedly on the arm of the sofa beside Brighton, practically buzzing with the anticipation of what might happen next.

"Maybe he's it," Andi whisper-yelled, blue eyes wide. "Maybe this is the one. He was making eyes at you for *how long* before he came over to talk to you?"

"Attraction doesn't mean he's my soulmate. They aren't mutually exclusive," Brighton retorted, staring at Gideon's name on her screen as she absentmindedly skimmed her fingers over her hip—and the soul mark that'd been there since puberty.

Everyone's mark was unique to them—and one other person.

Brighton looked at it as an insurance policy, of sorts. Something which cemented *everything* once you found your soulmate. Still, Brighton was protective of hers, reminded at every turn about the time she showed someone too soon.

Yes, experiencing *The Glimpse* was special. *The* event. Still, many waited to expose the last little detail, the final reassurance things were *exactly* as right as they seemed. It was the only piece of hope Brighton let herself have. A reminder that, if she was brave enough to leap, Brighton could have *The Glimpse* for real.

A soul mark's arrival was a big deal—up there with developing body parts and every other awkward part of puberty.

The girls in the locker room compared them as they appeared—a swirling knot behind an ear or the pair of arrows on the inner corner of a wrist. Brighton had been excited about the possibility, then.

For a while, as she awaited her mark to appear, Brighton

wondered if *The Glimpse* was the end to the gifts she'd be given; mark-less with the sight, but doomed to be without her other half.

As a young teenager, Brighton feared the mark would never show up. But on one, ironically grey day in March, a few days away from her fourteenth birthday, Brighton felt a sting on her hip. The arrival of a soul mark wasn't noticeable at first, but like the itch of a mosquito bite or holding your hand above a flame for too long, the subtle tingle gave way to something *more*.

She'd been tucked in her favorite chair at the front of the house, where the warmth of the afternoon sun would kiss her skin and leave her signature freckles behind.

Caught up in the excitement of the feeling, Brighton threw down her book and bolted to the bathroom. She gathered the hem of her shirt in breathless wonder, brushing her fingers over the mark with a quiet gasp and a trembling hand.

Still pink around the edges like a fresh tattoo, Brighton's mark was unique with only one match in the entire world —*theirs*—and she *finally* had one of her own; one Brighton's mother warned her to look at as a deeply personal thing, that showing someone was as precious as a first kiss or losing your virginity.

A nervous smile tugged at the corners of Brighton's mouth as she traced her way over each angular line. Her brows pressed together as she took in every crook and bend, committing the shape to memory.

A pair of triangles—more akin to mountains—sat balanced on each other's tip, mirror images of the other, precariously hanging by a single point. Brighton, still a little unsure after going without her mark for so long, idly wondered what her soulmate—whoever they are, *wherever* they are—thought once the mark had been revealed . . . what could it mean? Could they be looking for her, too?

As always, Brighton embraced the gift she was given and

lived her life as colorfully as she could. Even after a sliver of cynicism when it came to love and soulmates surfaced before she finished high school, the hope remained.

At seventeen, Brighton's life shifted and shattered. Right then, she decided when her dad, Thomas, lost the sight, there wasn't any point in holding out for a soulmate if it was only going to end in pain.

With age and a bit of wisdom beneath her belt, Brighton decided there was love outside *The Glimpse*. There had to be. Otherwise, what kind of sad, pathetic existence would she have? Remain rudderless until that *wow* moment?

So—while she dressed from head to toe in a brilliant, eye-catching rainbow—Brighton kept her options open.

Andi waited on bated breath when Brighton pressed send, sliding from the arm of the sofa up against her like they were reading a note from a boy in high school. Like any good friend, she furiously shook her when a floating trio of dots popped up to signify Gideon was responding.

Brighton was surprised it happened so quickly, but as she got to know him better, something she learned about Gideon was that his phone was never far away. Oftentimes, he fed off the high of the *ping* coming from his pocket.

Gideon was charming, and the conversation was going *far better* than Brighton imagined it would. A smile hovered on Brighton's lips. Andi noticed it without effort, lovingly jabbing Brighton in the ribs, blue eyes wide as she hissed, "*Ask him!*"

How long have you seen it? Brighton held her breath from the moment she pressed send. Andi practically squealed when the dots popped up almost immediately.

Seen what?

"He can't be that dumb." Andi rolled her eyes. "Then again, he's hot as fuck, so really . . . he might be."

"Alexandria!"

"What?" She coiled a dark brown curl around her finger

with a smirk. "I'm just calling it like I see it. Don't worry too much, Brighton. Have you seen how he dresses? There's no way he *doesn't* have *The Glimpse*."

"He could have someone like me who helps him. There's a lot of different ways to live around having *The Grey* when it comes to color, Andi." Brighton tugged on the perfectly paired cardigan to Andi's top, giving her a smile before typing out a reply.

How long have you been able to see color? I'm sorry to assume, but your outfit went together so nicely. Brighton bit her lip, sure she went on for too long. *I'm sure you get that all the time.*

The read receipt lingered on 'delivered' for a few seconds before flipping to 'read', staying there for what felt like forever. Eventually, the trio of floating dots in their happy little bubble popped up, disappeared, then sprang up once more.

Brighton felt like she was on the edge of something, that the universe was about to plop a beautiful gift in her lap. All she had to do was be a little more patient, then things would finally start happening. Brighton's hope grew higher by the second, fueled by the anxious excitement of the fabulously colorful Gideon Baumgartner keeping her waiting.

No one was quite as nervous as Andi, though, holding onto Brighton's arms with a white-knuckle grip. Her blue eyes watched every subtle movement in the redhead's face, especially when a message finally swooshed in.

Brighton's jaw clenched, forcing a smile through the disappointment when she met Andi's gaze. "It's fine. *I'm fine.*"

"Brighton . . ." Andi's voice was soft. Brighton slipped away, rising to her feet before they could make a bigger deal than it was.

"No, really." Brighton shook her head, taking a deep, stuttering breath; forcing an even wider smile. "Who needs a soulmate anyway? I'm *good*. It's for the best."

It *was* for the best; Brighton knew it. Her stomach twisted with disappointment anyway, spurred on by the memory of a different boy. It further leached away the brief flush of excitement Brighton entertained for Gideon.

"They're out there. I mean, I haven't met mine, and Gideon *seems* nice enough." Andi dutifully injected her with a sliver of sunshine.

"Yeah, that's true." Brighton glanced down at her phone, reading and re-reading the text Gideon sent.

I appreciate that, but I have a friend who works at Marshall Fields who helps make sure everything goes together nicely. Brighton laughed in appreciation of the sliver of humility, feeling the hint of a genuine smile come to her lips when she continued reading. *She costs me a pretty penny (personal shopper) but it's worth it. It caught your attention, didn't it? What do you think . . . dinner on Friday?*

Brighton thought of that other boy—of Jesse Butler.

After high school, in the shadow of her mom's death and her dad's lost *sight,* Brighton thought for sure she'd never be convinced the love of a soulmate was worth the risk of what *might* happen.

That is, until a few weeks into her Freshman year at University of Chicago when Brighton met *him.*

Like Brighton, Jesse had the sight since he was too young to know better. They even grew up going to the same summer camp—a coincidence Brighton shouldn't have let herself believe. But, butterflies, dimples, and halfway decent kissing had Brighton *convinced.*

Jesse was the one.

Night after night, twisted up in a twin-sized top bunk in his dorm room, Jesse implored Brighton to show him. He whispered sweet promises, singing the song of forever—*if only they knew for sure.*

Brighton's body said one thing, her mind another. With one cheap beer buzz, Brighton lowered the hem of her underwear and gave him a glimpse. It wasn't long after that Jesse showed her his own—a perfect match to the reflected mountains burned into her skin.

Brighton was *happy*, thrilled beyond belief that the search was over—until the ink of Jesse's forged soul mark ran at a summer pool party a few months later.

The betrayal was enough to cement Brighton's doubt that, maybe, a true happy ending wasn't meant for her. She'd have to settle for something safer.

After a lot of thought and some insistence from Andi she should at least *try*, Brighton took Gideon up on the offer. She liked Gideon, that much she could admit, even if he wasn't *him*. Brighton didn't need that. Companionship, though. Someone to fight off lonely nights and cold winters. Maybe Brighton could like him enough for that.

Gideon was charming, respectful, and dare Brighton say . . . *fun* their first night out. He'd walked her to her door, fingers brushing against hers as they strode down the hall side by side.

Brighton surprised herself when her fingers ached to hold Gideon's hand. She surprised herself further when Gideon tucked a strand of hair behind her ear and kissed her good-night—and Brighton happily let him.

"I love brunettes," Gideon murmured, green eyes alight. Brighton let the detail go, just once.

It felt natural enough, only a tiny bit forced, but Brighton anticipated it would take a little bit of effort.

Gideon wasn't her soulmate; Brighton knew it. Loneliness was still a thing, and she really, *genuinely* liked him. Together, they were content going against the grain. He was enough, and she could be happy with him if she tried. If *they* tried.

Oh, Brighton tried.

They worked well together, carried along by the same mutual flicker of attraction when they first met. It was a comfortable kind of familiarity.

Brighton knew the cadence of Gideon's voice, how he liked his coffee, and his mother's name (though, she *still* hadn't met her). Brighton was happy.

Gideon was a creature of habit, frequently caught up in himself, but it was one Brighton happily saw break the more time they spent together. Sweet and giving—more-so with things rather than time—Gideon showered Brighton with the kind of attention any girl would be ecstatic about.

Three years. Three years of beautiful dinners, luxurious trips, and . . . *other* kinds of fun they'd happily got caught up in. Brighton was *happy*.

Happy enough.

Who needs a soulmate, anyway?

Brighton's eyes flickered back and forth with the passing streetlights on I-90, settled comfortably in the passenger seat of the sleek Mercedes. Music thrummed in the background as she coiled a ribbon of auburn hair around her finger.

Happy enough. Brighton looked over her shoulder to Gideon. The man who'd been kind enough to fetch her from the airport at the last minute, who'd been thoughtful enough to bring Brighton a colorful bouquet of flowers he knew she'd appreciate, the man Brighton dedicated the last three years of her life to.

Brighton should have had her eye on Gideon. Instead, all she could think about was the sour bloom of disappointment when she came down the escalator and remembered he existed at all.

It would likely be etched in Brighton's memory forever, too caught up in the moment when a stranger asked her to dinner.

Everything about him stole her attention without effort. From the low rumble of his voice dipped in textbook Londoner, to the way he leaned in with a twinkle in his eye and a small, hopeful smile, the mystery man was unforgettable.

So wrapped up in it—in him—Brighton found herself nearly dumbfounded when *her boyfriend* called her name.

Brighton murmured her apologies to the mystery man, pink-faced as her heart hammered away like a runaway train. Brighton hopped right back into some sense of routine, looping her fingers through Gideon's as they walked to the baggage claim, hoping it would center her and remind her of what life looked like—that *Gideon* was what her life looked like.

Still, though, while Brighton waited at the carousel and Gideon went to fetch the car, Brighton could *feel* him—the one who called her *Colour Girl*. Their eyes met once . . . then again . . . and again. Each time, Brighton's stomach twisted, and eyes stung when she saw the clench of his jaw and sag of his broad shoulders.

Brighton's mind reeled with questions about him and their encounter long after she and Gideon made their way downtown Chicago, rolling through neat lines of glittering skyscrapers down Wabash.

It was one of Brighton's favorite places to be—like walking through the night sky with the smattering of lit-up, neon-bespeckled windows telling the world that inside, there were delicious, late-night snacks to be had.

So many questions—*all* the questions—floated through Brighton's mind, but only one came out when she spied the street sign as they passed through a brightly lit intersection.

"Where are we going?" Brighton asked.

"Home," Gideon answered, oh so casually leaned back in his seat with a single hand balanced at the top of the steering wheel. He glanced towards her with a smile. When the green of the stoplight got caught up in the emerald of his eyes, Brighton was reminded of one of the many things she liked so much about him.

Brighton let out a sigh, centering herself back in reality, far away from the bar at JFK. She wiggled back in the luxurious leather, closing her eyes to the lovely hum of the German-made car.

"Oh, good." Brighton opened her eyes, brushing her fingertips over Gideon's knee. "I could use a little time together. *I've missed you.*"

She did. *She had.* Two weeks was a long time, and Brighton was more than eager to get back to their comfortable routine, but her disappointment bubbled back up when Gideon flipped on his blinker and turned in the opposite direction from his Downtown apartment.

"Nah, gotta pass tonight, babe." Gideon scooped up Brighton's hand, pressing a kiss to her knuckles as the excuses flowed. "I have an early meeting and a workout to get in before then."

"*Oh.*" Brighton tried not to roll her eyes; choosing instead to give things a positive spin, giving his hand a squeeze. "Will you walk me upstairs, at least?"

Gideon's face bent into a look that made the answer stupidly obvious, and Brighton ashamed for asking. "Of course I will, babe. I'm not a total monster."

"I know you're not. That's not what I was saying." Brighton sank into her seat, watching the city go by to wait out the final few minutes.

Brighton took in the brick building through the window, flinching when Gideon's door slammed shut. Her eyes found her and Andi's flat in a second, smiling at the twinkling rainbow lights hung around the edges of the glass.

Gideon tugged the door open, holding out his hand to pull Brighton from inside. Grateful for the warmth of his touch, Brighton held it like a tether, hoping it would help steady the foreign ache of her heart.

Happy enough.

They remained hand in hand as they walked up the stairs.

Brighton went ahead, keeping her eyes trained on the fuchsia of her shoes as they moved over worn, taupe carpet.

One flight, then another. As they rounded the corner to climb up the final set to the fourth floor, Gideon grumbled a complaint about walk-up apartments.

Brighton let the comment roll off her back, turning with a smile as they came to the door with a colorfully painted *4D*. Andi sketched out the flowers, and Brighton brought them to life with color, more than happy to spread a little sunshine with something so wonderfully simple. Sunshine that was lost on Gideon.

Brighton set her bag at her feet, keeping her eyes with his— silently telling herself what they had was *real* and not related to the lingering disappointment that *wouldn't* go away.

Gideon spun her suitcase around, slamming the handle down before reaching up to straighten his tie.

"Thank you for the ride home, Gid," Brighton murmured, skimming her fingertips along his sleeve with a tilt of her chin —an invitation; a wish for more.

Gideon's hands circled around Brighton's waist, pressing a light as air kiss to her lips.

Normal. It's how it felt. It was them. It was *her*.

Brighton opened her eyes. "Wanna . . . *come in*? I won't force you to stay overnight. I know how you feel about that."

Gideon tucked a strand of her auburn hair behind her ear with a tempered smile that didn't *quite* reach his eyes. "You know I'd love to, but . . ."

"But what?" Brighton balked, leaning away from the welcome tenderness of his touch. "*Gideon*, it's been two weeks. I know you've got an early morning or whatever, but . . . can you do this one thing for me? I want to spend some time with my boyfriend. *Please*."

Brighton regretted the word as soon as it slipped from her

lips. Sure, she thought it all the time, and true, it's what he was, and yet—

"*Brighton.*" Gideon stiffened, taking a step back as he looked at her like a child who was about to get a proper scolding. "We talked about that. We talked about it so many fucking times."

"Right," Brighton quipped with a frown and a nod. "I'm sorry . . . I forgot."

"It's okay, babe. I . . . I just . . ." Gideon trailed off, pawing a hand through his blond hair. "You know how I feel about *that* word."

"I do . . ." Brighton chewed her lip, lifting her beautifully bright yellow bag from the floor in time for the door to spring open and Andi to appear in the frame like a breath of fresh air.

"Brighton, you're home!" Andi flashed Brighton a broad smile, blue eyes twinkling before they shifted towards the well-dressed man beside her. ". . . *and* you brought a spare. *Gideon.*"

Brighton suppressed a giggle when her petite friend grew to the size of a giant in the span of a few seconds and a single, icy look.

Andi's quick distaste for Brighton's long-term *not*-boyfriend was no secret. Mostly dark curls and bright blue eyes, Alexandria Whitaker, made up for her lack of height in attitude. Never afraid to share her thoughts, Andi fiercely defended her friends no matter the consequence.

"Good to see you, too, Alexandria." Gideon pursed his lips, giving Andi a pinched smile before turning back to Brighton.

"Can't say the same, sorry."

Brighton cast Andi a scathing look she shrugged off with a smirk. Brighton cleared her throat, turning her full attention to Gideon when he tugged her towards him by her belt loops.

"I should get going," he murmured, pressing a quick kiss to her cheek.

Letting her touch linger against grey wool, Brighton looked up at Gideon with the same aching disappointment that still hadn't *quite* gone away. "Are you sure you don't want to come in for a bit?"

"Please say no," Andi quipped under her breath from behind them as she stepped away and left the door wide open.

Gideon carded his fingers through his hair once more, clearing his throat as he glanced inside the apartment. "I'm good, Brighton. Sorry."

"It's okay," Brighton answered, bending on her tiptoes to leave a quick kiss on Gideon's lips a split second before he stepped away.

Brighton lingered in the doorway, holding to the frame as Gideon walked down the hallway, waving as he flashed her a brilliant smile before disappearing down the stairs.

Happy enough.

Perhaps, the more Brighton said it, the more she'd believe it.

"That went well," Andi droned from the couch, perched between colorful throw pillows and a blue, fuzzy blanket.

"You think?" Brighton pulled off her jacket and toed off her shoes before flopping down beside Andi. She rolled her head against the back, meeting Andi's gaze with a bitter smile. "I forgot how weird he is about that word."

"You mean, you forgot how weird he is *in general*?"

"Andi . . ."

"I mean it!" Andi sat up and animatedly flapped her hand towards the door. "How long are you going to give your time to that douche-canoe, Brighton? You deserve so much better."

"Gee."

"I love you, Bee, but . . . you're *settling*, and you don't have to!" Andi shoved a pillow at Brighton. "You're afraid of there being another Jackson."

"Jesse."

"Whatever." Andi made a face and waved her away. "What I'm saying is . . . you're afraid of the past. Not everyone is like that, Brighton. The right person isn't going to fake a soul mark like Jasper. They aren't going to fake commitment and love like Gideon . . . and they aren't going to die like your mom. I mean, they will, but like . . . as an *older* person."

Brighton clutched the pillow to her chest, heart seizing at the thought of her parents. She pushed her mouth against the seam, blinking away the threat of tears. "What's your point?"

"My point is . . ." Andi leaned closer. "Stay open to the idea, okay? You never know what's going to happen."

Brighton thought of the mystery man before instantly banishing him from her mind. "Gideon is a good guy—a safe bet. He's not going to hurt me. It's . . . a symbiotic relationship or whatever. I don't know what to call it, but it *works*."

Silent for once, Andi gave Brighton a pointed look that said more than words.

Brighton knew she was right. The problems were there. Their journey together was paved in red flags—one thing after the other to remind her time and again Gideon wasn't her soulmate.

But Brighton was happy enough, skirting along the edge of something safe and painfully predictable as long as it meant she knew what to expect.

"Fine," Andi groaned. "He's not the *worst* person in the world. He's no Jeffery Dahmer or Ted Bundy . . . *probably* . . . but he's definitely not for you."

"I appreciate it, but you ought to cool it on the true-crime podcasts." Brighton let out a breezy laugh, leaning into her friend. "I just . . . I feel like I need something to hold onto until . . . *if* . . ." She paused as the weight of her doubt sat on the tip of her tongue.

Brighton brushed her touch over the soul mark beneath her trousers—maybe the mountains imprinted there were the ones Brighton had to climb to find *the one*.

But.

29

She was twenty-five. Successful. Committed to a handsome man who was good to her. *Happy enough.* What else was there to want? If she never stumbled across her soulmate's path, Brighton *knew* she'd be okay. More than okay. Maybe even better off; *she'd survive.* She'd be happy enough.

"What is it?" Andi nudged Brighton with her elbow. "I can read you like a book, and you've got something *big* printed right across your forehead, babe."

"It's nothing," Brighton lied, pushing the stranger from the airport to the back of her mind, spinning a web of mistruths vivid enough she could wholly believe it. "Gideon is *good.* He needs time . . . we'll get there. I know he's not my soulmate, *I know* . . . but I'm happy with him. If I don't find *them*, then so be it. I'm good. *I'm great.*"

"Mhm," Andi hummed from beside her. Brighton knew, even though she might convince herself, her best friend was a tougher sell.

Andi's face shifted from a thoughtful frown to a smile so sweet, Brighton knew in an instant she wanted something.

"What is it?" Brighton said, lifting a single, questioning brow.

"So, my cousin Cain moved to the city last year, right?"

"I recall you mentioning him more than a few times, Ands."

"Right. So." Andi sat forward with an anxious, deep breath. "He's been pestering me about meeting his 'flat mate' . . ."

Brighton laughed when Andi motioned a pair of air quotes. "Okay, and?"

"A blind date, Bee."

"So?"

"I'm shy," Andi argued.

"That's a flat-out fucking lie." Brighton laughed so hard, her cheeks ached. "But let me guess, you want me to help you pick out something to wear?"

"Not quite . . ." Andi gave her a bashful smile.

"What did you do?" Brighton stood up and backed away, less than interested in what she was *sure* Andi was about to ask her. "I don't want to be a third wheel, Alexandria."

"You won't be! You'll have company," she argued, reaching out with a pout. "I told Cain the only way I was going to agree to meet his weird backward British version of a roommate was if he came along."

Brighton let out a resigned laugh and grumble as she gathered her fuchsia stilettos from the floor. "*Fine*. But you're buying my ticket, *and* I want popcorn—the big bucket. Deal?"

Chapter 3

"*S*hit, I'm so nervous," Andi said to her reflection, twining her fingers through her dark curls to make sure they were *perfect*.

"It's going to be *fine*." Brighton rolled her eyes with a playful smile from where she leaned in the doorway. Pushing her shoulder from the frame, she stilled Andi's hands. "Stop. You're beautiful. He's going to love you."

"You say that like it's . . . *you know* . . ." Andi argued, looking back at the mirror with a frown.

Brighton wished she could convince her, but all Andi really needed was for the night to begin so she could forget she was ever nervous and enjoy herself.

It wasn't an unusual thing for Brighton's friends to request a helping hand from her colorful eye, and for Andi—Brighton was more than happy to oblige.

They'd gone shopping a couple days before, picking out a gorgeous emerald green dress spanning the line between casual and cute, pairing it with a pair of cobalt heels and a borrowed pink coat from Brighton's closet.

The color combination packed a powerful punch, one so

pleasing to the eye Brighton wished she picked the outfit for herself.

Making a mental note to find a way to combine the same gorgeous blend of color she dressed Andi in, Brighton tried to go for something a little more casual.

She'd started with a pair of eclectic heels, plucked from a dedicated wall in her closet, which looked more like lemon meringue pie than something she should wear on her feet. Brighton's collection might've been the most colorful one belonging to *anyone*. With over thirty pairs, she had shoes to spare.

Getting dressed was one of her favorite rituals. It was an art form unique to her—one Brighton took seriously.

She lifted a pair of persimmon tights from a drawer, turning on her heel to face the rainbow of a closet that'd have Cher Horowitz *totally buggin'*. Brighton selected a turquoise skirt as light as air, a navy blue camisole, and a butter yellow cardigan to pull it all together. When she gave herself a once-over in the mirror, Brighton felt like she was ready to be *seen*.

Andi fidgeted the entire ride to the north side of the city. Brighton held her hand the whole way, acting as an anchor to help steady her usually confident friend through the final moments that felt so strangely pivotal to *everything*.

Brighton tried to keep the conversation light once the pair stepped down from the platform, yelling over the noisy *clackety-clack* of the 'L' as it passed overhead.

"No, you don't understand . . ." Andi moved her hands animatedly, no matter how firmly Brighton tried to steady her by looping their arms together.

"Enlighten me," the redhead laughed as they strode up North Wabash. "I don't think you're going to convince me any further why Aaron Burr is a better example of a Slytherin than Hamilton. Ham is the best kind of snake, and you're never going to change my mind."

"Hear me out . . ." Andi paused, pursing her lips together, surely rolling over every single lyric from the legendary Broadway show in her mind to build her argument. "Every line. Every song. *All of it*. Slytherin. Moot point."

"Okay, but, the ultimate question, here. It's a tough one, so pay attention," Brighton smiled down at the way their colorfully synced shoes were so perfectly in step—like them.

"I'm ready. Hit me with it."

"Lafayette or Jefferson?"

"Not fair."

"Why?"

"What do you mean *why*?" Andi looked offended. "How *dare* you force me to choose between two nuanced, interesting characters who both happen to be played by the *sexiest* man alive?"

"*Oh*, so this is about Mister Diggs, is it?" Brighton challenged her with a wry smile, looping her arm through Andi's as they proceeded toward the movie theater they planned to meet *the* cousin and his flat mate at.

Andi let out a massive sigh. "I swear . . . I would *marry* that man."

"Stranger things have happened, I'm sure." Brighton grinned, patting her friend on the hand as they rounded the corner, mere steps from the theater with only a couple minutes to spare.

As they drew closer, though, Andi stopped dead in her tracks.

Brighton's gaze snapped to her friend, carefully cataloging even the tiniest, subtle movement of Andi's face. Her blue eyes were wide, staring with each stuttering breath and slow blink as she looked further down the sidewalk.

"Andi, what is it? What's going on?" Brighton gripped her arms, an unshakable feeling of alarm seeping through her body like a cold November drizzle.

Brighton followed Andi's gaze down the sidewalk, stomach flipping when she saw a man caught up in the same, wide-eyed stare.

"*Holy fuck.*" Andi squeezed Brighton's hand so tightly, her bones began to ache. She tore her blue eyes away from the man at the end of the block. "Bee, *I can see it.*"

"W-what?" Brighton's breath caught in her throat, mesmerized and overflowing with the purest joy that her greatest friend —*her sister*—found *The Glimpse.* She hugged Andi's face in her hands, tears of happiness brimming on her lashes as she smeared away a single, silvery tear from her friend's cheek. "What are you doing here talking to me? *Go say hello.*"

"H-he . . . *I can't.*" Andi, usually the most confident person in the room, struggled with her words.

"You can and *you will.*"

"How can I? What will I say? *'Hey, nice to meet you, looks like you're my soulmate.'*"

"Something like that," Brighton grinned, holding Andi by the shoulders as she spun her around and gave her a little push.

Brighton crossed an arm over her chest, a giddy smile across her freckled face as she absentmindedly traced her fingertip along the bottom edge of her lip. She was happy for her friend—*thrilled*, even.

The Glimpse was something rare all on its own. To witness it happening to the person, Brighton had *chosen* to love the longest was more fulfilling than she could have imagined. Now she'd have a front-row seat to everything she ever wished for Andi—and for herself, once upon a time. Maybe it would be enough to tide her over.

They'd done everything together for as long as Brighton could remember. *Everything.* Perhaps this was the next step in their journey of togetherness, the sisters-found. Maybe it was the start of where their paths would split off, bound to go in separate directions at some point in their lives.

Still, Brighton's smile remained as she stood a few steps away from the beginning of Andi's forever, faintly aware of the time as it ticked by and how close they were drawing to the start of the movie they were supposedly attending.

It was an odd little dance, but a beautiful one. There had been a lingering handshake accompanied by broad grins, all sprinkled in the wondrously dumbfounded feeling Brighton was sure they both felt now their worlds shifted in such a monumental way.

He was tall, so much taller than dainty Andi. She practically bounced on her tiptoes, chin tilted toward him as he met her halfway with a slouch of his shoulders. Dark curls were wound around her fingers, bottom lip bitten as he spoke animatedly with a wide smile and a boyish giggle so effervescent, Brighton probably could have bottled it and powered the whole city.

Brighton searched down the block, idly wondering if the man they'd encountered—*Andi's glimpse*—was the flat mate of the cousin her friend was always talking about.

What are the odds? Brighton let out a dry laugh when she realized, if he was, the cousin was either a no-show or miraculously late to the life-changing moment she'd witnessed.

Brighton shrugged when she saw how caught up Andi was, deciding to take advantage of having come as far as they did and sit through the movie, if only to give the two some privacy.

Besides, life was short and beautiful; quiet joy was rare. Sometimes it came in something as simple as seeing a movie—even on her own. It's what her mom would want her to do.

As Brighton stepped up to the box office to request a ticket, Andi bounded over to her side. "Bee, wait!"

Andi wore a contagious smile. Brighton couldn't help but return it when she met the wide, toothy grin of the man beside her. She felt somewhere between amused and delighted when Andi reached towards him, not quite touching his sleeve, but *oh*, she wanted to.

He was beautiful, and up close, Brighton could see how wonderfully fortuitous their conversation had been when he'd literally stopped Andi in her tracks.

With skin like warmed bronze, deep brown eyes, and a gorgeous head full of long, tight curls zinging every which way, Brighton understood why Andi couldn't look away. Like Andi, he'd dressed to impress, with a suit jacket over a gingham button-down and a delightfully mismatched bow tie.

"This," Andi breathed, blue eyes wide with breathless wonder as she looked him over. ". . . is Elijah Martin. Eli, this is my roommate and best friend, Brighton. She's . . . she's basically my sister."

"Lovely meeting you, Brighton." Eli grinned at her, extending his hand to shake hers, even though he could barely keep his eyes off the petite brunette beside him more than a few seconds at a time.

"So nice to meet you as well, Eli," Brighton answered, taking a mental note of the lovely lilt of his accent—unmistakably British. There was no mistaking it, he *had* to be the flat mate. Brighton looked over his shoulder on her tiptoes. "Are you on your own, or . . .?"

"Shit, sorry." Eli fished in his pocket for his cellphone, tapping at the screen with a frown etched into his handsome face. "For such a successful bloke, Cain is late to everything. He'd probably be late to his own wedding."

"Speaking of late—" Brighton circled her hands at them. "I can see there's something a little special happening here, so if you guys want to bail, I understand . . . *but—*"

"Oh, hell yes, we're going. You can't get rid of me that easy, Bee. Plus, I owe you the big bucket of popcorn, right?" Andi gave her the broadest smile. "I'm a girl who keeps her promises."

"I love that," Eli murmured, catching his soulmate's hand up in his to press a lingering kiss to her knuckles.

Andi's cheeks flushed and Brighton couldn't help but laugh at the adorably stereotypical nature of it all as love at first sight unfolded right in front of her.

"I'm sure Cain will show up, so you won't be all by your lonesome." Andi fanned her cheeks, stepping up to the box office to purchase tickets with Eli by her side.

Still without the fourth member of their party, the trio settled into their seats—Brighton happily supplied with an enormous bucket of popcorn. The lights dimmed and as the film rolled on the first of many trailers, Andi and Eli still couldn't take their eyes off each other.

The movie was an odd choice for a first date, something Andi probably did on purpose, picking something popular enough the four of them would likely enjoy it, even if the blind date didn't go exactly as planned.

Since it was quite literally the best-case scenario for Andi and Eli, Brighton found herself endlessly amused when the Marvel Studios title card fluttered up on the screen.

She popped another piece of popcorn in her mouth, peering down the row of tightly packed chairs when a series of grumbles and complaints rang out from a few seats down.

Brighton lifted her eyes in the darkness, very briefly making eye contact with the man who settled in on the other side of Eli —who was completely unaware his friend had seemingly shown up. He was too wrapped up in Andi's gaze to even look at the movie.

They made it five minutes into the opening battle before the kissing began.

Brighton let out a sigh and kept her focus on the popcorn in her lap, casually popping piece after piece into her mouth as she tried to ignore the wildly flying hands to her left. When Eli's hand blindly tangled in her hair, she groaned and shifted over a seat.

Brighton settled into her new spot, digging into her bucket

of popcorn with fresh fervor as she focused on the heroes in the movie. Popping a kernel into her mouth, she tried to ignore the *passionate* sounds coming from beside her. Was that . . . was that a soulmate thing? Was that something she would miss out on by not being open to the thought?

While things with Gideon were *fun* enough, Brighton wasn't sure if they'd ever been completely *unable* to keep their hands off each other. Her stomach twisted at the thought there might be *more*, so she fed it with a fresh handful of popcorn.

Brighton huffed when a deep chuckle of laughter rang out in the darkened theater. There was certainly nothing remotely funny happening on screen, and the sound only added to her annoyance.

Leaning forward with a glare, Brighton met a pair of blue eyes four seats down. An explosion on-screen illuminated his face in the darkness, and she recognized him in an instant. When he *winked* at her, the aggravation gave way to a blooming warmth of shock and delight.

Of all people in the entire city, Brighton looked upon the face of her mystery man from the airport—stuck in an equally awkward position. When he smiled, she couldn't help but meet him with one of her own.

Practically larger than life, he hoisted himself from his seat and vaulted his long legs over the knotted-together couple like they were nothing but air. He landed with a *thump* in the empty seat beside her; leaning so close it nearly took Brighton's breath away.

This is nothing. It has to be nothing. He isn't looking at you in any sort of way, and no . . . he doesn't smell as good as you think he does. He's only this close to you so his hair doesn't get tugged on, too. This. Is. In. Your. Head.

The warmth of his skin so close to hers on the armrest made every inch prickle as her hairs stood on end to salute him. His eyes, sparkling in the flashes of gold from the movie, darted over her every freckle. A brilliant smile unfurled across his handsome face, like a lighthouse in a storm, pulling her closer with every passing second.

Even Brighton's body betrayed her, so she fed it with more popcorn.

"Fancy meeting you here. You come here often?" He let out a deep chuckle and he stuck a thumb over his shoulder. "I'm kidding . . . but can you believe these two? Not even twenty minutes in, and they're practically biblical."

"Oh God, let's hope it doesn't get to that point while we're still sitting here," Brighton moaned, stuffing another handful into her mouth.

"I—I don't want you to get the wrong idea, but . . ." he stuttered with a bend between his brows. He searched for his words as Brighton warily chewed her snack. "Any chance you'd like to get the hell out of here before this escalates past PG-13?"

"Are you kidding me?" Brighton's dark eyes widened, mumbling over the bits of popcorn in her mouth as she peered over his shoulder at Andi and Eli. "I would love nothing more right about now. Take me away, I beg you."

"*Marvelous*," he beamed, rising with an extended hand.

It felt oddly symbolic, like Christine Daae taking the Phantom's hand, or Rey refusing Kylo Ren's. What kind of temptations awaited Brighton on the other side—would she be able to resist? Then again, what did she have to lose when there seemed so much to gain?

Brighton tucked her popcorn beneath her arm with a deep breath and slid her fingers into his palm. It was so wonderfully warm, and she could swear she felt a subtle squeeze.

He pulled her to her feet, uncaring of the other audience members around them.

Brighton's breath caught when he tugged her close in the narrow aisle, meeting her wide-eyed gaze with an unexpectedly serious look.

"I'm Cain."

"I know," Brighton murmured with a breathless smile, losing herself for a split second to the way his hand felt around hers. Her mind traveled back to the moment at the airport when he reached out to take her hand the first time, silently cursing herself for not doing it right then. "I'm Brighton."

"*I know.*" He nodded.

"Hey! Down in front, asshole!"

They both let out a series of fitful, childlike giggles. Without a second thought, Brighton spun on her heel and *ran*, holding onto Cain's hand all the while as their feet carried them from the darkened theater and into the busy Chicago street.

Brighton wasn't sure when, but Cain took the lead, towing her down the sidewalk at a delirious pace. His hand never wavered in the way he held hers as he looked over his shoulder once in a while to offer another one of his dazzling smiles.

She couldn't quite put her finger on it—the strange familiarity about it all beyond meeting him in New York. It was welcome, though, and made her *sure* he wasn't just any person at all.

It warmed Brighton's heart in a way she couldn't describe and, even though she didn't realize it then, her world suddenly became more colorful than it ever had been before.

Chapter 4

$\mathcal{B}$righton swore they ran for ages, but she wasn't tired in the slightest. Cain's smile fueled her, and with his fingers twined through hers, it was only a matter of time before their feet left the sidewalk and they took flight.

Cain led her down the block, then another. Before Brighton knew it, her eyes were alight with childlike wonder when he dragged her through a pair of double doors and found herself looking over a brilliant array of neon colors painting every corner inside.

Already blinded by color in the best way, Brighton's ears were enveloped by the slow movement of heavy bowling balls rolling against polished wood, followed by the chaotic clatter of pins tumbling down at the end of each lane. The sounds blended effortlessly against the steady beat of *Crimson and Clover* coming from a rainbow-hued jukebox.

Brighton lifted her eyes to Cain, who wore what looked like the same permanent smile etched into her face after their first meeting.

Her smile was so wide, her cheeks ached. "I had no idea this place was here. *The colors* . . . they're amazing. The rest of the city can be so—"

"Grey?" Cain answered, crossing his arms with a shrug. "It really can be, can't it? One look at you, though—" he shook his head with a slow lick of his lips, "You're the most colorful thing I've ever seen in my life."

"How long have you had the sight?" Brighton trailed after Cain as he led her up to a counter where he handed over his silver credit card with a delightfully British, *cheers mate*, to the man on the other side.

Their conversation paused as they gave their shoe sizes and, in exchange, received a pair of hilariously colorful shoes. Brighton found herself distracted by how his were *so* much larger than hers. Cain didn't miss a single beat, picking up the conversation where they left off as they stepped into their designated lane.

"Most of my life. Can't quite remember exactly when, but it's been ages. My mum was *cross* when I told her, 'cos it took *weeks* before I announced I knew what blue was. They called all sorts of people and practically hired an inspector to try and figure it out." Cain chuckled, slipping off an over-sized sneaker. "Why? How long's it been since you met him?"

"What makes you think I have?" Brighton sat down beside him and tugged a lemon-meringue heel from her persimmon hued tights. She pulled on the bowling shoes, swiftly tying them before holding them out to appraise the rainbow on her feet.

"Oh, please." Cain gave her a look. "I can take one look at you and see it's no secret you have *The Glimpse*. Plus, can't exactly forget Flower Man at the airport."

Gideon. Brighton's mind went blank with dread, remembering he was off doing God knew what, and she—she was out with another man. While innocent enough, it didn't do anything to quell the odd surge of guilt in the pit of her stomach.

She stared down at her shoes and shoved the feeling down. "He's ... actually ... *not* my soulmate."

"No?" The lilt of Cain's voice drew Brighton's eyes back to him. He balanced an elbow on his knee, brow creased, tracing a finger along his bottom lip. "I suppose two people with the sight dating isn't the strangest thing."

Brighton playfully leaped to her feet and gave her turquoise skirt a spin. "I'll have you know color exists whether or not people can see it. Which ... Gideon *can't*."

"Mm, well ... yours are too well coordinated for you *not* to have it, darling." Cain stood and strode over to palm a massive, fourteen-pound, red bowling ball. He tossed it from hand to hand like it weighed nothing at all, but Brighton was too caught up in his words to notice for long.

"You think I match?" Brighton beamed, bouncing to his side to select a yellow, *much lighter* ball from the rack. "I think I might love you for saying so. It's so nice of you, Mister ..."

"Whitaker."

"*Whitaker,*" Brighton echoed, reminded again—of all the people in the entire world—her mystery man was Andi's cousin.

How many times had she heard of Andi's fabulously posh older cousin who lived across the pond, and *how lucky* her father's brother was to live there with his beautiful wife and sons?

Brighton's mind shifted back to what he said and her smile returned.

"It's no secret how much I love color." Brighton bit her lip, picking at a loose thread in the delicate print of her turquoise skirt. "I suppose I like to dress this way because ... if ... if the reason I have *The Glimpse* is because I've met them already, then they have it too. I just ... I want to stand out so they can find me, you know? I mean, that's what I told myself when I was a kid ... before other stuff. Now, I just like it. It feels like *me*."

"Makes sense." There was a tug at the corner of Cain's mouth—the faintest of understanding smiles. "I think it feels like you, too."

Brighton practically melted, smiling softly at his back as he stepped forward and effortlessly hurled the ball down their lane, obliterating the target with a loud clangor of pin against pin. She couldn't deny how Cain's subtle swagger somehow added to his whole aura, making her heart twinge in the strangest way when he goofily spun on his toes and gave her a thumbs up.

A burst of effervescent, girlish giggles erupted from her lips —almost freeing in the way they lifted her up from the inside out.

Brighton slid across the slick floor with a laugh, meeting Cain's gaze for a moment before lifting the yellow ball from the rack. She paused in the lane, holding it to her side as a thoughtful crease formed between her brows. "You know, I've known Andi my *entire* life."

"That's a long time," Cain nodded from his seat, leaning back into the candy-colored bench as he stretched his arms along the back. He was good looking—infuriatingly, so—and *had* to be sure of it.

Brighton banished the thought, turning on her heel as she sucked in a deep breath and lifted the bowling ball. She tried her best to center it with the single dot at the tip of markers inlaid in the shining wood, but when she wound up and let it loose, it veered from the path after a few feet.

Brighton held her breath, tip-toeing backward as the yellow orb spun toward the neatly stacked pins, knocking six over. One weebled and wobbled, making her wait on bated breath before—*finally*—it relented and fell with a clatter.

She turned with a wide grin and continued. "Through *all* that time—twenty years, at the very least—Andi never mentioned her cousin was *Superman*."

Cain let out a deep laugh. "Hardly."

"See, I disagree," Brighton argued.

"Why's that?"

"As I recall, about an hour ago, you *saved me* from a very awkward situation." Brighton planted her hands on her hips with a challenging lift of her brow. "Isn't saving damsels Kal El's thing?"

"True enough, there might have been a bit of a rescue." Gaze aligned with hers, Cain stood and sauntered to Brighton's side as her ball pirouetted out the return.

He leaned down and lifted it with a single hand, reaching out to wrap his other around her waist.

Brighton's heart hammered, *oh* so aware of the sliver of space between them and the heat radiating from his chest as he guided them into the playing area.

Cain lifted Brighton's hand and settled his chin on her shoulder, and—with his arms briefly aligned with hers—he twisted her wrist with a heated whisper, *"Now try."*

Together, feet oddly in sync and his hands on her waist, Brighton sent the ball hurtling down the lane toward the remaining three pins.

Cain lingered, letting his touch rest on the swell of her hip until—with a proud *HA!* in her ear—he gave Brighton a squeeze and stepped away as he murmured, "Of all the things I'm sure you are, Brighton, a damsel isn't one of them."

Rooted to the spot, Brighton's wits came back to her after an infinitesimal moment. Breaking free of the trance, she sat beside him with a wry smile. "So, if I'm not a damsel who needs saving, then what am I?"

Brighton was impressed by her audacity and boldness. Sure, she was confident enough to wear orange with red hair, but the more she thought about it, the more she was convinced Cain brought something out in her she didn't know she had—*a better something.*

He didn't blink, answering her with a slow smile as he stalked forward. Cain held Brighton's gaze as he drew closer and closer, leaving her waiting for his answer.

Cain's blue eyes flicked to the table behind her for a split second, the spell seemingly broken by a loud clatter of a strike two lanes down. He leaned away, holding a menu he plucked from the tabletop.

"You're the girl who's going to split a pitcher of beer and a pizza with me while I kick your colorful ass at this game." Cain grinned, giving the laminated paper a wiggle with a lift of his brow. "If you're okay with losing, of course."

"Oh-*ho*." Brighton shook her head, rising to snatch the menu from his hand, giving it a quick glance. "I've barely begun, Mister Whitaker. You haven't the faintest idea what I'm capable of."

"I'm sure I haven't, but good God, if I'm not willing to find out, Brighton." Cain's voice was low and his face darkened, summoning a shiver that ricocheted down to her toes.

She brushed the feeling away, silently whispering a name over and over in her mind to remind herself who she'd committed herself to, who *certainly* wasn't the man in front of her.

She told herself she would give things with Gideon her best shot. He was enough. A safe bet. Dependable. *Reliable.* Even if he wasn't *everything.*

"The thing you're going to find out, Cain, is you clearly have been eating at the wrong places in this city." She eyed a pizza traveling by on the tray. A pale imitation of what Chicago-style pizza was meant to be, Brighton shuddered when she saw the kitchen blasphemed the whole damn thing by putting cheese *on top.* "I can't speak for the pies at this place, but the bowling and the company are all right."

"Oh, are they now?" Cain offered a roguish smile.

"Mmm—" Brighton's cheeks heated again. "So far, at least.

Plus, they have my favorite beer on tap, and you're buying, hotshot."

She poked Cain in the chest, trying *so* hard to contain her sigh when the tip of her fingers pushed against the firm, solid mass of muscle beneath his black tee. Clearing her throat, Brighton told herself Cain definitely *didn't* have a self-satisfied look on his face as she scrambled for words. "I'll pay you back by taking it easy on you. Do they . . . do they have bowling where you're from? Isn't it all polo and sipping tea with your pinkies up?"

"Most certainly." There he went again, never missing a beat as his face stayed laughably serious, and he gave his pinkie a wiggle. "It's nearly an Olympic sport, and I happen to be an expert."

"You seem to be an expert at a lot of things . . ."

"I'd be happy to show you."

True to his word, Cain happily illustrated more of his natural skill—and subsequent silliness—when it came to plowing down the pins at the end of their lane over and over again.

Cain's score racked up. By the time they reached the tenth frame, not only had he won—he blew her out of the water.

"Beginner's luck," Cain shrugged with a smirk.

Brighton downed her beer. "I'm so sure. Best two out of three?"

Except, three games became five, and one pitcher of beer became two.

The conversation was impossibly easy—*natural*—like they were falling in step with each other, and the cadence was timed to the beat of their hearts.

Their time at the bowling alley came to an end long before Brighton was ready to call it quits.

"We need to do this again," she insisted as she slapped down her rainbow-hued bowling shoes back on the counter.

Cain answered with an easy smile that lit up his entire face. "I'd love nothing more."

Brighton shivered when they stepped out into the remnants of warmth left over from the late summer heat. Autumn was right around the corner, and with it, a season of change. The world around her would shift, blooming with an unbelievable array of color that never failed to leave Brighton in quiet awe of what the universe gifted.

The lakefront air fluttered Brighton's hair, bringing with it the sweet, smokey smell of the man standing beside her. She followed the direction of the wind and found Cain quietly watching her.

"What is it?" Brighton said, caught up in the intensity of his gaze.

The breeze must have had a mind of its own—but then again, they *were* in the Windy City. It circled around them, ruffling through his dark curls, pulling one down over his forehead.

Brighton found herself drawn to it, fingertips aching to touch it and slowly tuck it back into place. Her feet took her there by their own accord, and the wind seemed to agree, giving her a push. She looked over his face, carefully collecting even the smallest gesture to commit to memory.

Cain's blue eyes danced across her face and creased his lovely brow. "It's nothing. I . . . I've got a feeling, is all."

"What kind of feeling?"

His gaze fell to their feet for a moment, chewing on his words with a slow roll of his jaw.

"I can't put my finger on it, Colour Girl." Cain skimmed his thumb over the curve of her shoulder. "But I don't think I'm ready to say goodbye just yet."

To Brighton, the solution was simple. "How about you walk me home?

Cain smiled, blue eyes tinged with something like the

aching disappointment that burned through Brighton when she remembered the man waiting for her in a high rise on Lake Shore Drive. "I'd like that very much."

Without a second thought, they fell into the comfortable cadence of their conversation, only this time, their feet were in on the party.

"I wonder what Andi and Eli are up to." Brighton glanced at her watch.

Cain gave her a scathing look. "I love the man, and she's . . . well, *you know* . . . but those are details I'd rather not think about, thank you very much."

She laughed again. "And yet, you're the one who fixed them up . . . why?"

"A feeling." Cain smiled down at her for probably the millionth time that evening. Brighton swore she'd never tire of them.

The smiles of Cain Whitaker were something Brighton could collect, storing them in a special box like precious, long-distance letters from a secret love. There, she'd keep them safe, cracking open the lid of something that held such revered treasure, it would surely light her up from the inside out.

"Do those happen often for you, these . . . *feelings*?"

"Don't tease, Brighton."

They rounded the corner, and Brighton's thoughts went back to how she felt when Andi got *The Glimpse*—the thing everyone wished for their entire life. She'd felt a heady mix between joy and her own personal dolefulness, but with Cain by her side, things felt a little less hopeless. They felt *easy,* tinged with the promise of a friendship so pure and beautiful, Brighton wondered if—with Cain in her life, with that balance —happy enough with Gideon would finally start to feel like *happy.*

The conversation shifted from topic to topic without a second thought. Brighton asked Cain what kept him busy, and he rattled off marketing jargon completely lost on her, but hooked her attention when he mentioned Cubs tickets.

"I haven't been in ages. I'm so busy," Brighton grumbled midway through a crosswalk.

"So? Bunk off."

Brighton made a face. "I don't know what that means."

A deep, throaty chuckle rumbled up through his smile as Cain shrugged. "Play hooky, Colour Girl."

"*Cain*," Brighton breathed, wondering for a moment if it was the first time she'd said his name out loud. The taste of it on her tongue felt *good*, and she resisted the urge to say it again and again and *again*. "I—"

"—have no excuses." Cain finished for her. "I'll convince you one of these days, I promise. I can be *very* charming."

Brighton laughed again. "Of that, I have no doubts."

"I had a question, though."

"Shoot."

"You said you work in commercial design, right? More than curtains and throw pillows."

"Right." Brighton's heart flipped, thrilled Cain remembered. "What's your question?"

"I see how colorful *you* are." He smiled down at her, studying her every detail. "I've been wondering . . . does any of that find its way into your projects?"

"I-I can't tell you how much it means to me that you . . . *see me* . . . but I feel like, sometimes, I'm the only one who notices."

"You're kind of hard to miss, love," Cain answered in a voice so low, it was nearly a whisper. He lingered only a moment before playfully poking her in the ribs. "Answer the bloody question."

Brighton let out a breezy laugh with a nod. "Yeah, sometimes it does, if the project calls for it."

"What are you working on now?"

"Currently? Lakeview Children's is getting an entire overhaul. It hasn't been renovated in a long time. We're adding a modern addition with a high-level focus on waiting rooms, and . . ." Brighton trailed off with a bite of her lip when she closed her eyes for a moment and imagined the face of a beautiful woman—red-haired with glittering green eyes and a doctor's signature white coat—and found herself caught up in a memory.

Their little girl is very sick, Brighton. We are here to take care of her, but who takes care of their mommies and daddies?

"It seems like it means a little more to you than *merely* designing a space, Brighton." Cain squeezed her hand, brushing a thumb over her knuckles before letting go.

"Honestly? It's probably the most colorful project of mine. I think, when it comes to design, people seem to forget; usually, kids don't see color. I imagine parents waiting by their side through all this hard shit, and . . ." Brighton paused, her heart aching at the thought. "They suffer all on their own. I want to bring a little color to their lives when I'm sure it feels like it's being seeped away by illness."

"Sounds like you're taking care of them." Cain nodded. "Doctor Evans, delivering a prescription of sunshine in a bottle, err, waiting room."

"I design other parts of the hospital, too." Brighton laughed, looking up at the street sign as they neared the corner of another block, *very* aware of the fact their time was about to come to an end the closer they got to her apartment.

"I'm sure they're equally beautiful. I'd love to see it sometime, Bee."

Her feet slowed as they rounded the end of the block. Brighton regarded him with a look of wonder and the beginnings of another smile. "I don't think anyone but Andi's ever called me that before."

Cain looked perplexed. "How come? Does . . . flower man not call you by a nickname? Bee suits you."

"No man has ever called me Bee before. It hasn't ever felt right." Brighton fiddled with the sleeve of her yellow cardigan as the cold feeling of disappointment and guilt seeped in. It held firmly until Cain stepped closer and brushed his fingers over hers.

"Does it feel right, now?"

Brighton met his eyes, searching the facets of color inside them. With flecks of silver and a freckle of brown on one side, they—like Cain—were so much more than what they appeared at first glance. She'd noticed him then, too, no matter how hard she tried to put him off at the airport.

Fate seemed to have other ideas.

Did it feel right? Brighton couldn't argue with the way she felt, no matter how confusing. Still, worries tugged at her, reminding her of all the hurt in her rearview mirror.

No, Cain wasn't a safe bet. He was a risk—another hurt waiting to happen if Brighton let herself get too close.

If anything, at least they could be friends, right? Maybe Brighton would allow herself that much. She could still be happy enough with Gideon . . . and maybe a little more. Maybe meeting Cain was what she needed to fill the void. Already, it felt that way, and her heart was full—spurred on by the fire of their instantaneous connection, no matter how complicated everything else was. No matter how complicated *she* was.

Brighton stepped around Cain, smiling softly when he fell into step beside her. She fidgeted with a ribbon of her hair. "I like it."

"And?" Cain pressed.

"You could call me anything, and I'm sure I'd like it. Color Girl. Bee. *Brighton*." She hesitated with a wavering smile threatening to bloom like a springtime rose across her face when she remembered the way her name sounded on Cain's tongue. She might *more* than like it. Her stomach twisted, reminding herself that she couldn't. She *shouldn't*.

"I'll remember that." Cain nodded, glancing down at her as they made their way further down the block.

Brighton's steps slowed in the shadow of a red brick building, pointing over her shoulder. "This is me."

Cain stuffed his hands in his pockets, brows pleated together. "Do you mind if I walk you up?"

"I'd like that." Brighton tugged her keys from her bag as she walked up the concrete stairs. They jingled in her hand—a collection of custom-made rainbows as unique as the lock they opened.

Cain followed close behind. For the first time the entire evening, they were quiet, with only the sounds of their steps on the faded carpet and the distant thump of someone's music playing down the hall to keep them company.

Up one flight, then another, and another. Brighton turned and met Cain's eyes more times than she could count. Each time, he gave her a smile that made her stomach do somersaults.

Why did it feel like a date—and why was she stupid enough to let herself believe it?

Gideon. Gideon is a good guy. You are happy enough. Don't mess it up for a man you just met.

They walked down the fourth-floor hallway, close enough their shoulders brushed. Each time, Brighton's heart skip a beat. Sure, she and Cain were quiet, but the silence was comfortable, without the need to fill it with chatter.

She stepped slower and slower the closer they came to 4D, and once they came to the door, Brighton felt the urge to leave and find a way to give them more time.

Leaning her shoulder against the frame, Brighton lifted her eyes to look over his handsome face—from the stubborn curl falling over his forehead again to his square jaw and dimpled chin, making her hands ache to reach out and press her fingertip against it.

Cain stepped into the frame opposite her and traced his fingers over the swirl of colorful flowers around the apartment number with a smile. "Did you do this?"

"Andi helped. She drew, I colored. It's our thing and works out well for us." Brighton bit her lip. "Though, *now* . . . she's got herself a soulmate and will be able to do that for herself, now."

"Don't worry, Brighton," Cain murmured, moving his hand from the door to her face. Brighton leaned into it without thinking, body blooming beneath the warmth of his touch. "They're out there. Remember, while you're looking and waiting, I'm doing the same damn thing."

"I don't know about *looking,* but it feels good not to be alone in the whole having the sight with no soulmate part." Brighton lifted her chin with a whisper, drawing closer with a brush of his thumb across her cheek.

"You never have to be now I'm here." Cain's face was serious, blue eyes soft as he leaned in. "I'm so glad I met you, Colour Girl, and I don't plan on leaving you any time soon."

"*Promise?*"

The word fell from her mouth without thinking. Brighton wanted to understand why she said it, but never got the chance to consider the thought a moment longer.

The door swung open, and they instantly sprang apart. Brighton anticipated seeing Andi but found someone completely unexpected.

"Gideon?" Brighton balked, hands trembling. "What are you doing in my apartment?"

"You gave me a key," Gideon drawled with a shrug, green eyes snapping to Cain, sizing up the larger man from his head to his feet and back. "Who's this?"

"Cain Whitaker." He squared his shoulders and seemed to get two inches taller in the process.

"Whitaker, as in Alexandria Whitaker?" Gideon lifted a brow.

"Cousins."

Brighton froze, wide-eyed as the exchange took place; something more akin to peacocks sizing each other up than two men meeting each other for the first time.

"Interesting. You don't *sound* like a cousin," Gideon challenged.

"British mother. Our fathers are brothers. Grew up in London," Cain retorted without a second thought. "And *you are?*"

"Gideon Baumgartner." He stuck out his hand with a smug smile. "Thanks for returning *my* girlfriend."

Brighton barked out a gasp of incredulous laughter at the mention of the word coming from *Gideon* of all people. It died quickly, and she was left wishing she still had her popcorn as the tension climbed to new heights.

Cain stood his ground. The ghost of a polite semblance of a smile hovered on his lips as he ignored Gideon's extended hand and exhaled a deep breath from his nose—like he was gathering all the patience in the world to keep his composure. "Interesting. Last I checked, Brighton wasn't something that could belong to *anyone.*"

Cain broke eye contact with Gideon and met Brighton's gaze. The corner of his mouth quivered as he stuck out his hand. "I'll talk to you soon, Colour Girl."

Brighton slipped her hand in his with a baffled grin, shaking her head when he winked at her with a squeeze of his fingers.

A bit dazed, Brighton sank against the doorframe all over again as she watched him walk away, wearing the same swagger he'd shown at the bowling alley.

"Who the fuck is that guy?" Gideon leaned out the door with a sneer. "Your new best friend?"

Brighton shrugged with a laugh, meeting Cain's eye one last time before he disappeared down the stairs. "Yeah, maybe."

Chapter 5

There was something special about going to the ballpark. Brighton hadn't been to one in she couldn't remember how long. In her foggiest memories, she remembered laying out on the lawn in a faded white and blue pinstripe jersey, catching a fly ball in her beer. Being back, though, brought everything she loved about the game into sharp focus, and she couldn't be more grateful she decided to take the afternoon off.

Brighton grinned when her phone buzzed in her pocket. She smiled down at the screen with a flutter in her belly as she read over the words.

Saved you a seat.

The crowd's buzz grew louder as Brighton ascended into the stadium and her excitement palpable as the smell of roasting hotdogs and garlic fries wafted over her in a delicious cloud—and a drink was calling her name.

With a pair of frosty beers balancing precariously in her hands, Brighton stepped into the mammoth basin of the ballpark. She ducked her chin, thankful she'd worn a ball cap to help shield her eyes from the blinding sun hoisted high in the bright cerulean sky. Murmuring a flurry of "excuse me's,' she shuffled her way through the first row, settling herself into an open seat right across from first base as she handed a beer to her companion.

"Fancy meeting you here," Brighton echoed his words from the last time they'd met, taking a sip of her drink. "You come here often?"

"Hey, Colour Girl," Cain grinned, saluting his tall, plastic cup with a tilt of his head. "Thanks for this."

"You're buying the next round," she teased, flicking the sweat from her beer out over the field. She nodded out onto the wide-open expanse of emerald grass, her brows lifting beneath the brim of her cap as she let out a long whistle. "Wow. You really have the hookup, don't you? We're so close I can practically taste the sod. Is Rizzo gonna end up in my lap later?"

"Not if I can help it."

"That's no fun."

"Shut it."

"Make me," Brighton swore her cheeks were going to ache for weeks if they kept things up . . . *if* she let herself keep feeling happy and free the way she did when she was around him.

Cain's face darkened, leaning forward with a wickedly alluring tug at the corner of his mouth. "That can be arranged, darling."

Before she could blink, he grabbed the bill of her hat, yanking it down over her eyes. Cain let out a deep rumble of laughter when Brighton blindly punched him in the ribs in retaliation.

Brighton's mind swam for a witty reply but found herself *completely* distracted by the look in Cain's eyes when she lifted the brim. Her mouth hung open, but nothing came out as her cheeks flushed a rosy pink. The ballpark was sweltering, and Brighton was *sure* it had nothing to do with the weather.

"Hey man, you're in my seat."

A voice interrupted them, thankfully pulling Cain's attention away, who whipped out his phone to verify their seat numbers.

Brighton focused on the frothy lager in her hand, taking a deep drink in hopes it would both cool her nerves and the heat lighting up her freckles.

No matter the delightfully charged moment, she wasn't sorry she'd answered his invitation to play hooky with a resounding yes.

It turned out, the blessed interrupter was right about their seat—Cain's seat.

"I'll scoot over," Brighton insisted, reaching to gather her beer from the cupholder.

Cain held up his hand. "You stay put, Colour Girl. I'll come 'round."

The pair grew silent as Cain stood, and the space he once occupied was instantly taken over by the impatient person who'd demanded he move.

"Sorry," Cain grumbled awkwardly as he tried to shuffle past Brighton's knees, caught up in baseball stadium traffic as he waited for the rest of the row to scoot down a seat.

Brighton lifted her eyes to offer him a sympathetic smile when she felt the embarrassment radiating off him, but when their eyes met, Cain stumbled—lurching forward to catch himself on the back of her seat.

"*Shit.*" Cain pushed the fallen curls from his blue eyes, face *so* close to hers.

"It's . . . um . . . it's cool," Brighton mumbled, letting her fingers linger on the spot where they'd instinctually landed on his chest. She peeled them away, curling her hand into a fist and tucking it to her chest, practically holding her breath as their gaze remained intertwined for a split second more.

Brighton let out a breathless chuckle—half relief, half over-whelmed delight—silently cursing herself for noticing how much space he took up in the stadium seat, just as big—if not bigger—than the players in the dugout.

Cain's smile eventually returned, spreading high enough to crinkle around the corners of his eyes as he settled back into his seat and let his arm rest up against hers.

The first batter for the Cubs came up to bat, sending a foul ball careening into the upper levels over third base. Brighton sat back in her seat and crossed a leg over her knee with a deep drink of her beer, settling in for a magnificent nine innings of the greatest game in the world . . . until a wall of man leaned forward on his knees and concealed her view of home plate.

Brighton playfully jabbed her finger into his tree trunk of a bicep, trying and failing miserably at not thinking of how *firm* it felt. "Hey, down in front, *Kal-El*. Some of us are trying to watch a baseball game."

"You're not the only one here, darling." Cain peeked over his broad shoulder at her with a sly smile. "If you ask nicely, I could sit back a little."

Brighton rolled her eyes with a laugh, squirming when she met his mischievously expectant gaze. "*Please.*"

Cain's face split into a feigned grin of surprise, leaning back to open the view. "See? Not so hard, was it?"

"That's what you think," Brighton teased, pleased to feel them settle into a decidedly more friend-like zone. Her eyes shifted, and she let out a loud whoop when the crack of a bat rang out, and the Cubs secured a runner on First.

They sat in a comfortable silence while the first couple innings played out, more than happy to just *be* for a while, save for the occasional heckle Brighton would shout—

"I've seen more curves on my grandma!"

"I've seen better moves on a first date!"

"You couldn't strike out Stevie Wonder!"

Brighton couldn't help but laugh when Cain snorted into

his beer at her last jab at the Cardinal's pitcher, grimacing as he smeared foam from his face.

"You don't exactly watch this game the old-fashioned way, do you? Some of us are trying to pay attention."

"Speak for yourself, Grandpa. This *is* the old-fashioned way. Heads up!" Brighton nodded skyward as a foul ball lingered in the air before hurtling down into the section next to theirs. "I think you're confusing baseball with Cricket, *Old Sport*. Or did they teach you something different at Oxford?"

Cain laughed at her sublimely awful British accent, shaking his head as his shoulder settled up against hers. "King's College, actually."

"So, does that mean you went to school in a castle, or . . ."

"Kind of . . . it's an old school."

Brighton took another drink of her beer. "What brought you back here? You said your mom is English?"

"I did." Cain nodded. "She and Dad met at University, and . . . I guess you could say he was more than happy to stay in Mother England after he caught *The Glimpse*."

"Your parents are soulmates?" Brighton's heart swelled. "Mine too."

"It's pretty great, isn't it? Lucky bastards didn't have to wait too long."

"Yeah," she breathed. "Pretty lucky."

They settled in the cadence of the conversation, chatting back and forth about their lives. How Cain met Eli at University, and they followed each other to the states with exceptional job offers not long after graduation.

Baseball, luckily enough, was something they both loved. More of a football guy (the British version), Cain found a love for the game through his job, never looking back after attending his first game.

Their conversation flowed as effortlessly as breathing—

pausing when a player on the field would make a great play, only to fall right back into place like they'd never stopped.

Brighton tried to be on her best behavior, ever conscious of Gideon and the odd way he'd called her *his girlfriend* when he met Cain. None of her actions, even the flirtiest ones, happened on purpose—they came as easily as everything else when it came to her newfound friend.

Chewing on her thumb, Brighton leaned back in her seat and looked at Cain as he thoughtfully watched the game with a slow stroke of his chin. Brighton wanted to tell herself he wasn't the typical man she'd notice. Then again—she tried really hard *not* to notice anyone after Jesse.

Cain, though . . . he was so beautiful, he almost didn't seem real. He was an unexpected and undeniable infatuation. Handsome in his own, singularly devastating way, he was the opposite of the kind of man she'd ever dated.

Brighton sighed, watching how his blue heather tee strained across his broad chest with every breath. His blue eyes stayed intensely focused on the game while his dark curls fluttered in the warm, early afternoon breeze.

Cain glanced her way and briefly met her eye—offering a small but sincere smile and a bit of an awkward wave. The way he held himself and how he dressed made Brighton think the confident, flirty Cain was something only for her—not a show put on for other people.

No, if she had one, he wasn't what Brighton considered her "type" at all, but there was something about Cain that made her feel flustered. Her mouth and body kept running away with the idea no matter how hard she fought against it.

Brighton met Cain's gaze that burned with curiosity when she opened her mouth to speak— when the pitch-perfect crack of a bat rang out, followed by the collective gasp of thirty-thousand people.

Brighton's hand shot out in breathless anticipation, gripping the top of Cain's thigh—all eyes trained on the little white dot as it hurtled out over center field.

Moving as a single unit, the entire stadium rose to their feet. The cacophony of voices grew louder until the ball bounced off the broad yellow stripe lining the edge of the playing field.

The crowd went ballistic, cheering loudly as the Cubs' third baseman smiled towards their section, casually running around the bases with a flurry of fireworks exploding overhead.

Brighton jumped up and down with a squeal—landing straight in the arms of the man with whom she was trying *so hard* to stay just friends.

A broad smile broke across Cain's face, caught up with the entire ballpark as he curled his arms around her waist.

Brighton let out a carefree laugh that died quickly when she found her palms pressed against Cain's chest and her feet far, far away from the concrete. Her cheeks burned and skin prickled.

They lingered there, one against the other. Cain's eyes softened, never wavering while Brighton swore she felt the slight squeeze of his arms around her middle.

Blinking rapidly when another crack of the bat echoed into the decrescendo of the stadium, Brighton cleared her throat, and Cain looked anywhere but at her face when he set her back on her feet.

"I'm sorry," Cain murmured, fingertips lingering on her waist as he pushed her away from where she'd been pressed up against him. His eyes avoided hers, brows knit together, and jaw clenched before summoning an unconvincing smile. "I forget, sometimes."

"It's okay," she answered, cheeks still warmed and heart aching to get back to the fun, carefree feeling they'd been caught up in before. Brighton slipped her fingers into his hand and gave it a squeeze. "Cain, it's okay. Don't beat yourself up."

Cain chewed his words with the same feigned smile. "No promises, darling."

Brighton and Cain sat and silently watched the game. They'd alternate taking deep drinks of their beers and let out the occasional cheer for a great play. All the while, she was *so* aware of the warmth of his skin radiating against hers and every singular movement he made beside her.

Tension climbed, something unexplainable that shouldn't have existed with someone she barely knew, let alone when Brighton had—*whatever* Gideon was—waiting for her.

Cain settled back in his seat with a deep growl as he struggled to find a comfortable position in the tiny chair before leaning over to grumble in her ear— "You hungry?"

"*Starved.*" Brighton gave him a relieved grin.

Cain caught the vendor's attention at the farthest end of the row with a whistle, passing down a $20 bill. He offered a friendly smile, waving his fingers to say how many he wanted with a quick, "Keep the change!"

Brighton was happy for the distraction; the beginnings of her beer-fueled buzz making her a little too giddy as she unwrapped the warm foil to get to the goodness inside.

Snacks in hand, they fell into their uncomplicated cadence again, moving straight into a more innocent subject—

"Christmas or Thanksgiving?" Brighton asked with a poke at the tomato slices on her hotdog.

"Halloween," Cain answered without blinking.

She laughed. "That's not what I asked."

"Don't care."

"But if you had to choose?"

"Well—" Cain pursed his lips, rolling over his holiday logic. "There is a significant spread of food at both, that naturally lends itself to the merits of it being an even split. However, I am partial to the snowy weather come December. It gives one a reason to snuggle, and that's something I could get into, so—Christmas it is."

"Okay, I'll give you that." Brighton, happy with his answer, merely smiled with a random flip of her heart as she imagined a snowy Chicago afternoon with nothing to do but cozy up in front of a fireplace.

"Coffee or tea?" It was Cain's turn, and Brighton was relieved to have a reason to think of *anything* else.

"This might be very un-American of me, I know how most of us feel about their coffee, but I can't say no to a good English breakfast first thing in the morning."

Cain snorted into his beer, broad shoulders bobbing as he laughed. "Brighton, for Christ's sake—*phrasing*. You *are* talking about tea, right? 'Cos it's been said I, myself, am a full English breakfast."

"Oh my god." Brighton blushed harder than she ever had at the notion, punching him in the arm as her sides ached from holding back laughter. "*Yes!* Tea! English breakfast *tea!* Please . . . let me change the subject."

"Happily . . ." He wiped the corners of his eyes with a boyish giggle.

"Chocolate or peanut butter?"

Cain made a face like she'd offended him. "Both, clearly. How *dare* you suggest otherwise. Marvel or DC?"

"Here I was, thinking I'd given myself away by calling you Kal El . . ."

Cain gave her another collectible smile. "I'm flattered but can't agree."

"That confirms it." Brighton shrugged as she polished off the last bite of her hotdog.

"What's that?"

"You don't know everything," she mumbled over the food in her mouth. "How about you? Are you partial to one legion of heroes over the other since you, *you know*, are one?"

"Does Samwise Gamgee count?"

"Wasn't he a sidekick or something?" Brighton regretted the words as soon as they came out of her mouth when Cain gave her a look of such incredulity; she wondered if he had qualms over the beginnings of their budding friendship.

"*Brighton.*" He looked out over the field with a slow lick of his lips. "The thing about Sam Gamgee is . . . he is loyal, gentle, giving . . . *loving.* Without him, Frodo wouldn't have ever made it to Mount Doom. True enough, Mister Baggins was the Ring-bearer, but *Sam.* Sam is the story's hero. He carried Frodo the whole way, literally and figuratively. I'm sure it sounds silly, but . . . 'ole Samwise had a heart strong enough to resist the call of The Ring. He was strong enough to carry the emotional load, and because of his love and his hope . . . they made it as far as they did."

Cain trained his gaze on her, blue eyes flickering towards the corner of her mouth. Brighton's heart skipped a beat as he reached for her, cradling her face with a whisper—

"He pulled them through their darkest times and always believed, even when things felt hopeless, '. . . *how could the end be happy? . . . but in the end, it's only a passing thing, this shadow. Even darkness must pass. A new day will come. And when the sun shines, it will shine out the clearer.*'"

Brighton wanted to revel in the feeling of his flesh pressed against hers as tingles radiated out from his fingertips across her entire body like ripples of water on a freshly disturbed lake. She wanted to let her thoughts drift away on the delicious feeling his touch painted her in, but all she could focus on was his eyes shifting back to the corner of her mouth as he leaned forward.

"You've got a bit of mustard . . ."

"Shit." Brighton tried to scramble for a napkin, but Cain held her firmly.

"I've got it," he said, unhurriedly skimming the pad of his

thumb over her bottom lip, drawing it away to slowly suck it clean.

"That—that's some good advice your hero Sam has . . ." Brighton sputtered as she tried to regain her bearings.

"You never know when it might come in handy." Cain nodded, unblinking as he leaned away.

Brighton held onto his words throughout the rest of the game. They bounced back and forth through their twenty questions, sharing laughs and teasing jabs the entire time, but still —the words of Samwise Gamgee were ones she hoped she would remember Cain saying to her forever. Maybe she'd learn from them, maybe she could learn to be less afraid and finally brave.

After the game, even though he lived mere blocks from the stadium in Old Town, Cain insisted on accompanying Brighton home from the ride Downtown on the Red Line, walking the few blocks to her and Andi's apartment.

"I have something to tell you," Brighton confessed as he held open the door.

"I can't wait to hear it," Cain answered with another one of his impeccable smiles, following her up the stairs.

"It might . . . it might change your mind about me." She paused, wringing the hem of her jersey.

"I sincerely doubt there is *anything* you could tell me that'd make me change my mind about you." Cain's handsome face was stern, brows knitted together as he stopped her at the top of the stairs on the fourth floor. He reached out and gave her arm a gentle squeeze. "I mean that."

"Thank you . . ." she murmured, leaning against the door. "I haven't seen any of them."

"Any of what?" Cain was puzzled.

"Any of the Lord of the Rings movies." Brighton toed her red sneaker on the faded carpet, fixated on a dark stain. Her eyes didn't stay there long before the warmth of Cain's fingers curled around her jaw, tilting her gaze to meet his.

"*Hey.*"

"Y-yeah?" Brighton's eyes darted back and forth between his as he leaned closer. She wondered if Cain was about to kiss her, but before the feverish second—or the temptation—could last any longer, they blinked and took a quick step back with a hasty clearing of their throats.

Cain closed his eyes, pressing his mouth together with a roll of his jaw while Brighton fiddled with the buttons on her jersey. "Brighton, I—"

"No." Brighton's hand shot out. Even though her fingers trembled, she was *sure* about what she had to say. "I think . . . *I know* I forget sometimes, too. I like you *so much*. I don't want to fuck it up."

"You couldn't. Not ever." Cain looked so sure, so earnest; his eyes soft even though the rest of his face remained hopelessly solemn.

Brighton's eyes flickered down to his fists, distracted by how Cain curled and uncurled his fingers, but his words brought her right back to his face.

"I am aware of the time you've invested in your relationship or whatever it is. I can't say he gave the best first impression, and I confess—Andi didn't exactly have the best things to say about him, either. What I do know, is how *you* feel about him. That's enough for me."

Cain shifted, wedging his hands in his pockets before abruptly changing his mind—gathering Brighton in his arms for a bone-crushing hug.

Brighton didn't need to think about it. Her arms moved of their own accord, twining 'round his waist as she settled her cheek against the steady beating of his heart. It was a simple gesture, but it spoke more than words—feeding straight into their unexplainable bond and the friendship so effortlessly beginning to form.

The weight of his cheek pressed on the crown of her head, and Brighton felt his body release ounces of tension when he let out a deep sigh.

"I respect you, Brighton." The timbre of Cain's voice buzzed against her freckles. "This is what you want, and . . . with you as my friend; I'll be happy enough."

"*Happy enough*," Brighton echoed, lifting her chin to meet his gaze as she reluctantly unwound herself from around him. "I'd very much like to be your friend, Cain Whitaker."

Brighton felt a rush of relief and pride. They'd been smart enough to construct a much-needed boundary. Having the wall between friendship and *more* was something Brighton never thought she'd have to create. Now the line in the sand had been drawn—one she was more than confident they could happily keep to—she and Cain could foster their friendship the way fate seemed determined they did.

Twisting a daisy-freckled key in the lock, Brighton pushed it open.

Cain answered the action with a respectful nod and a smile. "Goodnight, Brighton. It's been an absolute pleasure spending the day with you."

Brighton made a face. She glanced at her watch, offering a bemused smile as she held the door wide open. "What makes you think our day is over?"

"You're not asking me to come in, are you?" Cain lifted a brow, hands finding their way back into his pockets. "Isn't that . . . *you know* . . . against the rules of guy-girl friendship or something?"

"We're friends, aren't we? Andi's my friend. I'm sure, at some point, Eli will be my friend too."

"Alright, true."

"So—" Brighton stepped away from the door and dropped

her keys in a dish before hanging up her bag and toeing off her shoes. "Get your ass in here. It's dinnertime, I'm starved, and there's some killer takeout nearby."

"Dinner?"

"Yes. *And*." Brighton strode over to the living room, plucking a black remote from a rickety coffee table. She gave it a wiggle. "There's HBO we 'borrowed' from my dad, and I'm pretty sure *The Lord of the Rings* is on there. What do you say to rectifying my friendship sin and educating me further on 'ole Samwise Gamgee?"

Cain hovered in the doorway, practically taking up the entire frame as each and every thought flickered over his face.

"Brighton, I—" Cain started with the tiniest hint of a smile.

"Unless you're busy," Brighton scrambled. Her heart flipped at the thought, so caught up in the excitement of the day, she hadn't stopped to think, maybe, Cain had somewhere—or someone—to go home to. "I'm sorry, I just assumed you . . . it's okay."

"Are you serious?" Cain finally crossed the threshold, stilling her hands from wringing the remote. "You're telling me —after an entire day—you're not sick of me yet. Now you want to watch my favorite movie? *Brighton* . . . not only do I want to, there's literally nothing that could tear me away from you."

"Fantastic." Brighton beamed, bounding into the kitchen. With a flourish, she tugged open a drawer. "Come on over and check out our extensive stock of takeout menus. We'll order in and get started right away."

⋈

Two hours later, tucked in her favorite spot on the sofa with a smorgasbord scattered across the coffee table —half-eaten bibimbap, dumplings, and crumbs leftover from a bahn mi that'd been devoured by Cain—Brighton sat transfixed.

Cain was casual through and through, arm slung across the back of the couch. His gaze flickered to Brighton from time to time as she clutched her favorite, red knitted blanket to her chin.

"I wish the Ring had never come to me. I wish none of this had happened."

"So do all who live to see such times, but that is not for them to decide. All you have to decide is what to do with the time that is given to you."

"Oh my god," Brighton breathed, brown eyes meeting Cain's amused smirk, scooting closer when her anxiousness over the Fellowship being trapped in the mines of Moria grew to new heights. "What's going to happen? I can *feel* it . . . like something's waiting in the wings. You don't give a big speech like that for nothing. It always comes before something monumental happens that shifts *everything.*"

"Patience, darling." Cain brushed his hand over her auburn hair. "All will be revealed in due time."

"I hate waiting," Brighton whined, chewing her thumb.

"All the best things are worth waiting for, love. This is only the start of the journey, and they've got a long way to go. It's not always going to be easy, but like how I told you Sam said . . . even though it's dark now, the light will come. Just you wait."

Brighton leaned against Cain's shoulder, biting her lip when Pippin dropped a stone into a deep well—awakening an army of orcs, trolls, and the dreaded Balrog.

She buzzed with excitement and palpable fear for the characters on the screen, caught up in every breathless second as they made their way to the Bridge of Khazad-Dûm.

Hope. Brighton's heart beat with it for the first time in a long time, keeping her on the edge of her seat with an unspoken wish they'd all make it out of the darkness. It shattered with the utterance of a single line, swathing the Fellow-ship—and Brighton, too—in darkness of another kind.

"Fly, you fools!"

The door of the apartment burst open as hot, silvery tears streamed down Brighton's freckled face. Her gaze shot towards the couple stumbling in the doorway who paid no mind to the people already occupying the space as they flung bits of clothing everywhere.

Cain slapped his hands over his eyes, and Brighton chucked a pillow across the room with a half-sob and a wail—

"Alexandria!"

Her half-naked best friend and her soulmate snatched up their clothes from the floor and disappeared down the hall with a giggle.

Brighton groaned, patting Cain's arm to let him know the coast was clear before leaning over to bury her tear-strewn face in his shirt with an exasperated laugh. "I love Andi, but I gotta get out of this apartment if they're going to keep this up."

"Chin up, darling. You're not alone, remember?" Cain pulled Brighton close and pressed his cheek to the top of her head. "We're in this together, now."

Chapter 6

Six months later

ime was a funny thing. Brighton swore it would go by the fastest when she wasn't paying attention, merely the center point as the world bent and shifted around her.

Summer bled into autumn, bringing with it ruby red apples and rich marigolds kissing the green of the trees across the city with every turn of the page in her calendar.

With each falling leaf, twisting and tumbling across the sidewalk, and every increasingly sharp gust of icy wind blasting in from Lake Michigan, Brighton felt the promise of new life waiting on the other side of what was sure to be a bitter winter. Where, if you paid attention, you could find the blooming of something new and beautiful, even in the darkest of winter days.

At least, it's how it felt for Brighton at the end of the summer when her best friend, Andi, experienced *The Glimpse*. Because of it, Brighton discovered something extraordinary; every color sharpened when she met Cain.

While it had a bit of a *heated* start, their friendship flourished like a garden in springtime, every new detail they discovered about the other more colorful than the last. Even as the summer sun started to dim, the bright light Cain filled Brighton with grew more radiant each day.

While one corner of her life blossomed, another stayed decently predictable.

Brighton and Gideon were good at that. They were good at normal. He'd work, she'd work, and they would text throughout the day. The predictable nature of their relationship comforted her, never asking more than what Brighton was able to give. And, when she was afforded the fortieth-floor view of the Chicago River, cozied up in Gideon's favorite U of C sweatshirt with nowhere to go, she couldn't be sorry he was what she chose. While he wasn't the textbook example of Prince Charming, Brighton knew Gideon loved her in his way. He made her happy.

Happy enough.

Blue felt like the right choice, one particular Friday evening in late February. The sun finally gave way earlier that afternoon, and Brighton idly wondered if spring was around the corner.

Brighton felt good—*damn good*—dressed in cobalt from head to toe. From the sheath dress hugging her every lithe curve, to the blue suede boots that came up over her knee, and the coordinating wool coat tying it all together—Brighton felt sexier than she ever had.

So sexy, when she stepped through the doors of Momotaro, even Gideon Baumgartner looked up from his phone and rose to his feet.

"You look amazing," he murmured in her ear, slipping a hand beneath her coat to hug the swell of her hip.

"Thanks," Brighton answered with a smile, turning as he pulled it from her shoulders. "I was feeling a little blue today."

"I wish I could see it." Gideon wore a faraway look as he settled into the seat opposite her.

"Me too," Brighton echoed, laying a crisp, white napkin in her lap, reminded again she and Gideon were merely place-holders for the other until when—and *if*—the real thing came along.

They fell into their same date night routine, talking about all the typical things—from her projects at work to new clients he'd acquired. To her surprise, Gideon even asked about Andi as their sake arrived.

Like clockwork, even when they were at their best, the conversation began to peter out halfway through the chef-selected sashimi. Brighton brought the petite sake glass to her lips, poking at a spicy tuna roll with her chopsticks as Gideon removed his phone from inside his breast pocket and lost himself to whoever or whatever he typed a reply to.

With some prodding, perhaps Brighton could convince Gideon to skip dessert and get them headed towards a *different* kind of distraction back at his apartment.

A subtle vibration from her bag—her favorite canary yellow —drew her attention away.

Brighton glanced at Gideon, still immersed in the screen in his hand, and figured there'd be no harm in taking a peek.

She plucked her cell phone from inside, swiping it open with a smile when she saw Cain's name emblazoned on the lock screen.

Nice of you to skip out on Happy Hour, Evans.

Brighton knew Cain's teasing tone in a second, knowing full well he knew exactly where she was.

Wish I could. I got a hot date, though.

Brighton typed out her reply, biting her lip when the trio of dots appeared in a second, bouncing happily as Cain responded.

Is your hot date you? Asking for a friend.

Brighton shook her head as her fingers danced over the screen.

Is the friend you or Andi? Asking for a friend.

Looking up at Gideon—still engrossed in his own phone—Brighton dutifully put hers aside, laying it face down on the white tablecloth before picking up her chopsticks to pop a piece of sushi in her mouth.

She reached out with her toe beneath the table, smiling to herself at the thought of the kinds of things the two of them could get up to later that evening if things went her way. Her touch against his leg didn't go exactly as she planned when Gideon barely flinched in response.

"Do you wanna get out of here, Gid?" Brighton prodded more firmly.

Gideon pulled his leg away, holding up a finger as he finished typing something else before twisting in his seat toward the kitchen. "Don't we have another course coming?"

"Yeah, I suppose we do," Brighton murmured, looking at her phone on the table when it buzzed again.

She lifted it, letting out a quiet laugh when, upon swiping it open, she looked upon a hilariously silly selfie with Cain, Eli, and little Andi smushed in the middle.

Andi says to ditch the spare and get your ass over here.

A quick glance across the table told Brighton that Gideon was right back where he'd been before. She let out a sigh and typed out a reply.

You and I both know it's not that easy.

Cain's reply came swiftly after.

I do, but I'm here if you need me to call you with a "family emergency," alright?

Brighton started to respond, but another text popped up right away.

Bee, get the fuck over here and have some real fun for a change. Love, Andi.

It was accompanied by a blurry image of Andi's toothy grin and Cain's hand trying in vain to snatch his phone away.

Brighton didn't think she'd laughed out loud, but must have when Gideon asked, "What's so funny?"

"It's nothing." Brighton slid her phone back into her bag.

"It didn't seem like nothing. You're laughing at your phone in the middle of our date, Brighton. That's not nothing," he argued.

"That's fair, but I'm trying here, Gid. You're taking a meeting or . . . *I don't know* . . . what am I supposed to do when my boyfriend is glued to his phone, and it's basically me and my sashimi?" Brighton's heart twisted when the word fell from her mouth. Even though Gideon broke his own rule in front of Cain a few months before, he still hadn't come to terms with the title and how he fit into it—too proud of their 'unorthodox' way of doing things to give in.

"I'm sorry." Gideon's gaze fell to his plate, working his jaw as he adjusted his tie, not bothering to scold her like Brighton expected. "I've got a lot going on. I'm honestly interested in what has you smiling. I love it when you do that."

"What, smile?"

"Yeah, of course. I want you to be happy, Brighton. I want to *make* you happy." Gideon leaned forward on his elbows.

"You do . . ." Brighton's eyes fell with a wavering smile as she pushed at a piece of wasabi on her plate, stretching it thin over the crisp, white ceramic.

"I know you probably weren't smiling about me, right then." Gideon drained his sake, rolling the small ceramic cup on its edge as he continued. "It's okay if you weren't. I know I've been more than a little preoccupied lately. Was it Andi? *Cain?*"

"Both of them, actually, plus Andi's boyfriend, Eli."

"You've been spending a lot of time with him lately," Gideon frowned.

"Who, Eli?"

He gave her a pointed look, "No, that other British bastard."

"Gid . . ." Brighton warned, even though what he was saying wasn't *totally* wrong.

She and Cain had lunch together at least once a week. His face was a frequent enough fixture in her office, the lady at the coffee cart had his order memorized. On top of their daytime meetings, if Brighton wasn't with Gideon on the weekends, chances were, she could be found with Cain—plus Andi and Eli—happily carving their way through the uniquest parts of the city.

"We're friends. *Just friends.*"

"I hope so." Gideon feigned an interested smile she saw straight through. "What did they want?"

"If you must know—" Brighton set down her chopsticks, squaring her shoulders as she poured the rest of the sake into her glass. "They invited me out to Happy Hour, but I told them I was busy."

The wheels turned in Gideon's mind as he mulled over her answer, getting distracted after a few seconds when his phone pinged from inside his jacket. He pulled it out, brows creased as he read.

"I know we talked about doing something else, but . . . I think I'm gonna be a little preoccupied with this work shit. It would be better for both of us if you go do what you want and have fun with your friends."

"A-are you sure?"

"Completely," Gideon answered brusquely, waving over their server to bring their check. "I'll get this. You go on ahead."

"Okay . . ." Brighton rose to her feet as Gideon came behind her and held out her blue coat, sliding her arms through the silk-lined wool, turning in time for him to press a chaste kiss to her lips. "I'll see you later, then?"

"I'll call you." Gideon smiled, depositing her yellow bag in her hands.

⋈

*A*nother quick text with the location, a brief ride on the L, and a two block walk—Brighton arrived. The bar around her buzzed with the Friday night crowd. It sent her spinning with excitement.

The designer in her preened at every detail—oversized sage-green velvet loungers tucked around wooden tables with flickering 'oil' lamps fluttering from their gilded wall sconces. Red light bathed every face as the sounds of big band jazz played from unseen speakers hidden expertly in faux bookcases.

Brighton blinked and stumbled into the height of 1920's Chicago—one wrong turn 'round a corner, and Al Capone would be sitting in an exclusive booth with a fat, smoldering cigar perched in his mouth.

Shouldering her way through the crowd, Brighton meandered to the bar, leaning her elbows on the shining mahogany. She ordered a gin martini with a smile, humming to herself while the bartender expertly shake Beefeater and vermouth.

"Fancy meeting you here," a deep voice hummed in her ear, catching her completely off-guard.

Brighton spun on her heel, broad smile blooming across her freckled face as she flung her arms out and greeted her best friend.

"Miss me?" Brighton grinned up at Cain, who looked impossibly at home in the old-fashioned decor.

"Terribly, darling." Cain gave Brighton a squeeze, pressing an unhurried kiss on each of her cheeks before grabbing her martini. "Shall we? I've got an impatient cousin who's been desperate to have our little foursome together."

"It's only been a couple days," Brighton groaned with a shake of her head. "I see her daily—what's the rush?"

"Apparently, there's an important talk to be had. Things are *serious."* Fingers twined together, Cain ushered Brighton through to the belly of the speakeasy, casting a wide-eyed grimace over his broad shoulder that instantly made her laugh.

Brighton wanted to explore every nook and cranny of the bar, but didn't have much chance. She barked out a laugh; grateful Cain had been holding her martini when—out of nowhere—a flurry of dark curls and loud squeals tackled her.

"Bout time you got here!" Andi punched Brighton in the arm before she took in her outfit. "*Damn*, Bee, you look good! Doesn't she look good, Cain?"

Brighton's cheeks heated when she lifted her eyes to meet Cain's as he straightened from setting her martini on the table.

Cain's mouth twitched, throat bobbing as he lifted a finger and motioned for Brighton to turn. He slid his warm hands beneath the collar, setting her skin aflame as he slipped silk-lined wool down her arms. "She looks divine."

Wrong. They couldn't. He shouldn't. Brighton's mind buzzed, and every fear flashed through her mind with a twist of her stomach. They were good as friends. *Amazing,* even. She couldn't risk giving in because Cain looked at her *like that.*

"Oh, this old thing?" Brighton spun around, summoning a smile to banish away *every* unwanted feeling. She settled in next to Cain in a roomy, leather chair, leaning away with a sip of her cocktail. "I had it . . . *you know* . . . laying around."

"Now, that's something I'd take as a sign you'd been kidnapped," Andi joked.

"I second that," Eli echoed with a lift of his drink. "Even I have known you long enough to know, with Brighton . . . it's all about the *fash-un.*"

"Okay fine, you got me. I might have popped by Blooming-dale's the other day. So sue me." Brighton rolled her eyes, setting the coupe glass on the table between them.

More than happy to be back together, even after a couple

days, the four of them lost themselves to the wonder of the environment—turning one drink into two and two into three.

With each one, Brighton felt her face warm and her nose tingle, smiles coming a little easier as they moved from topic to topic. She felt *marvelous*, gently swaying with the music as her body hummed from the delightful haze.

It might have been an hour, maybe two, but judging by the width of everyone's smiles, Brighton might have guessed they were leaning more towards three.

Fingers wrapped around the rim of her fourth martini, Brighton took a deep drink with a nod at Andi and Eli, perched together on a couch across from her. "What's this big news? You're not getting married, are you?"

Eli snorted into his drink, caught in a coughing fit; Andi answered with an offended gasp and a playful jab to his ribs.

"*Ha!* Not yet, but trust me—you two will be the first to know when that happens." Andi looked to her soulmate, laying a hand across his knee with a deep breath and a smile. "My lease is up in May. Elijah and I started looking at buying an apartment together."

"So, what you're saying is," Cain chimed in, his dark brows knit together as he whirled the ice in his whiskey, "You're *getting married* . . . but with real estate?"

"You could say that." Eli leaned and pressed a lingering kiss on Andi's lips.

"Good luck with this one, Andi. He wouldn't pick his towel up from the bathroom floor if his life depended on it." Cain lifted his glass. "Truly, though, I'm thrilled for you. Cheers."

Brighton sat forward in her chair, fixed on the olives in the bottom of her empty glass. "What about me?"

Her voice was soft. So soft, her friends met her with looks of pure confusion.

"What was that, darling?" Cain leaned down and brushed his fingers across her arm.

"What . . . about *me*?" Brighton looked up and met Andi's wide-eyed gaze.

"What do you mean, what about you?" Andi answered with a shrug.

Brighton knew it was selfish. She knew she should be happy for her friend. *More than happy.* Undeniably, so. Still, all she could think was how alone she'd be, and that . . . that was something she didn't want.

"If you move out, where am I supposed to go?"

Andi gave her a look. "I'm sure douche-canoe can take you in, right? God knows it's been fucking long enough for him to really commit."

Brighton thought she might cry. "You know for a fact Gideon isn't going to go for it. A night or two, maybe . . . but *live together*? Alexandria, he won't even let me call him my fucking *boyfriend*."

She was angry now, left with no answers and less solutions as Andi left her behind like so many others.

The unruly sting of irrational tears pricked the corners of Brighton's eyes. She leapt to her feet with a mumbled, *"I'm sorry,"* bolting back towards the heart of the bar.

Brighton stopped in the center of the dance floor, letting out a deep, stuttering sigh when she looked around and tried to decide where the hell she wanted to go. She couldn't go back and face Andi and apologize for her behavior, but she'd have to return at some point to gather her things she'd so foolishly left behind.

Anxiously carding her fingers through her auburn hair, Brighton closed her eyes in the red glow of the speakeasy. She sucked in a deep breath—entire body trembling as her tears threatened to give way.

"Hey."

Brighton didn't have to open her eyes; she knew his voice in a second.

Turning on her heel, her lip quivered when Cain stepped from the shadows. In the warmth of his gaze, Brighton's defenses crumbled. Briny tears finally fell free. She swept them away, shoulders sinking as she avoided his gaze. "I swear I'm happy for them."

"I know you are, darling." Cain lifted Brighton's chin, carrying away a tear with a gentle swipe of his thumb.

"I can't go back yet. I know I should, but I need a second."

"That's alright." Cain slipped his fingers around Brighton's waist when the song changed, and the rhythm picked up. "I know just the thing to cheer you up in the meantime."

Brighton peeked up at him when he snapped her to his chest with a press of his fingertips in the small of her back, less than immune to his growing smile. "You're not going to force me to dance, are you?"

"That I am, Ms. Evans. How'd you guess?" Cain smirked, reaching for her right hand.

Cain swayed them back and forth to the cheerful beat of the jazz, barely giving Brighton a second before launching her into a quick spin, bringing her back like a yo-yo.

Brighton couldn't help but laugh. "You're hopelessly predictable, *Mr. Whitaker*."

"Hell." Cain frowned, pushing her by the waist beneath his arm and back again. "Here I was, thinking I was devastatingly charming and *always* surprising."

"Practice makes perfect, you know," Brighton teased, feeling happier with each snap of a hi-hat.

"I'll try my best." Cain moved with an effortless grace for a man his size. Brighton couldn't be sure if they were doing the Charleston or the Jitterbug (probably neither) but couldn't care less.

Brighton spun like a top, laughing until her sides ached. Music thumped in her ears, and heart hammered so loudly, she couldn't be sure if she heard Cain right when he said mid-spin—

"Why don't you move in with me?"

"I—*what*?" Brighton came to a dead stop. "What do you mean?"

"I don't know what was confusing about that, Brighton." Cain stepped forward with an earnest look in his blue eyes. His fingers curled around her shoulders, holding her firmly as he sank to her level. "We've gotten really good at this *friend* thing."

"Have we?" Brighton bit her lip, stomach wrapped up in a weird state between butterflies and a brick of iron.

Cain pressed on. "You act like you have no place to go, like you'd have to be on your own . . . but here's the thing, Bee. I meant what I said when I promised I didn't plan on leaving you anytime soon, and if that means sharing a bathroom, then . . ." He shrugged with a half-smile. "Then that's what we should do."

Brighton stood back and twined a ribbon of auburn hair around her fingers, lifting her eyes to meet his before walking away.

Cain wasn't far behind, jogging up behind her as she slid up to the bar. "Is this a no?"

Brighton gave him a look, shifting her gaze back to the bartender as he slapped down a pair of glasses and filled them to the brim with tequila.

Lifting the shots from the bar top, Brighton handed one to Cain. She sucked in a deep breath, offering him a smile as she held the liquor aloft. For once in her life, Brighton was going to look past her fear and focus on the good. She'd take the risk . . . and worry about informing Gideon, later.

"To our friends Andi and Eli . . . new beginnings . . . and sharing a fucking bathroom."

Cain laughed, bowing his head with a clink of his glass against hers. "To you and me, Colour Girl. To *us*."

⋈

*T*he next morning, Brighton sat curled up in the downy softness of Gideon's California-king. She chewed her lip, staring out over an icy Navy Pier forty floors below.

Cain put her in a cab at the end of their night at the speakeasy. Body thrumming with a gin and dancing-fueled buzz—freed from the things that'd normally hold her back—Brighton knew exactly where she wanted to go.

The ride Downtown to Gideon's high-rise apartment was short. After a cheeky wave at the doorman and an elevator ride that went by in slow motion, Brighton found herself at his door.

Finally, with little convincing and a well-timed kiss, Brighton let Gideon peel away her layers and fill the ache that'd been building inside her all evening.

Her phone buzzed on the bedside table beside her. She plucked it from the glass top, tucking her knees to her chest as she swiped it open.

Are you sure you don't want me to come? I don't have to say anything.

Right. She and Cain had discussed a game plan for telling Gideon she'd decided to take up residence in his second bedroom. She'd panicked after excitedly throwing back a shot of tequila. Cain, as always, reeled her back in and helped her concoct a plan—take Gideon to their favorite breakfast spot and break the good news. Easy, right?

Except it wasn't, especially after falling so easily into Gideon's bed an hour later.

Sounds from the kitchen stirred her attention, spurring her to type out a reply.

I'm good, but thank you. I think this is important for me to do on my own.

"Hey, sleepyhead." Gideon's voice drew her away.

Brighton slid her phone back on the table, raking her fingers through her tousled hair. Her eyes darted over him, biting her lip as she took in his perfectly mussed blond hair and the way the hours Gideon spent on his Peloton bike were evidenced in every taut curve in his abdomen.

"*Hey*," Brighton breathed. "I'm sorry about barging in here last night without calling."

Gideon gave her the kind of smile that made her want to go back and relive every second. "I'm not. Not at all, Brighton. I was grateful for the distraction."

"Yeah?" Had Brighton misjudged him? Would he want her to be there, *distracting* him more often?

"*Yeah*." Gideon slid a steaming mug of coffee beside her phone, green eyes on her as he leaned in to press his lips to hers.

Brighton hummed, winding her arms around his shoulders to bring him down to the mattress—somewhere between the gentle pecks hello he normally gave her and the unhurried burning ember of desire she craved at night.

She lingered there, letting out a needy whimper when, as things started to heat up, Gideon pulled away.

Brighton gathered up her coffee. If she couldn't hang onto her not-boyfriend for more than a second, surely the warm ceramic would keep a little longer. Besides, the weight of her news seeped into her every atom, colder than the winter waters of Lake Michigan. The coffee could help with that, too.

"So . . ." Brighton blew away a huff of steam, wishing it was a strong English Breakfast. "I was wondering if you'd given any thought about . . . about maybe the two of us spending a little more time together."

"Like . . ." Gideon trailed off, trailing a ribbon of her hair between his fingers before kissing her again. "You wanna go on vacation, again? Cabo? London?"

"No. Not vacation, Gid. More like—" Brighton glanced over

his shoulder into the shadow of his closet. "More like a . . . *permanent* kind of visitor pass."

His brows scrunched, but his smile remained. "Leonard knows you, Brighton. He wouldn't ever not let you in."

Brighton set down her coffee, searching for answers in the eight-hundred thread count sheets. "This isn't about the doorman, Gideon. I'm asking if you would ever consider *living together.*"

A cold sense of realization floated down over his features.

"*Oh.*" Gideon swallowed, scrubbing a palm along his jaw. "I mean . . . we're having fun, right? We've got a really good thing going on. What's the rush on forever?"

Brighton's shoulders fell. Her teeth found the inside of her lip, again. "The rush is . . . Andi closing our apartment. She and Eli are buying one together.

"So?" Gideon shrugged, offering an unconvincing smile. "Get a roommate."

Brighton's lips parted, on the edge of saying she had, but found herself caught up in bitter disappointment. Even though she tried to do the right thing . . . apparently it wasn't enough. She thought of Cain and his offer she'd so enthusiastically agreed to and smiled.

"I did. I have." Brighton twisted a ribbon of hair around her finger. "Eli's moving out, so Cain has an extra room on the North Side he said I could have. I think I'm going to take him up on it."

Gideon's smile fell, and eyes went cold. "He does, huh?"

"I wanted to see if . . . if you . . . *if we* . . . before I made anything official." Brighton laced her fingers through his. "What are you thinking?"

Her eyes danced over his face, trying to decode what was going through his mind, hoping to gain some clarity. His gaze softened, but the distant ping of his cell phone rang out and snapped them out of it.

Gideon rose, flashing her an oh-so-casual smile, like nothing in the world could bother him. "I think you should go for it. North Side, right? Old Town?"

"Yeah." Brighton nodded, curling her fingers into her palm. His attention threaded with every chime, itching to be done with the conversation so he could answer the call—even though Cain was at the center of it.

Her stomach twisted. Even Gideon's jealousy was no match for his all-important work ethic.

"That much closer to Wrigley. That's great, Brighton." Gideon lingered in the doorway, giving her a nod before disappearing into the hall with a yell. "Lemme know if you want help moving your shoes!"

Brighton's phone buzzed, drawing her attention away from Gideon's disembodied voice from his office down the hall. She gathered it and stepped to the sprawling wall of windows, hoping the fortieth-floor view would help quell the cold sting of disappointment.

She *knew* her long-term *not*-boyfriend wouldn't go for moving in together—she'd told Andi as much the night before. What she didn't figure, was how he'd react to the news that— since he wouldn't have her—she'd be moving in with Cain.

Everything is going to be fine. Think of all the incredible things we have ahead of us, Colour Girl.

Cain's text set her at ease from the first word, sending a smile blooming across her face—she knew she made the right decision.

. . . but you'd better start packing. Lord knows it'll take ages for you to move that closet. I might need a second apartment to fit it all.

Chapter 7

May

Brighton stood on the sidewalk, arms crossed, tapping the toe of her yellow converse with a frustrated *whoosh* past her lips and a shake of her head.

The hum of the bright orange U-HAUL's engine went silent, axle creaking, when Cain hopped from the driver's seat of the pickup and walked around to stand beside her.

Cain wore a puzzled frown, following her gaze to the truck and back. "What is it?"

"It's not big enough."

He made a face. "What do you mean?"

"I mean, it's not *big enough*."

"That's what she said?" Cain chuckled, but the sound puttered out when she glared up at him.

"Cain Henry Whitaker, this isn't the time for jokes. We are going to be at this *all* day . . . and most of it is going to be spent in fucking traffic while we go back and forth to Old Town," Brighton argued, glancing up at the windows of her and Andi's fourth-floor walk-up.

"I'm an excellent driver," Cain teased. "All your clothes will be *fine,* darling."

"Don't *darling* me." Brighton poked him in the chest. "Excuse me for wanting time to unpack and get settled in."

"If you wanted the day to go faster so you could spend time with yours truly, all you had to do was say so, Brighton." Cain winked.

Brighton groaned, spun on her heel, and headed inside with a slam of the door.

Cain bounded up the stairs two at a time to catch up with her, pulling her to a stop with a tug on her wrist as she rounded the corner on the third-floor landing.

"What is it?" Cain's blue eyes studied her freckled face as he caught his breath.

"Nothing."

"Liar." He swiped a stray red curl behind her ear. "I know you, Brighton Evans. I can see when there's something on your mind. At this very moment, I see you are, in fact, full of shit."

"Am not." Brighton chewed her lip and turned her attention to the canary yellow of her sneakers.

"*Brighton . . .*" Cain gave her a look, holding her chin firmly between his thumb and forefinger. "Out with it."

She spent one second too long wrapped in his gaze before letting out a sigh of such massive proportions, the relief was instantaneous. "Is this the part where I tell you I hate change?"

Cain tilted his head with a frown. "Have you changed your mind? We don't have to—"

"No, *no.*" Brighton splayed her fingers across his chest, summoning a wavering smile. "It's not that in the slightest. It's just . . . closing this chapter and starting on a new one. It's daunting, you know?"

"You're talking to the man who moved to a new country after University, love." Cain laid his hand over hers. "I know it can feel like a lot, like a sudden hard-right turn, but you're adaptable. You're smart, creative, and honestly? You ought to give yourself more credit. You say you don't like change, but what's ending? No one is going anywhere, not really. Andi and Eli will only be a few blocks away. And me and you . . . we'll be together. What's more to want?"

Brighton's gaze fell. "The ability to linger?"

"How do you mean?"

"I wanna . . . I don't know . . . *press pause*. Rewind. Go back and relive all the best bits." Brighton stepped away, swimming in nostalgia as she trudged to the fourth floor.

As always, Cain was close behind. "What's the difference between that and dwelling? Why not look forward?"

Brighton shrugged, stopping in front of the colorfully painted *4D*, tracing her fingers over every green vine and rainbow-hued flower. "Sometimes, I feel like I have a scrapbook in my mind . . . a box of old home movies. I don't see the harm in wanting to dust them off on the last day. Sure, it's a fresh start . . ."

"A damn good fresh start for all parties involved, I'd say."

"You're not wrong, but this place—" Brighton paused to level her quaking voice. "There's a lot of great memories here with Andi."

"Mm, true, you two are like sisters." Cain nodded.

"I would follow her anywhere. But . . . she doesn't need me anymore. So, yeah. I want to linger. I want to remember every second we had in this place, you know? Remember the good ole days while we—well, *she*—was busy waiting for the next right thing. Life steered her in this direction, and I'm gonna miss the hell out of her, even if she's only a few blocks away. I'm going to miss the memories in the four walls of this place, forever. All the firsts. All the lasts." Brighton tucked a strand of hair behind her ear, taking one last glance at the door before looking to Cain. "There's quite a few with you in them, too, *Kal El.*"

"Me?" Cain gave her a face of feigned surprise, pointing towards himself with such suave, she might have mistaken him for Han Solo.

"Yes, you." Brighton laughed with a shake of her head. "This is where you promised you weren't going to leave me. I didn't know it then, but it was our new beginning, too."

"So's this."

"I know." She nodded. "But this was *the* beginning."

Cain wrapped her up in a firm hug, burying his nose in her hair. "It won't be our only beginning, love. I'm *positive* there's more around the corner. Trust me."

Brighton lifted her chin and looked up at him with a content smile. "I do. *I know.*"

"Besides." Cain released her, reaching for the knob to push the apartment wide-open. Brighton took in the empty space with a lump in her throat as they lingered in the doorway. "Most of the work is done already. Before you know it, we'll be eating takeout with *The Return of the King.*"

"Hey, *no.* You promised."

Cain groaned, throwing his head back with a roll of his eyes. "Fine. I relent. We'll watch your blasted Kryptonian."

"*Finally,*" Brighton joked, stepping inside, making a beeline for her bedroom where the bulk of boxes remained.

Behind her, Cain whistled when he looked over the collection of wardrobe boxes filling every square inch of the worn wooden floors. "How big do you think my apartment is, darling?"

"You saw my bedroom before now, right? You saw the organized masterpiece, which is my closet. I'll make it fit." Brighton gently jabbed Cain in the ribs. "*Our* apartment."

"Right, sorry," he joked, stepping past her to lean against the boxes. "Though, I can't say I had the pleasure of spending any extended amount of time in your bedroom, Brighton. I'm sure I'll frequent it more often now it'll be across the hall."

"Oh, really?" Brighton tried to quash the flush in her cheeks before it could fully take root. "Are you planning on helping me unpack, then?"

"If you'd like." Cain hoisted a pair of boxes into his arms, playfully pushing past her. "But first, we've got to get all of this shit over there, and it's going to take ages."

"That's why I said to get the big one!" Brighton exclaimed, gathering her own box before following Cain into the hall, breaking into a wide smile when Andi and Eli burst through the door. "What are you two doing here?"

"You guys helped us clear out *both* places. You don't think you're rid of me yet, do you, Bee?" Andi came forward, giving her best friend a half-hug around the load in her arms.

"I sure hope not." Brighton shifted, balancing the weight on her hip. "I'm . . . *we* are thankful for the help. Though there's not much."

"There's a-fucking-lot!" Cain interjected from the doorway beside Eli, whose shoulders shook with laughter.

"It's not *that* much," Brighton retorted with a giggle. "He's being dramatic."

"Says the girl who said I didn't bring a big enough truck," Cain shot back. "Come on, you lot, get a fucking move on. I haven't got all day."

"Oh, you wanna hurry so we can go watch *Man of Steel*?" Brighton's smile grew.

Cain's face bent into a haughty smirk. "On second thought, take your time, lads. Anyone want a'cuppa?"

"Love one," Eli chimed in, sitting against the wall on an invisible chair.

"Oh my god, you two assholes. Get to work, could you please? Bee is going to need at least six hours to organize her closet." Andi gave them both a look of such ferocity, they both vaulted to their feet, taking their conversation down the stairwell.

Brighton laughed when she heard Eli's voice echo up with a *'bunch of bollocks'* before turning towards Andi. "I'm really happy for you, you know."

"I do." She nodded, taking in the mostly empty apartment. "Lots of good memories here. It wasn't easy to let it go."

"I know."

"Where's Gid?" Andi offered a tempered smile. Brighton could tell she was *trying.*

"He offered to help, which was sweet . . . but something came up." Brighton twined her copper braid around her palm. "If I'm honest, I didn't expect him to come."

"Yeah, me either."

"Andi!"

"What? I'm being honest, too." Andi leaned against a box, watching as Cain and Eli came back in, giving the girls their best dashing smiles as they disappeared down the hallway to Brighton's bedroom. They emerged seconds later, another load in their arms—Cain giving Brighton a playful wink before disappearing into the central corridor once more.

Andi leaned closer, nose wrinkled. "While we're being honest, I gotta point out something that's been bothering me for a while."

"Okay, shoot."

"Cain is a better boyfriend to you than Gideon's ever been."

"Andi . . ." Brighton's mouth hung open to argue, but Andi pressed on.

"The evidence is *abundant*, Bee. You two are always together, all snuggled up on the couch watching movies."

"We aren't snuggling."

"Happy Hour twice a week."

"*With* you and Eli."

"You're moving in together. Can't exactly say the same for you and douche canoe." Andi shrugged.

"Cain is a good friend who saved me the hassle of looking for a new apartment." Brighton floundered for reasons.

"He brings you lunch at work . . ."

". . . he works five blocks away!"

"And then . . ." Andi said with a catlike smile, like she was about to present the juiciest bit of information yet. "There's the fact he is totally, completely, irrevocably in love with you."

Brighton's mouth hung open. "He's not. We're not. We're *friends*."

"Yeah, well. I'm just saying, if my best guy friend was as hot as Cain . . ."

"Andi, he's your *cousin*, GROSS."

"That's beside the point, Brighton. What I mean is, he's attracted to you, and you'd be a fucking liar if you say you're not equally attracted to him. You're hot. He's hot. Why the fuck not?" Andi crossed her arms, hiding her grin as Cain and Eli swept back into the apartment.

Brighton couldn't help but meet Cain's dimpled gaze when he walked by, painfully aware of how Andi watched their every move.

"Do you two—I don't know—plan on helping?" Cain joked, another one of many wardrobe boxes in his arms.

"We're right behind you," Brighton assured him with a smile.

"Yeah, sorry . . . girl talk and all that. Gotta make sure my girl Bee gets hooked up with the *right* guy here soon," Andi interjected.

"Whoever he is, has to go through me," Cain agreed with a sly smile. "We Whitakers have high standards when it comes to the partners for our best friend, don't we, Andi?"

"Too right you are, Cain," Andi answered with her own, horrid attempt at his accent.

"You guys are terrible." Brighton blushed, turning away to hide it while the guys disappeared again.

"My point is . . ." Andi stated once their voices faded away.

Brighton planted her hands on her hips. "Did you have one?"

"*My point is* . . . douche canoe—sorry, *Gideon*—doesn't deserve you. He never has. Where's he been through all your important shit? *Nowhere.* Cain has always been there for you, more-so than Gid ever has in less time. A nice apartment with a decent view does not a good boyfriend make, Bee."

Brighton mulled over Andi's words, working her jaw back and forth before admitting, "Okay . . . I'm not saying there wasn't the possibility of *something* at some point, but—" She sucked in a stuttering breath. "I know it's hard for you to believe, but I *like* what I have with Gideon. It's predictable. It's safe. We're *okay* with the fact that we aren't each other's soulmates, and it works. At this point, I've invested so much time in Gideon . . . I can't walk away because of a random attraction I had at some point to this other guy."

"*Brighton.*" Andi's eyes were soft, like she felt *sorry* for her.

"I *know* what you said." She waved her away. "You said to be open to the idea, but I—I *like* how things *are.*"

"What if Cain's the one?"

Brighton's stomach twisted. Her every atom argued. "He's not."

"How do you know?"

"Wouldn't there . . . I don't know . . . been some other, *more obvious* sign?"

"Maybe, but you'll never know unless you try, Bee." Andi pulled her down into a hug, murmuring against her shoulder. "You're already a sister to me . . . but think of it . . . we could *literally* be family. Plus, you'd make the prettiest babies."

"*Aaaand* I'm walking away . . ." Brighton gave Andi a look, promptly sliding the box they'd been leaning on out from under her elbow, laughing loudly when Andi stumbled and gave her the most loving rendition of the middle finger between giggles of her own.

⋈

*F*ive hours later, four trips back and forth from Old Town, three knowing looks from Andi each time Brighton and Cain interacted, two coffee breaks, and countless trips up and down the stairs—they were *done*.

As Brighton stood in the doorway of an empty *4D,* she still wasn't *quite* ready to say goodbye. She rubbed a hand against her heart when heavy footfalls creaked over the carpet-covered floorboards in the hall, closing her eyes when she felt him lean against the opposite side of the frame.

"It's not all bad, is it?" Cain gave her a little push with his elbow.

Brighton shook her head, her voice quiet. "Not in the slightest. There's so much good here. *So much.*"

"Well," he breathed. "For what it's worth, I'm glad you had this place, that you had Andi."

Her gaze shifted. "How come?"

Cain gave the apartment a nostalgic look of his own before turning to her with a smile. "Well, because you know Andi . . . I know *you.* Sure, it took a while, but we're here now, aren't we?"

"True." Brighton nodded, wrapping her fingers around the brass knob.

With an excited flutter in her belly, Brighton gave the apartment one last look. She shut it with a perfunctory *click,* closing the door on a chapter in her life—both literally and figuratively.

Brighton looped her arm through Cain's. "What do you say we get on the road before Andi and Eli beat us over there?"

"I'd love nothing more, Bee. *Really.* It's about time we gave this adventure a proper start."

"Mm, I couldn't agree more. We've certainly wasted enough time, haven't we?" Brighton said as they made their way down the stairs, side-by-side.

She lifted her hand as they stepped out into the late spring sunshine, motioning for Cain to toss her the keys.

Once in the cab, Cain stretched from the passenger seat as soon as she pulled away from the curb. Brighton's breath caught in her throat as his arm brushed across her front, trying as she might to keep her eyes firmly planted on the busy road.

"Safety first," Cain rumbled, pushing the metal tongue into the anchor with a loud *click*. "Could save your life one day."

"Yeah, and you're distracting the driver. Keep your hands to yourself, sir," Brighton rattled off, keeping her hands firmly at ten and two as she drove them to his—no, *their*—apartment, hoping to rid her mind of the way her skin buzzed from the sensation of his taut, muscled arm against her skin.

⋈

*M*any hands made for light work, and it wasn't much longer before Cain stepped through the threshold of the apartment and declared—

"This . . ." he paused for dramatic effect with a wink at her flushed face, ". . . is the *last* of Brighton's blasted things. Sorry, darling, this is your home forever. To hell with doing that all over again."

Unable to hold in her excitement of *finally* being done with a backbreaking day of work—legs aching and covered in sweat—Brighton leapt into Cain's arms, holding him firmly as he met her with equal enthusiasm.

His body was unbearably warm, wrapped in a sheen from the day's work, but Brighton couldn't care less.

"Welcome home, Colour Girl," Cain murmured, smile playing on his lips.

"Happy to be here," Brighton answered, hopelessly lost in his gaze until a loud cough rang out from inside the apartment.

Brighton looked up at Andi and Eli, both with arms crossed and gazes less than thrilled as the brunette nodded towards the door behind them.

She glanced over Cain's shoulder and felt her stomach drop when she looked upon a well-dressed Gideon in the doorway with a massive, beautifully wrapped gift basket in his arms.

"Sorry, I'm late."

"Gideon, hey!" Brighton dropped down to her feet and jogged over to his side, pressing a swift kiss to his cheek. "I didn't think you'd be able to come! We've just finished."

"Yeah, like, you're *just* in time to do nothing but stand there and look pretty," Andi said with a frown from the arm of the couch.

"*Alexandria.* " Eli hissed in her ear, rubbing his hand over her knee.

"Sorry." She summoned the *least* enthusiastic smile she could. "Thanks for coming, Gideon. I am sure *Brighton* is really happy to see you show up for *something*."

"Could I take this?" Cain stepped forward, motioning for the absurdly large gift basket packed full of all sorts of goodies Brighton knew had been packed by Gideon's assistant.

"Yeah, sure," Gideon passed it over, jaw clenched as he let out a deep breath from his nose. His green eyes shifted around the apartment and the collection of furniture—Cain's furniture.

"I, uh, thanks for that." Cain thumbed over his shoulder, stuffing his free hand in his pocket with a forced smile as the two men stood in a silent stand-off. "So . . ."

"It's a nice place, Brighton." Gideon's turned his attention to her with a tempered smile.

"Thanks, I'm lucky he had the extra space. Pretty sure I'm not contributing enough to the rent, though." Brighton answered, nervously twisting the hem of her red t-shirt around her fingers.

"So, it doesn't bother you that you are living with someone else's girlfriend?" Gideon's green eyes snapped to Cain.

Cain answered in kind, face darkening as he squared his broad shoulders, getting taller by the second—fully aware of the small little detail that the only person who'd been allowed to refer to Brighton as such was Gideon, himself. "I didn't exactly see you jumping to take her in when she needed a place to go."

Brighton's stomach churned as she cast a glare over her shoulder to where Andi giggled not so silently at Cain's comment.

"Hey, so . . . we were going to get some takeout from Tiparos, I know how you love that place." Brighton changed the subject quickly in hopes it would help diffuse the sudden rise in tension since Gideon's arrival. "Did you want to stick around? I'm sorry there's not much work left to do. These guys were efficient."

"Can't." Gideon softened, reaching for Brighton's waist with a smile reserved for her as he pressed a quick kiss to the corner of her mouth.

"*Shocker,*" Andi whispered from behind them.

"I'm sorry to hear that," Brighton mumbled, pushing Gideon out into the hall so they could be relatively alone.

Her fingers lingered on his sleeve, casting a quick glance over her shoulder at Cain before turning back to her *not*-boyfriend. "What's going on?"

Gideon looked over her head into the apartment. "What do you mean?"

"*Someone else's girlfriend.* Are you kidding me?" She rubbed the back of her neck before pushing him further from the open door. "Why do you get to say that? It's been a non-starter for you for how long?"

Gideon shrugged. "It's only a word, Brighton."

Brighton chewed the inside of her cheek, eyes everywhere but on him. "I guess."

He hooked his knuckle under her chin, lifting her gaze. His voice was quiet, and green eyes crinkled. "I love you, you know."

Brighton swallowed the sudden lump in her throat. In all their time together, he'd never said it before, and she'd never been brave enough to even *think* it. "Thank you?"

Gideon let out a huff of laughter. "Don't worry, you don't have to say it back. What I'm saying is . . . to me, the most important part of all this is me . . . and *you*. Does a shared address or a label society approves of prove what we feel?"

When Gideon smiled at her, Brighton couldn't help but smile back. "I suppose. But please don't make a big deal out of things with Cain, again. We're *friends*. And you're the one who told me I should *go for it*. It's not fair if you care all of a sudden."

Gideon sucked in a deep breath through his teeth. "*Fine*. I won't make a big deal out of things if he doesn't. Deal?"

"Whatever." Brighton let her touch linger on his sleeve, skimming her finger over a slight wrinkle. "Are we still on for Friday, then?"

"More than likely," Gideon answered with a nod, skimming the pad of his thumb over her cheek. "I'll let you know if anything changes, okay?"

"Okay," Brighton murmured. "I'll see you."

"Good luck unpacking that closet, babe." He winked before turning on his heel to walk down the stairs.

Brighton turned and met Andi and Eli. Her brows puckered. "What, you guys aren't leaving already, are you?"

"Afraid so," Eli answered, nodding towards Andi. "This one booked us a fancy dinner in a few hours, so we have to go make sure my bowtie coordinates properly with my glasses. You know, the important things."

"Oh, that's exciting!" Brighton looked over Andi to Eli, who tapped his finger against the side of his nose. Her heart did a little flip. "I'm so happy for you. I really, really am. Have the *best* time."

"It's only dinner, Bee." Andi made a face, tilting her head inside. "Now get in there and properly christen that apartment."

"Ew."

"I meant with like, unpacking your closet, *calm down*." She grinned with a giggle, stepping backward as Eli towed her towards the stairs. "I'll give you guys a few months before I officially try to get you two married. Just wait, it's gonna happen. I can *feel* it. Can you hear the wedding bells, Bee? *Ding dong, ding dong . . . Cain and Brightoooon.*"

Brighton shook her head and stepped back into the apartment, gently shutting the door behind her.

"What'd she say?" Cain asked as he gingerly unpacked a box of her favorite mugs, placing them side-by-side with his in the cupboard.

"Oh, nothing." Brighton leaned against the island counter, watching with a happy sigh as he unwrapped another colorful piece of ceramic. "So . . ."

"So." Cain nodded, crumpling up the paper before tossing it back into the box. "Shall we move some boxes to your room, then?"

Brighton cast a look over her shoulder into the shared space stacked *full* of boxes. "I suppose they're taking up all the space in the living room, aren't they?"

"No matter." Cain walked around the slab of black granite, lifting a box from the floor with a tilt of his head. "Follow me, Your Ladyship."

Spinning on the toe of her yellow converse, Brighton collected a box marked *Brighton shoes* and followed Cain down the brick-lined hallway. She paused in the first doorway, peeking inside with a confused laugh.

Eli's former bedroom Brighton helped empty the day before was fully furnished with a dresser, nightstand, and a sprawling king-sized bed.

"This is your stuff . . ." Brighton stated, halting Cain's steps one door down.

"Correct. Superb skills of deduction, Ms. Evans. I'm impressed. Truly."

"This isn't the master bedroom." Brighton looked again, brown eyes wandering over the sleek, wooden frame and the deep gray velvet duvet that looked achingly soft to the touch.

"*Amazing.* You're correct again," Cain teased, motioning towards the open door in front of him. "Be a good lass and come take a look at the things I've been up to since you've made the horrible mistake of living here."

Brighton narrowed her eyes with a suspicious smile. "If this is a horrible mistake, then I don't know what is," she drawled, stepping into the bright, clean, and *empty* master bedroom.

"Over here, darling." Cain pushed the small of her back with his free hand, watching her as he set the box to the floor.

She followed his gaze to a side wall, peeking her head in the darkened doorway of what used to be Cain's closet as he flipped a switch and a bright light flickered to life.

Brighton's mouth dropped open with a gasp, eyes wide as she set the box she'd been holding at her feet, gingerly stepping around it like she was walking on hallowed ground. With a trembling hand, she skimmed her fingertips along an empty shelf, slowly turning to look at Cain, who leaned *oh-so-casually* in the doorway.

"*What did you do?*"

He shrugged. "It's no matter, really."

"Cain Whitaker, this . . . is *not* the way things looked in here before. Did you . . . did you gut the entire thing?"

"I had a little help. It's no big deal."

"*No big deal*?" Brighton scoffed, stepping further back into the space as she cocked an eyebrow and held out her arms—voice cracking as her eyes brimmed with tears. "You built me a *closet*."

"Andi had a hand in it." He stepped forward, lifting his eyes, and looked at the rainbowed glass fixture hanging from the ceiling, casting a shower of glittering light over every surface. "They're from the web. All I had to do was put it together."

"I don't even know what to say," Brighton murmured, holding her elbows as her eyes darted over every corner.

"Don't say anything, darling," Cain answered, wrapping her up in his arms, pressing a kiss to the crown of her head. "I'm happy you're here, and I wanted to give you something to make you feel properly at home."

That was the thing, though. As Brighton lifted her chin and took in Cain's smiling face, it wasn't the closet that made her feel at home. It wasn't the building or the furnishings. It wasn't the gift basket from Gideon left untouched in the kitchen or her mugs beside Cain's in the cupboard.

It was him.

Chapter
8

The next year...

*B*righton closed her eyes as she walked down the sidewalk, breathing in the cold December air with a smile. Snow was coming; she could feel it. Soon, the city would be blanketed in purest white.

Brighton let out a sigh while striding down the sidewalk, past decorated windows and trees twined with rainbow-colored lights. Things in her life were falling into place. As time passed, she felt better about the decisions she'd made and couldn't see herself anywhere else than where she was.

Perhaps, now, after so much time, she let herself be more than happy enough.

Dressed for the Christmas-themed party she was about to attend, Brighton didn't only feel stylish—she felt *beautiful.*

A black velvet top hugged the curve of her shoulders, leaving each and every sun-kissed freckle from summertime open to the air. Her auburn waves were tied back in a simple red ribbon perfectly matched to the lipstick on her mouth and the Jimmy Choos on her feet. The pièce de résistance, though, was the bright emerald taffeta skirt hugging her waist and flared out just past her knees.

It was attention-grabbing, but Brighton didn't mind, focused only on securing the attention of one specific person.

Freckled cheeks flushed from the cold, Brighton stepped inside the breezeway of a sleek restaurant.

"Name?"

Brighton looked over to the host with a wide smile and the faintest flutter of excitement in her belly. "Whitaker."

"Fantastic, they're waiting at the bar for you." She motioned into the sleek, silver and black Art Deco dining room.

They?

Brighton walked past a sweeping staircase, keeping her eyes trained on the back wall of the restaurant as the excited flutter gave way to a bucket of boulders. There was no mistaking Cain, even in the sea of people on a busy Saturday evening at Christmastime.

His suit stretched across his back, seams aching down the length of his arms. Cain looked *good*, there was no denying it, and Brighton didn't see the point in trying. He was the most beautiful thing in her life, and out of her many talents, appreciating beautiful things was her favorite.

But.

There, beside Cain—talking *with him*—was Gideon.

Their posture was perfect, standing as tall as their bodies would allow—shoulders square and chins up. Brighton's mind buzzed, sending her fingers tingling as she tried to think of what the two of them could *possibly* have to talk about. More than anything, though, Brighton could carefully catalog every crease of Cain's brow and twitch in his jaw while Gideon animatedly prattled on about something she couldn't hear.

Like he felt her presence, Cain lifted his gaze to meet Brighton's before she even had the chance to speak. At once, his face softened, blue eyes dancing over her every inch. Gideon followed soon after, face blooming into a smile.

"Well hello, gorgeous." Her long-term someone's chest puffed out, slipping his hands beneath her ribbon-tied hair without hesitation to pull her in for a kiss.

Brighton pressed her hands to Gideon's chest, humming as she pushed him away.

"S-sorry I'm late," she breathed, brushing her knuckles against her cheek—now blazing hot even though she'd just come in from the cold.

"Worth waiting for, certainly." Cain hadn't moved from the spot where she'd found them, allocated to the background when Gideon—rightfully, so—took advantage of the first moment to give his *someone* a proper greeting.

"Hey, Kal El."

"Hi, Bee." Cain kept his hands in his pockets, leaning close to brush an unhurried kiss on her cheek, then the other.

It was brief. So brief. *Too brief.* So much less than the kind of hello she'd come to expect.

Brighton's cheeks ached from her smile; arms aching, too, wishing to hug him the way she wanted. "How was New York?"

"It was alright." Cain's hands remained deep in his pockets, shoulders hunched as he worked to contain his smile. "I went to our place."

"Your place?" Gideon, standing in Brighton's periphery, chimed in.

"Yeah . . ." Brighton nodded as he reached for the collar of her crimson wool coat. "It's a bar at JFK."

Gideon looked puzzled, like he never thought to consider there might be any place in an airport other than the Sky Club Lounge. He stripped the coat from her shoulders, leaving them alone while he took it to the coat check.

"You're a sight for sore eyes, darling." Cain's voice was low.

"Am I?" Brighton slid her palms down emerald taffeta before looking back at him.

"A beautiful one, at that. You look incredible," he answered, taking a step closer.

Brighton clutched her bottom lip between her teeth, letting out a slow breath through her nose. "What were you two talking about?"

"Me and flower man?" Cain let out a huff of laughter.

"Gideon, yeah." A ribbon of auburn hair found its way around her finger, her stomach twisting with every heart-stopping second she waited for Cain to answer.

The playfulness of his grin faded. "Which of us is the best man for you."

"*Cain.*" Brighton flinched when the sharp *pop* of a champagne cork rang out across the lounge. "I'm serious."

"So am I." Cain's blue eyes sparkled as he casually ran a finger between the fabric of her blouse and her shoulder, giving it the gentlest of tugs to straighten the line as he murmured, "Sorry. Trying to lend a hand."

Brighton brushed her hand against the ghost of his touch, mind reeling with questions. "Thank you."

"We ready to party?" Gideon strode up, straightening his tie.

Brighton wound her arm through Gideon's, heart still thumping as their odd little trio made their way upstairs. With every step, Brighton was *oh* so aware of Cain's eyes on her.

She could hear the hum of a jazz band playing *Winter Wonderland* before she reached the top, caught up in the sweet sound and the gold and red Christmas decorations dripping down from the towering ceiling.

Together, they stepped through the doors and into a spacious, private dining room with a gold and red Christmas tree in every corner and stacks of gorgeous decorations everywhere.

"Wow, she really outdid herself, didn't she?" Cain's brows lifted as he turned his gaze to the ceiling.

Gideon leaned down and whispered in her ear, "Tacky, isn't it?"

Brighton's eyes snapped away from the beautiful decorations to his. "This is my best friend's party. *Be nice.*"

Gideon forced a smile, snagging a champagne flute from a passing tray. "I'm always nice to Alexandria."

The bride, whose attention Brighton was briefly able to catch, quickly sent them on their way with strict instructions to mingle, eat, and have fun. After a quick exchange of smiles, Brighton and Cain went their separate ways into the party.

She happily rubbed elbows with old friends from college and reconnected briefly with Andi's parents as Gideon disappeared and took a call. As she made her way through the crowd, Brighton's eyes would always find Cain's.

They'd bump into each other—sometimes literally. He'd give her a grin. Other times, he'd press his hand on the small of her back, sending her on her way as they worked the room.

Cain and his collectible smiles . . . to Brighton, the ones he gave her that evening were for the books. She found herself inexplicably drawn to them, which wasn't *entirely* out of the blue. After all, it was his smile that caught her attention when they met.

Brighton tried to be a dutiful friend and properly mill about the room with Andi and Eli's guests, but after Gideon left the hall to answer a third phone call in a row, and the fourth time she bumped into Cain, she didn't want to say goodbye. Thankfully, he gave her a perfect reason to stick around.

Bringing his lips to her ear to hear him over the steady din of the crowd, Cain murmured, "Fancy a dance, beautiful?"

Brighton cleared her throat, tugging her bottom lip between her teeth with a nod. "Love to."

Hands twined together, Cain towed Brighton to the center

of the dance floor, pulling her in a wide circle before sliding his hand to the small of her back. Fingers splayed out across black velvet, he pressed her up against his chest as the tempo of the music slowed to something more romantic.

"Fancy meeting you here," Brighton murmured, looking up at him as she slipped her fingers into the palm of his other hand.

Cain let out a low chuckle when—in a single sentence—she brought them straight back to their first meeting. "You come here often?"

"For dancing? Yes." Brighton nodded, chest rising in a deep, contented breath when Cain gave her waist a push and sent her into a slow spin under his arm before pulling her back in.

"Blimey, you don't say. *Me too.*"

Brighton felt at home with Cain, wrapped up in the comfort of his arms. She leaned her head against his shoulder as they swayed back and forth.

"I've been thinking," Cain hummed, slowly thumbing his touch up and down her back. "About all this."

"Oh? About Christmas, marriage, *soulmates* . . . which is it, Whitaker?" Brighton teased, lifting her eyes to give him a smile. It melted like a snowflake on a summer sidewalk when she saw him remain pensive. She chewed the inside of her lip as a knot twisted in her stomach.

"All of it, actually." Cain pushed her into another lovely, slow spin before bringing her back home in his arms.

"*Oh.*" Brighton swallowed the growing lump in her throat. "What about it?"

"I'm just . . ." His brows creased together as he looked over her head across the room. "It was a lucky shot with Eli and Andi—how it brought us together. I'm so thankful for it, for them . . . for their *Glimpse*. Sometimes, though, I wonder if there's something else to it."

"What kind of something else?"

"I . . . uh . . ." Cain breathed with a clench of his jaw and a tempered smile. "Maybe a fate kind of thing."

"Fate or not." Brighton feathered her fingertips through the dark curls at his temple. "I'm so glad I met you. I'm grateful to know Andi and that you introduced her to Eli, because without it . . . I wouldn't have met you, and I . . . I don't think that's a life I'd want. One without you, I mean. You're my best friend, and I—"

Cain smiled with another sigh, leaning down to press a long, drawn-out kiss on Brighton's forehead before rumbling, "You're mine too, darling."

They settled back into the soothing rhythm of the dance, smiling and laughing each of their cares away, happy to just *be*.

It didn't last long before Brighton asked. "What did you mean by fate?"

Cain leaned closer, brows drawn together. "That's complicated, Bee."

"Try me."

"If you say so." Cain pushed Brighton into another breathless spin, summoning a fit of girlish giggles when he sank her into a dizzying dip. His face hovered close to hers, and a dark curl slipped forth from his hairline. "What I mean is . . . some people talk about this life not being the only one we get to live . . ."

"You mean, like . . . reincarnation or something?" Brighton laughed, but it died with the decrescendo of music, moving into another lilting, romantic tune. "You don't think this world with pre-destined soulmates isn't already enough?"

"No, I think there's more to it, is all. I've . . ." Cain's blue eyes fell to the floor as he thoughtfully considered his response, bringing his gaze back to Brighton's with a look of such earnest intensity, it practically pulled a gasp from her lips. "I've never shaken this feeling like I've *always* known you. Hasn't it always felt so impossibly easy between us? *Effortless?*"

"Y-yes. It has."

"I swear—if I'm right—if we were friends in another life, if we're friends in the next . . . I'd remember you. I'd remember in the next life, and the life after that, and *the life after that*. If not . . . if this is all we get, then I'll never stop wishing for more because I'd take all the lifetimes I can get with you by my side."

Brighton's lips parted, heart hammering away with each breath. Cain tucked his hand beneath her chin, gently skimming the pad of his thumb over her cheek as his jaw clenched with a chorus of unspoken words.

Had they stopped dancing? Brighton wasn't entirely sure. Then again, she wasn't totally convinced her feet were still planted firmly on the ground. Her eyes darted back and forth across Cain's handsome face, looking over every line—both ones she recognized and others she'd watched form.

Brighton's hands ached to trace them, committing them to memory, storing them lovingly beside the collection of smiles she'd put away from the first moment they'd met.

Love. It was something she was sure she felt for Cain . . . but of what kind? Her loyalty and fondness for him were undeniable. Still, with Cain's words fresh in her mind, his gaze twined with hers, and bodies pressed so firmly together, Brighton started to wonder if it was a different feeling altogether. There it was, on the tip of his tongue—so plainly illustrated in his gaze —Brighton swore she could hear him say it.

Three words. Eight letters.

Lips parting softly, they drew closer as Brighton murmured so quietly, she wasn't sure if he'd be able to hear her. *"Cain,* I—"

A voice interrupted before she could finish or question the thought any further. Banished from her mind in an instant, they sprang apart, and Brighton spun and met Gideon's eyes with a smile.

Chapter 9

"**Y**ou don't mind if I cut in with my girl, do you, Whitaker?" Gideon slid his hand around Brighton's waist, pulling her snugly against his side.

"Not in the slightest," Cain answered with an unruffled, composed smile.

Gideon looked down at her, giving her a foreignly tender squeeze, pressing a kiss to the freckled curve of her shoulder. "Thank goodness."

Brighton's eyes stayed on Cain throughout the interaction, unable to look away when he tensed under Gideon's extra attention.

"So, uh . . ." Brighton her ponytail over her shoulder, trying to focus on Gideon's face through every anxious beat of her heart. "I am so glad you're back. I thought for sure the office would keep you on that call a little longer."

"I said I'd be here, and I'm here, Brighton." Gideon looked offended, giving her another firm squeeze around the waist as he forced another smile. "I'm a man of my word."

"I know you are. It's . . . usually . . ." Brighton shrugged, caught up in her guilt.

"It's alright, baby. I know I've been absent, but don't you worry. I'm going to be around a lot more often." Much to her surprise, Gideon cupped her face in his hands, soulfully staring into her eyes before bringing his lips to hers.

In literally any other situation, Brighton would be happy for the attention, but here, like this . . . she *knew* it was all a show put on for Cain. The thought angered her, spurred on by the want to protect her friend, but from what? Jealousy? Why? They weren't together, no matter how close they toed the line between friendship and more—no matter how often Brighton fought the feeling they ought to be.

It wasn't always easy. There were times when she would catch herself looking, but over and over again, her choice to be with Gideon won out. He was predictable—*safe*—a source of comfort and calm after what Jesse Butler did. Gideon Baumgartner put Brighton back together, and that wasn't something she could let herself set aside . . . even if he couldn't admit to seeing a future for them.

Regardless, Brighton was happy with him.

Happy enough.

Brighton pulled away from the kiss, humming with a wavering smile and a press of her lips, holding firmly to Gideon's wrists as she pulled free from his grasp.

"I'm glad to hear it," she stated, eager to put a sliver of space between them, ever aware of Cain steps away—a captive audience for the charade.

Brighton wanted to believe it, she really did, but at what point did Gideon's attention turn from something she wanted him to do because he loved her—to something he did to make someone else jealous?

"Is that . . . is that Brighton Evans?" A voice interrupted her thoughts, and Brighton thought she might faint from the relief when one of the many guests recognized her.

Brighton turned around, thrilled to chat with Andi's cousin

three-times removed. Gideon followed close behind, and Cain was never far away, both of them determined to remain by her side as they milled through the room.

The three of them went about their way, caught up in an odd dance. Brighton would try and create a little extra space, desperate for an ounce of breathing room from Gideon's unexpected extra affection.

Another guest would call for her attention, inevitably pulling Brighton away from the bubble. Part of her was thankful to have a second to breathe—to think—but never long enough before Gideon would be by her side again.

There wasn't more than a minute or two without his hand planted firmly on the small of her back, showering her with affectionate kisses Brighton would wholeheartedly welcome . . . if they didn't feel so out of place.

The situation was so odd; Brighton almost thought it felt like a game. They milled through the cocktail party, plucking *hors d'oeuvres* from a platter here, a glass of champagne there, and no matter the space she tried to put between her and Gideon, like a bloodhound, he always found her.

"*What is going on?*" Brighton hissed into Gideon's ear when his hand found her waist again, lifting her eyes to meet Cain's across the circle of people. He wore a deep frown with a twitch of his jaw. Her eyes darted back to the blond, stomach twisting.

Gideon looked taken aback. "What do you mean?"

"Come on, Gid," Brighton argued quietly, brow furrowed as she leaned away. "You never act like this. You never touch me like this."

"Babe, I touch you *plenty*." Gideon's face melted into a Cheshire Cat smile with a tilt of his head and a quick glance over her body. "I mean . . . if you wanna get out of here, I won't argue. This party is a little too fucking much. Whoever I marry better not want something like this, I swear."

Brighton clenched her jaw, dark eyes ablaze. "Are you serious? *Whoever* you marry?"

Gideon looked down at her with an infuriatingly casual shrug. "I mean, yeah. Why wouldn't I be?"

Without a second thought, Brighton pushed him away and stormed to the back of the room. She shoved her way through groups of people, not caring about the hushed murmurs as she eagerly chased a quiet corner where no one bothered her.

Somewhere past the restrooms and before a service elevator, pacing back and forth in the relative quiet of a hidden back hallway, Brighton struggled to catch her breath as the click of her ruby-red stilettos rang out over the marble floors.

She liked Gideon. Loved him, maybe. He was a good guy who made her happy. One night of being a complete ass didn't negate everything else they had.

Brighton repeated it over and over in her head, needing to banish the anger boiling beneath the surface that stole her every breath with each rapid beat of her heart.

"*Hey...*"

Spinning with a ruffle of emerald taffeta, Brighton practically melted like ice cream in a warm porcelain bowl when she saw Cain's concerned face hovering on the edge of the corridor she'd hidden in.

"*I'm sorry.*" Brighton whispered with a stuttering breath, dashing the silvery streaks of angry tears from her eyes.

"Bee, *no* . . ." Without a second thought, Cain stepped forward and held Brighton by her shoulders, blue eyes darting back and forth between hers. "It's okay. Focus on me and *breathe*. Don't be sorry for a single moment, alright?"

Brighton gave Cain a shaky nod, lips parting as his face hovered above hers. Cain coached her through a few slow breaths until her heartbeat began to normalize, and she felt like she could really, truly breathe again.

"I don't know what his problem is," Brighton murmured,

fanning her flushed cheeks as the pair of them hovered on the edge of the festivities.

"Aw, no, darling. Your boyfriend is the life of the fucking party, isn't he?" Cain teased with a wry smile.

Brighton glared up at him. "I thought you were on my side?"

"I am, I am! Don't you worry, Colour Girl." He held up his hands in mock surrender. "I want to support you in whatever you choose, same as always."

"*Thank you.*" Brighton softened, wrapping her arms around Cain's waist before, with a deep breath, she looked up at him with her chin balanced on his chest. "We should get back out there."

Ever the constant force of calm in her life, Cain answered with a reassuring smile, holding out his elbow with a charming, "Shall we, m'lady?"

"I suppose." Brighton snaked her arm through his, leaning against his bicep as they stepped back out into the fray.

Cain leaned down and rumbled a shiver-inducing whisper in her ear, "If you want to get out of here, tug on your ear three times, and I'll whisk you away."

"*My hero.*" She laughed, giving his arm a squeeze.

Brighton instantly felt more comfortable by Cain's side. Still, her suddenly attentive *not*-boyfriend was relentless, swooping in to join a conversation not long after she and Cain stopped to mingle with an old professor of hers from the University of Chicago.

"And where are you working now, Brighton?" She, a woman with a well-earned tenure in her weathered hands and face, asked.

"I am part of a fantastic architecture firm in The Loop. Bazaroff & Graham. They've got an incredible reputation, and I'm currently heading up a full renovation at Lakeview Children's."

"Oh, that sounds *wonderful*. You ought to be proud." The professor smiled with a slow tap of her finger on the side of her Manhattan. "Now, how about you two? Has your best friend tying the knot lit a fire under this one here?"

She motioned to Cain, who graciously smiled and shook his head. "I'm afraid there's no fire to light. Though, I'd be damn lucky to marry her if I had the chance."

Brighton blushed under the professor's scrutinizing gaze, glancing at Cain before meeting Gideon's look of pure jealousy he cast from across the cluster of guests.

"Professor Field, this is Gideon Baumgartner, my partner." Brighton motioned for Gideon to step up beside her. Twining her fingers through his, she forced him to smile with a squeeze of his hand. "He's a U of C grad, as well."

"Pleasure." Gideon nodded, tone clipped.

"Oh, *oh!* I apologize! I thought . . ." She motioned between Brighton and Cain, her mouth wide open and ruddy cheeks a rosier hue as her gaze moved to Brighton and Gideon—realizing her mistake.

"No, please don't apologize, Professor. It happens more than it should." Brighton scrambled to fix the situation and ease Gideon's discomfort.

"My goodness, let me start over, sweethearts. *Now*, how long have you two been together?"

"Five years, nearly," Brighton answered.

"My goodness, such a long time for you young people!" The professor gave her an encouraging smile.

To her surprise, Cain chimed in, and Brighton felt her cheeks flush all the brighter.

"I'm a little curious in regards to the Professor's earlier question." The softest, almost imperceptible smile hovered on his face. "Is this what you want? Does Andi getting married make you crave the same kind of thing?"

Brighton rolled it over in her mind, slowly licking her lips as the words sat on the tip of her tongue. It would be a lie to say she hadn't thought about it. Her heart fluttered when the answer became all the clearer. "If I'm honest, I think—"

"*Actually.*" Gideon's arm snaked around Brighton's waist as he sipped his vodka rocks through his teeth. "Brighton and I pride ourselves to be outside of the loop of the monotony of traditional relationship goals. There are ways around *The Grey*, and I don't believe in the tiring search for a so-called 'perfect person' when there are perfectly satisfactory partners across the city. We don't use words like *boyfriend* or *girlfriend*. In fact, we don't even live together, and we like it that way. Marriage is such a blasé concept, don't you think? Personally, I—"

Cain held up his broad palm with an icy stare, stopping Gideon in his tracks with a tilt of his head, reaching out to help free Brighton from her not-boyfriend's grip.

"Oh, thanks mate, but actually, I was asking *Brighton*." His blue eyes shifted from Gideon to hers. Cain gave her a confident nod telling her to continue as the professor waited on bated breath for her answer.

"*Actually*—" A different voice chimed in, and a small hand curled around Brighton's arm, tugging her away. Andi looked over the faces in their small circle of conversation with a forced smile. "Sorry for the interruption, but I need to borrow my best friend, please, and thank you."

Brighton was more than thankful for the distraction, though her stomach twisted at the thought of leaving Cain and Gideon alone for the second time that night.

"You're welcome," Andi gave her a smug smile as they found a quiet corner next to a glittering Christmas tree.

Brighton breathed a happy sigh as she looked up over the twinkling lights, helpless to do anything but smile at the simple joy it brought.

A finger in her arm brought her back to reality with a hiss

of pain between her teeth. "Fuck! *Ouch*, Alexandria. Can you not?"

"I'm the bride. Pay attention to me for two seconds, please. It's important."

"*Fine*." Brighton rolled her eyes, but her grin fell away when Andi hoisted a large, colorful box from beneath the tree.

Andi laughed when Brighton took it with a groan and a swear. "What the fuck is in here, Andi? *Bricks*?"

"Booze, mostly." Andi shrugged, gathering up her crimson skirt to slide down the wall with a grumble. "Damn, my feet hurt. Is this night almost over? I'm tired of being on my best behavior."

"You're almost there, don't worry," Brighton laughed, balancing the parcel on her hip as she settled in beside her. She grasped the end of a yellow ribbon between her fingers, slowly pulling it open before lifting the lid.

Andi wasn't kidding. Inside was an expensive-looking bottle of Mezcal and a vast collection of mini bottles of tequila that brought an instant smile to Brighton's face.

Little by little, she made her way through the box. She pressed her nose into a green satin robe, squealed over a bottle of blue nail polish, and promptly secured a sleep mask around her head before she got to the best part—a framed set of pictures with two pairs of their faces.

One of the photos had to be at least twenty years old. In it, both of them were missing most of their teeth, and their faces were covered in a summer's worth of freckles with the lake where they spent their childhood behind them.

Brighton felt overwhelmed, remembering the day her mom snapped the photo. The girls had waited patiently as the roll of film filled up over the next week, and not so patiently for the One-Hour-Photo stand to develop it.

It was a summer like all the others. The pair of them swam like fish, leaping from the end of the dock in every ridiculous way they could think of. They'd rejoice over a shared peanut butter and jelly with their feet dangling over the water, and complain when their parents would call them in by the dimming light of day.

Brighton wished she could go back, more homesick in a single moment than she had been in the time it'd been since her mother died and her dad, Thomas, sold the empty lake house.

The other photo was recent. Brighton recognized the elbow-length of her hair, the diamond ring on Andi's left hand, and the deep green seats of Wrigley Field in a second.

She thought back fondly to when Andi had handed off her phone to her fiancé. Sandwiched between Eli and Cain, the two women wrapped their arms around each other for the photo seconds before a fly ball came their way.

Brighton ran her thumb over the photo when she saw the same little girls in the broad grins of the friends who were more like sisters than anything else.

There—behind her shoulder—was Cain.

Around the edge of the frame, were words printed in a swirling script that read, *"I found my mister, but I still need my sister. Will you be my Maid of Honor?"*

Reading the words took Brighton's breath away, and she quickly felt the pinprick of tears. Usually, she couldn't care less about such things—but this was *Andi*. Her oldest friend. Her found sister. Brighton couldn't imagine her life without her, let alone on the most important day of her life.

Eyes shimmering with emotion, Brighton looked up at her best friend with a small voice, *"Andi..."*

"It's cheesy, I know, but I . . ." The bride-to-be stuttered through her own tears, dashing them away with the back of her hand. "I can't do it without you, Bee. Would you?"

"Oh my god." Brighton threw her arms around the

brunette's shoulders with a dramatic grin to try and laugh away the absurdity of crying. "I thought you'd never ask!!"

They sat there for a few more minutes, reminiscing over summers on the lake. It gave Andi the opportunity to rest her feet before, eventually, the groom-to-be came searching for her.

Eli pulled Andi to her feet, enveloping her in a hug that summoned a smile wider than anything Brighton had ever seen her friend wear the entire time she'd known her.

Brighton mulled over the answer she'd been prepared to give her professor earlier—and Cain's that followed swiftly after.

Does Andi getting married make you crave the same kind of thing?

Brighton watched Andi walk away, gazing adoringly at Eli in a way she was *sure* only soulmates looked at each other. Part of her *craved* the feeling, she'd wished for it since she was a little girl, but something still held her back.

Thinking over the faces of the men in her life with a smile, Brighton was only half-sure what she would want, and happy enough playing it safe with Gideon.

The idea was appealing, to joyfully join hands with the right man for the rest of her life—soulmate or not.

Who needs a soulmate? Brighton traced her fingertips over the hidden soul mark on her hip. Surely, it wasn't the most significant thing if she was already really, truly happy.

A soulmate would be an added bonus.

Brighton meandered her way through the remaining guests, saying a chorus of goodbyes and farewells. Eventually, she made her way back down the stairs, eager to get home and out of her shoes.

She slid her arms through the sleeves of her favorite crimson coat, letting out a breezy sigh as she stepped out onto the street.

Oh, what a wondrous sight it was. In a matter of hours, not only had Brighton's feeling been right, but the entire city had been blanketed in a fresh cover of snow.

Lifting her face to the sky with a beamingly bright smile, Brighton watched the fluffy flakes gently tumble from their skyward home, twisting and turning on the slightest breeze as they took the long way down to Earth—perching themselves on her eyelashes. She closed her eyes as each one kissed her face, breathing it all in as her grin grew wider.

"Brighton . . ." His voice pulled her from her winter wonderland before she was ready to let go. She tilted her chin down, waiting until the last possible second before opening her eyes.

Gideon stood—wrapped in his own Brooks Brothers wool with a silk scarf—leather glove extended expectantly. Brighton knew in any other circumstance; she'd be following him home . . . but then came a different voice.

"You ready, Bee?"

Brighton looked back and forth between the two men in her life, both arguably of equal importance. With one, she had a history. With the other . . . it was beyond words. Still, Brighton found the decision nearly impossible to make.

Her eyes darted back and forth across the street, searching for answers she was sure the advertisement on top of a passing yellow cab wouldn't give her . . . but time might.

⋈

Later . . .

*B*righton wasn't sure when she'd fallen asleep or how. It might've had something to do with the champagne she'd been drinking at the party. Perhaps it'd been the warmth of her favorite knitted blanket across her lap . . . or the slow, steady beating of a heart beneath her cheek that sent her dozing somewhere between '*Now I have a machine gun, Ho-Ho-Ho*' and '*Yippee-ki-yay Mother Fucker!*'

Sleep made Brighton's thoughts fuzzy. She wasn't convinced she was on the couch any longer, and her blanket was missing. However, the still, sure beating heart was the same—*ba-dump, ba-dump, ba-dump*—beneath her cheek.

Hands. Hers were in front of her, with one tucked against her chin and the other pressed against something warm. Perhaps a tuft of chest hair? She blinked in the darkness as her body shuffled back and forth like a dance— like her dance earlier with Cain where he held her so firmly . . . not unlike how firmly she was being held right then.

Before she could wake any further, Brighton felt the softness of her pillow beneath her cheek, opening her eyes enough to see the still-falling snow outside her bedroom window. She burrowed into her blankets with a muffled groan, vaguely aware of the gentle press of a kiss upon her head and the tender whisper of "*I love you, darling*" before falling asleep once more.

⋈

*T*he snow continued into the next afternoon, falling in quiet, dreamy flakes outside their window. Brighton spent most of the morning curled up beneath her favorite red wool blanket, trying and failing to focus on her book as her final waking moments the night before played on a loop in her mind.

Balancing her jaw on her knuckles, Brighton looked to the other end of the sofa where her feet were tucked beneath Cain's knee. He had his nose stuck in a worn copy of *The Return of the King*, none the wiser to how her heart flipped every time she glanced his way.

Bad. It was a bad idea to let herself give into the feeling. Dangerous, even. She'd been on the edge of it at the party, so wrapped up in the feeling of being wrapped up in Cain, Brighton let her fears slip away.

She was scared for good reason, though. After her mom— after Jesse—the risk of feeling the same kind of hurt was too great. What she and Cain had was good. More than good—it was *everything;* too important to gamble with by making it more complicated than it needed to be.

Cain's eyes lifted from the page, luminous like a cool lagoon as the afternoon light bounced off crisp white paper and lit his face. "You alright?"

Brighton pulled her feet out from beneath him, mustering a smile. "Yeah. I'm fine. I'm good."

He lifted a brow. "Liar."

Brighton stomach flipped, and she leapt from her cocoon to dart down the hall to find a distraction. Moments later, she emerged with a gift box she'd snagged from her underwear drawer.

Cain gave her a look as Brighton slid in beside him, snapping his book shut when she tossed the parcel in his lap. "What's this?"

"Bribery," Brighton giggled, chewing the inside of her lip as he inspected the multicolored wrapping and slowly pulled on the end of the blue ribbon.

"Bribery, eh? For what? To drop the subject? Got a bad picture you don't want me to show anyone?" Cain mused with a lift of his brow and one of his heart-stopping, collectible smiles.

"This is me begging you not to make me watch Die Hard at Christmas *ever* again," Brighton grimaced.

"*Ouch.* You bite your tongue. John McClane is a national treasure." Cain's mouth hung open in mock-hurt, pressing his fingers to his chest to make it all the more convincing.

Brighton waved him on. "Maybe for the rest of America, but not for me. Open it, already."

"Did you drag the paper through a crayon factory? This is

pushing it . . . even for you." Cain hooked his finger into the seam to rip it open, smile fading away as he swiped his thumb over the gold *B* embossed in the leather case. Cain's eyes glittered as he cast her a sidelong gaze. "Breitling . . . *Brighton* . . . this is too much."

"I really, *really* don't want to watch Die Hard." Brighton leaned closer, anchoring her elbow on his shoulder as he opened the box with a creak.

Inside—with a black face, luxurious leather band, and a glimmering crystal crown—laid the watch Cain had always talked about owning but was never quite able to convince himself to buy. Tucked beneath it was a folded-up photograph of Brighton.

Cain peeled it open, letting out a quiet huff of laughter at the ridiculous face she was making in it.

"Okay, the picture is obviously a joke, you *definitely* don't have to keep that . . . but . . . I hope you like the watch." Brighton twisted a ribbon of red hair around her finger.

"Oh, *I'm keeping it.* I'll put it in my wallet, too. That way, I always have you with me." Cain wrapped his arm around her, pulling her into a hug as he murmured into her hair, "I don't know how I can ever thank you. It's beautiful, Bee."

Brighton lifted her chin from the warmth of Cain's chest and the steady rhythm of his heart. "I can take the picture for you and save you the hassle. You'll be sick of it by Valentine's Day, I promise."

"Not a fucking chance, darling." A deep chuckle rumbled around in Cain's chest as he pulled her close again, pressing a kiss to the crown of her head. "You can have it when I'm dead."

Chapter 10

February

She'd been to fancy restaurants time and time again, but this one—*The Signature Room at the 95ᵗʰ*—was a special kind of place. Brighton had only seen pictures and heard from friends who ventured to the top of the John Hancock building. Reservations were an unattainable thing, and as the lift declared her arrival and the doors slid open—she could see why.

Brighton's shoes—a favorite red pair to match her coat and lipstick—clicked along the marble floors, twined with every beat of her heart as the restaurant opened around and below her.

It took her breath away, but Brighton barely had a chance to get a proper look at the 360-degree view before a snide voice interrupted her quiet wonder.

"Can I help you, miss? This establishment is by reservation, only," the hostess sneered.

"Actually, sweetheart, I'm meeting someone." Brighton peered over her shoulder and into the dining room, lifting her hand to wave at the handsome man sitting at a table along the wall-to-wall windows.

"Name?"

"Baumgartner, Gideon."

The hostess's icy demeanor melted at the mention of his name.

"Mister Baumgartner? *Oh*, I'm terribly sorry. This way, please, Ms. Evans," she bumbled with a dip of her head, ushering Brighton down a sweeping staircase into the dining room below.

After how poorly the night had gone in regards to Gideon at Andi and Eli's engagement party—and the absurdity of the possessiveness he displayed—he'd made good on his promise to be around more often.

They'd spent the last two months together more often than they were apart. Gideon popped by for lunch, met her at the end of the workday, and called in the evenings "to say goodnight."

To Brighton, he was like the Gideon she met five years prior —the one with whom she'd shared an instantaneous attraction, who held her attention and showered her with his own. The one who made her feel safe and put her back together after life had torn her hopeful heart apart.

With time and Gideon's effort, Brighton finally allowed herself to be open to the idea of more than their *normal*. So, when he asked her to dinner in the clouds on Valentine's Day— no matter how cliche it felt—Brighton couldn't find any reason to say no.

They were happy. Happier than before. *Happy enough.*

Brighton swept down the stairs and into the dining room. Flickering candlelight and the distant hum of romantic music enveloped her in the elegant ambiance.

Gideon stood with a smile, placing a kiss on her lips before slipping his fingers beneath the collar of her coat to pull it from her shoulders. "Hey, you . . ."

"*Hi.*" Brighton shivered when he pressed his lips to the curve of her neck.

"You look incredible, as always. What color is that?" Gideon inquired with a smile as he held out her chair.

"Pink." Brighton grinned up at him, running her palms over the deep magenta dupioni silk. It felt appropriate for the day. Playful with a pleated skirt that fell just below her knees and hidden pockets, sophisticated with its square neckline leaving some things to the imagination, and sexy with a nipped waist and an open back, Gideon wasted no time in brushing his fingers against.

Gideon strode around the table, settling into his seat as he unbuttoned his navy jacket. Brighton took a deep drink of the martini waiting for her, letting out a slow breath as she let the flavor coat her tongue and warm her chest. "Sorry, I'm late. The L was delayed, and it was impossible getting a cab with the snow."

"Don't worry about it, babe. You're here now, aren't you?" Gideon smiled, glancing out over the immaculate view of Chicago sprawled out around them. "You're worth the wait, and this view made it easy."

Brighton followed Gideon's gaze, effortlessly caught up in the wonderment of it all. The city seemed so vast and *so small* —a sea of flickering lights in the darkness, like stars on a still sea.

They quietly made their way through seven courses of delectable food in impossibly small portions. Over the sea bass, they discussed a play they'd seen at The Chicago Theater a few days prior, and the possibility of taking a trip together come summertime while Brighton enjoyed pan-seared duck.

Brighton absentmindedly pushed around bits of a deconstructed chocolate hazelnut *something* when the unexpected swell of romantic violin music drew her attention to a fleet of waiters with armfuls of red roses pouring from the kitchen. "Oh my god, Gid, *look*..." She nodded towards them with a giggle, "It looks like some poor bastard is about to propose. It's so adorably cliche."

Brighton's brown eyes widened when she looked across the table and saw a quiet Gideon, jaw clenched, and face flushed scarlet. He rose to his feet with a forced smile, buttoning his suit jacket as the army of serving staff with their roses arrived at their table.

Brighton's heart dropped in her chest when a pair of champagne flutes were set in front of her, and Gideon cleared his throat and lifted her shaking hand in his own.

"Brighton ... the last five years together have been a whirlwind for me. We go so well together. I can see us galavanting across Chicago the rest of my life with you on my arm. I-I love you, and I can't ignore that anymore." Gideon spoke loudly, drawing the attention of every table around them.

Brighton's face went cold as Gideon stepped closer and sank down on one knee. "Oh, *Gideon*, no ..."

"Babe ... *sweetheart* ..."

"Gideon, stop. Please get up." She leaned forward, heart hammering away in her chest—so, *so* aware of *all* the eyes upon her.

"Brighton," he pressed on, pulling a Tiffany-blue box from the inner pocket of his jacket.

"Gid, please."

"Would you do me the honor of ..."

"For the love of God, would you please get up off your knees," she hissed.

Gideon finally got the message, looking back at the hoard of waiters with a silent jerk of his head to tell them to take the flowers away. He lumbered up from the floor, dusted off the knees of his Armani suit, deposited the turquoise box onto the table, and casually sat back down as the dining room returned to a hushed din.

"I don't understand." Gideon scrubbed his neatly trimmed beard with the tips of his fingers. "I thought this was what you wanted?"

Brighton offered him a sympathetic smile. "Is this what *you* want?"

Gideon fidgeted with the buttons on his suit jacket, brows furrowed as his eyes searched the tablecloth in front of him. "I —*yes*, of course, it's what I want. Why the hell would I be asking if it wasn't what I wanted? You're beautiful, talented, and . . . *I love you.*"

Brighton sat back in her seat, chewing the inside of her lip as the little blue box—something so small and seemingly inconsequential—held her attention like a ticking time bomb.

She lifted her eyes to meet Gideon's, heart aching when she saw his hurt looking back at her. "You do?"

"*Yes*, Brighton. Listen . . . I realize I've been a shitty boyfriend or whatever. I know I haven't done much to deserve you." Gideon idly picked at a stray crumb on the white tablecloth before meeting Brighton's gaze again. "I know I don't deserve you. I can see how much happier you are when you're not with me. It was clear as fucking day back in December. Call it a wake-up call. Call it inspiration—I don't care. We've been doing this so long . . ."

"We have." Brighton nodded. He had her attention, and his words *spoke* to her on a different level than Gideon ever had.

"My point is . . ." Gideon worked his jaw, leaning forward to lift the ring box from the surface of the table, opening it with a creak before setting it in front of her. "I want to marry you. I know I've taken forever to get here. I know I've been an idiot. I know I haven't been fair to you, and *I'm sorry*. I *do* love you, and I promise I'm going to do better, Brighton. *Please* . . . think about it, okay?"

Brighton looked at the ring inside the box, brows pulled in as she took in every overwhelmingly beautiful detail—a flawless, *large*, cushion cut square diamond glittered in the candlelight and only muddled her thoughts further.

Sure, Gideon's apartment was to die for, and he spoiled her from time to time—but *things* weren't the reason Brighton stayed. Why, though? Was it because she loved him too, or because she felt safe in the predictable nature of their relationship?

Brighton couldn't deny the time they'd been together, and Gideon's frank discussion of his own personal wake-up call—even if it was five years too late—made the choice a muddy one.

"*Okay . . .*" Brighton said softly, surprising herself as she blurted out the word with a nod.

"You will?" Gideon's face was triumphant as he leapt to his feet, taking her face in his hands to pepper her cheeks with kisses.

"Please be patient, okay?" Brighton wrapped her fingers around his wrists, laughing in the light of his joy, putting a little space between them. "Give me a little time. I won't keep you waiting long, I promise."

Gideon carded his fingers through her hair with a smile. "I'll take it, babe."

"Until then," Brighton murmured as she rose to her feet. She lifted the champagne to her cherry-hued lips and drained it to the very last drop. She set it back down with a deep exhale, pressing a short, simple kiss to his lips. "I'm going to go home and sleep on it. Okay?"

"You got it, beautiful." Gideon grinned like he'd put the ring on her finger, calling after her as she walked away. "We still on for this weekend?"

"Yeah." Brighton nodded as she slipped her arms through the sleeves of her red wool coat. "I think we are."

⋈

Three blocks, one ride on the red line, and a long, snowy walk through Old Town later, Brighton finally made it up the stoop of their building. With the twist of the key in the lock and a push of her shoulder against the door, she stepped inside into the blessedly warm air.

One flight of stairs, then another, and another, Brighton felt lighter when she saw the bright, cerulean door of their apartment. Toeing off her shoes with a shiver, Brighton shook off her coat and plopped down onto the couch next to her overgrown tree of a roommate.

Cain sat with his long legs perched on the coffee table, laden with a six-pack of beer and an open box of cheap pizza. He leaned to the side as Brighton tucked her feet beneath her and settled in against his side, giving her a curious look with a tilt of his head.

"Back so soon? I didn't expect you home until at least tomorrow. How'd the filial, time-honored Valentine's Day dinner go? Was it *achingly* romantic?"

Brighton gave Cain a pained smile with a lift of her brows, wordlessly snatching the bottle of beer from his hand. Taciturn and lost in thought, she downed the bottle in its entirety as he looked on with quiet surprise.

Cain let out a strangled laugh. "That well, huh?"

"I love your choice in romantic movies," Brighton scoffed at the TV as Jeff Goldblum stumbled through a warehouse apartment, well into his transformation into "Brundlefly." She snatched a slice of pizza from the box and took a huge bite.

"Listen, *The Fly* is cinematic gold, and I, for one, find it to have many romantic attributes. Don't think I can't see you trying to change the subject, Bee. What happened?" Cain feigned hurt, popping open another beer and taking a healthy swig.

Brighton chewed thoughtfully, sucking in a deep breath through her nose before mumbling past her half-eaten pizza— "He proposed."

Cain snorted, choking loudly on his beer. "He *what*? Poor bastard."

Brighton shifted in her seat, leaning away from him with a fixed stare. "What do you mean, *poor bastard*?"

"Poor bastard for asking a question he ought to damn well already known the answer to." Cain squared his shoulders, leaning his head towards her. "You *did* say no . . . right?"

Brighton's chest tightened, every part of her buzzing with a thread of anxious frustration. "Say no? Why should I? We've been together how long? Isn't marriage the next logical step?"

Cain sat forward with his elbows on his knees, jaw clenched as he stared at the floor between his feet. Brighton could see the way his thoughts ran away in his mind and the flicker of fury in the curl of his lip and flash of his eyes.

"Logic?" Cain growled, tucking his long fingers into a fist before bringing his burning gaze to meet hers.

Tension buzzed between them. Thick and as chilly as the weather outside, Brighton worried—with a single, wrong word —things would fall apart altogether.

They stood on the edge of their sacred silence, the kind Cain had dutifully stayed behind for a little too long. Eventually, it was bound to break in glorious, horrific technicolor.

"Are you . . . are you *angry* with me?" Brighton rose, taking a step back as Cain looked to his boots, silently fuming in a way she'd never seen him before. Sure, he'd teetered on the brink of losing his temper on a rough day, and he'd *loudly* expressed his frustration at the end of the *Skywalker Saga*, but this . . . this was something else entirely.

Cain jumped to his feet, pacing back and forth like a caged animal in a zoo. Brighton could feel the way his irritation—*his rage*—simmered beneath the surface in every twitch of the vein in his temple and crack of his knuckles.

Cain's feet finally stilled on the spot furthest away from her. He planted a hand on his hip, chest heaving as he brought his free hand to his lips like he was trying to physically keep the words in, but nothing, no one, would hold back what he needed to say.

"This is a mistake," Cain muttered, eyes firmly planted on his feet.

"What is?" Brighton snapped, sharper than she meant.

Cain shook his head. "You marrying that *fucking* twat."

"A *twat?*" Brighton let out a titter of delirious laughter as the instant sting of frustration bit at her. "Since when have you thought Gideon was that bad?"

Cain flinched at the mention of his name, shaking his head when he finally lifted his gaze to meet hers with a smug shrug. "Since always."

"That is news to me." The beginnings of Brighton's own anger simmered around the edges of her vision, buzzing with every realized, hurtful, and *true* thought Cain harbored. "What makes you think you get to have any sort of opinion on this? You aren't my boyfriend. You're not my *soulmate*. You don't get to make the rules where I'm concerned."

A flicker of hurt passed over Cain's face.

Brighton regretted the words as quickly as she said them, but now they were playing hardball, and there was no going back.

Cain sucked in a deep breath, pressing his long fingers to his chest with a bitter, wavering smile. "I thought I was your *best* friend."

"You are, but . . ." Brighton shook her head, silently begging herself not to go any further, but with her heart pounding in her ears, she couldn't help herself. "Gideon has been around a lot longer than you have, Cain."

"Oh, has he? What's so great that time counts over everything else, Brighton? He must be real fucking good in bed for you to stick around as long as you have, though you wouldn't know it based on how often I hear you touching yourself through the walls." Cain's voice grew louder with each word, flinging an accusatory finger down the hall with a vicious growl.

"Don't you think for a *second* my sex life is *any* of your business. That *any* of this is your business. This is my life, Cain. *Mine*. Where do you get the right to care where I spend my time and who I spend it with?"

"As long as it's on Lake Shore Drive, right?"

"You know that's not why I'm with him."

"Isn't it, though? He's treated you like garbage for how long? You've never been happy with him, Brighton. Everyone can see it. Why can't you?"

Cain knew her. He knew Brighton better than anyone. Like a favorite book with worn edges and faded letters, Cain could see between her lines like no one else did. His words stung all the more because they were *true*.

"*H-he loves me*," Brighton argued as the hot sting of tears welled up in her eyes.

"No." Cain shook his head with a wry, furious smile. "*I* love you. What that is—" He pointed out the window to wherever Gideon might have been in the city. "*That* isn't love, Brighton. Not in the slightest."

Cain's confession hung between them, and wordless tears streamed down Brighton's face to land amongst melted snowflakes on her sleeve.

"Don't say that." Brighton's hands trembled with every thunderous beat of her heart. "I wish you wouldn't."

Cain pressed his knuckles to his lips, shoulders sagging. "What . . . *I love you*?"

"You shouldn't." Brighton's voice quaked. She wished her

tears would stop. She wished she wasn't caught up in the grip of her fear, filled to the brim with every terrible thought as the best thing in her life fell to pieces. She had to fix it. They could fix it. "Take it back; nothing has to change. *Please.*"

"It's too late for that." Cain shook his head as a solitary tear slipped down the end of his nose. "I'm *in* love with you, Brighton. I have been f-for ages. You might as well know."

"I wish you'd never told me after that party." Brighton choked out a sob, smearing away her tears. *"Why?* Why ruin what we have . . . why make it complicated?"

"It's not like I have a choice in the matter, Brighton. Do you think I wanted this? Do you think I wanted to fall in love with a woman I can't have . . . with a woman I try to love how I can— how she *lets* me—a woman I've watched make mistake after mistake? *I don't want this.* I don't want to watch you throw your life away because you're afraid of what might happen if you let yourself be *truly* happy." After a beat, Cain lowered his chin, taking a small step forward with a small, tentative smile. "I think you love me, too. I think you're terrified to admit it."

Brighton gripped the edges of her coat, swaying on her feet as her breath hitched. *"I can't."*

The flicker of hope in Cain's face fell. "So. The twat's a better alternative, is he? Is he more suited to your lifestyle that you're not afraid to be with *him?*"

"What do you want me to say? What, that he has a good job?" Brighton cried, storming into the kitchen as her breaths came in sharper waves—desperate to put a sliver of space between them before things got worse.

"I have a good job." Cain pressed his hand to his chest, truly shouting now with every ounce of brief calm long forgotten as he followed her. "Why don't you marry me, huh?"

"Oh *fuck off.*" Brighton rolled her eyes, grasping the countertop at her back.

Cain shifted on the balls of his feet, jaw clenched with a

slow shake of his head before he brought a stormy sea of blue to warm amber.

"*Right then.*" Without a single glance at Brighton, he stormed past, a deep furrow in his brow.

Brighton kept her gaze stubbornly trained on a far spot on the wall, flinching when the door slammed shut.

Typically, silence wasn't something which bothered her. Brighton often found a peace in the quiet, but *this* was something else.

The remnant of their argument lingered in the air like weaponized gas. It stuck to her hair and her skin, clinging to every breath she tried to take as Cain's absence—and the gaping hole he left in her heart—sunk in. Brighton's anger gave way to panic, desperate to go back, to fix things before she said the wrong thing, before they spat such lethal words at one another they'd never be able to take back.

Cain was gone.

Chapter 11

*B*righton's brain fired on all cylinders, whispering poisonous things over and over as the sound of the door rang in her ears. It was her fault; she drove Cain away, and —because of her—he'd break his promise and never return.

In the firm grip of her silent panic—without Cain there to calm her like he had during the engagement party in December—Brighton frantically searched the apartment for something, *anything* to ease the ache in her heart and allow her to breathe again.

Brighton tore at the neckline of her dress with trembling hands, gasping for air as her panic clouded her vision. She stumbled down the hall, shedding her layers with each slow step. First, she flung the crimson coat blindly to the walnut floor, then her fingers clawed at the clasp at her neck and the zipper at the small of her back.

Brighton knew what she needed.

The thought anchored itself in her mind as she stepped out of a pink silk puddle and wrenched open the door to Cain's bedroom. The smell of him assaulted her senses as soon as she crossed the threshold, easing her panic as quickly as it had arrived—but it wasn't enough.

Brighton's eyes went straight towards a tall, black dresser in the corner of the room. She wasted no time sliding it open, skimming her fingers over the fabric of Cain's clothes. Even in the dark, her touch recognized the dark blue sweater Brighton *loved* when he wore. She gingerly raised it to her nose with a sob.

Without a second thought, Brighton pulled it on, letting it skim across her skin and settle over her hips. Her chest heaved and quaked, hands still trembling as the grip of her panic held on by an iron thread.

She looked over Cain's bedroom, lit by a yellow light outside his window as a fresh layer of snow fell. It felt like *him*, and even though he wasn't there, Cain lingered in every corner, haunting it like a ghost.

Brighton's fingers toured every inch—along the foot of the bed, up the other side to his bedside table. Tucking her hands around the black-banded watch, Brighton lifted it from the worn copy of *The Silmarillion* and skimmed her thumb over the crystal face.

Tick-tick-tick

It mocked her, carefully calculating every thunderous second without Cain, reminding her of each sin and mistake with every shiver of the second hand.

Brighton felt drunk with despair, practically swimming in the headiness of her wish to do things over and the aching need in her heart for Cain to return, wrap her up in his arms, and hold her until the feeling passed.

She settled for the next best thing, peeling back the grey velvet duvet a few inches before sliding her bare legs beneath it. The combined softness of the mattress and the covers hugged her every curve, bringing with them a bitter sense of relief she wanted to believe.

Brighton grasped the curve of Cain's pillow, pulling it to her chest with a sob as, with a single intake of breath, his smell overwhelmed her completely.

Brick by brick, the walls Brighton clung to came tumbling down—the ones holding back her tears—flooding her with wave upon wave of regret. Every word. Every syllable. The hurt in his handsome face. It pummeled her all at once, bringing with it sharp sobs and silvery tears pooling under her cheek and into the fabric of his pillow.

So deep in the trenches of her regret was she, Brighton didn't hear the creak of the front door, the slow, heavy footsteps as they came down the hall, or the quiet sigh of the man who *loved her* looking over her quaking body in his bed.

The mattress had barely bent under Cain's weight when Brighton felt the warmth of his arms. He settled in behind her, pressing his nose between her shoulder blades with a deep, settling breath of his own.

He brought the cold with him, and it seeped through the fabric of his sweater and onto her skin.

"I'm sorry I walked out, darling," Cain's deep voice buzzed against her back.

Brighton hiccuped into his pillow. "You promised."

"I know," Cain answered, giving her a squeeze, holding her more firmly as he pressed on. "I shouldn't . . . I shouldn't have said the things I did."

"Me neither," Brighton echoed, slipping her hand over Cain's on her stomach with a wavering smile from the sudden wash of comfort she felt in his presence. "I'm so sorry."

"If you want to marry him, you should, Bee." Cain hesitated, brushing his thumb over the curve of her hand. "I just . . . I don't want to see you waste any more time being afraid."

"I know." A single tear slipped free. "I'm trying."

"My point is . . . I was a jealous asshole, and I'm sorry. I know this means things will change between us. I know it will

141

mean you won't be here with me, and I don't think I am ready to lose you." Cain pressed a kiss against her back.

Brighton shifted, rolling in the weight of Cain's arms. She settled her head into the space beneath his chin. It was hard to resist the urge to breathe him in, to memorize the feeling of his heart beating against her cheek—so she didn't. "You'll never lose me, Cain."

"Nor me, darling."

"You promise?" Brighton lifted her chin, slotting her foot between Cain's as she tried to meet his gaze in the dark.

Cain's fingers brushed against Brighton's cheek, and breath kissed the baby hairs framing her face—holding her more firmly with his jaw pressed against her forehead.

"*I promise.* I'll always be around, Colour Girl. No matter what. And, if things don't work out with him, we can grow old together, if you want."

Brighton hummed a smile, settling back into the nook under Cain's chin. "That doesn't sound so bad."

Her breathing still shook from the remnants of her tearful panic when he'd abruptly stormed from their apartment. The poison of the biting words they exchanged lingered over every inch of her, even though she'd shed her clothes.

Cain pressed his nose into her hair as he thumbed gentle, slow circles on her back. "Is this okay? Is this something we should be doing?"

"I don't know," Brighton whispered, tucking her fingers into the fabric of his shirt with another faltering breath.

Served with a reminder of her tears, Cain pulled her closer and pressed the day's scruff against her cheek. Brighton laid paralyzed, transfixed as he traced the tip of his nose along the edge of her jaw.

Cain carried her attention as he pulled away, handsome face lit by the dreamy halo of falling snow outside the window. Every unspoken thought flittered across his face, written in the lines between his brows and creases around his eyes.

There, wrapped in Cain's arms, his gaze . . . *his love* . . . Brighton forgot to be afraid. Her eyes darted to his mouth, hand twisted in his shirt, and she *wondered* . . . what if, just for now, things were different?

Brighton feathered his temples, weaving her fingers into his curls as Cain drew her closer. Arm coiled firmly around her waist, Cain's free hand skirted up the curve of her hip and beneath the hem of her borrowed sweater.

They answered the call, the secret song their bodies sang from the moment their eyes met at El Deseo del Corazón— every inch too far as they folded their bodies together. Brighton trembled, fears and heart's desire squabbling over what was best. There, in the moonlight, with Cain's breath tangled with hers and limbs knotted in such a way, made her wish *he* was what was best.

But no. They couldn't. *They shouldn't.*

Brighton broke the spell the moment the honeyed whimper fell from her lips, panting into Cain's chest as the remnants of their too-brief and too-long heated moment settled around them.

Brighton had Gideon. And Cain . . . he had the hurt *she* caused him.

A sob shook them free. Cain answered the wordless need without a second thought, holding Brighton more firmly with an innocent press of his cheek on the crown of her head. The ghost of a deep chuckle rumbled around in his chest. "Are you . . . are you wearing my jumper?"

Brighton felt the tug of a smile, nuzzling deeper in Cain's arms to quell the sting of her tears as she murmured. "Shut up."

"Okay."

With her nose pressed against Cain's chest, Brighton let out another sigh—surely her thousandth one. While his presence brought a peaceful calm, washing away the tension from their argument, her melancholy remained. It was an unshakable feeling, like a shadow hanging over her head not even Cain's touch could chase away.

A slow blink in the gold-tinged darkness made Brighton's world a bit of a blur, bringing with it a yawn of such massive proportions, she knew sleep wasn't far away. Brighton trusted that, should she fall asleep in Cain's embrace, she'd wake up in her own bed the next morning, though she wasn't sure she wanted to.

With the slow rise and fall of Cain's chest against her cheek, Brighton gave into the quiet calm sleep promised, letting it carry her away to wherever her dreams would take her. The last waking thought she had was the hope that, wherever it was, Cain would meet her there.

It felt like Brighton drifted for a mere moment when her eyes opened again to greet the dawn.

Brighton stretched, elongating every inch of her long limbs from the tips of her fingers down to her toes. She blinked in the strands of morning light as they streamed through the window, rolling over in the warmth of the rays like a lazy cat on a summer day.

A brush of her fingertips over grey velvet sent Brighton shooting up in bed, clutching the blanket to her chest as she took stock of the bedroom around her, which *definitely* wasn't hers—and the empty spot beside her.

Had it been a dream? The proposal. The fight—and what came after. A glance down at her bare legs and the dark blue sweater bunched up over her hips told Brighton some of what she remembered was real, but Cain's absence said something else.

Maybe it had been wishful thinking—a delirious, tear-fueled fantasy that, after the poisonous words she spat at him, he would want to come back.

The faint, familiar buzz of her phone pulled her from Cain's sprawling bed. The wood floor was cold on the bottoms of her bare feet, sending a shock through her already frazzled system as she stepped towards the doorway.

Brighton anchored her hands on the edges of the frame, peeking out into the darkened hallway, hoping there would be some sort of sign of Cain—the smell of coffee, the hum of the tv, or the clink of dishes in the sink. But, to her despair, it was quiet, save for the drone of her phone only steps away.

Tiptoeing over worn walnut, Brighton crouched down, hugging her knees as she reached for her red wool coat where she'd left it. Brighton blindly fished her hand into the bottom of her pocket, pushing past a folded up post-it note and a gum wrapper before finding her phone.

It buzzed again as she drew it out into the open. With a tap of her thumb, the screen lit up, illuminating the corridor as she looked over the handful of waiting messages.

There was one from Andi, reminding Brighton of their appointment at an exclusive wedding dress boutique on Saturday, and another from her dad asking if she was free for breakfast soon. While Brighton intended to send him a quick message back saying she'd meet him before her appointment with Andi, two other texts held her attention.

Gideon and Cain.

Brighton fell back against the wall, balancing her elbows on her knees as she ran a finger from her free hand over her bottom lip as she read over each message.

Cain's words sent a sharp rush of relief washing over her, reassuring Brighton that she hadn't imagined the night before.

Morning love. Slept amazing last night, but work calls. I'll be back Saturday evening. Can't wait. Lord of the Rings re-watch?

Right. Brighton should have remembered Cain had a trip to New York on the docket for weeks, but after how things fell apart the night before, she'd forgotten completely.

Gideon.

Brighton chewed her lip when she thought of when he had so earnestly told her he loved her, and that he wanted to make up for the time he'd squandered—making good on the relationship they'd built.

Her brown eyes darted over Gideon's message with a smile.

Breakfast? There's a plate of French toast at Daley's with your name on it.

They frequented the worn red and white booths every weekend when they first met, back when things were a little simpler, still fresh, and more than a little exciting—*The Glimpse* be damned.

Brighton could swear her stomach had a direct line to her phone, grumbling loudly as she thought about her favorite breakfast dish she hadn't had in *years*. She pulled herself to her feet, pausing in the doorway to Cain's room.

Brighton lingered in the frame, nodding to herself as she stepped inside, made the bed, and slipped the navy blue sweater over her head.

Lifting it to her nose, Brighton breathed in the combined smell of him and her—*of them*—and smiled fondly at the thought of her best friend, her anchor, her port in a storm who was Cain Whitaker. Cain *loved* her, and she didn't deserve it in the slightest.

I'll always be around, Colour Girl. No matter what. We can even grow old together, if you want.

Brighton closed her eyes—never mind the fact she was standing in Cain's bedroom in nothing but her underwear—and let herself entertain the idea.

The details were fuzzy, but Cain's face was clear. She. Him. *Them.* Bound together by something more than friendship. By love. His blue eyes crinkled around the edges, burning brighter than Brighton'd ever seen them.

Happy.

Like always, the image shifted, leaving Brighton alone in the dark—back in Cain's bed, alone—caught up in the dread that he was never coming back.

Brighton thought of her dad—of the final, heartbreaking moments when her mom had been carted off in an ambulance in the driveway. At seventeen, she'd had a front row seat to what it was like to have *The Glimpse* and see it torn away in the blink of an eye. Brighton would never forget the sound he made when everything shifted, clutching his heart like a piece of his soul had been torn away.

No, Brighton couldn't give in. Not at the risk of the pain that could be waiting for them on the other side, soulmate or not. Brighton would protect Cain, and she'd protect herself. It was for the best.

Gingerly folding the sweater against her chest, Brighton set it on the bed with a smile before returning to her bedroom.

A quick trip into the closet Cain had built for her, and Brighton was on her way—dressed in a muted mint sweater and dark green trousers with her favorite crimson coat to fight against the bite of the remains of a brutal Chicago winter.

Stepping foot in the diner took Brighton back in time, overwhelming her senses in the best kind of way—from the *click* and *clatter* of dishes to the symphony of cinnamon and sweet vanilla wafting from the kitchen.

She and Gideon fell into an easy conversation. Between the setting and the company, Brighton felt like they'd traveled back in time. It stirred a *good* feeling inside her, one she couldn't quite shake—the same feeling of predictable safety she'd come to depend on.

Brighton leaned forward in the booth, pressing her knuckles to her chin as she absentmindedly stirred her tea. Lifting her eyes to look at her long-time *someone*, Brighton smiled, holding out her hand expectantly. "Can I see it again?"

Gideon's blonde brow furrowed. "See what?"

"Gid, I know it's in your pocket. Give it up." Brighton wiggled her fingers at his sport jacket.

With a knowing smile and a gleam in his green eyes, Gideon pulled out the bright, turquoise box and slid it across the table.

Brighton's hands trembled as she nervously swiped her tongue over her bottom lip—sighing softly as she opened it and revealed the beautiful ring inside.

He'd done his job well. Gideon Baumgartner was a man of taste. After all, he'd chosen her in a world of soulmates, hadn't he?

Brighton pulled the ring from the box and held it gingerly between her fingers, chewing the inside of her lip as she looked to him with a shake of her head. "I'm not your soulmate."

"I know." Gideon nodded, his face earnest and, for once, *sincere*.

"That doesn't bother you?"

"Not at all."

"What if I meet mine? What if *you* meet yours?" Brighton watched the way the stone caught the light streaming in from the window, scattering a million beams of refracted light around their booth.

Gideon shrugged. "Then we cross that bridge when we come to it. Until then, I'll think we'll be happy enough, don't you think?"

"Happy enough." Brighton half-smiled with a tilt of her head, sucking in a deep breath as she slid the platinum band on the third finger of her left hand.

Brighton met Gideon's eyes with a smile as she slid from the booth, taking his face in her hands to press a kiss to his lips, hoping, if she kept thinking she'd be happy enough, eventually it would be true—maybe.

Who needed a soulmate, anyway?

Chapter 12

Saturday

The ring on Brighton's finger was heavy in more ways than one. In the two days since she'd accepted Gideon's proposal, she'd spent the rest of the day—and night—by his side, happily celebrating the way all newly engaged couples should.

For the first time in—well, *ever*—Brighton felt completely welcome in his apartment. Gideon cleared out a drawer for her —officially—and even gave her a toothbrush he'd bought the same day he picked up the little blue box from Tiffany's.

Brighton had to laugh. The idea a toothbrush and a drawer held more weight than the three and a half carats on her finger was too amusing not to.

She'd spent the night without any pressure to leave once morning came. Gideon made her breakfast, and they'd sat together in his bed and discussed the future. Like with most things, they didn't agree on everything, but Brighton was determined not to spoil the illusion.

Friday evening, though sure she could have stayed longer if she wanted to, Brighton bid a temporary goodbye to Gideon—

her fiancé—idly wondering with a hammering heart and a cold sense of dread that, eventually, she'd have to tell Cain. But how?

Back home in Old Town, Brighton tossed and turned in her bed, thoughts consumed with the image of Cain returning home the next night, surely noticing the diamond on her left-hand seconds after stepping through the door.

Cain was upset—*angry*, even—when Brighton merely considered the idea. What would her accepting Gideon's proposal do to them? He said he wouldn't leave her behind, again. While Brighton trusted his word, part of her worried the relationship with Gideon was bound to break them, and it'd be her fault.

Eventually, when Brighton drifted off to sleep, it was fitful, and she found herself ripped back to consciousness with a yell —caught up in dreams of red and blue flashing lights and an unshakable feeling of dread covering every inch of her skin like icy cold rain.

Saturday morning arrived with the promise of a full day. Brighton agreed to meet Andi for lunch after a morning packed full of wedding dress shopping.

First, Brighton had a *very* important man to see.

The Shedd Aquarium was one of her most-beloved places, with grand limestone walls, and the shimmering rainbow which made up so much sea life. Fish always fascinated her, even at a young age. Blessed with *The Glimpse*—even as a little girl—Brighton begged her parents to take her to the aquarium and let her look upon the oceanic rainbow with her brown eyes wide in wonder.

Brighton—dressed in a yellow-gold, gossamer pleated skirt with a faded Guns'N'Roses tee and a pair of red converses— found herself smiling so wide, her cheeks ached. She strode into a vast, pillar-lined rotunda, making her way beneath the glass ceiling.

She drew toward a figure illuminated by the deep, flickering blues of the water. Brighton knew the square shoulders and large frame by heart.

"Hey, stranger." Brighton poked him in the ribs with her elbow, smiling up at a worn, familiar face.

"Hey, Pumpkin." Thomas Evans grinned down at her with brown eyes just like hers. "You're late."

"I know." Brighton grimaced. "I'm sorry. I didn't sleep well, and it didn't make it easy to get out the door."

"What's your excuse the rest of the time, kiddo?" Thomas gave her a pointed stare, handing over a paper cup with a wink. "Can't say you were busy getting the refreshments."

"Mmm, thank you. English breakfast?"

"Is there any other kind?" He gave her a knowing look before turning back to the Caribbean Reef. "Amazing, isn't it?"

"Yeah." Brighton looked through the crystal clear waters, eyes darting from one flash of color to the next as brightly-colored marine creatures lazily made their way round and round the cylindrical tank.

Brighton snuck a glance at her dad, feeling a piercing ache in her heart as his eyes danced over the hundreds of fish inside—unable to see any of them in their true beauty.

"I miss her," Brighton whispered, turning her eyes back towards a parrotfish as it glided by.

"Me too, kiddo. All the time." Thomas looked down at her. "But I know she's here. Somewhere in all this."

Brighton looked up at her father and saw the map of his life all over his face. A thousand smiles creased around his eyes; countless nights studying during med-school and twenty-four hour shifts etched in his forehead. Each one of them was precious in their own way—all of them a story to tell or a lesson to remember.

"You think so?" Brighton took a sip of her tea.

"Know so."

They stood in easy, uncomplicated silence, with the shared

loss weighing on both of their hearts. Things were never quite the same after she was gone, but they made the best of it the way they knew how.

"How's that boyfriend of yours?" Thomas broke the silence with a gentle push of his shoulder.

"He's . . . uh . . . *not* my boyfriend."

"Oh, right, right . . . he's a funny one with the titles, isn't he? Nice guy, though. Good job. Has a good head on his shoulders." Thomas nodded knowingly.

"Actually, we've kinda come to a different kind of arrangement, Dad." Brighton anxiously coiled a ribbon of her red hair around a finger. "We're getting married."

Somehow, saying it out loud made it all a reality. It wasn't a figment of Brighton's imagination. It wasn't some game. The ring on her finger was *real*, and the promise Gideon made was real along with it. Why didn't she feel more excited?

Thomas pursed his lips. "You sure?"

Brighton cocked her head to the side with a nervous huff of laughter. "Pretty damn sure, Dad."

Thomas took another drink, smacking his lips together with a frown and a furrow of his brow. "I thought for sure you'd marry this little guy who hung around the lake one summer. I guess some things don't pan out the way we think, huh?"

"What little guy?" Brighton's gaze snapped to his, her stomach churning. "When did this happen?"

Thomas chuckled. "Hell if I know. There was a party at the Whitakers. You don't remember?"

"*Dad.* Obviously not. You can't just *say* stuff like that."

"He's not your soulmate, though, is he?" Thomas nodded at a passing fish.

"The little guy?" Brighton's heart leapt again.

Thomas made a face. "The other one. Gideon."

"*Oh,*" Brighton murmured, eyes falling to the floor. "No. He isn't."

Thomas roped an arm around her shoulders. "That's not going to bother you, sweetheart?"

"I've got *The Glimpse*. I can see. Isn't that enough?" Brighton argued, nervously fiddling with the ring on her left hand.

"I don't know, honey. You've worn a rainbow to say, 'look at me, I'm right here!' since you were a little girl. I'm not so sure it's something I can see you giving up for the rest of your life, Brighton. I'm afraid you won't be happy if you settle."

"I'm not settling, Dad. I'm . . . I'm happy enough. Having a soulmate is overrated."

Thomas's body language shifted, shoulders squared and jaw tight as he nodded. "Is it?"

"Dad, *no*. I'm sorry . . . I didn't mean it like that."

"I know what you meant, Brighton." His voice was low and tone curt. "You are young. Is finding love outside of *The Glimpse* possible? Sure. But you are living proof yours is *out there*."

Brighton sighed. "I'm so tired, Dad. I held out hope . . ."

"Have you, really? To me, it seemed more like you were too worried about what happened with me and your mom to really *try*." Thomas leaned down and looked her square in the eye with a knowing smile. "Keep holding out, honey. Who knows, it could be like any lost thing. You spend all this time looking, but . . . once you finally find it, it was usually right in front of you the whole time."

Brighton chewed the inside of her lip. "You sound so sure."

"I *am* sure." Thomas wrapped an arm around her, pressing a kiss to her head. "What I'm trying to say is . . . *stay open*. Take chances. You never know. Sometimes the most precious treasure is hidden in plain sight."

ho knows, it could be like any lost thing . . .
Brighton crossed her arms with a frown, chewing the edge of her thumb as she sorted through each conflicting thought. She tilted her head from side to side, decoding the pattern in the carpet beneath her red Converses.

"What's wrong with your face?" Andi shuffled out of her dressing room in a cloud of dreamy tulle—more cupcake than person.

"Nothing." Brighton sat up in her chair, summoning a smile as she looked over the way the dress completely overwhelmed Andi's petite frame. "You look incredible."

"Fuck off, I do not. This is horrible." Andi made a face at her reflection, waving away an overly enthusiastic consultant who held forward a veil.

"It's not that bad," Brighton laughed, shaking her head. "But . . . as the person who has to hold it while you pee, I beg you to pick something . . . *less fluffy.*"

Andi opened her mouth to respond, meeting Brighton's gaze in the mirror before she spun around on the platform, gathered up the mountain of fabric around her, and promptly marched over. She crouched down, nearly getting lost in the fluff, and firmly grabbed Brighton's left hand. "What the fuck is this?"

Brighton looked at the diamond ring with a shrug. "Jewelry."

"Brighton." Andi gave her a scathing look, lifting her hand with a wiggle. "This is an *engagement* ring."

"Yeah," Brighton breathed with a nod and a bite of her lip. "It is."

"Gideon?"

"Who else would it be?"

"Are you kidding me? You really are thick, you know that?"

Andi rose from the cloud of tulle back towards the dressing room. "Literally anyone else, Bee."

She flinched when Andi snapped the curtain closed, caught up in the inescapable feeling— of all things anyone would hope for her best friend to feel when getting engaged, Andi seemed *disappointed*.

Brighton wandered into the showroom, fidgeting with her engagement ring. She walked through the forest of pale ivories and gossamer blush gowns, reminding herself that, if things went according to plan, she'd be back in the boutique in no time.

Brighton's eyes moved over each texture, reaching with a tentative hand to brush her touch over delicate embroidery and breathtaking appliqués, letting out a slow, shaky breath when she felt how achingly soft they were beneath her fingers.

Was she doing the right thing, or was it a betrayal to herself —fears or not—to settle for something second best—even if her soulmate *wasn't* a sure thing? Was being happy enough truly *enough*?

A ping from Brighton's pocket jolted her from the jumbled mess of her thoughts. She pulled out her phone and felt the beginnings of a wavering smile.

Cain's face was a sight for sore eyes. The selfie was laughably cute—taken at a wonderfully awkward angle that illustrated the sharp edge of his jaw and the marvelous width of his smile. It was of the collectible kind, transforming every corner of his handsome face.

I'm at "our place" in New York. Not quite the same without you here beside me, Colour Girl. Can't wait to be home.

Brighton quickly typed out a reply.

It's not the same without you here, either. Need me to pick you up?

The happy trio of dots popped up in an instant, followed quickly by Cain's answer.

Nah, I'll grab an Uber. Have the popcorn ready.

Brighton found herself absentmindedly reaching for the mark burned into the skin on her hip, wishing things would have been different. Clearer, even. It was so easy for them. Effortless.

There wouldn't be anything effortless about the conversation they would have, no matter how good of a friend Cain was. No matter how Brighton tried. No matter how peaceful things seemed on the surface. Cain was bound to be hurt by her decision, and Brighton wasn't ready to see it on his face again. Not yet. *Not ever.*

Another ping rang out. Brighton lifted the screen, and her eyes danced over Cain's words.

I know you're busy with Andi. I'll leave you to it, but I have to say . . . I can't stop thinking of how well I slept the other night. Best sleep of my life, Bee. 🩶

Brighton's eyes were glued to the little red heart at the end of the text, chewing on the inside of her lip as she read the message over and over and over.

"*Hey.*" Andi's voice prompted Brighton to put the phone away and summon a wavering smile. Andi was tied up in a white satin robe, arms crossed over her chest. "I'm sorry about before . . . how I reacted. I realize this is your life, and it's your choice."

"I just want *someone* to be happy for me. Can you be happy for me?" Brighton's voice wavered, brows drawn together with a quiet involuntary sob before Andi surged forward and wrapped her up in a hug.

"Of course I can be happy for you," Andi murmured into her shoulder, pulling away to wipe away the beginnings of Brighton's tears. "I love you, Bee. I want to see you get to the part of your life you've dreamed of when we were little . . . I want to see you meet your soulmate and live your life in the most glorious technicolor."

"I mean, I kinda already do." Brighton chuckled, glancing down at her outfit.

Andi laughed. "Yeah, but you know what I mean. And let me tell you . . . soulmate sex is *not* something you want to miss out on if you can help it, Bee. So, stop being a chicken, and *open your eyes.*"

"Oh my god, gross. Please spare me the details."

"I will if you try a dress on," Andi teased, spinning her friend around, pointing to a silvery-grey gown tucked between the field of ivory and white. "*That one.*"

"Andi, no. Why?"

"You're a bride, too. Whether I like it or not, so let's like . . . do bridal things together. Come on . . ."

"I can't."

"Why the fuck not?" Andi leaned back and planted her hands on her hips.

"I mean, look at it . . . it's *grey,*" Brighton argued.

Andi shrugged. "Exactly. Try it, and I'll shut up. Come on. *It'll be fun.*"

At Andi's insistence, Brighton found herself wrapped up in an identical white robe inside the dressing room, arms crossed as she stared at the silver gown that *somehow*, she'd been roped into putting on. It was simpler than she would have chosen; with no color and little embellishment. She pursed her lips as she looked it over on the hanger with a shake of her head.

What the hell? What do I have to lose? Brighton stripped the robe and pulled the dress from the satin hanger.

It was heavier than she thought it would be, but as she stepped into the skirt and slipped the thin straps over her shoulders, Brighton found herself caught up in the delectable feeling of the silk sliding across her skin. Brighton didn't dare peek at her reflection—turning, instead to slide open the curtain.

Andi waited, dressed in a new gown that took Brighton's

breath away. It was the opposite of the previous cupcake she'd tried on—a simple, elegant A-line with delicate lace running down to her wrists.

"Holy shit . . . *Brighton*." Andi's eyes widened when the redhead emerged from her dressing room.

"Is it bad?" Brighton tried to cover the plunging neckline.

"Oh my god, *no*. You look incredible. Come here." Andi waved Brighton over onto a wooden pedestal, holding her by the waist as she spun her around.

Brighton's lips parted as she took in her reflection. Her hair hung down over her shoulders in dreamy waves. She swore the color of the gown made it appear brighter than it ever had. The dress wasn't grey. No, it was *silver*, like spun stardust God wove just for her.

With the rest of Brighton's colors stripped away, every strand of hair, each fleck of gold in her eyes, and every freckle was accentuated. There was no color to distract or draw anyone's attention—*just her*.

The gown hugged every lithe curve, following the swell of her breasts before flaring out at the waist to the floor where it stretched out behind her in satin waves. Too caught up in the sight of her reflection, Brighton didn't see Andi wave over their consultant with a veil, but *oh* . . .

"Brighton, *look at you* . . ." Andi's blue eyes shimmered. "This was made for you."

"You think so?" Brighton threaded the thin, gossamer fabric of the veil between her fingers as it settled around her shoulders.

The dress was beautiful. Breathtaking, even, but the simple accessory added something special Brighton couldn't quite put her finger on. It was light as air, framing her wide-eyed face with delicate silver flowers floating down around her like they'd fallen from the sky and been drawn to it.

The flash of a camera shook Brighton from the trance. Her

eyes darted to Andi, who held her cellphone aloft with a coy smile. "Did you take my picture?"

Andi merely grinned, her blue eyes on the screen as she typed out a message. "Maybe a little."

"Tell me you didn't send it to someone," Brighton pleaded, gathering the skirt to step off the pedestal.

"Just to your other not-boyfriend," Andi giggled, jerking the phone away when Brighton lunged for it.

"We're . . . we're friends." A flush rose in Brighton's cheeks when she thought of Cain seeing her *like this,* or worse— putting two and two together before she had a chance to tell him the news. "Give it."

"*Are you?*" Andi teased, grinning down at her phone when it buzzed in her palm. "Aww, look at what he said."

Brighton wrenched the device from Andi's grip, heart pounding when her dark eyes darted over the text before releasing a sigh of relief.

She looks incredible. I wish I were half that lucky.

"He loves you, you know."

"We're *friends,*" Brighton echoed, handing Andi's phone back as she backed away, turning to her reflection.

"To you, maybe . . . but have you seen the way he looks at you?" Andi slid up behind her with a tempered smile. "And I don't mean in the way that I love you . . . Cain *loves* you. I know you've made your decision, but . . . if you're going to settle for someone who isn't your soulmate . . ." Andi leaned her cheek against Brighton's shoulder. "I'm just saying there are other, *better* options. And, who knows . . . maybe it could be greater than you expect. Be honest—is Gideon *really* who you see at the end of the aisle?"

Brighton looked at her reflection—at a bride. Her mind reeled with uncertainty as she chewed the inside of her lip raw. She took a trembling breath and pushed away every bit of fear that held her back, and tried to picture the day of her wedding.

So much of it was clear. Brighton could hear the music. Hell, she could even *smell* the flowers and saw every beautiful ounce of color.

There, at the end of the aisle, dressed to the nines in a crisp, black tuxedo . . .

. . . was *exactly* who Brighton expected.

Chapter 13

"*I* have to go."

The words fell from her mouth before Brighton even realized she'd said them, but the sense of urgency she felt couldn't be denied.

Brighton would have run through the snowy streets of Chicago in a wedding gown if she had to. All that mattered was that she made it to where she needed to go—and say what she needed to say.

The veil was the first thing to go. It fluttered down to the floor as Brighton rushed back to the fitting room, fingers grasping at the clasp at the small of her back.

They shook so much, Brighton could barely get a proper grip before a pair of hands stilled hers with a whisper, "Here, let me."

Andi freed Brighton from her satin prison, sliding the silver silk from her shoulders, swooping it from the floor as she leaped out and snatched up her clothes.

With her red converses back on her feet and her coordinating wool coat 'round her shoulders, Brighton hugged Andi, murmuring her apologies before bolting out the door into the blinding winter sunshine.

Her eyes darted across the street and up the block both ways, and she let out a grunt of frustration when there wasn't a single cab to be found. Brighton tugged her phone from her pocket, checking the map on her rideshare app, heart pounding when she saw the closest cars were more than a few blocks away.

Brighton looked eastward towards the lake, the winter wind fluttering the hair around her face as she mentally counted the blocks and the amount of time it would take to get there if she made a run for it.

With nothing to lose and everything to gain, Brighton took off. Her feet pounded the pavement as her heart thudded in her ears. She gasped apologies as she pushed past tourists, sliding around a corner on her heels before bolting forward again.

Brighton zig-zagged through pedestrians on the sidewalk, all of them dressed warmer than her, but she couldn't be bothered by the sting of the wind on her cheeks.

The doorman nodded as Brighton flew by, uttering a confused, "Ms. Evans," as she rushed into the lobby, giving him an apologetic wave when she finally came to a halt inside the lift.

It might have been the longest elevator ride of her life. Each floor ticked by slower than the last. Eventually though, it announced her arrival at the fortieth floor with a *ping*, and Brighton wasted no time in flinging herself out of the car and down the hall.

Out of breath and trembling, Brighton raised a fist and pounded on the door. Over and over, her knuckles collided with solid wood while muffled voices filtered through to the outside, furthering her impatience.

Except, when it opened, Brighton found something—or someone—wholly unexpected.

A woman—petite and tan, with bright green eyes and hair blended from black at the roots to a deep caramel at her waist

—stood between Brighton and the rest of the apartment. Ribbons and braids were twisted into her wild curls, and she wore a ring on every finger.

She was beautiful, someone out of a folktale or fresh from Burning Man . . . and most *certainly* not someone Brighton ever expected to find in Gideon Baumgartner's apartment.

"And you are?" The woman asked.

"Who am I?" Brighton's breath came in sharp waves as she looked her up and down. "Who the fuck *are you?*"

Pushing past her, Brighton saw Gideon—out of breath, pink-faced and disheveled in a way she'd never seen him before.

"B-Brighton," Gideon stuttered, hair mussed, wearing only a pair of shorts that looked like they'd been put on in a rush.

Brighton turned back to the mystery woman, who wore a fringed robe . . . and not much else. Brighton's stomach twisted, and her head swam. It didn't take an idiot to put two and two together.

"Who's this?" Brighton demanded, brows drawn together, heart hammering away from a bewildering blend of anger and relief. She searched in the entryway for something—a credenza, *anything*—to hang onto.

"This . . . this is Juniper-Rain." Gideon stepped closer. A flicker of recognition passed over his face. "*Wow.* Your hair . . . *so vibrant.* I mean—I always knew it was going to be amazing seeing you like this, but this . . . this is something else."

Brighton stepped back, heart skipping a beat as she looked back and forth between her fiancé and the mystery bohemian princess standing between them, when—all at once—it dawned on her what happened.

"*You can see.*" Brighton let out a breathless, disbelieving huff of laughter. "A text would have been nice. *Sorry, Brighton. Date night's canceled, met my soulmate.*"

Brighton wanted to be the kind of person who'd be happy

Gideon finally found the person destined for him, but all she could think was of all the time she'd wasted. How long had she given it her all? How long did she trust Gideon and consider him the safe option, only for it to all fall apart like she feared? He was just another disappointment, another hurt—another Jesse.

"I'm sorry about the timing." Gideon drew closer, green eyes soft.

Brighton choked out a cutting bark of laughter. "You couldn't have waited, could you? Is this what I get for putting up with you and your non-committal bullshit for the last five years? You could have *called*. I would have understood, but you didn't even give me a chance."

"Brighton, I—" Gideon scrambled for something to say, pawing a hand through his hair.

"No. Don't even try, Gideon. This is enough, just . . . *fuck this*." Brighton's eyes stung, but she blinked away her tears— refusing to give him any more of her.

Brighton looked at Juniper-Rain. "It's lovely meeting you. *Really*. I hope you, Gideon, and his phone will be *really* happy together."

Brighton shoved past Juniper-Rain into the apartment where she'd spend countless hours over the previous five years, slipping the ring from her finger before extending it to Gideon with a bitter smile. "No offense, douche-canoe, but . . . I don't think we should get married anymore."

"I hope . . . you know . . ." Gideon murmured, curling the diamond ring in his palm.

Brighton bit her lip. "Yeah, well. You don't really have to worry about that anymore, do you?"

Before Gideon could answer, Brighton walked into the hall without a second look, keeping her eye on the future.

As the lift carried her back down to street level, Brighton

pulled her phone from her pocket, glancing at the time with a flutter of freedom in her heart.

Cain was on his way home, and she still had plenty of time to travel to O'Hare to meet him if she hurried, so Brighton stepped to the curb, silently calling a taxi to her side.

With traffic better than she could wish for, Brighton breathlessly watched the city melt away. Green highway signs flew overhead, and she counted each plane she spotted in the sky— silently wishing and hoping one of them wasn't Cain's, and she was too late.

It wasn't the first time Brighton ran through the sweeping corridors of an airport with Cain waiting on the other side. Though, the first time, Brighton didn't have any idea how her life would change in the single span of a moment and a blessedly delayed flight.

A single conversation. That's all it took to send Brighton spinning. All it took was an evening in a bowling alley and an afternoon at a baseball game for Brighton to know she never wanted to be without Cain—friend or otherwise.

Friends. If that's all they were bound to be, would it be enough? Would Brighton be satisfied?

Brighton watched the arrivals screen, silently willing the words to flip from *on-time* to *arrived* as she counted the minutes until Flight 0327 from New York pulled into the gate.

She might have looked a little crazed, impatiently pacing the base of the escalator. Brighton felt like she had been waiting all night when another flurry of passengers floated down the moving stairway.

Brighton ran her fingers through her hair and fidgeted with her coat. She ran over a list of things she wanted to say and do . . . wringing the silken lining of her pockets over and over, until she spotted an unmistakable set of square shoulders cresting the top.

Brighton smiled at him with a bite of her lip, remembering fondly when they'd stood on them together and Cain so boldly asked her to dinner. *Oh,* how things had changed since then and were on the verge of changing again if Brighton was brave enough to try.

Cain's face was pensive, quietly fiddling with the hem of his coat as he looked out over the other travelers. His eyes passed over her, summoning an instantaneous laugh from her lips. Brighton wondered if she should have gone the way of John Cusack in *Say Anything* and brought a boom box to hold over her head.

Brighton's laughter seemed to do the trick, snapping Cain's gaze to hers. He shook his head in surprise with a wide smile. It only grew as he shouldered past the other passengers on the moving stairway to get to her side.

Brighton squealed when Cain swept her up in his arms, holding her firmly as he buried his nose in her auburn waves with a deep, rumbling growl. Brighton could have stayed there forever, face smushed into Cain's neck with her fingertips twisted in his dark curls without thinking.

Setting her to her feet, Cain's held her face, skimming his thumbs over her freckled cheeks. "You're a sight for sore eyes, Colour Girl. It's been too long."

"It hasn't been *that* long," Brighton murmured, blinking softly when Cain's face hovered so achingly close to hers. Could she? *Should she?*

Cain drew closer, skimming his tongue over his bottom lip. "Every moment away from you is too long, Brighton."

Brighton blinked up at him with a whisper. "*Same.*"

Cain's jaw clenched, eyes darting back and forth between Brighton's, brows drawn together. "I'm sorry about before. About what I said . . . about leaving without saying goodbye. I was an ass."

"I am too," Brighton whispered.

"What are you doing here? Didn't you have plans with Andi?" Cain asked.

Brighton shrugged. "I had a little bit of extra time."

"Oh yeah?" Cain gave her a wry smile that made her heart skip a beat. Maybe three. He was so close, and for once—not off-limits.

Brighton let herself linger in the warmth of Cain's gaze and the twinkle in his blue eyes a little longer before pulling his hands away. "The last time we were here, you asked me to dinner. Do you remember?"

"I could hardly forget, Colour Girl. I told you I wouldn't."

"Well—" Brighton's eyes fell to the toes of her red Converses. "I'm here to take you up on the offer before we head home for our movie date . . . err, *night* . . . movie night. My treat."

A slow smile bloomed across Cain's face. "I'd love nothing more."

⋈

Together, as the dimming daylight set the sky ablaze with striking golds and warm splashes of tangerine, Cain and Brighton set off in the same Uber he intended to take home alone.

They went to Gino's East and lost track of time over a few pints and a deep-dish pie. Glasses stacked up in front of them as the time ticked away. Brighton couldn't help herself. Every time the confession crawled to the tip of her tongue, she'd drown it with another beer. Then another. And another.

The conversation was as easy as it had always been, maybe even easier than before without the thing Brighton shackled herself with for years. She was *free*. Free, but still too chicken to tell Cain what happened.

Brighton could feel her body buzzing from the effects of the alcohol. She moved fluidly, always a little further than she meant; laughing a little louder and smiling a little wider.

Knees slotted comfortably between Cain's, Brighton drained the last few drops from her glass, setting it down harder than she meant.

"Are you trying to get me drunk, Colour Girl?" Cain chuckled, offering an easy, lopsided grin. "You're giving hobbits a run for their money."

Brighton let out a loud laugh and a hiccup. "M'drowning my sorrows."

"Are you?" Cain was puzzled, leaning closer with a furrow of his brow. "D'you want to talk about it?"

"*Nope.*" Brighton polished off the word with a crisp *pop* of her lips. The words she needed to say bubbled up, so she motioned for the bartender. Maybe drowning her fears in tequila would help.

Cain swore when Brighton slapped a pair of glasses down and slid a bottle of Mezcal over scuffed mahogany. He watched her, hand perched on Brighton's knee as she ripped open the cork and put a healthy splash into each one.

Brighton hissed through her teeth after throwing one back. "I *just*. . . wanna have a drink with *m'friend*. And I—"

"Hold on."

In the split second before Cain's touch brushed against her skin, every nerve in Brighton's body was electrified. Her head spun, and as Cain's thumb collected a trip of golden agave nectar from her chin, Brighton's resolve crumbled.

One touch and Brighton's intoxication became so much more than the warmth in her chest and the taste of tequila. It rushed across every inch of her skin, furling out from her core in a way she was sure to regret tomorrow.

Except, it wasn't tomorrow. It was *right now*, and with *everything* lingering between them like the promise of a summer storm, Brighton swore time didn't exist at all. Fate pressed pause, letting them linger in the moment as Cain Whitaker's hot hands caressed the long line of her throat, pulling her in as her eyes roved over every inch of his lovely face.

Brighton counted his every faded freckle, idly wondering if God flecked a paintbrush across his skin to make him so beautiful. With a shiver, Brighton imagined herself—imagined *them* —mapping out those marks like an explorer charting the stars, carefully cataloging each one with a kiss.

Cain's eyes darted to her mouth.

If you're going to make a move, you better do it fast.

Brighton's fingertips made contact first, tracing the supple curve of his plush, *oh* so kissable lips. It would be a lie to say Brighton hadn't thought about kissing them before, dreaming of letting them wander over her every freckle.

Brighton tugged her own between her teeth, leaning closer as she reverently went over every centimeter, lingering on the blessed space of Cain's cupid's bow. With a whispered sigh, Brighton brought her touch down, pulling the pliable flesh of his mouth open with a single press of her hand.

It happened in the blink of an eye.

Cain's hands wound around Brighton's waist and tangled in her hair, pulling her closer, until—

"*Cain,*" Brighton murmured his name like a prayer, a breath away from nothing and *everything.*

Brighton held Cain's gaze, slipping from her stool, unable to look away from how he watched her every move, placing his foot on the floor with every intention to follow her.

"What are you doing?" Cain's eyes darkened. "What are *we* doing?"

Tell him. Tell him and stop being afraid. Brighton's every atom buzzed. She needed to feel the February air on her face, to catch her breath, to pull Cain into a darkened hallway and deliver on the promise of his touch—but not like this.

Brighton stepped back. "We . . . we should go home. I want

to go home. It's late."

Cain stood, draining the shot of tequila she poured for him —"sober" once more. *"Yeah.* I think that's a grand idea, Colour Girl."

⋈

*H*ours later, they leaned on each other, hands *everywhere* as they zig-zagged up the stairs of their building, fueled by the beer that warmed their bellies from the pizza parlor—and the pub they stopped at before their return home.

They'd barely made it three steps from the lobby when Cain, drunker than Brighton had ever seen him, with his arms wound 'round her waist, started to sing.

"OHHH, you can search far and wide, you can drink the whole town dry, but you'll never find a beer so brown as the one we drink in our hometooooooown!"

Brighton wasn't sure if she should silence Cain or laugh; neither seemed like a perfect option.

"Would you hush?"

"Ne'er, mi'darlin . . ." Cain drawled with a grin, skirting his palm along the wall to help keep balanced.

Brighton was grateful for it, unsure if, even drunk as she was, she wouldn't want Cain unexpectedly on top of her . . . not in that way, at least.

"I didn't think it was possible," Brighton grumbled.

"Think wot's possible, luv?"

"That you could get *more* British."

Cain made a face and huffed the curls from his forehead. "Not likely, methinks."

Brighton towed him around the next curve of stairs and the next, practically pushing him by the time they made it to the third—while Cain sang the whole way.

"Duuump the crocks in a boiling bowl, pound them up with a thumping pooooole. And when you've finished, if they're whoooole, send them down the hair to roll. That's what Bilbo Baggins hates!!!!"

Cain leaned against the wall, watching as Brighton unlocked the door to the apartment with a roll of her eyes and an exasperated laugh. "Would you be quiet?"

They stumbled into the darkness and the door snapped shut behind them—and Brighton got her wish.

There, in the hushed quiet, a tension of a different sort buzzed between them. Cain's hand gripped Brighton's waist and breath tickled her face as she stumbled back against the wall.

Brighton adjusted to the muted moonlight streaming into the living room in delicate silver rays. Cain came into focus, blue eyes darting over her with a slow lick of his lips.

"You're beautiful, you know that?" Cain rumbled, tucking a strand of hair behind her ear.

Brighton shivered when his balance wavered and body momentarily pressed against hers. Cain anchored himself on her hip—just over her soul mark—sending Brighton's every inch thrumming in a way she'd never felt before.

"T-thank you." Brighton's cheeks burned. "So are you."

"I love you, you know." Cain's hands slid to cup the curve of her jaw. "*I* know you're afraid. So, m'going to try not to love you so much, but I don't *want* to stop, Colour Girl."

"You don't have to." Brighton swallowed the lump in her throat, eyes stinging with every ounce of her regret, with everything she wished she'd done with Cain. The alcohol urged her on, stealing her fear. "I think I can be *brave*. With you."

"I—I think . . ." Cain staggered with a slow blink of his blue eyes. "I think it's time for bed . . . and I think . . . I'd like to kiss you goodnight."

"I think that would be okay," Brighton murmured, heart racing when Cain stepped closer. Her eyes slipped closed, breath shaking as the alcohol dulled her senses, a gasp catching in her throat when—of all the places she wanted Cain Whitaker to kiss her right then—he pressed his lips to her cheek.

"G'night, Colour Girl," Cain growled, skimming his scruff along her jaw, offering one final heavy-lidded, scorching look before pulling away.

Brighton turned to lock the door as Cain set off down the hall, shedding his layers *so* similarly to how she had done a couple days before—leaving a trail behind him as he peeled away his coat, his tie, his shirt . . .

The muted light in the hall illuminated every cursive line of Cain's body, casting shadows of finely toned muscle across valleys of velvety skin. Every curve bent and moved with each step he took, drawing Brighton closer as each millisecond ticked by.

Brighton followed close behind, wanting more than anything to follow suit, to follow *him* and do what she'd thought about countless times—but something stopped her.

Not like this. Not today.

Brighton hovered in the doorway as Cain stood at the edge of the bed, handsome face etched with a frown as he looked at the blue sweater she'd left behind.

"You could have kept this, you know." Cain's eyes snapped to her, broad chest catching the moonlight. Brighton's eyes took in every detail, fingers aching to see if it felt as soft to the touch as she imagined.

"I do." Brighton smiled, holding fast to the frame like an anchor barring her from temptation. "Maybe someday I'll claim it. But for now . . . it's still yours, Cain Whitaker."

"Fair enough." Cain nodded towards the bed, "You headed to sleep?"

"Seems like the right thing to do. It's late and . . . it's been a long day."

"True. Well—" Cain sucked in a deep breath, blue eyes glittering. "You could join me again. Best sleep of my life, Bee. Could test that theory."

Her heart flipped, and if she hadn't let herself think about it, Brighton would have crossed the threshold—and all sorts of *other* lines if the buzzed, heady feeling had its way. "No, I don't think that's a good idea."

Cain's eyes fell, but his smile remained. "Until tomorrow, Colour Girl. Sweet dreams."

"You too, Cain," Brighton smiled.

As she turned to walk away, he spoke again. "Do me a favor?"

"Anything," Brighton answered, brown eyes bright as she leaned through the doorway.

"Try and be brave."

Brighton thought about the precipice they seemed to be on —a sliver of a fresh start. She'd turned the page and closed the book on a volume long overdue to be shelved.

Here they were, with their own story and nothing but their future ahead of them—whatever it might hold. Before then, everything was merely a prequel, a prologue to the story Brighton wanted to tell.

"I'll try." Brighton offered one final look as she stepped away and into her own room. Closing the door with a quiet *click*, she sighed, eager to calm the aching in her heart and the fuzz on the edges of her vision.

They were friends. True friends. *Best friends*. Ones who'd drawn a line in the sand years before with a good reason to do so.

As Brighton slipped between the covers and pulled a pillow to her chest, she wondered what would happen if they demolished the line and built something new.

Fueled by the warm, dull thrum from their trip to the pub,

Brighton fell asleep—jetting off to a dream world where she could finally get to find out.

Chapter 14

*B*righton couldn't sleep. She tried for a little while, briefly carried off to the shores of her childhood home. Cain was there, and instead of almost kissing, they did *so much more.*

Their dream selves stripped each layer away, thumbing every cursive line like something precious, something to be savored. Just as things were about to go from good to incredible to . . . *more* . . . Brighton snapped back to consciousness with a *very* specific itch to scratch.

So, under the secret serenity of darkness, *she did.* Only, Brighton's new, seemingly incurable, hunger wouldn't be satiated. Until—with the help of a piping hot shower and the image of Cain's face hovering over her in the moonlight—she chased it away again with the tips of her fingers, hoping it would cure the feeling so she might be able to sleep.

The thing about cravings, though—is they find their way back over and over.

Brighton, practically *addicted*, chased the thought as often as it surfaced that night and well into morning, praying the walls and her pillow would help suppress the way Cain made her sing—without him knowing.

What would Brighton do if Cain *did* know? Her cheeks heated at the thought. She smushed her face into the pillow with a groan, but when another thought surfaced, the cravings washed away like she'd done the Polar Bear Plunge.

Somehow, since she'd *literally* run to him at the airport—sans engagement ring and fiancé—Brighton still hadn't told him that things between her and Gideon were *finally* over.

Would it be too late? Brighton's stomach twisted at the thought, never wanting Cain to feel like he was second choice—he was the *only* choice. Brighton knew that now.

Waiting wasn't an option. They'd waited long enough. Maybe . . . maybe Brighton could do something special, something beyond their normal day-to-day that'd help her gain the courage to let it all out and be brave like she promised.

As the early morning sun crested over a fresh layer of snow and Cain slept off his beer-fueled haze, Brighton set to work.

Never much of a baker—or anything in the kitchen—Brighton quickly feared she'd bitten off more than she could chew. But, Two YouTube videos and half an episode of The Great British Baking Show later, Brighton thought—maybe—she had a handle on things.

"I got this. I can do this," Brighton whispered, wiping flour from her forehead as she set to work kneading raisins into an impossibly sticky dough.

Brighton collapsed against the counter when she finally got the infernal sweets into the oven—after figuring out she did, in fact, have to turn it on—slamming back an early morning shot of Mezcal to ease her baking-induced anxiety.

The thing about recipes, though—they often require the use of a timer: a crucial detail Brighton missed during her intense study.

Settled onto a barstool to work on a sketch for a client, Brighton found herself so involved in the delicately drawn lines on her tablet, she didn't notice the smell until it was too late.

Brighton bolted from her seat, tearing open the oven to pull her kind-hearted but poorly executed goodies from inside. The edge of the pan kissed the tip of her finger through a thin kitchen towel, pulling a hiss between her teeth as she dropped the smoking buns on the stove.

Brighton pressed the sting of the burn against her lips and the smoke detector caught wind of her kitchen faux-pas.

"Fuck..." The screeching alarm startled her into action.

Brighton jumped onto the counter—noisily scattering glass jars of cinnamon and nutmeg—frantically waving her hands at the alarm, praying, *somehow*, Cain would sleep through the clatter. But, regardless how feverishly she flapped her hands, it persisted.

Brighton anchored one hand to the top of the cabinet, stretching to the very tips of her toes as she reached to disconnect the damned thing. No matter how far she stretched, swore, or—hell—used the Force, Brighton couldn't snag the noisy little thing.

"What in the hell is going on here?" Cain's voice interjected from behind her.

Brighton spun on the stone counter, face flushing a deep scarlet when she remembered she'd slept—and been baking— in a stolen shirt of Cain's from the laundry. And *he* wasn't wearing one at all.

"It was supposed to be a surprise." Brighton's cheeks blazed, trying and failing spectacularly to avoid taking in every inch of Cain—especially the way his grey sweatpants slung low over his hips, offering the glimpse of a freckle along the waistband and *other* things further beneath.

Veiled in sleep, Cain's brow furrowed in the bright morning light—further illuminating the cornflower blue of his eyes. His usually neatly coiffed curls draped every which way, and *oh* how Brighton ached to brush them back into place.

His hair, though, wasn't the only thing Brighton wanted to touch . . . and her fingers weren't the only thing that craved him.

Cain rubbed a broad palm across his bare chest, holding Brighton's gaze as he ambled into the kitchen, barely stretched, and twisted the smoke alarm off its base. He held it out with a laugh and a smug grin, taking in her appearance.

Brighton was sure she looked more than a little frazzled—from the messy bun atop her head to her obvious lack of pants and the fact she was most certainly covered in flour.

"You chose *now* to try your hand at baking?" Cain asked with a lift of his brow. "You remember what happened last time, right? It took weeks to get the smell out."

"You shut up, we are never talking about this ever again. Come here—" Brighton motioned towards him with a laugh and placed her hands on his shoulders. "Can you help me down, please?"

Cain coiled his hands around Brighton's waist, tugging her to his chest to lift her feet from the counter and ease her to the floor.

Brighton let her hands rest against him, caught up in the feeling of his downy chest hair beneath her fingertips. Cain, too, lingered almost as close as the night before, with a smile playing on his lips, like he *knew* what she'd been up to all night —just she and her fingers.

With a cough and cheeks aflame, *again*, Brighton pulled away and dusted the layer of flour from her shirt, propping her hands on her hips to survey the complete disaster in their kitchen.

Flour scattered the counter, with bits of unused dough, a stray rolling pin, and a tray of what should have been hot crossed buns—burnt to an absolute crisp on the stove.

"Well, fuck me." Brighton blew a ribbon of hair from her face.

Cain grumbled a spellbinding chuckle. "Don't tempt me, darling."

Brighton disguised the searing heat in her cheeks with a frown. "I wanted to make something to remind you of home. So much for that idea."

Cain gently knocked his shoulder against hers, blue eyes crinkling at the corners. "Chin up, Bee. I'm honored you tried, but what's there to remind me of when 'home' is wherever you are?"

"Flatterer," Brighton groused with a shake of her head when she was struck with an idea. "*What if* . . . we go have a brunch date?" She answered the ache in her fingertips and brushed them against his temple. "Maybe cure your hangover?" Brighton's hands trailed down his bare torso, thumbing the edge of his sweatpants *just* above where her own soul mark existed.

"*Stop.*" Cain's fingers snapped around Brighton's wrist and tugged her hand away before she could get a better look of what lay beneath. Brighton's heart did a *very* specific kind of twinge when Cain reassured her with a brush of his thumb against her cheek. "I think brunch sounds marvelous, Colour Girl."

Brighton reluctantly headed down the hall with a smile, motioning toward the flour on her face. "Listen, you get dressed. I'm going to wash away the evidence of the Great Hot Crossed Buns Massacre of 2021, then we'll get breakfast. My treat."

Brighton chewed the edge of her thumb as she stared at the rainbowed curtains of fabric in her closet. Her stomach flipped, twisted, and turned, going over every version of the future conversation with Cain in her head.

Brighton had an outfit for every occasion, each one more vivid than the last. But what was she supposed to wear to tell the love of her life she'd finally made the choice to be brave—to love Cain back the way he deserved?

Her fingers moved against bright pink crepe, blue velvet, and orange chiffon. All of them *beautiful*. Brighton shook her head. She didn't *need* any of the bright colors. Cain could already see her, he saw past all of it. Cain saw *her*.

So, Brighton picked something simple—a plain white tee, jeans, and a no-fuss pair of black heels.

Brighton smiled at her reflection, curling the flyaways at the end of her braid around her finger. When she stepped into the hall, a fresh sheet of steam curled from the slightly ajar door of the bathroom.

Brighton knew she shouldn't look. The old building had its quirks—including doors that wouldn't *quite* latch. But, when she heard the water shut off and a screech of the shower curtain sliding open, Brighton's eyes wanted to know if what she'd been thinking about all night had been accurate. A peek wouldn't hurt, right? Cain would be none the wiser.

With a lick of her lips, Brighton held her breath, and *looked*, petrified the stream of light into the darkened corridor might give her away. Either that, or the thunderous drumming of her heart.

Like a mountain stream tumbled and twisted 'round every bend and curve on the rocky facade, so did the tiniest rivulets down the contours of Cain's back. Not only had Brighton's imagination not fabricated how beautiful he was, it hadn't done him justice. Her mouth watered, but she felt thirsty—leaning closer toward the opening in the door as Cain scrubbed a towel over his shoulder.

So achingly close to Cain, now Brighton freed herself from her poor choices and finally chosen to be *brave* . . . why not skip brunch and jump in with both feet?

Brighton's fingers hovered over the door, eager to demolish the line in the sand she'd drawn and draw a circle around them, instead. Someplace safe for the two of them, as they were meant to be, and give she and Cain the chance to explore each other in ways where words failed.

Before, Brighton's mind wandered. Now, it *ran*—enthusiastically chasing every heated thought the longer she watched how the taut muscles in Cain's back bent and shifted with every minuscule movement.

In it, Brighton pushed the door open and all it took was the look in her eyes to tell Cain everything she wanted to say.

I'm sorry. I'm sorry I was afraid. I'm sorry I didn't let myself see. I'm sorry I didn't let myself love you.

In it, Cain didn't hesitate. He took her in his arms without a second thought, peppering her skin in delicate kisses that sent her every atom spinning. Layers came away, and . . . the more Brighton let herself entertain the idea, the more her resolve crumbled.

. . . until Judy Garland ruined it.

Cain's eyes snapped toward the slightly-open door at the first note of *Over the Rainbow*.

"*Fuck*," Brighton hissed under her breath, trying to balance between a tip toe and sprint to her bedside table before Dorothy got to the second verse.

"Bee?" The bathroom door swung open behind her, bathing her in bright light. It might as well have been the Bat Signal, telling Cain *exactly* what she'd been doing.

. . . the dreams that you dare to dream really do come true . . .

"Hey!" Brighton plastered a smile on her face, hoping it would banish the heat in her cheeks—and in her belly—when she turned around and could have looked *anywhere*, but stared straight at the laughably small towel Cain casually held from his hip. "You . . . uh . . . you almost ready?"

Someday I'll wish upon a star and wake up where the stars are far behind me.

Cain's brows creased, carrying away droplets of water

hanging from the wet tendrils hanging in front of his eyes. He gathered a bead of water from his lips with a swipe of his tongue, clearly interrupted before he finished drying off. "Nearly there, Colour Girl. What were you doing out here?"

Where troubles melt like lemon drops, oh high above the chimney tops, that's where you'll find me.

Brighton's phone rang and rang. Her face burned, and she wished a cyclone would sweep in and drop a house on her.

"I . . . uh . . . was getting my phone." Brighton thumbed over her shoulder. "Better get that before voicemail picks it up."

"*Yeah.*" Cain half-smiled. "You'd better."

Brighton stumbled into the master bedroom, thunking her head against the wood as the latch clicked.

Judy crooned louder than before, demanding Brighton answer before she sang a song of her new, perverted hobby of peeking on her roommate fresh from the shower.

"H-hello?" Brighton caught it in the nick of time.

"Hey, Pumpkin."

Brighton practically melted into the mattress. "Hi, Dad."

"You texted and said you wanted to talk?"

"Yeah." Brighton pushed her toe across the rainbow shag rug. "I have something to tell you."

"Oh?"

"I, uh—" Brighton looked at the door, swallowing the lump in her throat when she thought of Cain in the next room. "Gideon and I are done."

"*Oh?*" Thomas's voice lifted. "I'm sorry to hear that, kiddo."

"Don't be. I'm not. It needed to happen a long time ago. I wish I could go back and tell myself to end it sooner. He was good for me after Jesse, but . . . after that, not so much. Plus, he met his soulmate, so I feel like he got the better end of the deal."

"Did he?" Brighton *heard* the knowing look Thomas gave her.

Brighton shook her head, unable to keep the smile from her face when she heard Cain's distant hum from the next room. "No, I don't think he did."

"That's my girl. When are you going to tell him?"

Brighton smiled, cheeks heating again. "Tell who?"

"Brighton Faye Evans, you know exactly who. You've always known. You needed time to realize it." Thomas paused, probably giving her the look that warned of oncoming, sage advice. "You had to learn something, first."

"*Cain,*" Brighton breathed, heart twisting when her fears of all the things that could go wrong leached away her joy. "What if I'm too late?"

"I can say for certain, when it comes to love, there's no such thing as too late when that person is right in front of you. Live your life now. Take chances. You never can tell what's going to happen." Thomas gave Brighton an inch of breathing room to take it all in and pressed on. "Shit happens. Accidents. Freak snowstorms. *Cancer.* Life is this strange journey with twists and turns. There's no reason you need to be in the car alone—especially when you clearly love the guy."

⋈

*T*he warm ceramic in her hands held Brighton like an anchor. Her thoughts ping ponged as the storm outside continued to hold her attention.

She and Cain been nestled into a booth for five minutes and forty-two seconds. Brighton still hadn't spilled the beans even though they practically melted her from the inside out. Brighton knew what she wanted to say, practicing it in her head a thousand times on the walk over. She knew what she wanted, but part of her was terrified of ruining a good thing, tearing their precious friendship to shreds when—like many good things—it inevitably fell to pieces.

Brighton glanced across the table, meeting his blue eyes before looking back down at her tea. She rotated her spoon in small circles, sorting through all of the 'almost, maybe' moments of their history.

She smiled, remembering falling asleep in Cain's arms after their fight and how she wished she could've woken up beside him.

With a slow blink and the ghost of a smile, Brighton imagined what it would have been like if she *had*.

The weight of Cain's hand on her waist. His mouth would quiver at whatever he dreamt about. Brighton would marvel at the shape of Cain's lips as he breathed. Her hands would ache and she would surely have to resist reaching out to brush a dark curl from his forehead.

Eventually, temptation would win out. Brighton would give into the allure of Cain's inky locks and regret it when he'd stir with a quiet grumble.

But what, then? The possibilities in Brighton's mind were endless. Maybe Cain's lips on hers with Brighton's leg slotted between his as their hands wandered. And, in the early morning light, they could explore what it meant for them to be more than friends.

"*Brighton.*" Cain interrupted her delirious daydream, making her flinch and nearly spill her tea.

"Shit, Cain. You scared me." Brighton carded her fingers through her hair.

"*Scared you?*" Cain cocked his head, brows furrowed simultaneously in confusion, mild concern, and amusement. "You were definitely in it, Bee. Where'd you go?"

"It . . . uh. It was my dad who called me earlier. He gave me fascinating advice. I'm trying to decide if I should take it or not." The half-lie laid heavily on Brighton's tongue, so she washed it away with a sip of her tea.

Cain leaned back and whistled. "Your dad is a wise bloke. If he gave you advice, you'd better listen. He strikes me as the kind of man who knows everything."

"He does." Brighton nodded with a laugh.

"My mum's that way."

"Yeah?"

Cain nodded. "I got some advice from her a while back. I'd bet a hundred quid right now she was right."

"Did you take it?" Brighton leaned forward on her elbows. "Her advice, I mean."

"No." Cain smiled wistfully. "I've regretted it ever since—the time I've wasted. So, believe me. You'd better listen to your old man."

Best friends fell in love all the time—Brighton heard the stories all her life. If those other people made it work, couldn't they? *Yes.* She knew they could. They'd pass whatever test that came their way with flying colors.

Peering at Cain from over the edge of her cup, she took another sip. Brighton knew it was time. Time to be brave.

She leaned across the table and twisted her fingers with Cain's. "I have to tell you something."

Brighton expected her heart to run away. She expected her hands to clam up. She expected every nervous feeling to overwhelm her and tell her she was wrong, but as Cain's eyes lifted to meet hers, the only feeling she felt was *sure.*

As Brighton opened her mouth to speak, to declare herself and make everything as it should be, his jacket pocket pinged and tore his attention away.

Cain pulled his phone from inside and *smiled,* giving Brighton a quick glance before setting it face-down on the table. "Sorry. You were saying, darling?"

"How much do you remember about last night?" Brighton chewed her lip.

Cain made a face, draining his mug.

"Not much." Cain's frown deepened when, as he tried to fill

it back up from the carafe on the table, it offered only a few drops. "Why? . . . I didn't start singing dwarfen pub songs, again, did I?"

Brighton laughed. "You did. And—" She hesitated, thinking of how Cain told her he loved her. She wanted to say it back . . . could she? *Should she?* "Do you remember talking? A-about being brave?"

Brighton piqued Cain's interest, drawing him forward with a half-smile. "Being brave? Did I say that?"

"Yeah, and you went full *Hansel and Gretel* with your clothes down the hall." Every detail Brighton revealed made her feel lighter. Her trepidation melted away. Could this be it, could this be the start of their forever?

Cain's face flushed a deep scarlet, muffling his voice as he hid behind his hands. "Fuck me, that's embarrassing. Sorry 'bout that. You didn't . . . did you *see* a lot?"

"It was dark, so no. But you *did* try to get me to sleep with you." Brighton giggled when Cain's mortification climbed, anchoring him with her touch. "Not like *that*. Like the whole 'best sleep of your life,' kind of way. Which—brings me to the thing I wanted to tell you."

Cain's gaze craned as a waiter passed them by. He gave her hand a squeeze with a still-bashful smile. "Hold that thought, darling. I'm going to see if I can get us some fresh coffee."

Brighton curled her fingers into her palm, holding onto the feeling as Cain slipped from the booth.

Cain's phone buzzed on the laminate, drawing Brighton away from his subtle saunter. She stared as it vibrated again . . . and again. Then, Brighton thought of how Cain smiled at the earlier message—the kind of smile he usually reserved for *her*.

Brighton leaned back in the booth, stomach twisting as she regarded the device like a ticking time bomb. Her fingers itched and trembled, wanting to reassure herself that it was probably Eli or Andi, but too afraid to look.

Brighton blew out a short breath, snatching it from the surface before Cain came back to the table and instantly wished she hadn't. Her eyes darted across the list of notifications—all from someone named *Rebecca.*

Can't stop thinking about our little "meet-cute." I still can't believe I ran into you by chance.

I confirmed our reservations for Tuesday. Can't wait to see you, Cain. I've got a lot to show you.

It's a sexy setting, I know you'll love it. Do you want baguettes?

Brighton's mouth went slack. She weaved in her seat. Her every atom went cold and she battled the need to cry. Sliding Cain's phone away from her, Brighton stared at her open palms, hoping they held the answers as her fears bubbled back to the surface.

She *was* too late.

"Who died?" Cain's voice pulled her back to the present.

Brighton's gaze stayed on the table, folding her fingers together as Cain slid a fresh cup of tea in front of her. She lifted her eyes and met Cain's beautifully lopsided smile, summoning the last ounce of bravery she had left. "Gideon and I are over."

Cain's smile fell, brows puckering together. "Brighton—"

A million things went through Brighton's mind—all the *should-haves* and *could have beens.* Every beautiful thing she imagined in her wildest daydreams flittered away in a wisp of smoke.

Cain reached for her; Brighton pulled away.

"Listen." Brighton anchored her hands around the warm ceramic as the name Rebecca floated around in her mind. "I've been thinking about our fight . . . about the things you said. I—I thought I finally knew what I wanted, but I get it. I understand. I know what you're going to say. I don't want to talk about it anymore. *I can't.* I think, at this point, it's better if we stick to our boundaries—*better* boundaries—and just be friends. It's too complicated, otherwise."

Cain leaned back in the booth, rubbing his fingers against the table's surface. "Are you sure?"

Brighton nodded, forcing a smile. "For once, yes."

"Complicated . . . *right*." Cain pawed a hand through his dark hair, chewing on his words before blurting out, "If it's what you want, I'll honor that, Brighton."

Brighton. Not Colour Girl or Bee—*Brighton*. That only cemented things, souring Brighton's stomach further as she imagined him happy with another girl. And Brighton—she'd have to live with the unfathomable truth she'd wasted the time Cain spent loving her by being *happy enough* with someone else. Maybe this was her punishment, reaping what she'd so foolishly sown.

Brighton flipped open the menu, distracting herself with a decision that held a lesser weight—french toast or eggs Benedict. Maybe, on a full stomach, she'd feel better about the whole thing.

Chapter 15

June

"*P*ass the chips."

The clouds flew by Brighton window as they passed herds of cows, touristy cheese shops, and the green, rolling pastures of the Midwestern countryside. Brighton smiled when Cain let out a grumble from the driver's seat.

"Get your feet off the dash and pass the chips, yourself." Cain tapped his long fingers on the leather-wrapped steering wheel, keeping his gaze ever-vigilantly on the road. "Distracted driving kills, you know."

"Yes, I know. You've told me a *million times* before. I get it," Brighton muttered, unbuckling her seatbelt to climb halfway into the backseat.

"See, I don't think you do, darling," Cain growled from behind her.

"How so?" Brighton shuffled through the bag of snacks Cain packed.

"Your colorful arse is in my face right now, and I find myself *thoroughly* distracted by it."

Brighton snatched a bright blue bag of salt and vinegar

chips, promptly plopping back into her seat with a laugh. "If it's so distracting, then don't look at it."

"I can't help if it has its own center of gravity," Cain teased with a sidelong gaze before leaning over and pulling her seatbelt back across her body. Brighton held her breath at the close contact, unable to ignore the frisson of goosebumps down her legs as the firm muscle of Cain's arm brushed across her chest. "*Seatbelt.* Could save your—"

"—life one day, I know. You've said it before. Yes, Cain Whitaker, *sir.*" Brighton saluted before ripping open the bag and stuffing a handful of chips in her mouth. "Think you'll miss me all the way from your room?"

Cain laughed. "It's just down a different hall than we're used to."

"It might be floors, *Kal El,*" Brighton teased. "You could fly up to my balcony if you're lonely."

"Are you kidding?" Cain asked. "This'll be like a vacation. My room will be far enough away from yours; I won't hear your snores."

"*Hey,*" Brighton warned through a fresh mouthful of chips. "I don't snore. Besides, you won't be able to hear me over whatever gorgeous girl you meet at the reception."

Brighton's stomach twisted at the thought, but she banished it with a smile.

Cain, however, didn't have an ounce of amusement in his blue eyes. "There won't be a girl, Bee."

Brighton made a face. "How come? Weddings are perfect for this kind of thing. You're single . . . who knows . . . maybe *she* is gonna be there."

"No." Cain shook his head, glancing her way for the briefest second. "I already have a girl."

Brighton's stomach fell, and her smile faltered. "*Oh.*"

Cain's handsome face cracked into a smile. "Don't fret, darling. *You're* my girl."

Brighton's heart flipped. She turned her attention out her window, wishing it were true.

Things had been *normal* between them since she ended things with Gideon and decided that friendship with Cain was worth protecting. Plus, he had Becky. Well, *Rebecca*. At least, Brighton thought he did.

As the weeks wore on, and Brighton's every sense fixed on every ping of Cain's cellphone and the way his face would change as he read, she started to wonder if things with *whatsherface* didn't work out, after all.

Brighton felt good about her choice. Mostly. But, every once in a while—like right then—the feeling would sneak back in, rooting itself in Brighton's mind with every lingering touch and wayward glance.

The way Cain looked at her—the way Brighton imagined them together. No matter how hard she tried, no matter how she reminded herself of all the things that would inevitably go wrong, Brighton went back to a list of moments—*proof* they ought to be more.

They made excellent time, crossing the distance from busy Chicago and its suburbs over the state line into Wisconsin in what felt like record time.

Out of snacks and more than ready to stretch her legs, they pulled up a long, gravel drive to a stately lodge. Cain looked over the massive log cabin—akin to something belonging in a national park—and held out an arm for Brighton.

She slipped her hand through the crook of his elbow, lifting her wide-eyed gaze to the broad, luxurious facade. Three floors —maybe four—stretched out across a few acres of thick woodland.

Brighton recalled Andi rattling off a series of details about the *perfect* venue she'd found—one that felt like home— complete with an elegant banquet hall for dancing, a carriage house for the men, and a lush forest that made it all feel like a fairytale.

"You know, when Andi said she wanted to get married in something like a castle, I thought she was being metaphorical," Brighton breathed as Cain knocked on the door.

It swung open, and the pair of them were swept inside by two pairs of hands. They gave each other a wayward glance as they were abruptly separated by the bride and groom.

A cocktail party—somewhere between a rehearsal dinner and a full-blown reception—was in full swing. Brighton barely had a chance to murmur a single hello before Andi pulled her into a blessedly quiet corner.

The bride looked imploringly at Brighton. "There's . . . there's a problem."

"What kind of problem?" Brighton answered with a furrow of her brow, mind flying to the usual kinds of issues plaguing a bride the night before her wedding. She was ready to solve all of them like any Maid of Honor should. "Whatever it is, we'll get it figured out."

"I mean . . ." Andi's face bloomed into a sugary sweet smile. "It's not a *problem* problem, I guess. Eli thought it would . . . be *funny*, maybe? But then . . . it sorta worked out this way, and there's no going back, and I'm really sorry, please don't be mad."

"Don't be mad? Why would I be . . ." Brighton took a step back, planting her hands on her hips with a frown. "*What did you do?*"

⋈

*F*ive minutes later, Brighton trudged up the stairs, half-amused, half-annoyed as she walked the long corridor of the third floor to a heavy wooden door with a golden plate reading, *The Fairytale Suite*, in exquisite, curly lettering.

With a jingle of the key, Brighton pushed it open, closing it with a soft slam. She leaned against it, face melting into a smile when she met Cain's equally perturbed gaze from across the room.

"They think they're so fucking funny, don't they?" Cain groused, dropping his luggage onto the floor with a *thud*.

"It won't be that bad," Brighton laughed, setting her own overly-stuffed suitcase down on the bedspread of a sprawling, king-sized log bed. "It's not like we haven't been in close quarters before. I mean . . . we *live* together, Cain. Will this really be that different?"

"Brighton . . ." Cain growled, animatedly waving his hands. "There's only *one bed.*"

"So?" Brighton leaned forward and unzipped her bag, pulling her clothes from inside to hang in an adjacent wardrobe.

"So . . . what . . . are we supposed to *sleep together?*" Cain snapped, pacing back and forth across the lush, ivory carpet.

"What are you so upset about?"

The bed was more than big enough for the two of them, plus a plush, velveteen, wine-red sofa at the foot of the bed, and a large clawfoot tub situated in the corner by a towering window.

"I mean . . . if the idea of sleeping in the same bed as me bothers you *that much*, I'll sleep in the tub, okay? And here I thought we could have a repeat of the '*best sleep of your life . . .*'"

"Stop." Cain scowled, hands on his hips. "Don't be ridiculous. You're not sleeping in the tub. I will."

Brighton barked out a loud laugh, planting the last of her rainbow-hued shoes in the bottom of the wooden wardrobe before turning back to him. "Now, who's being the ridiculous one?"

Cain paced in a quiet fury until Brighton reached to still him.

Her heart fluttered when she felt Cain's racing pulse slow and the warmth of his skin bloom beneath her fingertips. Brighton gently skirted her hands up the hard planes of his chest to cup the curve of his face.

Cain's gaze softened once he was centered in hers.

"It's going to be fine and isn't a big deal, okay? We aren't strangers. We're *us*," Brighton whispered.

Cain blinked back at Brighton before wrapping his arms around her waist to pull her into a hug.

Brighton reciprocated it with one of her own, nestling her cheek against Cain's shoulder, murmuring with a laugh. "I won't bite or steal the covers, I promise. Plus, if it's really an issue, you can stay in the wardrobe. It's so big, I think Narnia is back there somewhere."

It felt like home, tucked in the warmth of Cain's arms, probably more than it had any right to be, and Brighton quickly found herself second-guessing every second.

With a quiet clearing of her throat, Brighton pulled away and peered up at Cain through her lashes. "We'll make the best of it. Okay, big guy? In the meantime, we ought to get dressed for dinner, yeah? We're late."

"If you say so." Cain heaved a great sigh, pulling her to his broad chest again. He tucked the tip of his nose into Brighton's hair, giving her one last blessed squeeze before releasing her. "I'll take the bathroom to change if you want."

"Okay," Brighton whispered with an almost bashful smile as he bent down to gather his bag from the floor.

It shut quietly behind him and left Brighton deliriously alone, realizing being apart from Cain was something she didn't want to be.

Not anymore. Never again.

Chapter 16

*B*righton absentmindedly swayed her feet from the edge of the bed, fiddling with the hem of her dress. When the door to the en-suite bathroom swung open, her eyes shot to the man taking up every inch of the frame.

When Brighton looked at Cain, she didn't *see* anything different than what she'd seen a thousand times before—from after-work happy hour to Andi and Eli's engagement party.

Still, Cain held himself a certain way. Maybe the way *she* looked at him changed when he stepped out and met her gaze.

Brighton slipped to the carpet, a smile playing on her crimson-hued lips. "*Wow* . . . did you . . . is that a new suit?"

Cain shook his head, tilting it to the side as he looked over Brighton's carefully chosen dress for the night. "Mm, no. But you . . . *wow*, yourself."

Cain gave her a slow spin, and the honey-hued fabric fluttered at the hem. When he stopped her, hands on her waist, Brighton wished she could linger. No party. No guests. No other obligation than the two of them, anchored in the charged silence together.

The warmth of Cain's hands bled through the fabric as if

she wore nothing at all, like they brushed against smooth, unencumbered flesh. Brighton wished they *were*. She wished he'd lean down and pepper her bare, freckled shoulders with kisses until they found themselves so inexplicably caught up, they'd never make it downstairs for the party.

Brighton wondered what was going through Cain's mind as he held fast to the small of her back. He smelled of shave soap —a blessed blend of spices, smoke, and earth that made her mouth water. Brighton's fingers ached to touch the edge of his square jaw to see if it was as smooth as it appeared to be.

"Thank you," Brighton murmured when fear broke the spell and stopped her from taking another step closer to find out if her daydreams were worth exploring.

"I don't think I've seen that one before," Cain smiled, scrubbing his fingers along the edge of his clean-shaven face as he, too, put another few inches between them.

"This old thing?" Brighton joked, skimming her palms down golden taffeta. It was beautiful, and she *had* to have it when she spotted it in a department store window that spring.

Effortlessly elegant, the dress hugged the outside curve of Brighton's shoulders with a wide band of fabric that bent and dipped down into a shallow v over her bust. It nipped in at the waist and flared out into a classic A-line. Brighton paired it with her favorite pair of red stilettos and matching lipstick. The holy blend of every colorful facet—from her hair to her makeup and her shoes—made Brighton feel like a golden, autumnal sunset.

Together, they stepped out into the hall. Cain looked down at her, blue eyes crinkling. "You ready, Colour Girl?"

Brighton chewed the inside of her lip, and she glanced back at the four-poster log bed in their suite. "You sure you don't want to stay? Have another Return of the King rewatch?"

Cain shook his head, handsome face creasing into a broad smile. "Not even Samwise Gamgee can keep me from wining and dining with you tonight."

"Fine, fine," Brighton laughed. "Might as well, or we got all dressed up for nothing."

Cain held out an arm. Brighton slid her hand against the bend of his elbow, finding an easy home there as they stepped around the corner.

The clink of cocktail glasses and the din of Andi and Eli's guests grew louder as the pair descended a sprawling staircase. Brighton's dress flounced with each step, and Cain dutifully held tight to her hand while she navigated every stair in her stilettos.

Hand in hand, they made their way to the bottom, but Cain paused at the base of the final stair. "On second thought." He turned around, fingers still twined with Brighton's. "Revisiting Middle Earth doesn't sound so bad."

A smirk tugged at the corner of Cain's mouth, but Brighton could see the faraway look in his eyes.

Cain stepped up in front of her, lifting his chin to meet her gaze.

Brighton's hands felt impossibly small as she drew her touch along the line of his broad shoulders and up his neck, across the freshly-shaven line of his jaw. She lingered there, pulling them closer as she held Cain's face—Brighton's whole heart—in her hands. "What is it? A few seconds ago, you were ready to 'wine and dine' with me . . . now you want to go back to the room . . . the room you didn't want to share with me . . ."

Cain found Brighton's waist, knotting his fingers together in the small of her back. He chewed his words. "Do you . . . do you ever feel like you're losing track of time?"

"What do you mean?" Brighton feathered her touch on his temple.

Cain sucked in a deep breath, shaking his head. "Sometimes, I feel like it's slipping through my fingers. I blink, and *years* have gone by. It's gone by too fast, and all I want to do is be here in this life . . . *with you* . . . forever."

A smile bloomed across Brighton's face. "That doesn't seem like too much to ask. I want that too, Cain."

"Sometimes, I worry it's more complicated than that." Cain rolled his face in Brighton's hands, pulling her firmly against his chest as he summoned an unconvincing smile. "I don't know. It's this odd feeling I've got buzzing in the back of my mind."

Brighton wasn't convinced, leaning down with a brush of her thumbs against his cheek. "Wasn't there a part in . . . *Fellowship of the Ring*, I think? Arwen said 'something, something . . . trust . . . something . . .'"

Cain gave her a true smile. "*If you trust nothing else, trust this. Trust us.* Yeah, I remember it well, darling."

Brighton shrugged, trailing her fingers down to Cain's chest, lingering on the ruby-red of his tie. "Think like Aragorn and Arwen, maybe? Trust this. Trust us. *Trust me.*" Brighton's dark eyes lifted back to Cain's. "I'm not going anywhere. I know time goes by quickly, but . . . at least we're together, right? I don't plan on changing that anytime soon. Do you?"

Cain shook his head. "No, I don't, Colour Girl. Not if I can help it."

"Good," Brighton wrapped her arms around him, grazing her lips against his cheek. "I'm your girl, remember? So let's go enjoy ourselves. Do the thing Gandalf says . . . choose what to do with the time that's given to us, right? Use that time to drink Andi's booze."

Cain's shoulders bounced with laughter, taking a step back as he finally released her. "Can't argue with Old Greybeard. Party, it is."

Brighton stepped down from the staircase, taking Cain's hand in hers with a broad grin to join the festivities. They were already late, and there wasn't any more time to waste.

⋈

A few hours later, with a full belly, a faint buzz, and Cain by her side, Brighton wandered through the cocktail hour, happily chatting with other guests.

Cain looked down at her with a lazy grin as he handed over a fresh glass of champagne, taking her hand in his with a tug as he leaned down to whisper in her ear. His lips came so close, Brighton's own parted, when his breath kissed the tender flesh of her earlobe.

"Come 'ere. There's someone I want you to meet." Cain's brows drew together, blue eyes heavy-lidded and mouth caught in a semi-permanent, bubbly-fueled smirk.

"Cain Whitaker." Brighton rubbed the crease in his forehead. "If you're not careful, your face is going to stick like that."

"M'serious." Cain towed Brighton through the guests.

"What is it, your mother or something?" Brighton jibed playfully, trailing after him across the elegantly wood-paneled hall.

"Something like that," Cain chuckled with a wry smile over a broad shoulder as they strode up to a small, stately woman on the other side of the room.

She was *beautiful,* with a kind face, glittering blue eyes, and silver-white hair hanging past her shoulders. Brighton thought she looked oddly familiar.

"Brighton, this is my mother, Carrie Whitaker." Cain looped an arm around Brighton's waist, bringing her forward from the spot she'd nervously rooted. "Mum, *this* is Brighton Evans."

"*Carrie Whitaker.*" Brighton looked from Cain to the woman and back again before anxiously extending a hand to shake hers.

"I've heard so much about you, Brighton," Carrie let out a laugh, squeezing Brighton's hand with a creased brow. "Evans, you say? Not any relation to Margot, is it?"

"My mom, actually," Brighton answered, stomach aflutter.

"Oh, yes! The lake house, right? Thomas is your father, then?"

"Yes, and *yes*," Brighton replied, giving Carrie a tempered smile as she pressed on. "Dad sold the house after Mom passed away."

"Oh, I'm sorry to hear that, darling. How long?" Carrie cupped her hands around Brighton's with a comforting, motherly brush of her thumb.

"Ten years this spring," Brighton said, leaning into Cain's touch on her shoulder.

"Certainly more than a few good memories at that house, though, I hope?" Carrie smiled, releasing Brighton's hands as she lifted a glass of champagne from a passing tray.

"Oh, definitely." Brighton nodded. "That place will always be special to me."

"It's certainly beautiful, I'll give it that. I'm sorry we didn't spend more summers in the States. That one we were able to, though . . . it was special. Wasn't it, Cain?"

Carrie looked up at Cain as he stepped to her side, patting his cheek as he leaned down to wrap his arms around her tiny, waif-like frame.

"Can't hardly recall, Mum. I'll take your word for it."

Cain tilted his head, giving Brighton a quizzical look, when his mother unexpectedly stood up straighter.

"*Petit-fours.*"

"What?" Cain shook his head with a laugh.

Brighton grinned. "I *adore* petit-fours. I'm not sure if Andi has any on the menu tonight, though."

"No, no." Carrie leaned forward, pointing a finger at Brighton. "*You're* the petit-four girl. I knew I recognized the red hair from somewhere. Cain, you remember . . ."

"Not likely," Cain grumbled from behind her, brows

pinched together and sunny demeanor gone. "That was a long time ago."

Carrie turned her attention back to Brighton. "The summer of ninety-seven. You wanted them so badly, your father had said no, and you couldn't reach them on your own—so Cain, here helped you. Between the two of you, the whole tablecloth came down, and *all* the desserts along with it. Cain had icing behind his ears for *weeks*."

"Mm, no. No recollection at all, Mum. Sorry." Cain shrugged, cheeks tinged pink as he met Brighton's gaze with a clench of his jaw.

Brighton's mind buzzed as she tried to recall the day. It had been the Fourth of July. The weather was unseasonably cool, but the sun finally broke through the clouds and sent a sheet of glimmering diamonds across the surface of the lake. There were fireworks, barbecue, and . . . *petit-fours.*

"I . . . I think I might remember it, only a little. Why didn't I realize we'd actually met before?" Brighton asked him, pressing her fingertips to her temple.

"It was a long time ago, darling," Carrie answered, squeezing Brighton's shoulder. "Sometimes, childhood memories are funny like that, but I assure you . . . I'd remember those freckles anywhere. It was after that summer Cain confessed he'd been seeing things in color for quite some time."

"I hardly remember a specific timeframe, Mother," Cain groused with a deep set frown, clearing his throat as he looked across the room like he was searching for an escape route.

"It's foggy for me. I was so little," Brighton murmured with a bite of her lip. "I remember the day, I remember the cake—why can't I remember anything else before then?"

"Maybe there wasn't much for you to know until then, dear," Carrie winked, looking to Cain for a split second before her son shrugged away her touch, mumbled his apologies, and strode away.

Brighton gave Carrie an apologetic look, murmuring a quiet *I'm sorry* before following after him with a swish of brilliant golden-honey taffeta. She glimpsed the heels of Cain's shoes as he rounded the corner of the handsome, wood-carved stair-case, following close behind with the *thud* of her favorite red stilettos on the carpet.

Brighton charged down the corridor, sliding around the corner to their door—*The Fairytale Suite*—and sent the heavy door swinging on its hinges.

Cain paced inside, his eyes flashing when he met her gaze.

Brighton slammed the door, brows creased as she stood against it and crossed her arm.

"What the hell is your problem? You take me to meet your mother, and then, what . . . *storm off*? I don't understand." Brighton motioned her hands in the direction of the still-ongoing party. "Did she say something? Did *I* say something?"

"It was the subject matter, Brighton." Cain slowed the frantic pace of his steps, planting his hands on his hips as he chewed his lip. "What she insinuated is the problem."

"What do you mean?" Brighton went over the conversation in her mind, and a flurry of emotions flooded her. They'd met before—long before the afternoon in an airport bar. Was he—could *they*? It couldn't possibly be that easy. Could it?

Brighton's mind reeled. Pulse racing, fingers trembling. Every part of her wanted to delve into the mere suggestion and find out if Cain's mother was right, but the tiniest sliver of doubt bled into the back of her mind, in case it *wasn't* that simple.

Cain'd gotten upset as soon as Carrie inferred perhaps, *they* —but no. Brighton would have known, wouldn't she? *Wouldn't he*? How could it be that a plate of petit-fours would trigger a wash of brilliant color . . . and *neither* of them be the wiser?

"It's really something I'd rather not talk about right now,

Brighton. What part of that didn't you understand? It's why I *walked away.* Can you . . . *for once in your life* . . . leave well enough alone?" Cain threw his arms out as his voice grew louder than she'd ever heard.

Brighton sucked in a trembling breath as silvery beads of tears pooled on her lashes.

"A couple months ago, you said you loved me. Isn't this the best case scenario? What part of us maybe being soulmates is so fucking upsetting, Cain? Is . . . is the thought that maybe . . . maybe this thing—" she motioned between them with a trembling hand, "That this thing between us is something *more* than we originally thought . . . is the thought I might be your soulmate—*your Glimpse*—is *that* the part that upsets you?"

"That's not it." Cain kept his burning gaze trained on Brighton with an anxious twitch of his jaw. "That's not it at all."

"Then show me your hip. I want to see it." Brighton took another shaky breath as her chin quaked, brushing her fingers against the fabric that hid her soul mark away. "Let's get it over with and find out for sure. Nothing has to change."

"*No.*" Cain shook his head, stepping away.

"Take your own advice. Don't be a fucking coward. *Be brave.* What are you so afraid of? *Just show me,*" Brighton pressed, moving forward, only to feel the sharp jolt of hurt when Cain took a step back with a shake of his head.

Brighton's lips parted with an *oh* as the silence stretched between them and Cain turned his eyes to the floor, unable and *unwilling* to meet her gaze.

All at once, Brighton's worst fears came true. Every wrong choice, every mistake. They all had one thing in common. From Jesse to Gideon—now Cain.

The problem was her.

This wasn't how it was supposed to go. This wasn't how Brighton imagined it every time the thought of she and Cain being *more* crossed her mind. Their Fairytale Suite had turned into something more like a nightmare, one Brighton wished she could wake up from or rewind. She wished she could go back and know sooner; she wished she could remember the day at the lake. She wished he would have reacted in *any* other way. She wished for *so* many things—but more than anything, Brighton was tired of *wishing*.

"I get it," Brighton whispered, brushing her palms over the golden fabric of her skirt, turning towards the bed. "I don't want to fight. I'm really tired. Tomorrow is going to be a long day, so I'm going to bed. You do what you want."

"Brighton . . ." Cain's voice called out to her, like a rumble of thunder echoing over the horizon with the whispered promise of a summer storm.

Brighton followed the sound and saw Cain—her best friend and maybe her greatest love—standing like a broken man, barely holding it together.

With a hand on his hip, dark brows creased together, and fingers pressed to his lips like they were forming the words he so desperately wanted to say, Brighton found herself waiting for *something*—anything—to make it feel better.

Cain sucked in a ragged breath and lifted his tortured gaze to meet Brighton's. "That's not it at all. I'm . . . I'm afraid that if I show you . . . you *won't* be her. The mere thought of you not being my *Glimpse* . . . it fucking terrifies me."

Cain's confession hung like a weight between them. Brighton knew she could fight, she could tell him all the ways he was wrong to feel afraid. It's what Cain would have done for her, what he *had* done for her a million times. Brighton knew she should want to gather Cain in her arms and comfort him. She knew she ought to tell him it'd be alright—even if his fear was true. But, all Brighton could bring herself to feel was her exhaustion.

Brighton held his gaze, murmuring a quiet, "Goodnight, Cain."

Still in her cocktail dress, Brighton toed off her shoes next to the bed and climbed into the sprawling four-poster. She settled her head against the softness of the pillow, hugging her arms around it to hold it to her chest as her tears finally fell— silently but free.

Chapter 17

*S*leep claimed Brighton, but only for a little while. It wasn't long before she rolled over and silently counted the stars embroidered in the satin draped over the bed. She hadn't changed her dress, too busy floundering through the unbearable silence to bother.

The stubborn ass stood there for longer than she could count before flipping off the light and disappearing to; Brighton didn't know where . . . mostly because her own hard-headedness kept her from rolling over to look.

Brighton twisted the hem of her skirt between her fingers as her mind ran through each second of their fight, wondering how it got there in the first place—and why finding out mattered so much to her when she'd told herself for *years* having a soulmate was overrated.

What if a soulmate meant something different? Was it only a single moment or a culmination of them that gave life color?

Brighton loved Cain. She had for the longest time, even if she couldn't put her finger on the instant when they went from friendship to something *more*. The more she thought about it, though, Brighton wasn't sure if it had ever been that simple.

They were happy together. More than happy. Brighton and

Cain were *complete*. Did she really need *The Glimpse* to tell her how she felt in her heart?

Brighton sat up in the darkness of the suite and looked at the different shapes in the room, letting her eyes adjust in the muted shards of silvery moonlight streaming through the milky glass. Brighton laughed when her gaze landed on the porcelain tub in the corner—and the hulking man asleep inside it.

Cain's feet were propped along the edge, knees bent to fit all six feet, four inches of him inside. Brighton gasped a dulcet sob of bewildered guilt and amusement from the peek her perch offered.

Sliding from the deep green bedspread, Brighton wiggled her toes in the plush carpet as she tiptoed to Cain's side.

The quiet of Cain's breathing found Brighton's ears, summoning an aching bloom in her heart that flourished every time they were together. A whispered sigh fell from her lips as she drew close enough to see him—positively boy-like—with one arm draped over his torso and the other over his head. Tie removed and two buttons undone, Cain still wore his suit jacket from the party, offering a glimpse of downy chest hair that made Brighton's fingers ache with the need to touch it.

Perching on the porcelain's cool edge, Brighton chewed the inside of her lip and reached out with a trembling hand to trace the long line of Cain's nose. She followed the rounded curve of his mouth with the tip of her finger, idly wondering what his lips would feel like against her own.

Cain's brows creased under her touch, drawing him from the quiet shores of sleep to drowsily open his blue eyes.

"Hi." Brighton balanced her elbow on the edge of the tub, bringing herself closer.

"Hey, you," Cain mumbled in return, pulling himself to sit with a groan, pawing his fingers through the mess of dark curls hanging in his eyes. "What's up?"

"I—I wanted to talk . . . if that's okay." Brighton let her hand linger on Cain's chest, centering herself in the steady beating of his heart.

"Sure . . . *of course* . . . I'm—I want to say I'm . . ."

"Hold on—I want to go first." Eager to ride the sudden wave of brazen confidence, Brighton firmly held Cain's gaze, and when he nodded, pressed on. "I—I'm not sure where to start, but . . . I need you to know that . . . I love you."

"I love you, too, Colour Girl," Cain answered without a second thought, his handsome face impossibly earnest as Brighton continued.

"No, *I love you,* Cain. Like . . . the *big* kind of love. The—deal with your brooding, make you bad soup when you're sick, give you the bigger half of the cookie, let you win at Monopoly— kind of love. The *forever* kind of love. The soulmate, *Glimpse* kind of love."

Cain's eyes—a stormy sea of blue in the moonlight—filled with a flurry of emotion, cataloging Brighton's every move as she gathered her skirt and slipped a bare foot into the tub.

The heat of Cain's gaze drew Brighton in as she followed the first foot with the other. Kneeling between his knees, Brighton walked her hands up Cain's chest to bring her body flush with his.

Brighton beamed, face hovering so delightfully close to Cain's—so close, she could count the lines etched into his face and the ghost of the day's facial hair beginning to grow around his delectable mouth.

With a tilt of her chin and a gentle press of her hand, Brighton cupped the curve of Cain's jaw, blinking in the silvery strands of light as she skirted the pad of her thumb over his bottom lip.

They parted under her touch, accompanied by the gentle tug of a tentative smile. Cain was wordless, allowing Brighton to say everything she wanted as his eyes darted across her face.

"*My point is,* it doesn't matter. Not to me. I know it scares you—it scares me too—but does it really matter? Nothing changes between us, and the existence of a birthmark in a matching place doesn't affect the love I hold in my heart." Brighton drew closer, watching how Cain's eyes flickered to her mouth. "And *now*, Cain Whitaker, I'm going to kiss you . . . just to prove it. Okay?"

Cain remained motionless, save for a small nod as Brighton lifted her chin and slowly brought her lips to his. Though tempted to leave them open to witness the moment, Brighton's eyes fell closed, and their lips met for a breathless moment, and *oh*—they were everything she imagined and more. Brighton found it nearly impossible to pull away.

Brighton hovered a whisper away, taking Cain in as he tucked his bottom lip in with a swipe of his tongue.

"Was that alright?" Brighton murmured, skimming her thumb against his stubble.

Cain opened his eyes, brows knit together as he slotted his long fingers in her hair, drawing her back in with a rumble— "I think I should like to try again."

"Me too," Brighton echoed, closing her eyes with a shiver and another gentle press of their lips.

Brighton lingered there, breathing him in—a blessed blend of sweet, smokey vetiver and cedar—with a small, satisfactory smile when Cain's hands shifted and coiled around her waist.

Cain pulled Brighton closer, leaning into the kiss like he was memorizing the feeling, locking away the taste of her for the rest of his life.

Brighton rolled her forehead against Cain's, letting out a trembling breath as she pressed her palms against his broad chest. "That was—"

Cain left Brighton little time to catch her breath, twining his long fingers in her hair to bring his mouth crashing against hers all over again. Before, it'd been a tentative examination—new, slow, and butterfly soft. Now—

Cain's hands were made for Brighton, knowing each way to press and move her, molding her into shape like a master sculptor creating a priceless piece of art. She gave into each caress of his fingertips and gentle tug of her hair, falling further with each one.

Cain deepened their kiss with a leisurely flicker of his tongue against the seam of her lips, letting out a low groan when Brighton responded in kind. The air buzzed deliciously as they eagerly explored the new, tantalizing sensations.

It was unlike any kiss she'd ever felt before. Brighton felt it in the way their bodies were so well-attuned, moving seamlessly as their hands wandered, and they lost themselves to the enchantment blanketing them in a wholly unexpected, most welcome way.

With a chorus of quiet moans, Cain cradled Brighton with a broad palm in the small of her back and lifted them from where she'd been nestled between his knees. In a single, fluid motion—without disrupting their kiss—he rolled Brighton to her back. Anchoring a hand on the edge, Cain held her firmly to his chest as he eased her onto warm porcelain.

Cain's hand skirted the curve of Brighton's shoulder, drawing a musical whimper from her lips. Cain devoured the sound, delving further with every press of his fingertips, movement of his mouth, and delicate twining of their tongues.

"Hold on." Palm pressed to his firm chest, Brighton pushed Cain away, catching her breath with a bite of her lip. "F-friends don't kiss like that."

"*Brighton*," Cain growled, leaning down to kiss her soundly all over again, slowly drawing away with a low, heated groan. He slowly opened his eyes, handsome face hopelessly solemn as he leaned in with a tilt of his chin. "I've never been *just* your friend. *Ever.*"

"Never?" Brighton's breath staggered.

"*Never.*" Cain skimmed his thumb across her flushed cheek. "I have loved you every second of every minute of every hour since the instant I laid eyes on you."

Brighton's eyes darted back and forth between his, feathering her fingers through his dark curls to push them from his face. "All this time?"

Brighton didn't understand. If . . . if Cain had loved her from the first fortuitous moment in an airport bar—the thought of him forging forward in friendship with her, regardless of Gideon and all the other obstacles standing in their way, made her want to cry. Brighton wanted to weep over the time they wasted—the time *she* wasted.

Cain steadfastly stood by behind the line they'd drawn in the sand, despite the pain he surely felt.

Brighton's heart lurched when she thought of Cain's anger at her non-denial of Gideon's proposal. With it, every ounce of evidence firmly fell into place.

Despite everything, Cain patiently waited for her— Brighton hadn't deserved *any* of it.

Cain always had a way of knowing exactly what was on Brighton's mind, and there in the moonlight of the *Fairytale Suite* was no different.

"*Hey.*" Cain tilted Brighton's gaze to meet his. "Stop it. I know what you want to say. You want to say I could have walked away. That I didn't have to linger. Here's the thing . . . *I wanted to*, Brighton. There was never a time I wanted to be away from you. I said you wouldn't be alone, didn't I? I promised I wouldn't leave, and I like to think I delivered on that as long as I was able. Not because of any chivalrous nonsense—because *I wanted to*. I loved you. I *love* you. I would have waited through a hundred rubbish boyfriends or a hundred years. None of it matters. It never did. We're here now, aren't we? *That* is what matters."

Brighton blinked up at Cain, heart thumping and skin thrumming as she whispered, "Say it again."

"What?" A smirk tugged at the corner of Cain's perfect mouth. "*I love you?*"

Brighton nodded, eyes wide when Cain leaned down and brushed his lips against the curve of her ear.

"*I love you, Bee.*" Cain shifted, grazing his jaw from one side of her face to the other, pressing his lips against her cheek. "*I love you, Colour Girl.*"

Brighton could lose herself to the feeling of his body pressed against hers and the way he whispered, but she was barely allowed a moment's breath before his lips devoured the whimper he summoned.

Cain pulled away just as they were getting started, pupils blown wide in the moonlight. "I love you, Brighton. I have forever. I *will* for the rest of my life."

"I love you too," Brighton answered, coiling her fingers in the thatch of dark curls, every inch between them too far.

Cain fervidly claimed her with his tongue, twining it with hers in a kiss so deep, Brighton thought she could drown in the way it made her feel.

With every pass of Cain's lips over hers, she thought she might either melt or combust from the sheer ferocity of it all, melting into his touch with an impossible hunger that could only be satiated by one thing—*more Cain.*

Cain anchored himself between her knees, groaning against her lips as he pulled her closer. His lips were warm, and he tasted of champagne as he lifted her back from the base of the tub.

Brighton's head buzzed, but it'd been hours since the party and its libations. Perhaps *he* intoxicated her, drunk on the heady feeling of him pressed between her thighs.

Cain's mouth wandered, breathing a gravelly hum as he left a trail of molten kisses across the golden, freckled flesh of her shoulder. Brighton's body bucked when his scruff grazed against the skin he'd practically set alight from his first touch.

Brighton's palms skimmed up the curve of Cain's broad chest, sighing against his lips when she tucked them beneath his suit jacket. She pushed it down, eager to explore what lay beneath.

In a flurry of limbs, swears, and the slip of fabric against porcelain—they tumbled. Cain—caught up in navy blue wool —braced himself on the edge a little too late and dark curls collided with warm auburn.

"*Fuck*, Bee. I'm so sorry." Cain reached for Brighton, face creased with concern as his hands searched for the source of her hurt.

Brighton rubbed at her forehead with a grimace and a chuff of laughter. "S'okay, I'll live. Here I thought *I* was the hard-headed one in this relationship."

Cain's blue eyes searched her face, tracing his touch over the offending injury. "Are you sure you're alright?"

"Promise." Brighton nodded with a grin. "Though I might not be if Andi sees. If there's a mark tomorrow, I'm blaming you."

"Duly noted." Cain gave Brighton a gorgeously lopsided smirk, lifting his chin to survey the room. "Although . . . I think this might be a sign we ought to stop for now."

"What do you mean?" Brighton sat up, eyes alight as Cain stood and stepped out of the tub.

"What I mean, Colour Girl," Cain rumbled, slipping his suit jacket from his shoulders. "If the bathtub proves hazardous to your health, t'would only be right to take you *to bed*."

Cain swooped down and collected Brighton from the base of the clawfoot tub. Brighton let out a squeal and a titter of girlish laughter but found herself silenced by the look in his eyes the second she was cradled against his chest.

Skimming her tongue over kiss-bruised lips, Brighton's eyes

danced over every inch of Cain's handsome face—memorizing each detail from lines to freckles. Drawn to his lips, Brighton traced her fingertip over the curve of his cupid's bow with a smile.

She'd imagined kissing him before—beneath the spray of a hot shower or tucked deep beneath her rainbow quilt so Cain wouldn't hear. It was the thing dreams were made of. Living it, though, was an experience all its own.

Now she'd tasted him; Brighton wasn't sure if she'd ever be able to get enough of the feeling.

With a tilt of her chin, she brought her mouth to his. Cain answered in kind, letting out a ravenous growl as he blindly carried her across the room.

Trust—it was something they had in spades. Brighton knew Cain would never let her fall. Not in the traditional sense, anyway.

The mattress bent under their shared weight. Cain pressed Brighton to his chest as he balanced on a knee to slowly lower her onto the bedspread.

A smile tugged at the corners of Brighton's mouth when she saw Cain hovering a breath away—dark curls forming a blessed halo around his face.

With him, she'd never been without words, the conversation flowing too naturally for any lulls to fill. But, in the muted moonlight of their *Fairytale Suite* and his eyes so full of emotion so close and so ripe for kissing, there was only one thing Brighton could think to say.

"I love you."

To Brighton, it felt like she'd been asleep at the wheel, driving in the dark without anything to guide her. All at once, she was wide awake. There, filling her everything with a beamingly bright light, was Cain—her living embodiment of sunshine, the light on her dark days, and guiding force in every way.

Together, they'd found forever and would use the rest of it to explore every inch and each facet of color they painted each other's lives with. Beyond regrets of the past, with the promise of the future, and everything in-between.

><

*B*righton woke earlier than she expected but couldn't be disappointed—not with her breathing seamlessly intertwined with the rise and fall of the broad chest she nuzzled.

Steady like a drumbeat, Cain's breathing was as ever-constant and sure as the heartbeat beneath Brighton's cheek. She could lose herself in the heady splendor of it all. Brighton's every inch buzzed with anticipation of Cain's next breath, his next movement—his next anything at all.

Part of Brighton wanted to be embarrassed she'd been brazen enough to climb into a bathtub with her best friend and spend the hours after making out like teenagers. Though, as she gingerly trailed a path down Cain's chest—connecting freckles like constellations in the night sky—Brighton felt only the purest joy. *True happiness* because she'd finally been brave enough to try.

Cain spoke the language of Brighton's soul and was fluent in the prose of her body—knowing which string to pluck to make it sing. Brighton was *whole*, part of something she knew she belonged to—a matching puzzle piece or twin flame born in the heart of the same star.

Brighton marveled at the way Cain's skin sent her synapses tingling as she trailed her touch to his serene face, beautifully boyish in the golden strands of early morning light.

Brighton wondered how different things would be if they'd remembered the moment they met. What if Cain's family came to the lake house more than one summer? What if *those*

Whitakers lived next door? What would change? *Everything* would.

If they *had*, Brighton knew they'd know by then.

Brighton could picture it—their *other* selves. Maybe even their future selves.

Their outline on the lake's edge. She'd nestle between Cain's knees with her head tucked against his chest with his nose in her hair—palms resting against her swelling belly. Brighton shivered. Yes—a family. In a world where she finally had it all, where Brighton was finally brave, they'd have that, too.

Tears blurred the image away, unable to keep herself from wishing they *had*—that she and Cain had more time. Brighton looked at Cain's still-sleeping face, smiling when his fingers instinctually squeezed hers—reassuring like he sensed the ache in her heart.

Brighton brushed a dark curl from his forehead, laughing when Cain stirred and let out a deep, rumbling groan. He circled his arms around her and burrowed deeper into the covers. Brighton splayed her fingers against Cain's heartbeat, smiling when her head swayed with the rhythmic rise and fall of his breathing. Brighton couldn't resist finding his face again, running her fingers over each faint line—holding her breath as she lingered against his lips.

"Cain," Brighton whispered, pulling on his taut lip before pressing a kiss against them—ready and eager to pick up where they left off in the early morning hours.

Cain grumbled incoherently, slinging a muscled arm over his eyes.

Palms against his chest, Brighton shifted—anchoring her knees on either side of his waist. She circled her nose against Cain's before placing another kiss on top of the first. "Cain . . . *I'm hungry.*"

Cain groused again, brows scrunched as he cracked an

eyelid. "It's barely dawn, darling—are you seriously thinking about food?"

"Not really, no," Brighton crooned. She twisted her thumbs in the hem of Cain's stolen sweater—*her favorite*. When they retired in the early morning hours, Brighton pulled it from Cain's suitcase when he wasn't looking. Now, Brighton slipped it over her head and sent it flying across the room.

Brighton had Cain's attention, then—rapt and burning as she walked her hands up his chest and peppered his face with kisses.

Cain relented, twisting his fingers in her hair to capture her mouth in a languid, sleepy kiss. Heat won out against sleep as he curled his arms around Brighton's waist and flipped her to her back.

Dizzy with need and anticipation, Brighton's eyes darted over his face, silhouetted with a halo painted in the early morning light, and hooked her fingers in his hair.

"Did you mean it?" Cain leaned into her touch, voice trembling as his eyes slipped closed.

Brighton's heart fluttered. "Did I mean what? That I love you?"

Cain nodded, seeds of doubt sewn between flecks of silvery-blue. "You feel like a dream, Colour Girl. Like it's all too good to be true."

Uncertainty swarmed Cain, surely planted there by *her*. Brushing her lips against his, Brighton tried to send every ounce of love through the line so Cain, like her, could be brave and let himself believe it. "Cain Whitaker, you are the only thing in my life I've *ever* been this sure about. You . . . you're the foundation of everything *good* in my life. It isn't a dream. If it is, I don't ever want to wake up because *I love you*, I will *always* love you, and there will never come a day when I change my mind about that."

"Promise?" The beginnings of a smile flickered across Cain's handsome face.

"I promise," Brighton echoed with a quiet titter of laughter, rubbing her nose against his. "I'd be happy to show you."

Cain laughed—a deep, lovely sound. He left Brighton little time to enjoy it before crushing his lips to hers.

The kiss had no sudden burst of dazzling fireworks or sparks. Steady and sure, it spoke of everything Brighton ever needed, everything she wanted and wouldn't let herself see. It saturated her every atom in something more than color—*in love.*

Brighton's heart thundered in quiet anticipation of Cain's next move, a sweep of his hand, and press of his lips against hers.

Cain's mouth wandered, answering the call of their shared desire as he trailed molten kisses down the column of Brighton's throat—mapping every freckle. Every touch sent an electrifying shiver through her as Cain moved his bare chest down the length of hers. He kissed his way down her torso to her legs—methodically traversing the flesh there, too.

Cain thumbed the hem of her underwear, twisting lace around his fingers—and froze.

"*Brighton.*" Cain's voice quaked.

Brighton met his wide-eyed gaze and whisper-soft huff of disbelief as he exposed her soul mark. With a trembling hand, Cain outlined the shape burned into her skin, a quavering smile pulling at his mouth as she whispered, "*Tell me.* Tell me it's yours."

Cain pressed a heated kiss against it. "Look for yourself."

No. It couldn't be that simple. Brighton sat up, taking Cain with her as they rolled. Cain's chest heaved, and Brighton's fingers trailed a course down his torso to the waistband of his sweatpants.

Brighton curled her fingers into her palm, bringing it to her chest with a shake of her head. "I'm scared."

Cain leaned on his elbows, eyes soft. "You don't have to be —not anymore."

His touch guided hers, pushing the cotton hem until the light illuminated the mark on his alabaster skin—one identical to hers.

It *was* that simple, and Brighton couldn't keep her tears at bay.

The Glimpse. Her glimpse. After a lifetime of convincing herself she didn't need what everyone else craved—he'd been right under her nose the whole time.

It hadn't been so obvious as being knocked over the head when the grey curtain lifted— soulmate waiting at the center of a symphony of color on the other side.

No, Brighton and Cain had something more akin to a slow discovery, a chance meeting more out of a movie than real life. The obstacles in their way were many—the biggest one was Brighton, herself.

"*Cain.*" Brighton let out a sob, letting Cain sweep her into his arms to pepper her every freckle with kisses, silencing her tears before they could take root.

Cain brushed the hair from Brighton's face, blue eyes gleaming as he pressed his lips to hers. Brighton lost herself in the feeling, wrapped up in the weight of his arms and the promise of forever with her soulmate by her side.

Cain twisted his fingers in her hair, deepening the kiss into something more libidinous than before—until Judy Garland ruined things, again.

Brighton swore and lifted her phone from the table with a resigned sigh—like a reminder her favorite library book was overdue and couldn't be renewed anymore.

Cain pressed a kiss to Brighton's forehead with a chuckle. "Mm, right. *The wedding.* Duty calls, my darling."

"Do we have to?" Brighton grumbled. "I want to *celebrate*."

"As do I." Cain laughed again, pressing another deliriously short kiss to Brighton's lips. "And we will, Colour Girl. I assure you. We have our whole lives ahead of us to make up for lost time."

Chapter 18

The morning went quickly, aided by a mountain of croissants and a never-ending flow of mimosas and girl talk. Still, Brighton found herself distracted by the fleeting thought of Cain—*her soulmate*—passing through her mind every few seconds.

Andi was the first to notice something different.

Red hair twisted up in voluminous curlers and a fresh face, Brighton looked out over the lawn, idly tapping her finger on the side of her champagne glass. An elbow poked Brighton's in the ribs, drawing her gaze to the petite woman beside her.

"*So . . .*" Andi pressed with a playful grin on her freshly made-up lips, looking every bit the blushing bride in her silken robe.

Brighton looked down at her with a shy smile and a casual shrug. "*So*, what? Why are you looking at me like that?"

"So . . . how did last night go?"

"So—none of your business, that's how," Brighton retorted with a titter of laughter.

"It most certainly *is* my business." Andi crossed her arms with a challenging lift of her brow.

The redhead leaned back and chewed her lip with a smirk. "Enlighten me."

"It's my wedding day. The bride gets what she wants. That's me. I'm the bride," Andi pointed a finger at her face with a brilliant smile. "*This* bride wants you to tell her how things went in your *Fairytale Suite.*"

"You *did* do it on purpose!" Brighton's brown eyes narrowed in mock offense. "I knew it!"

"I—Eli is the one who came up with the idea. He's been desperate to get the two of you together for the longest time. And I mean . . . *the longest time.* I have a feeling, though . . . our plan worked, didn't it?" Andi's grin grew wider, nodding slowly as she pressed on. "Getting the two of you alone *did something.*"

"Andi, we *live together.* We are *literally* alone all the time," Brighton argued with a wry smile.

"Yeah, but *alone* alone . . . in a place like this. Tell me it didn't work. Go on, I'll wait." Andi planted her hands on her tiny waist, giving her maid-of-honor an expectant look. When Brighton came up with no words and flushed, Andi's face melted into an even wider, victorious smile. "I *knew it!* Oh shit, wait 'til Eli hears! He might cry out of happiness. It—*fuck*—it could be the happiest day of his life."

Brighton rolled her eyes with another bout of laughter. "It's your wedding day, Andi. It's supposed to be the happiest day of his life."

"Yeah, but . . . I think this might take the cake over us getting married," Andi giggled, practically beaming from the inside out when she flung her arms around Brighton. "I'm not mad about it, either. *Oh, holy shit*, I am so happy for you guys. I can't even begin to describe how much!"

"I don't know what happened . . . how I didn't know," Brighton murmured, tracing her soul mark through her robe. She still couldn't believe its twin was on the other side of the lodge.

"*Know what?*" Andi gasped, wrapping her hands around her maid of honor's wrists. "Know what, Brighton?"

"It's—" Brighton swallowed, her heart hammering away as the words sat on the tip of her tongue. Saying it out loud made it *real,* and saying it to Andi meant *everything.* Acknowledging it filled Brighton with a strange apprehensive joy—like she was on the edge of forever.

Saying it with her own words would set Brighton off to the next chapter of her life. She was ready, she was *sure,* and . . . it meant Andi was really, truly, going to be her family, just as they'd always thought themselves to be.

"It's *him,* Andi. It's always been him. Right under my nose this whole time . . . *my whole life.* Me. You. All of it led right here."

For the first time in her life, Andi fell speechless. Her eyes glittered with a fresh wave of tears, shaking her head in disbelief. "Cain is your soulmate? I—*how?*"

"Fate, I guess." The flush in Brighton's face felt brand new when her thoughts rushed back to that morning.

"Do you . . . do you want to trade places or something?" Andi playfully tugged off her engagement ring and held it out. "Wanna get married?"

"Oh my god, Andi, no," Brighton, pushing the glittering piece of jewelry back. "Today's your day, remember?"

"Damn right it is," Andi teased. "You guys have so much time to make up for. You better start quick and, like, have lots of sex."

"Oh, um . . . we . . ." Brighton scrubbed the back of her neck with a bite of her lip. They hadn't quite made it that far, and she was *not* disappointed about it.

Andi held up her hands in a plea. "Spare me the details, though. I beg you. He's my *cousin.* Makes you think about all those summers at the lake, though, doesn't it? Do you wish we could go back so you could know then?"

"I don't think so." Brighton shook her head, imagining the days she and Andi spent together. "You were my soulmate, then, Andi. I wouldn't change it for the world. Cain and I have now . . . we'll make the very best of what we're given now we know."

"That's fair." Andi carried a tear from the corner of her eye with the tip of her freshly manicured finger, wrapping Brighton up in another bruising hug. "At least I don't have to hear about Captain Douche Canoe, anymore. I can't tell you how happy I am that's *over*. Speaking of which . . ."

"Speaking of Gideon?" Brighton laughed, caught up in a surge of happiness.

Andi released Brighton from their embrace and wandered to a bag in the corner of the room. She rifled through the contents before pulling a small, gift-wrapped parcel from inside.

Andi tossed it to Brighton with a wink. "Since I did you the favor of playing nice with him for so long, it's time for you to pay the fuck up. Those are for Eli. Would you mind terribly finding a groomsman who'd pass them along? A . . . *Best Man*, perhaps?"

"Andi . . . I—I'm not exactly dressed." Brighton looked down at her bright pink satin robe and brushed her fingers against the nest of mammoth curlers in her hair.

"You look fine to me, Bee." Andi waved her away.

Brighton gave the bride a scathing look which melted into a grin with a shake of her head. She tucked the edges of her robe closer and stepped out the door toward the back of the sweeping lodge.

The early afternoon air kissed Brighton's skin, sending a frisson of goosebumps down her arms when she stepped from the shadow of the house and into the sunshine. Lifting her face to the light, Brighton let it warm her from the inside out before approaching footsteps drew her attention back to the present.

Like he had known she was coming, Cain strode across the loose gravel of a path cutting through the garden, dressed in a sharply tailored tuxedo. Brighton loved the way his silk bow tie hung beneath his collar, still untied with the top two buttons of a crisp white shirt undone and the rest straining against the width of his chest.

Lost in thought somewhere far, far away, a smile hovered on Cain's handsome face as he lifted a hand to skim a thumb along his bottom lip. Brighton chewed the inside of hers, wishing she could be a glove upon Cain's hand so she might be able to feel it, too.

When Cain's eyes met Brighton's, he let out a playful gasp, covering his mouth to stifle his laughter when he took in her appearance.

Brighton hovered her hands over her curlers, trying in vain to hide as Cain erased the distance between them. "Oh, go to hell. Don't make fun of me."

"I like them. They're adorable," Cain teased, tucking a stray strand of her hair behind her ear. The laughter died as they held each other's gaze, and the memory of the night before hung between them.

Brighton looked down at her feet, bouncing on the toes of her ballet flats as her entire body buzzed. Her eyes darted back to Cain's face with a climbing heat in her cheeks.

Cain cleared his throat, hands in his pockets with a chuckle that lasted a little too long. "So . . . how're things over there? Is it like, Bridezilla or whatever they're called?"

Brighton laughed, relieved he chose humor to try and break the delectable tension. "Andi is a very gracious bride who's probably had a little too much champagne and may or may not have let the power go to her head—she forced me to come out here like *this*. But it meant I got to see you . . . so that's a bonus."

"Oh, I'm a bonus?" Cain gave her a lopsided smile on his

freshly, clean-shaven face, holding Brighton's gaze another electric moment.

Brighton blinked up at Cain for a beat before thrusting the gift box into his hands, freeing her own to play with the seam of her sleeve. Brighton couldn't understand why she suddenly felt so bashful, meeting Cain in the daylight for the first time since they went from just friends to *soulmates,* almost lovers.

Not only had Brighton and Cain crossed the line they'd drawn in the sand—they *demolished* it. As shy as she was, Brighton couldn't keep herself from thinking of all the other lines she wanted to cross with Cain.

No, *write* with him.

Bold. Cursive—ones that twisted and turned. Brighton wanted to color so far outside the lines with Cain and explore all the blank pages of their story.

Brighton chewed on the inside of her lip, again. She idly wondered if it would eventually begin to ache, but didn't care. A faint pink blush warmed her cheeks. "These . . . these are for Eli. From Andi. Not from me . . . I mean . . . *duh* . . . but . . . you know . . ."

"Okay," Cain answered with a nod, rolling the box over in his hands before pocketing them inside his velvet suit jacket.

She was still her. He was still him. They were them. Nothing had to be different. And yet, *everything was.*

Brighton's gaze locked on Cain's as he stepped forward, close enough she could feel the warmth of him through the thin fabric of her robe. She peered up at Cain through her eyelashes and the glow of early afternoon sunshine, brown eyes darting over every fleck of silver in his. A quiet whimper fell from Brighton's lips when Cain cupped the curve of her jaw and anchored his other hand on the swell of her hip.

Cain's touch lingered there, skimming the pad of his thumb over her soul mark before leaning down to press a warm kiss to her lips.

Brighton hummed quietly as the breeze swept around them, bringing them closer together as Cain coiled his arm around her waist and pulled her body flush with his. It was quicker than Brighton would have liked, the opposite of the way they'd languorously explored one another the night before —both in the tub and out of it—but she lost herself in it all the same.

Breathless and reeling, Brighton traced her fingertips over the delightful burn upon her lips when Cain pulled away, offering one of his collectible smiles before striding away. "I'll see you later, Colour Girl . . ."

Chapter
19

A couple hours—and at least another mimosa—later, Brighton was primped, polished, and dressed to the nines in a jaw-dropping gown.

With the whole *Fairytale Suite* "faux-pa" and resulting night spent twisted up with Cain, Brighton was convinced Andi picked the sexy style on purpose. Black satin oozed over Brighton's every curve, leaving very little to the imagination; with thin straps sank into a deep v from Brighton's shoulders past the swell of her breasts, a low-slung open back, and a thigh slit up to *here*. Black was never Bee's first choice, but like the starlight silver gown she tried on at the bridal boutique with Andi, it seemed to accentuate all of *her*. Maybe it wasn't a bad thing.

Brighton joyfully performed her duty as Maid of Honor, transforming Andi into a bride as a photographer snapped picture after picture of each tiny detail.

With everything accounted for and memorialized to film, the bridal party ventured toward the ceremony.

Hand-in-hand, Brighton and Andi were quiet as the rest of the group walked ahead, with only the distant din of wedding guests in a wooded grove steps away to keep them company.

Brighton thought back to the seconds before Andi's first date with Eli, how her friend had been wrapped up in nervous anticipation until she spoke to him. Andi as a bride was a wholly different woman. Her blue eyes were bright, shoulders square, and chin lifted high with every self-assured step.

One by one, each bridesmaid bid Andi a joyful farewell, turning up a wooded path leading to the heart of the forest where the guests—and Eli—waited.

Brighton tucked her nose into a fragrant bouquet—a stunning collection of tender blush-colored roses, burgundy calla lilies, and wine-soaked dahlias—smiling away the threat of tears as the music swelled to signify the start of the ceremony.

Brighton turned to Andi, swimming in nerves as she wrapped her childhood friend—her sister—in a firm hug. Pulling away, she straightened the edge of Andi's veil and fluffed the hem of her lace-covered gown before giving her a nod.

"We good? Want a slushy? It's not too late for us to make a run for it," Brighton teased, knowing Andi was *precisely* where she wanted to be.

"I'm good. *I'm great.* Unless you want to swap places and marry my cousin and make us *officially* family. Wanna do a double? I'm sure the Justice of the Peace won't mind. I know I said today was my day, but I'm feeling generous."

Brighton saw Andi's sincerity. While the idea of promising to spend forever with Cain was a tempting one, she wanted Andi to have something special of her own.

"I'm honored you asked, but no," Brighton laughed, giving the bride one last hug before turning a corner to head down the wooded aisle.

Andi regaled Brighton with every detail of the stately lodge when she and Eli discovered it the summer before. None of it did any justice to the forest's true beauty.

A thousand twinkling lights hung between the Beech, Ash,

and Tamarack—lending an ethereal glow in the already magical hues of the summer evening. Together, with the delicate luminescence of electric light kissing the tips of the leaves gold between the green, the wooded grove felt more akin to Lothlórien than rural Wisconsin.

The music grew louder as Brighton turned a final, winding corner. Rose petals the same pinky-hue as the ones in her bouquet wound up the aisle in elegant swirls. Rows upon rows of wooden benches—filled to the brim with smiling, expectant faces—lined either side. At the head stood two interlocking wooden hexagons dripping with flowers on either corner.

There, waiting at the top—was Cain.

In the span of a single breath, everything else faded away.

Cain was as handsome as ever, maybe even more so because of the love in his eyes—the love he felt for Brighton.

Music played around them, fluttering through the trees with whispers of wedding guests as Brighton went by. She couldn't pay them any mind, not with Cain's gaze holding her like a tether.

For a breathless moment, Brighton could *see* it—their future.

The black satin of Brighton's gown became pale silver; Cain's tux a midnight blue. A melody shifted through the trees as daylight faded to nothing, leaving only the two of them with a blanket of stars above. The heavens provided more than enough light to see by, canvasing the sky like sugar spilt over dark, polished stone. Cain provided the rest.

In him, Brighton had everything she needed—everything she *wanted*. She found shelter in his arms; his kiss fed her very soul. In a single, collectible smile, Cain breathed life into her. With him, Brighton's search would end. Instead of traveling a path toward him, she and Cain would walk the rest of the way together.

Like the shining, golden strands of light streaming through

the trees, Cain called to her like a beacon. All the while, with each and every step, the only thing Brighton could think was, *yes*.

With a few blinks, Brighton tore herself away from her soulmate's gaze and found the face of his best friend, Eli. His impossibly charming wide smile was more reserved, practically buzzing with feverish anticipation. As Brighton passed him by, she gave Eli's shoulder a squeeze, as if to say, *she's coming*.

The music shifted, laying a hushed quiet as guests rose to their feet. With it, Brighton turned her gaze toward the bride at the end.

Alexandria Whitaker was someone Brighton always considered to be beautiful. From the inside out, Andi was *radiant*. As a bride, wrapped in the delicate evening light, Andi was *otherworldly*. With her dark curls twisted into an elegant knot at the base of her neck, it exposed her lace-framed collarbones to the summer air. There, peeking out from beneath delicate embroidery, was a pair of intertwined hexagons—the soul mark whose twin Eli bore.

Brighton's eyes searched past the bride and groom, landing on Cain with a sigh. Even if she could, Brighton wouldn't ever want to look away—mouthing '*I love you*' while the ceremony continued. All the while, all Brighton could see, all she could feel—was Cain. In his eyes, she found forever—she felt *complete*.

Then, with rings exchanged, tears shed, at least *two* curse words from Andi, a *long* kiss, and the jump of a broom—Andi and Eli were *married*.

By pairs, they filed up the aisle. Brighton couldn't help the bubbly grin from her freckled face when Cain held an arm out when they met in the middle.

"Fancy meeting you here," Cain rumbled, pressing a kiss to the crown of her head.

Brighton laughed. "You look like this guy I know. Do you come here often?"

"Mm." Cain nodded, smiling down at her. "It's got an unbeatable view."

Brighton's cheeks ached as the heat crept up beneath her freckles. "How was the traffic on the way from Krypton? I hope you got good mileage on your spaceship."

"Oh, *the best*," Cain answered, skirting his hand down her back to settle around her waist.

Brighton barely settled into the quiet when Cain looped his fingers through hers and tugged her into the tree line. She tried her best to keep up, leaning down to loop her black satin skirt around her free hand as Cain led her over fallen logs and green ferns.

"*Cain*," Brighton pleaded. "My shoes aren't . . . *ugh* . . . they aren't made for hiking!"

"Fine by me." Cain barked out a laugh, sweeping Brighton off her feet.

Peals of girlish laughter fell from her lips, but they quickly faded away when Brighton met Cain's electric gaze.

When the din of wedding guests had all but faded away, Cain set her to her feet. With a lift of her chin and a bite of her lip, Brighton met his eyes. The tension grew thick like the taut string on a violin—requiring merely the right touch to make it sing or snap it completely.

No sooner had Brighton got lost in the dreamy paradise of his eyes, Cain stepped forward and devoured her with a searing kiss. Brighton's lashes slipped closed in a second, moaning as his hands held her face firmly between them.

Cain pressed into her, sending them backward against a sturdy tree trunk. Brighton's whole body buzzed with an electrifying thrill as the weight of him demanded more with every curl of his tongue and touch of his hands.

Brighton tried to keep up, to carefully catalog each

delectable second, but as Cain's hands wandered down her torso and anchored on the swell of her hips, the only word on her mind was *more*.

A white-hot coil curled deep in Brighton's belly, spurring on every moan, feverish kiss, and desperate claw of her fingertips against black velvet.

Cain leaned into her, the heat of his hands slipping through a slit in her gown. His touch skimmed along the flesh of her thigh; growling against her lips as he eased Brighton's feet up from the forest floor.

Brighton's toes hooked behind his leg, pulling him closer and winding her hand in his dark curls. Her head lolled against the tree as his mouth wandered down and across her collar bones. "*Cain . . . w-we should.*"

Cain's lips trailed across every freckle, his baritone buzzing against her shoulder when he answered, "We should what, darling?"

Cain coaxed another whimper from Brighton's lips when his touch drew further north, skimming a single finger between the heat of her flesh and thin lace of her panties.

"*Nnghh . . . fuck . . .*" Brighton found his lips all over again, letting out a breezy moan when her body answered with a buck of her hips. "Mm, never mind. I'll tell you later."

A familiar voice echoed through the tree line, halting their feverish actions. Cain froze, holding her thigh firmly, panting into her shoulder when it called out again.

Lifting Cain's face, Brighton turned his gaze to meet hers.

Cheeks flushed, Cain winced, chewing on his emotions with a whisper, "*Brighton . . .*"

"No. Don't do that. Don't do that thing where you brood and let yourself get swallowed up by Catholic guilt." Brighton held his jaw with trembling hands, pressing another kiss to his lips as he eased her feet down to the ground. "We got a little caught up. *It's okay.*"

Cain shook his head with a grimace, fingers lingering on her waist. "I didn't mean . . . I forgot . . ."

"You forgot, what?" Brighton pressed, amber eyes darting back and forth between his. "That we *love each other*? That we're *allowed* to do this now? Trust me. I haven't forgotten, and I don't plan to."

"After . . . after the ceremony . . . *how it felt* . . . all I could think about was kissing you." Cain tilted his head, a wry smile playing on his lips. "I didn't mean to get carried away."

"*Carried away*?" Brighton brushed her palms along the achingly soft velvet on his broad shoulders, straightening his jacket with a chuckle. "If that's carried away, I can't wait until later."

The tips of Cain's ears kissed pink. "Yeah?"

Brighton nodded, a flush of her own staining her cheeks. "I've been thinking of doing something like that for a *long* time."

Cain choked out a laugh. "*Yeah?*"

"It's true." Brighton laughed along with him, walking her fingers up his chest. "*But . . .*"

"But?"

Brighton cast a wary look toward the lodge. "I think the newlyweds are expecting their Best Man and Maid of Honor to be in the group photos."

Cain followed her gaze over his shoulder with a frown. "You think so?"

"Just a hunch." Brighton twisted her fingers in his hair. "Think you could, uh, get *carried away* again and give me a lift back to the path?"

Cain's gaze darkened with a smirk, wasting no time in hoisting her into his arms like she was nothing, jumping effortlessly through the bracken and bramble.

All the while, Brighton was breathless with laughter, so far beyond happy enough, she was dizzy with it.

⋈

*H*ours later, the delicate chime of silver against crystal rang out across the hall. Cain captured Brighton's hand in his, pressing a lingering kiss to her palm with a low whisper—

"Go grab some champagne, Colour Girl. That's my cue."

Brighton sat at one of the tables with a perfect view, balancing her chin on the heel of her hand. She traced slow circles along the rim of her crystal glass with a chuckle as Cain floundered with a microphone and a slip of paper from his breast pocket.

With an awkward tap of his finger over the top and a groan-summoning squeal of feedback from the speakers around them, Cain lifted it to his mouth and began to speak.

"Hello . . . uh, *hi* . . ." Cain balked when the microphone squeaked again, swearing loudly enough to cause a chorus of laughter from the crowd. He dropped it to the table with a *thud,* stuffing a hand in his pocket with a lift of his chin, projecting his booming voice like he'd done it his entire life. "My name is Cain Whitaker, I'm the Best Man, and . . . I . . . and I am Andi's cousin, Eli's long-suffering best friend from University, and the reason for the nuptials you witnessed earlier this evening, so . . . *you're welcome,* you two.

"I promise no one need be nervous about any stories I might tell . . . unless you married Eli today. *I'm kidding!* But really, Andi . . . I couldn't be more grateful to you for being precisely the kind of woman my best mate needed and exactly the kind he doesn't deserve in the slightest."

Cain's eyes shifted to meet Brighton's for a split second, pausing to take a deep breath before turning back to the bride and groom with a smile.

"Eli can hold his drink to a dangerous degree . . . and I mean that. The fact that I can't remember how we arrived in a pub in

Southampton by the end of the night on his 18th birthday is proof. Let me say, if someone says it's a good idea to try one of everything at each pub ... *it's not* ... but I digress ...

"I'm here to talk about you two. About love. How lucky are we to be here and witness something so wonderful?"

Cain sucked in a shaky breath, pausing to slowly chew his words. He drew his hand from his pocket to press his fingers to his mouth, lifting his eyes to find Brighton's in the crowd.

"With *The Glimpse*, fate leaves us little choice when it comes to the process of picking the person we spend the rest of our lives with, but ... not everyone is as lucky as these two right here.

"I know we all live our lives waiting for the grey curtain to be lifted, but I believe it is so much more than that. Because ... when you believe you're happy enough with the wrong person, it doesn't matter if there's *The Glimpse* or not—you might as well not have it at all.

"Sometimes, you can go your whole life and never realize the color you've been blessed with. Until one morning, you wake up and realize *years* have gone by, and all you've got is an endless list of missed opportunities.

"I've got a list of my own." Cain paused, eyes falling to the tablecloth. His broad shoulders heaved with a sigh and a twitch in his jaw. Cain summoned a smile, looking back over the rustic hall as he continued—

"I know what it means to love someone who's brought the most glorious technicolor to my life in countless ways. She is the light in my darkness and will be long after we've gone on to live whatever life is next for us. I am, without a shred of doubt, the luckiest man alive to have been given the gift of her friendship. I pray I never took it for granted."

Brighton shivered when Cain's blue eyes met hers.

"I know now without any shred of doubt, no matter who we are, what we're doing, or who you're with ... I will always love you. In this life, and the next, and every single one after that . . . and, as a wise, *English* man once wrote in a tale which means a whole lot to me, '*I would rather share one lifetime with you than face all the ages of this world alone.*'"

The audience was silent, save for the quiet titter of a few voices, the clink of silver on china, and the thunderous beating of Brighton's heart.

Cain held her gaze for another beat. She swore she saw him nod before grasping his long fingers around the bell of a champagne flute, clearing his throat loudly before turning back to Eli and Andi.

"Ladies and gentleman, please be upstanding. To the Bride and Groom. May they never take their love for granted. Live every second like it's your last, and love each other like this is the only life you'll be given." Cain raised his glass to their friends before turning his blue eyes back to her, lifting the crystal flute higher with a bow of his head.

As she lifted her glass to her lips—taking a drink of the effervescent liquid, letting it tickle her tongue before she swallowed it and welcomed the warmth that blossomed in her chest—Brighton thought of him. Of *them.*

Cain embraced Eli and swept Andi into a bone-crushing hug with a broad smile on his face—letting out a booming laugh when the bride mouthed, 'you're fired.' Brighton couldn't help but welcome the slow, blooming ache in her heart when she looked at Cain.

Her soulmate.

With a flutter of her heart, Brighton wondered how long they'd loved each other. She supposed falling was the easy part. Effortless as breathing, falling as quickly as the rain from the sky, so subtly they didn't even notice it happening.

In a world where everything hinged on the ability to see color—a gift she'd already been given—Brighton had been stubbornly unaware Cain had been there beside her all along.

She dressed from head to toe in the most eye-catching combinations she could with the smallest sliver of hope—when her soulmate *did* come along—they wouldn't miss her.

Cain *had* come along, and he hadn't missed her. Not for a single moment.

Their connection was as clear as could be. It caught her attention way back on the night when she happened to sit on a neighboring stool at a random airport bar. It happened all over again when the pair had been dragged along on Eli and Andi's first date ... where Cain hopped over the seats to be beside her, and he whisked her away to the most colorful place in the entire city of Chicago.

That night, Brighton wondered if Cain would illuminate her world and make it more colorful than it had already been. With her fresh perspective and the wild surge of love in her heart, Brighton knew it was true. He really had.

Chapter 20

A couple hours later, after a few too many glasses of champagne and a dizzying amount of dancing, Brighton and Cain plodded up the stairs of the lodge.

Brighton slipped the keys from Cain's fingers when he pulled them from his pocket. He stepped up behind her and *oh so slowly* peppered the curve of her shoulder with delicate kisses as she twisted the key.

They wobbled into the suite, both unwilling and unable to separate one from the other after a night of wayward glances and dancing in ways so much more than what mere *friends* would do.

The door snapped shut with a *thud* and an assist from the heel of Cain's polished, black brogues—leaving them finally, delightfully alone.

Brighton trembled when Cain's thumb ran up the length of her spine to the base of her neck, sending an electrifying shiver down to her toes.

He curled his long fingers over the curve of her shoulder and swept her auburn hair over the opposite side. With the tip of his nose, Cain traced the curve of her bare shoulder and around her ear, stopping to kiss and gingerly nibble the tender flesh at the base.

Brighton turned and brushed her lips against Cain's, moving to trace her mouth along the edge of his jaw. She delighted in his strangled groan as she tenderly sucked on the lobe of his ear, whispering, "I have something to show you," before slowly pulling away to look into his eyes.

A slow, coquettish smile curled the edges of Brighton's mouth, unzipping her gown at an achingly slow pace. Her eyes locked onto Cain's scorching gaze with a shiver, stepping further away with every gained inch of her exposed back.

Cain watched Brighton's every move, standing perfectly still like a hunter stalking his prey, with only the tiniest flickers of ravenous hunger crossing his face while his eyes roved over her body. The flash in his blue eyes only spurred her to go slower and elongate the moment of their coming together, which was, quite literally, meant to be.

Brighton's body felt like a live wire, set to blow with the slightest of touches. Even her own fingertips sent a tantalizing shiver down her arms when she slipped the black fabric from her shoulders. His gaze burned into her as the gossamer material slid past her hips to pool at her feet—revealing her soul mark in the hushed moonlight.

Cain took a step forward, mouth hanging open and fingers twitching to touch her, but Brighton held up a hand with a quiet tut of her tongue.

"*Patience*," Brighton cooed, stepping free of the onyx puddle. "We've waited this long, haven't we? It proves that . . ."

"It proves what?" Cain rumbled, lowering his head, eyes darkening with desire and an achingly unhurried tug on his bow tie.

"*Good things come to those who wait*," Brighton hooked her thumbs into the band of her strapless bra, eager to move on but unable to keep herself from prolonging things a little longer.

Brighton wanted to remember the look in Cain's eyes forever, memorize the electrifying buzz in the air, and carefully catalog every delectable second—locking them away in the same place where she kept his smiles.

With a flick of her thumb, the band came free. Brighton let out a quiet whimper when she dipped her palms over the peak of her breasts, caught up in how Cain looked at her as she stripped away each layer.

Brighton felt the charge in the air and Cain's need to erase the distance between them. Still, she couldn't help but linger in the intoxicating power from holding him on a tether; reeling him in slowly—unwilling to rush the start of their forever.

Oddly aware of the frantic beating of her heart, Brighton held her breath when Cain took another step forward, making her fully cognizant of his impatience—and his *need* to be with her. To touch her. To *taste* her.

"I should have done this a lot sooner," Brighton hooked her thumbs in the waistband of her panties, twining the fabric around them to force the hem to dip and offer the tiniest glimpse of what was waiting for him below.

"I want to help with those." Cain pulled on the end of his sleeve, practically ripping away the luxurious, black velvet of his tuxedo before tossing it over his broad shoulder.

"What, these?" Brighton circled and gingerly pushed the silkiness of her green thong over the curve of her ass, guiding them down to her feet. She chanced a peek of her would-be lover from behind her calves, giggling quietly at the wonton look upon Cain's face.

With a salacious bend of her body, Brighton stood, turning slowly before perching her bare ass on the curve of the clawfoot tub they'd been in the night before. She gasped, shivering when the warmth of her skin met cold porcelain. "If I had known getting you naked would have been as easy as kissing you *in here* last night, I would have interrupted a post-workout shower a *long* time ago and moved up our timeline a little."

"*Woman*, I swear to God," Cain growled, tugging his pleated tuxedo shirt open before undoing the cufflinks at his wrists. "You're testing my patience. Do you have *any* idea how badly I want to touch you right now? How badly I've *always* wanted to touch you?"

"H-how long?" Brighton shivered as Cain stalked towards her one, sure-footed step at a time.

"From the first moment I saw you at that bar . . . and the moment after when I asked you to dinner when we landed in Chicago . . . and the moment after at the movie theater."

"All that time?"

"Always, Brighton. *You* . . . you and all your colors. It's something I've always loved about you. From then . . . *to now*." Cain's eyes were glued to hers as his silver cufflinks fell from his fingertips with a quiet *clink* on the floor. His gaze roved to the long line of her throat, wandering back up as he rolled his sleeves to his elbows. "You're a masterpiece, Brighton. A *symphony* of color. Do you have any idea how much of it you bring to my life?"

"I—I thought my soulmate might notice," Brighton whispered as Cain painstakingly erased the space between them, lifting her eyes when he stopped a breath away.

"*I noticed*, Brighton. I've always noticed. Christ . . . I wish . . . I wish so many things, but all I can think about is kissing you."

"Then why don't you?"

Cain barely allowed a second for Brighton's words to echo around the room before he took her face in his hands and pulled a moan from her lips with a demanding kiss.

Brighton melted against him, lips parting as she twined her fingers in his curls, devouring the groan from his mouth.

Cain's hands roved across the toned muscle of her back, pulling her flush against his chest while his mouth wandered, mapping out the golden expanse of freckled flesh in the bend of her shoulder.

Brighton's every inch buzzed as Cain skimmed his over her body—pliable and wholly willing to bend to his every whim.

Cain was thorough and meticulous in his exploration, leaving no portion of her uncharted. The heat of his hands danced over her torso, causing the slow, unfurling heat in Brighton's core to grow more with each second.

With an encouraging press of his palm against her stomach, she leaned against Cain's chest. His long fingers were splayed out so wide and his touch so enticing, Brighton felt like she was wrapped up in a blanket made of Cain.

Brighton's breath stuttered when Cain pressed his touch against her soul mark with a hungry growl in her ear. "This is mine, as mine is yours. *Forever.*"

Cain's mouth and tongue moved over the tender flesh of her throat. She let out a quiet titter when his fingers delved further down her belly, dipping them to tentatively circle the tiny bundle of nerves at the height of her sex.

"Fuck, you're so wet for me already. *So ready,*" Cain uttered, holding her firmly in his arms as her body began to quake and squirm from his dexterous touch. "I've dreamed about this for so long."

"I've—I've thought about it too," Brighton whimpered, words slurring into an airy whine. Her cheeks blazed at the thought of confessing what she'd done to the thought of Cain in the darkness of her bedroom. When she imagined Cain sharing even a sliver of the same thought, of doing the same, Brighton's knees threatened to give out.

"Did you touch yourself like this?" Cain pressed his nose to her ear, dipping a single finger into her wet cunt. "Did you think of me?"

When Brighton answered with another moan, Cain only

delved further and pressed harder, drawing another series of delectable sounds from her lips.

"You know what I want, Brighton. Say it," Cain demanded with a slow knead of her pebbled nipple between the fingers of his free hand. "*Say it.*"

"*Yes,*" Brighton choked out a breathless sob, rolling her head against Cain's shoulder when her pleasure crested from his tireless ministrations. Her mind reeled, body buzzing with every libidinous thought coming to life in the palm of his hand.

With the utterance of a single word, Cain's motions instantly stilled. Brighton cried out, bucking her hips against his palm.

"*Oh no,* my love. You can finish when you've answered me properly," Cain tutted with a slow shake of his head. "*Yes, what*?"

"Yes—yes, I thought of you," Brighton gasped, her voice tinged with a delicious strain of desperation.

"*Good girl.*" Cain rewarded her with a slow suck and nibble of the tender flesh between her shoulder and throat. He resumed his handiwork, slowly delving a second finger to join the first, pulling moan after moan from Brighton's lips, timed perfectly with each movement. "I'm going to keep getting you to make those pretty little noises for me. I could hear you, you know . . . through those thin walls . . . I could hear you come apart. Every time, I'd hope it'd be for me."

Cain's words, alone, nearly made her fall apart at the seams, but he held her together.

Brighton *knew* being with Cain would be good. She knew kissing him would be something dreams were made of, but the reality was so much more. Every touch, every breath, every word sent her spinning.

"It is . . . I always . . . *god* . . ." Brighton lost all sense of her words as Cain carried her to the edge all over again—pushing her to her orgasm with a short series of thrusts.

Brighton's body bucked and trembled when Cain thumbed her center, keening as she tumbled back to Earth. With her fingers coiled in his hair, Brighton pulled Cain to her lips, hungrily delving her tongue to tangle with his.

Cain answered with a growl, hooking his hands beneath the curve of her ass to hoist her into the air.

Never straying from their heated kiss, Brighton frantically yanked open the buckle of Cain's belt. She scrambled for the zipper as Cain blindly stumbled towards the bed. With a triumphant giggle from Brighton, she shoved his trousers down.

Cain, unwavering in the way he kissed her—a furious clash of tongues and teeth—stepped free of them, toeing off his shoes in the process, only to stumble from his stubborn persistence to keep kissing.

They landed in a heap of laughter, bouncing gently on the mattress. Brighton looked up at him, surrounded by an ethereal halo of moonlight.

With Cain staring down at her with swirls of bright blue in his eyes and dark curls hanging around his beautiful face, Brighton felt wholly overwhelmed by her love for him.

With the tips of her fingers and the gentlest touch, Brighton brushed a curl from Cain's forehead, offering a hint of a smile. She let her touch linger, tilting her chin to meet him for a slow kiss.

Before him, Brighton had only ever loved on the surface. With Cain, things were *different*—a holy combination of what was right for her, unique in all the world.

With him, she could remove her armor. In him, she was whole—more than a person, more than herself. Beside him, hand-in-hand as they looked toward their future, she wasn't afraid anymore. Not only was she brave—Brighton was *fearless*, ready to take on anything, so long as Cain was by her side.

The joy in Brighton's heart overwhelmed and terrified her

all at once. She'd gotten used to living without her soulmate—to being *happy enough*. She never thought of finding him as anything truly tangible or real. Any form of eternity was like a far-off dream. Now, with Cain in her arms, Brighton never wanted to let go.

Cain met her with a smile of his own, resting his brow against hers, aligning their noses as he let out a trembling breath. "*I love you*. I will forever. And in our next life, I know I'll love you just as much, if not more."

"You think we'll get another? I've heard stories . . ." Brighton sighed, unable to remember a time before then. Surely, with a man as memorable as Cain Whitaker, she would?

"Brighton Evans," Cain said sternly with a hint of a smile. "I would know your face whether it was my second life or my hundredth. No matter where I am. Where we are. What we are doing. *I'd know*."

"Liar." Brighton tugged at her bottom lip, smile melting away when Cain's face grew somber.

"I've never lied to you."

"*Okay*," Brighton whispered with a nod, letting her lashes flutter closed when Cain leaned down to claim another kiss.

It was easy to get caught up in where they'd been before—a flurry of limbs and lips. Cain trailed molten kisses and delicate nips over every freckle dusting her body.

They bent around each other, twisting and rolling like elegant acrobats, twining themselves together as they found the brand-new rhythm of *them*.

When Brighton grew impatient of Cain's careful and seductive study of her body—how she moved beneath his hands and under his mouth—she let him gather her in his arms and settle in for what they both so desperately craved.

Cain was so close, so warm, and *so right*, arms twined around Brighton, the pair painted by shards of moonlight as she settled her knees on either side of his hips. He held her firmly, posing a silent question in his eyes. Brighton answered wholeheartedly with a searing kiss as she slowly sank down and took him deep inside.

Brighton gasped, fingertips trembling as she held onto his broad shoulders, and her body adjusted to the feeling of being *so full*. Cain, her lover—*her soulmate*—took her face in the palm of his hand, drawing her in for a deep kiss. Skirting the tip of his tongue over the seam of Brighton's mouth, Cain choked out a groan when she tentatively rolled her hips.

Cain tucked his forehead in the curve of her shoulder, holding firmly to her waist when Brighton moved again . . . and again, increasing the pace until they settled into something between a slow exploration and a passionate frenzy.

Brighton wasn't alone in wanting to remember every moment, to linger in the feeling, even though she was sure they'd recreate it a hundred thousand times, maybe more.

Cain met her in every delectable motion, moving their bodies together in the way they were always meant to—rousing a sense of pleasure Brighton didn't know existed.

With every slow rock of his body with hers, Cain moved his mouth over every part of Brighton he could reach, pulling quiet mewls from her lips with each one.

Coiling his fingers in her auburn hair, Cain gave it a gentle tug, summoning a breathless whimper from her lips as he gave himself access to the long column of her throat. He peppered it with kisses, basking in her taste as they chased the culmination of their pleasure—*together*.

Unable to resist touching him for long, Brighton carded the loosely coiled ribbons of thick, dark curls through her fingers. She pulled Cain's gaze to meet hers as another orgasm curled in her belly, growing tighter and tighter with each salacious movement until—with her amber eyes wrapped up in cool, lagoon blue—she fell apart at the seams with a mournful keen. Cain swiftly followed with a low groan, shoulders trembling as he buried his face in the crook of her neck.

When they finally stilled, glistening and momentarily spent, they fell back onto the bedspread. Brighton beamed, twining a lock of Cain's hair around her finger, only to have her hand captured by his to press a lingering kiss in her palm.

Cain's eyes met hers, and Brighton felt it again—the same swell of love and warm ache in her heart. Somehow, wrapped up in Cain's love, Brighton knew her life would never be the same again.

Chapter 21

ain's smile—perhaps the most collectible one of them all—played on his lips as he brushed his fingertips up and down her arm. Brighton's skin buzzed from the heights of their shared passion and all the twists and turns in the journey it took to get there.

Her lips parted, followed swiftly by the flash of her tongue over the taste of his kiss, already hungry for more. Perhaps, now she'd finally experienced the brush of Cain's lips against hers, Brighton's appetite would only increase—never fully satiated as long as she lived.

Cain let out a low hum as he enveloped Brighton in his arms, cradling her lithe frame against his broad chest as he stole another kiss for himself.

There was so much Brighton wanted to say, so much she wanted to do, but as her eyes searched through the dreamy folds of steel and cornflower, she found herself without words. There wasn't anything left to say. No focus. Only the constant, delirious ache of waiting fueled by years of their unfulfilled desire.

"What are you thinking?" Cain spoke first, the warmth of his voice reverberating beneath her fingertips.

Brighton shifted closer, slotting her leg between his with a quiet groan when he met her with *just* the right amount of pressure between her thighs.

"I'm thinking . . ." Brighton hummed, looking down in the silver shards of moonlight as she traced a delicate zigzag through his chest hair. ". . . I'm thinking that I'm feeling really, ridiculously *hungry*."

"Oh, are you?" Cain grinned, coiling his thick arms around her waist to flip her to her back.

Brighton let out a titter of laughter that fell away when, with the lift of his hand beneath her chin, Cain kissed her. It was the sort of kiss Brighton wished could last forever. Between the way he held her, to the way his tongue leisurely danced with hers—it was something she would never tire of.

Brighton breathed a dulcet sigh when Cain pulled away with a wry smile, rising to his feet. "As a matter of fact, I'm feeling rather famished, myself."

Sitting up with the blanket clutched to her chest and auburn hair falling in elegant waves around her freckled shoulders, Brighton watched Cain move through the strands of light streaming in through the window, focused on how they lit every contour and curve of his body.

Every inch of him made her ache with the need to touch, to trace her fingers over every band of hard, corded muscle, explore every minuscule imperfection, and map every inch with languid kisses so she might make Cain feel the way he did for her.

"Where are you going?" Brighton's voice softened, tinged with an odd sense of hurt when Cain slipped on the sleek, black underwear she'd happily watched him remove only an hour ago.

"Nowhere without you, darling. Get a move on. The kitchen awaits."

Brighton gave him a look with a puzzled tilt of her head. "The kitchen? Cain, I—"

Her breath caught in her throat when Cain's eyes narrowed and he sauntered back to her side, silently holding out a hand with the tiniest quirk of a smile. "*Come here.*"

Brighton slipped her hand into his palm, keeping her eyes trained on him as he pulled her to her feet. She shivered when Cain's bare chest brushed against her cheek as he tugged the sheet from the bed they'd happily *unmade* together.

A dark curl fell over his forehead when he *oh* so slowly wrapped the fabric around her. Cain topped it off with a leisurely kiss on her lips and a smile. "See? Now you're dressed."

Fingers twined together, Cain and Brighton tip-toed downstairs. Due to the late hour and quiet air, she could hear the faint rush of wind through the forest outside.

The moon, much like it had done upstairs, illuminated every shining, stainless steel surface of the industrial kitchen—providing enough light to find their way.

With his hand around her waist and another kiss, Cain lifted Brighton onto the counter, hanging onto the taste of her lips until the very last breath when he pulled away to open the door of the refrigerator.

"Find anything good in there?" Brighton bit her lip, swaying her feet as she looked over the way the bright light illuminated every contour of Cain's broad shoulders and the curl of his hair.

"Undoubtedly," he hummed, turning 'round with a victorious smile and a mammoth plate of wedding cake.

"Score!" Brighton's smile grew with the flutter in her belly as Cain settled between her knees.

Cain's eyes flickered to hers as he peeled away the noisy sheen of plastic wrap. Brighton held her breath in anticipation —even for cake—because, in the most impossibly sexy way, he dipped his finger into the frosting and drew it to her mouth. He watched her take him into her mouth with a hum as she sucked every bit of the decadent dessert from his fingertip.

Cain answered with a groan and a slow lick of his lips, sweeping another dab of frosting from the plate for himself. "Beautiful," he murmured.

"It's delicious, although, I am not sure if I'd call it beautiful," Brighton answered.

"I wasn't talking about cake, darling."

"*Oh . . .* well . . ." She blushed, looking down to collect a dollop of frosting, holding it out to Cain with a coquettish smile.

He held her gaze, opening his mouth to take it, but not fast enough when Brighton playfully sucked it clean with a *pop* of her lips.

"*Brat,*" Cain growled, grabbing her by the wrist to tug her against his chest to devour her mouth in a heated kiss. Her lover stole a moan from her lips—and the sweet taste of the frosting, too—moving his mouth against hers until she was dizzy with need all over again.

Wrapping her arms around his shoulders, Brighton brought him closer. She split her knees, mewling quietly when Cain settled the hard length of his body between them.

She practically sang when they finally came up for air, balancing her forehead against his as she caught her breath. "Cake is nice and all, but it's not exactly what I meant when I said I was *hungry,* Cain. *This,* however . . . might satiate a girl's appetite."

"Will it, now?" Cain rumbled, rolling his head down the curve of her face, tracing the line of her jaw with dreamy kisses, bending further and further down until he came to where he'd so carefully tied the sheet around her.

"*Yes.*" Brighton shivered, lifting her hands to twine her fingers in his dark curls as he continued his exploration.

Cain, nestled firmly between her knees, tucked his fingertips into the knot of fabric over her heart. He looked at her with a gleam in his eye and a facetious smile as it came apart with a flick of his finger.

The honeyed whine that fell from Brighton's lips was involuntary, merely an automatic gesture when he reached for the cake and trailed a slow path of frosting between her breasts.

"*Oh, dear me* . . . someone ought to clean that up." Cain shook his head with a tut of his tongue. He trailed lazy, molten kisses up her throat until he found her lips all over again.

Cain hugged the curve of her jaw, skimming the tip of his tongue along the seam of her mouth as he eased her down—laying her out on the counter like a meal he was about to devour.

And oh, *did he.*

Cain savored her like the most refined delicacy, taking his time as he explored every flavor, memorizing each nuanced taste until Brighton found herself simultaneously well-fed and ravenously hungry—eager to devour something for herself.

For once in her life, Brighton demanded her pleasure—her happiness—knowing full well Cain provided everything she needed. He carried her so far beyond her ideal of being *happy enough*, Brighton didn't even know what to call what laid beyond, finding herself without words altogether.

Words, though, were something Brighton and Cain didn't need.

Cain lifted her from the countertop, wrapping Brighton up in the softness of his touch—and the sheet he'd taken from their suite—carrying her back up the sprawling staircase where they fell back into the brand-new rhythm of *them*, communicating in ways to fill the gaps where words so hopelessly failed.

It wasn't until the first delicate beams of dawn stretched its arms into the vast blanket of inky blue they finally began to tire.

Brighton watched early morning light draw the promise of

a new day—a new life—up like a curtain. She brushed her fingertips over her arm, smiling with a sleepy, content yawn when she felt the heat of Cain's chest upon the bare skin of her back.

"Come back to bed, darling. I miss you too much already." He wrapped his arms around her waist, nuzzling the tender lobe of her ear before following her gaze with a thoughtful hum.

"Spooky, yet so beautiful," Brighton whispered, taking in every inch of the blood-red sunrise.

"*Red sky in the morning, sailor take warning,*" Cain rumbled in her ear, pressing a lingering kiss behind it before slipping away.

"What?" Brighton asked, twisting to watch him stride —*gloriously naked*—back to bed as a cold shiver went down her arms.

"Storm's coming, Bee. That's all. It'll be gone by the time we wake up," Cain waved her over as he slid into the wonderfully unkempt bed. "Now, *get the fuck over here.*"

Brighton shook her head, giving the brilliantly bright crimson sky one last wary look before snapping the curtains closed.

Just as Cain said, a storm rolled in, rattling the windows of the wooded lodge well into the afternoon as they slept soundly in each other's arms. Every once in a while, Brighton would wake and spy Cain's beautiful face, and try—and fail—to resist brushing her touch across his lips.

It felt like heaven. With one so twined around the other, it was hard to tell where Cain ended, and she began.

Brighton wished she could slow down time and linger for another day or two, hiding in their suite away from prying eyes. Eventually, though, their hours-long marathon—and subsequent day's sleep—had to come to an end, as Chicago called, and there was no time left to waste.

"Come on, love. It's going to be dark soon, and we've got a

lot of ground to cover," Cain growled in Brighton's ear as he walked past her on the porch with her suitcase in-hand.

Like earlier, as dawn broke, the sky spoke to her. The days' storms had passed, but Brighton felt the charge in the air—like they were all on the cusp of something *more*. Distant rumbles whispered something was coming, fluttering the auburn waves around her face as tiny pinpricks came from the hairs on her arms standing on end.

"We could have left earlier if you would have kept your hands to yourself," Brighton teased, following Cain to the back of the sleek, black Range Rover. She coiled her arms around his waist, nuzzling the gossamer, navy blue fabric of his sweater—her favorite she planned to claim permanently—with the tip of her nose.

"I have no regrets," Cain laughed, gathering Brighton up for another searing kiss in a growing list of *many* memorable ones. "Except for maybe not kissing you sooner. Like . . . three years ago sooner—over twenty years ago *sooner*."

"Don't worry." Brighton wound her fingers in his hair as he hoisted her from her feet. "We've got plenty of time . . . and now I get to kiss you whenever I want. I think our chances are good for making up for lost time."

"Too right," Cain answered with a squeeze around her waist before setting her toes back down. "Now, let's get a move on, so I can get you home and take you to bed . . . *our bed*."

"*Our bed*," Brighton echoed as she followed Cain to the passenger side, cheeks flushed as he held the door open for her. She slid into the leather seat and asked, "What are we going to do with the extra room?"

"I'm sure we'll figure something out. Maybe we'll get a dog or a tiny other *something* to put in there in the future." Cain kissed her once more with a grin, pulling at the strap beside her shoulder. "In the meantime—"

"Seatbelt, *I know*." Brighton rolled her eyes. "Like I could forget."

"Good." Cain gave her a nod and one more quick peck before closing the door and walking around to the other side.

Brighton gave the lodge one last look as Cain turned the key in the ignition, setting them on their way as the light of day faded—and the rain of a freshly brewed storm fell.

Cain's hand felt so warm and *so right*, wrapped around Brighton's as they drove down the dark country road back to the city. Music played quietly through the stereo. He hummed as he skimmed the pad of his thumb over her knuckles, keeping a vigilant eye on the road along the way.

Nestled into the camel-colored leather, Brighton watched as they rolled over each mile of the smooth, black river of asphalt.

The darkness had an almost meditative quality to it. With the occasional white speed limit sign, the steady patter of rain on the windshield—punctuated by the occasional smear of a wiper—and a blue-green flicker when the headlights illuminated the face of a passing deer hidden in trees.

"I have some vacation saved up . . . we should do something . . . go somewhere—just us." Brighton's heart fluttered when the muted light from the dash lit the contours of Cain's handsome face and the creases around his mouth when he smiled.

"Go somewhere, hm? What shall we do?" Cain mused with a squeeze of Brighton's hand.

"I dunno . . . New York, maybe? Vermont? I don't care, as long as I'm with you."

Cain shifted his gaze to meet hers before turning back to the road, pulling his hand free to reach into his pocket.

"I have an idea of what we could do," he murmured, turning her palm skyward to place a small object inside. "What we *should* do."

Brighton turned it over in her hand, squinting in the darkness as she ran her thumb over the circle. Pinching it between her fingers, she held it up to the light and let out a quiet gasp when a brilliant stone caught what little it could and sent brilliant glimmers across every inch of the car's interior.

"*Cain...*"

"Marry me." Cain turned his gaze away from the road to hold her eyes with an excited and expectant gleam.

"But . . . we only just . . ." Brighton stuttered, playfully slipping it on the third finger of her left hand to hold it aloft. *Of course*, it fit perfectly. "Where did you get this? Have you been carrying around an engagement ring?"

"So what if I have?" Cain pawed his fingers through his hair. "I met a jewelry designer a couple months ago in New York. I started talking about you, and it was like kismet. I . . . I had this *feeling*, Bee."

"*Oh.*" Brighton traced the edge of the emerald cut diamond at the center of the art deco beauty. Her stomach twisted at the thought of their talk after things with Gideon ended. About Rebecca, and her subsequent refusal of Cain. She was wrong, *so* wrong. "We can't get married at the drop of a hat. Isn't there some sort of dating requirement?"

"A dating requirement? *Brighton*—we've lived together for years. We know each other better than anyone. You're my soulmate, and *I love you*. I don't want to spend another second without you . . . don't you think we've wasted enough time?"

Brighton opened her mouth to speak, awash with a sudden blanket of goosebumps crawling up her arms.

She wanted to argue. She wanted to tell him it was too soon, but as Cain had said during his speech—when it came to picking the person you want to spend the rest of your life with, the weight of the decision was something of the greatest importance—and there was no one more important to her than Cain Whitaker. What else was there to say but yes? After all, the simplest choice was often the right one.

Cain met Brighton's gaze with a bright gleam in his eye, gently chewing on his lip as he twined his fingers with hers.

Time slowed. Brighton blinked in the darkness, lips parting with a brilliant smile and her answer—resolute and unwavering—until a sudden flash of light lit Cain's beautiful face and his attention darted back to the winding curves of the dark, country road.

Cain's mouth fell open, and brows creased as he jerked the wheel to avoid the oncoming car.

Chapter 22

The world bent around her in slow motion.

Brighton's body floated from her seat, straining against her seatbelt as the Range Rover skid along its nose. Her arms sailed above her head, surrounded by a glittering wave of broken glass that pierced her cheeks.

She searched for something to hold onto, blindly reaching for Cain as their car careened end over end. A cacophony of shattering glass and screeching metal against asphalt, they moved as easily as a stone skipping over the smooth surface of a lake.

Brighton felt every brutal movement as it happened, unfolding over a series of never-ending seconds. The taste of blood coated her mouth—coppery and metallic. She gritted her teeth and waited for it all to stop, wishing she could just fall asleep and rid herself of the sound of mangled steel and wet pavement.

All at once—in flashes of light and a painful blow against the side of a crumpled door—everything came to a sudden halt. They were left only with eerie silence as pieces of Brighton's rainbow-hued clothing fluttered down around them. They floated gently on the wind, like leaves in Autumn, with only the gentle *pitter-patter* of rain against mutilated steel to cut through the hushed quiet.

Brighton groaned, squeezing her eyes shut as she freed herself from the seatbelt. Her entire body screamed as she shifted, hands trembling as she blinked past blood-soaked lashes to get her bearings.

Brighton's heart raced, fighting against every movement as she looked across every broken surface. They'd blessedly landed back on their wheels, but the roof had collapsed from the force of each twist across the narrow country road. Blinking in the darkness, her vision adjusted, and everything came into sharp, devastating focus.

Cain sat slumped in his seat, deathly still, with a collection of tiny cuts marring his face.

Brighton pushed through her pain to gently press two fingers against the base of his throat. Her breath came in sharp, agonizing bursts as she frantically waited for a sign he was still there, letting out a choked sob when she felt the faint pulsing of a heartbeat.

"*Cain,*" she sobbed, hovering her hands over his body, brushing them against the delicate knit of his navy sweater —*her favorite*—now ripped from the fury of flying glass. She prayed the pulse she felt wasn't her own. Her palms trembled with the desire to shake Cain from his deadly sleep—desperate to hear him speak, but too afraid to touch him. She needed something, *anything*, to tell her he was alright.

Hands pressed to his chest, Brighton's head fell, silently praying to anyone who'd listen. Tears slipped down her cheeks, stinging in the tiny cuts on her face. A low moan pulled her from her reverent pleas, summoning a strangled sob when she looked up and saw the parting of dark lashes over cornflower-blue.

"*Ouch . . .*"

"*Oh,* thank you, God . . . *Cain* . . ." Brighton cried, clapping her hands over her mouth with a tremble of her chin and a relieved huff of laughter threatening to break free. "Shit, I was so scared. Are you—how do you feel?" She hovered over him, desperate to cover him in kisses and whisk them back to the night before.

Cain's brows puckered when he shifted in his seat, lifting his head from the headrest to survey what was left of his car.

"*Fuck,*" he growled, pressing his fingers to his temple. "This is not how I thought today was going to go. I'm—I'm fine, Bee. Just bruised, I think. I'll be okay. What—what about you?"

"I'm—I'm good. Shook up, but fine."

"I'm so sorry, Brighton. I didn't mean—" Cain floundered, his gaze shifting around the car. He lurched forward to search the nooks and crannies in the broken remains of the vehicle, knocking bits of broken glass out of the way as he frantically dug. "The ring . . . W—where? My phone . . . Brighton, we gotta call someone. We need to warn Andi and Eli. I gotta tell them that I—we need to call for help."

"Cain, *stop.*" Brighton stilled him, cupping the curve of his face to halt his frenetic behavior. "Calm down. Andi and Eli are fine. They're on their way to Croatia . . . their honeymoon, remember? They're okay. We're *okay.* The car sent a call out as soon as it happened. Help is coming, don't worry. Though, it's probably best if you stay still."

Cain's focus shifted to her with a slow nod. Pulling Brighton's left hand from his cheek, he rolled it to look upon the diamond that'd miraculously made it through the accident unscathed.

Cain lifted his eyes to hers with a hopeful huff. "Is this a yes?"

Brighton leaned over the center console to get closer, grasping Cain's hands to press a hurried kiss against the rough skin of his knuckles.

"Yes. *Forever.*" Brighton nodded with a tearful smile,

grateful her broken body allowed her to close some of the distance between them.

Cain's blue eyes shone as they darted back and forth between hers, exhaling softly as the corners of his mouth quirked up into the tiniest smile.

Brighton held Cain's gaze, brushing the strands of dark hair hanging around his ears. She looked upon him like he was something precious—something to be savored. Her eyes shifted to his mouth, carrying the whispered promise of his name as she pressed her lips to his.

After a lingering moment, Brighton reluctantly pulled away, relishing the feeling of Cain's hands against her back as her fingertips lingered on the side of his face.

Cain let out a quiet rush of air with a broad smile, blinking slowly in the muted light.

It was almost romantic, with the quiet of their breathing and the gentle patter of rain on the roof—just the two of them —still basking in the revelation they'd found each other after a lifetime apart. Their smiles only grew when, on a distant rush of wind through the midnight rain shower, the sound of sirens echoed through the night.

Cain's smile faltered, blinking slower and slower until his faded blue eyes slipped closed and head slumped against the leather seat.

Brighton's breath caught with a ragged sob, scrambling to bring Cain back to consciousness with desperate whispers, pleading with him to return.

"Cain . . . *Cain* . . . wake up. Help is coming. They're so close. You hold on . . . *please stay with me*. You have to stay awake." Brighton's voice cracked with each despondent word, growing more inconsolable when she pulled her hands from his face.

Brighton looked down in horror at her palms, scarlet and sticky from the blood that seeped from Cain's ears. She let out an anguished cry, suddenly awash with an exquisite rush of pain and unfathomable fear of loss.

Every fear Brighton ever harbored came hurtling back, writhing around her like noxious ropes, mooring her deeper into the pits of her own darkness with every twisted thought. Her stomach churned, wrapped up in the bitter taste of an indifferent world that took away more than it gave.

Brighton felt like a teenager again, witnessing her mountain of a father crumble as an ambulance carted away her mother. Her shredded heart from Jesse's betrayal. Even Gideon—the one who put her back together and should have kept her safe— duped her in the end.

After all of it, after every ounce of fear that held her back— once Brighton decided to be brave—the universe took it away *again.*

Cain wasn't gone. He couldn't be gone. *She could still see.*

Brighton frantically felt for Cain's pulse like she'd done before, but with the way her own heart screamed in her ears, she was less sure the pulsating beneath her fingers was his and not her own.

Brighton lifted her eyes, twisting her body to peer through the shattered remains of the windshield, and felt a bright surge of hope when the sight of red and blue flashes crested the peak of a hill a mile away.

The lights closed in, filling the broken interior with bright beams of color until—in the blink of an eye—Brighton's world shifted to grey.

Chapter 23

A cry tumbled from Brighton's lips, broken and despondent, more than mere tears—the kind of desolate sob coming from a woman deprived of all hope. She tore at his body while paramedics swarmed the car, pulling her away from his side—where she belonged. They murmured to her, pleading to let them help, but she couldn't hear beyond the blinding, searing pain in her soul.

Brighton fought tooth and nail to get back to Cain, desperate not to lose sight of him, convincing herself there was still color in her world—*that he was still in her world*. Still, the first responders managed to wrap her neck in a stiff brace and pull her from the wreckage onto a backboard.

Her gasping wails rang out into the deadly quiet of the night air. Tears stung her flesh as they mixed with the gentle rain upon her skin when they loaded her into an ambulance.

Hovering over her, a kind-hearted paramedic offered a tempered smile as he pulled a flashlight from his breast pocket. With a click, he peered in both eyes as her body gently swayed with the drive. Moving in a flurry, he took her vitals and pieced together a gash in her arm with a few butterfly bandages and a firmly wrapped piece of gauze.

His dark eyes hovered close. "It's okay. Take a breath—*calm down*—or I'll have to sedate you, and I really don't want to do that."

Brighton slowed her frantic attempts to be free from the gurney, worried he'd act on the kindest threat she'd ever heard. When she listened, his eyes crinkled around the edges, and he turned on the flow of the oxygen tank.

"I'm Riyan. We're gonna get you taken care of, okay?"

Brighton, hurting in more ways than one, looked to the proffered mask in his hand, blinking slowly as he lowered it to her face. He gently tucked the strap behind her head, letting his hand linger on her hair, offering an encouraging nod as she sucked in a trembling breath.

Brighton's grief settled, giving way to numbness.

The emotional paralysis was a funny thing, something Brighton only ever experienced when her mother died. It protected her, wrapping around her like a suit of armor. Brighton *needed* it, now. She couldn't allow herself to consider the thought of Cain being gone. So, she welcomed the daze that went so well with *The Grey*.

Still, it didn't stop Brighton from wishing *The Glimpse* would return, wash her in a blinding array of colors, cleanse her of what had happened, and restore her life to the way it had been in the morning. But no, the numb protected her. It shielded her from the truth.

Rushed through a pair of sliding doors, Brighton met another flurry of faces and a chattering of medical talk—*lacerations to the face, neck, and arms. Possible contusion to the frontal lobe. Blunt force trauma to the chest.*

Moved from room to room, she was transferred from the backboard and cut from her clothes. Brighton resigned herself, too exhausted to fight any longer—not with grey being the only thing she could see.

Rectangular lights went by in a flurry overhead. All of it was a blur, softened by morphine they'd dosed her with once she arrived. She wished she was still in the car, wasting away so she might be able to go wherever Cain had gone.

⋈

*H*ours went by. Eventually, Brighton found herself in the quiet of her own room. With the help of medication to dull her senses and wash away her pain—the physical kind, anyway—she finally drifted to sleep.

"*Try and be brave.*"

Brighton found him there, in the most vivid color she remembered him to be.

Dream Cain didn't speak, but she felt his love reverberating through every movement of his hands against her skin and press of his lips against hers.

The rush of passengers along an airport corridor. A cold, orange drink in her hand and a collectible smile to her left.

"*I get this feeling like I've seen you before.*"

Cain's smile infected Brighton's every atom, spurred on by the effortless conversation that carried on to another airport. There, when he reached out to shake her hand, Brighton took it and accepted his invitation to dinner.

She blinked, and the memory shifted. Brighton felt the blooming ache in her heart as she leaned against a green door, chewing the inside of her lip as she let herself get caught up in the temptation of new love—accepting Cain's with open arms now she'd found him.

"*It feels good not to be alone.*"

"*You never have to be now that I'm here . . . I'm so glad I met you, Colour Girl, and I don't plan on leaving you any time soon.*"

"*Promise?*"

Dream Cain tucked a strand of auburn hair behind

Brighton's ear, beaming with his wordless answer, sealing it with a tender kiss upon her lips. She wanted to linger, but—

Brighton blinked in her dreams again and found herself in the golden-hued light of a summer day, filled to the brim with effervescent laughter as the crack of a bat sent a ball careening to the furthest reaches of Wrigley Field.

Cain was there too, arms wrapped around Brighton's waist with her feet far, far away from the concrete. Hands pressed to his chest; she decided to give in to temptation and celebrate quietly with a kiss that blossomed like a summer rose in sunshine.

Rose-colored memories came one after the other—flashes of the life they'd built without ever knowing what they really were to each other. Though, what was there to know that Brighton didn't already feel? The love in her heart for Cain was incomparable, incomprehensible, and irreplaceable.

The dream Brighton held in her heart her entire life—the reason she swathed herself in color—was *gone*, extinguished as easily as a candle put out by wet fingers on a flame.

Things shifted, and Brighton found herself in their apartment, sitting on the kitchen counter with Cain by her side. She sipped from a piping hot cup of tea as he did the same with a smile—something they'd done a thousand times before. It was so real, and the smell of her tea so fragrant, Brighton could have sworn it could have been real—until the picture changed again.

Only, her mind didn't show a past that never happened or things she wished she'd done. Brighton wasn't allowed to stay amongst what-ifs and second chances. Instead, it gave her a glimpse of what could have been—a family painted in glorious, heartbreaking technicolor.

Brighton sat in long, green grasses, gently skimming the palm of her hand over the swell of her stomach while watching

Cain with a dark-haired little boy who stretched up with tiny, wriggling hands to be held by his father.

In her dream, Brighton lifted her hand from the warmth of her belly—a baby that'd never be—and brushed her palm over the tops of the grass. It *felt so* real. She plucked a stem from the ground and slipped it between her fingers. The color was as mesmerizing and breathtaking as her memories, but from where?

She reluctantly turned away from the vision of Cain as a father—walking hand in hand with the small boy down a wide dock jutting out into the diamond surface of a lake—rising to her feet with a groan. The ache in her body felt *real*, blooming at the center of her back through her hips—different than anything she'd ever experienced.

Brighton followed a set of stairs zig-zagging through the trees. It felt oddly familiar, like she'd been there a thousand times before, though couldn't quite place it—until she got to the top and saw an achingly familiar house tucked amongst the Poplar and Oak. With faded cedar shingles and wide windows with green trim—it filled Brighton with an unshakeable sense of nostalgia.

Home.

What a cruel joke, taking her back to where things began— to where her mother had been alive . . . to where she and Cain met as kids, even though they hadn't realized it at the time. A breathless sob fell from her lips. Brighton held onto a wooden railing, hugging her free hand around her frame as her body wracked with desolate cries.

The warmth of a hand on the curve of her belly drew her attention away from the grief. Cain—the dream him, anyway— calmed her in a second, reaching for her face with a smile.

Brighton shook her head, silvery tears slipping down her cheeks as she wished in vain it was real, choking back another sob when she looked into his eyes. "Why? Why are you doing this to me? Can't we—can't we go back to before? Try again? Do something differently? I can't do this without you. *I don't want to.*"

Brighton's frustration grew when Cain only gave her a knowing look, holding her gaze as a different voice entered her mind, and she found herself remembering the teachings of J.R.R. Tolkien—

"So do all those who live to see such times, but that is not for them to decide. All we have to do is decide what to do with the time that is given to us."

⋈

*B*righton woke with a start, the remnants of her dream lingering in every atom. Her grief surged with every expelled breath, climbing to new peaks with every heartbeat measured with a loud beep on the monitor next to her hospital bed.

She blinked up at the ceiling tiles, shapeless and white in her ashen, achromatic vision. A drip stand mounted next to the screen showed the steady waves of her blood pressure and the rise and fall of her breathing.

Signs of life.

It proved, after everything, *somehow*, Brighton was stuck in the land of the living, caught up in the *beep-beep-beep* that spelled out how alive she was . . . and how alone she felt.

A gentle squeeze of her hand, so welcoming and warm, stirred Brighton's heart in a way she heard on the monitor. She wondered—with the color of *The Glimpse* in her dreams fresh in her mind—things might have happened differently than she remembered. Maybe the accident had all been in her head. A bad dream.

Brighton turned against the scratchiness of the pillow

towards the hand holding hers so firmly. She opened her eyes and took in the figure sitting beside her bed.

"Hey, kiddo."

Looking worn and worried beyond belief at her bedside, with his reading glasses perched on the end of his nose, was her father—Thomas Evans.

His brown eyes—now grey to her—looked like he'd been awake half the night. Scrubbing his long fingers through scruff along his chin, Thomas let out a quaking breath as he took in the bruised and battered vision of his daughter in the hospital bed.

"*Dad...*" Brighton croaked as a single tear slipped down her cheek.

"They called me as soon as you got here, Pumpkin. You're .. . *thank God you're okay.*" Thomas cradled her IV-wrapped hand, lifting it to press it to his cheek while his own tears fell. "I got here as soon as I could."

"W—where am I?"

"About twenty miles north of Madison." Thomas's eyes searched her face, knowing she wanted—no, *needed*—to know more. "The accident happened further north, but they thought it best to bring you here."

"Cain?" Brighton pressed, a sliver of foolhardy hope splitting her voice as she sat up with a groan. The sound of her rapidly rising heartbeat beeped incessantly on the monitor, increasing as Thomas slipped the glasses from his nose.

"There wasn't anything they could do, Brighton." Thomas wrapped his arms around her more firmly, holding her together before he said the thing which would surely make her crumble. "Cain is dead."

Brighton pushed him away and rolled to her side with a sob, curling her fingers around the handrail on her bed, even though the tubes connected to her wrist protested. She buried her face in the only waking shadow she could find, unable to look at how clouded things had become.

Thomas held her as best as he could as she cried, keeping her close with comforting whispers in her ear, like the time she'd fallen from her bicycle and skinned her knee as a kid. Only, Brighton wasn't a little girl, and the hurt was so much more than a scrape or a cut.

Brighton felt broken down to her soul; a piece of it had been torn away, leaving a gaping hole behind that would never heal.

This was her life now. Colorless and grey without him.

Chapter
24

*T*he steady, digital beep seeped into Brighton's dreams, always announcing the beat of her heart. No matter how much she tried to banish them or how they taunted her, the dreams remained, twined with her signs of life.

Brighton's brows scrunched with a groan when she focused on the distant sound of quiet conversations happening in the hall and the occasional alarm blaring out from two rooms down.

She'd been in the ICU for twelve hours. That's what they told her. They'd moved her from the ER, tearing her away from the torturous, color-filled dreams where Cain waited with a family they'd never have, and Gandalf the Grey provided more of his unwanted wisdom.

Maybe it was some sort of inception—a dream within a dream. Doctors said Brighton suffered a brain bleed. Perhaps it caused her heartbreakingly beautiful nightmares. Of course, Cain wasn't real—he was a *symptom*.

The waiting felt endless. Time ticked away, and Brighton felt stuck, caught up in an odd sort of limbo—trapped in the First Circle of Hell. Perhaps, Cain was waiting, too, caught on the other side, wandering Elysian Fields until it was her turn.

Sleep came in waves, accompanied by images of Cain painted in the most vivid color—breaking Brighton's heart all over again when she'd come to and be reminded the world was grey without him.

Upon waking, Brighton ran through all the scenarios in her mind . . . of ways to fix her waking nightmare.

What if she had seen three years ago what'd been in front of her the entire time? What if they stayed another night at the lodge? What if they left in the morning instead of sleeping the day away? What if she never found out Cain was her soulmate? Would they never have fallen into bed together, would they have woken up in the morning—the same as they'd always done—driven home, and carried on with their lives?

Brighton would have accepted that. She would accept being happy enough if it meant he was still alive.

><

*T*he knock at the door was different from the perfunctory kind when one of the staff came through. This one was shier, tinged with an odd sort of hesitation.

Brighton looked to Thomas, offering next to nothing as he rose to his feet and opened the door.

She heard voices—brittle and hushed. "Can I see her?"

Brighton's eyes shifted towards the door, meeting Thomas's gaze as he looked over his shoulder before turning back to the familiar voice at the door.

"I think that would be good for her."

"How is she?"

"About as well as you could expect. They want to send her home."

"Do you think she's ready?" A different voice, rounder and more masculine, chimed in.

"They seem to think so," Thomas answered with a shrug. "Medically, anyway. Grief is something different. Especially this kind of grief."

"C-can I?"

Thomas cast Brighton another look over his shoulder before pulling the door open with a nod. "Come on in."

Andi's face stirred something in Brighton she didn't expect. When she rounded the corner, she could see her childhood friend—*her sister*—was grief-stricken.

What Brighton noticed most of all were what she remembered to be steel and cornflower blue eyes so achingly familiar but as grey as everything else.

The wall Brighton built helped with that, too.

Andi stepped forward, wringing her hands with a forced smile and tears brimming in her eyes, undoubtedly caused by Brighton's appearance.

Mottled, purple bruises and cuts across her face had only deepened with each passing day. Brighton hadn't been brave enough to look at her own reflection more than one excruciating time. The ever-constant ache was reminder enough to know they existed, whether Brighton acknowledged them or not.

"Hey, Bee." Andi's voice wavered as she stepped towards the hospital bed, motioning with a trembling hand. "Can I?"

"Sure," Brighton croaked, testing the broken limits of her voice for the first time in a day or so. She pushed herself to sit with a quiet groan and a wince, wishing morphine still pumped through her body to numb her.

She avoided Andi's gaze, focusing instead on a loose thread in the blanket covering her legs, twisting and tugging at it with both hands as her oldest friend gingerly sat beside her.

Brighton froze when Andi carefully wrapped her arms around her. She let out a quiet, dry sob, unwilling and unable to

let any ounce of her pain loose. She couldn't cry. No. There'd
been enough tears already. There could be no more falling apart
because—if she did—it would mean Cain was really gone.

It didn't matter how the evidence stacked up. It didn't
matter that Brighton's entire world was painted in grey, that her
father was there, or that Andi had returned from her honeymoon to be by her side. No. Brighton had given enough and
would refuse to allow anything past the fortification she'd so
carefully constructed. She'd hold it together. She'd be strong,
even though her heart had been shattered.

Brighton stayed as still as a statue as they lingered in the
painful awkwardness of the embrace until Andi pulled away to
look across her battered face. Brighton let her eyes flicker to
hers before returning to the solitary thread she was holding to
so fiercely.

Andi spoke again, breaking the heaviness of the silence.
"How are you?"

Brighton remained wordless, meeting Andi's gaze with a
slow shake of her head. It's all she could muster.

"I'm sorry, that was a dumb question, Bee." Andi reached
for her hand, but Brighton found herself instinctually pulling
away, curling her fingers into her palm.

The brunette stiffened, surely in need of her own comfort,
but Brighton couldn't bring herself to care.

They sat in silence—Andi struggling to find something to
say, and Brighton with no more words than what she'd already
given.

Thomas and Eli stood in the hall, giving the two women the
space they might have needed if they had done what everyone
else surely expected—break down tearfully in each other's
arms and comfort the other in their shared grief.

Part of Brighton wished she had more to offer. She wished
her silence didn't fuel the already gaping hole in her heart.

Even if she wanted to—the walls were too thick and unwilling to break. Not yet.

Eventually, the thread Brighton had been tugging at gave way from the woven blanket, breaking the tension as Andi rose to her feet.

Brighton looked up, unsure if she was ready to be as alone as she thought she wanted. Andi gave her a pointed look—some potent combination of hurt, grief, and frustration—before rubbing slow circles on her temples.

"I can't imagine what you're going through right now, Brighton. I know I can't. The thought alone . . . it—it terrifies me," she murmured, tears falling unbidden. "I know I am expecting too much from you right now . . . but . . . *I need you*. I don't want to do this alone. You don't have to do it alone, either."

Brighton's gaze fell back to the thread, wrapping it around her finger until she saw a subtle change in the shade of her flesh. "Aren't I, though? You still have your soulmate."

"That's not fair," Andi argued, voice stained with hurt.

Brighton knew she shouldn't have said it, but now the poison had started to fall from her lips; the gaping wound in her soul split open, leaking out every awful thing before she could stop it.

"None of this is." Brighton's voice broke. "My whole life. None of it is fucking *fair*. What did I ever do to deserve this kind of punishment, huh? I'm not doing it. *This* . . . whatever this is. I'm not going to answer stupid questions, and I'm not going to hold your hand through something that happened to *me*. I just—"

Brighton balked when Andi charged forward with a determined look on her face. They stared at each other for a beat before the brunette stepped closer and was met with a flinch.

Hurt flickered through her stubborn determination. "Would you hold still? I brought something for you."

"I don't want anything." Brighton shook her head, watching as Andi reached for a bag she'd brought with her.

"Too bad. You won't talk to me. You won't let me do anything else, but you're going to let me do this." Andi pulled a brush and a can of dry shampoo from inside, offering a wavering smile. "You look like shit, Bee. *I know you.* I know you always feel better when you dress up a little."

"*Andi...*"

"Would you shut up? Just . . . close your eyes, and we'll get it over with."

Brighton reluctantly let her eyes fall closed as Andi reached for her hair.

Ever vigilant of the cuts marring every inch of her, Andi gave the can a shake and spritzed a fragrant spray at the roots. Then, with the tips of her fingers, Andi rubbed gentle, shallow circles in Brighton's hair.

The comfort of her touch was a welcome one, no matter how Brighton initially fought against it. With a shiver, her body relaxed when Andi eased a brush through the tangled mess.

Over and over, the bristles caressed every curve, taking the redhead back to when she was a little girl, and her mother would hold her and slowly run her fingers over her temple.

Whether it was to ease the ache of a scrape on her knee or the memory of a bad dream, the touch was like no other, and Brighton couldn't help but let herself get caught up in it as her friend—*her sister*—recreated the feeling.

While Andi twisted Brighton's hair into a braid, something completely unexpected happened. The walls she'd so carefully built began to crack, and her tears—though unwelcome and unwanted—fell free.

Chapter
25

*B*righton felt like a wet rag that had been rung out dry—their last moments haunting her when she closed her eyes—replaying like a distant echo on the wind with the promise of a life that'd never come.

I know now without any shred of doubt, no matter who we are, what we're doing, or who you're with . . . I will always love you.

Eventually, even though her heart ached with a piercing pain throbbing in her chest, doctors decided Brighton was well enough to go home.

With a trembling hand and a cheap ink pen, Brighton signed her name on the line, looking to the doorway of her room, half-expecting Cain to stride through and cheekily apologize for being late with one of the collectible smiles she loved so dearly.

Wrapped up in clothes Andi brought and her favorite wool coat—once crimson, but no longer—Brighton sat forlornly on the edge of her hospital bed. She found momentary comfort in her newly acquired freedom from tubes and wires she'd been trapped in for the last few days.

Still, it was paralyzing to think of going back to their apartment. Being amongst Cain's things, his smell, *his bed* . . . it was too much to fathom while sitting in the cold, sterile environment of a hospital—still broken and bruised from the accident that killed him.

Brighton absentmindedly picked at the black square on her hand, evidence of the medical tape that held her IV in place, when a quiet knock rang out from the door.

Brighton vaguely recalled the man smiling from the doorway. With a crease in her aching brow, she tried to pinpoint him from the endless parade of faces that flashed overhead through her blood and tear-stained lashes.

"I brought you something." Riyan, the kind paramedic who'd calmed her, smiled, holding out a small paper bag.

Thomas took it from him with a smile and handed it to her.

Brighton pulled out a bundle of fabric, clapping a hand over her mouth to stifle a cry. She tasted the salt of her tears on dry, cracked lips, tracing a jagged line of delicate stitches puckering the material down the center.

Dragging her fingers away, Brighton sucked in a trembling breath, lifting the fabric of Cain's sweater—*her favorite*—to her face with a muffled sob.

"I thought for sure they threw it away," she whispered, pulling the garment to her chest as she looked at Riyan lingering in the doorway.

"Usually, yeah. I thought you'd want to have it. Not as a reminder of what happened, but what was. It gets better. It will, anyway."

"I don't know how to thank you." Brighton's voice was quiet.

Riyan's eyes crinkled around the edges. "You don't have to. Just—pay attention. There's still color if you know where to look. He'll show you the way."

⋈

*W*ith the mail, Cain's sweater, and his possessions from the hospital piled in her arms, Brighton went home.

The closer she came to their door, the heavier her feet became, dragging from one stair to another like they weighed a thousand pounds at least.

Brighton turned the corner, and her heart lurched when the door—*their door*—came into view, finding herself suddenly regretful she hadn't asked Thomas to stay.

She rifled through her bag they'd recovered from the scene and fished her keys from the bottom. Taking a deep breath to steady her shaking hand, Brighton turned the key with a *click* and opened the door.

Shutting it with a perfunctory *thud* felt like Brighton was closing the door on a chapter of her life—the one with Cain in it. Brighton choked back a sob as she looked over the once-colorful rooms of their shared apartment. Her bag fell to the floor, and she did the only thing she could think of—

Brighton toed off her shoes—a plain pair of Keds handed to her by a nurse—leaving them in a heap by the door. She stripped away the clothing that smelled of hospital. All bleach and iodine—more sterile than she could stand.

If the sight of color Brighton once loved so dearly was taken from her in her own home, there was no way she was going to go another second wrapped up in a reminder of how it'd been robbed from her in the first place.

Clothes strewn to the floor, Brighton stumbled over her heavy feet, unwrapped the warm knit from her arms, and pulled it over her head. Her legs threatened to give out with each weighted step. Dragging her toes along the floor, she struggled to catch her breath until she finally collapsed under the weight of her grief.

Brighton's despair pummeled the hypothetical walls she'd

built at the hospital, tearing them down with each stuttering gasp.

The tears came, too—trailing hot streaks over the scratches and cuts marring her skin. Brighton knew they were for Cain, but they were for her, too.

She cried for the time they wasted. She cried for the time they lost. And she cried for the life she'd never get to have with him by her side.

They came in waves—mainly for Cain from the uncontrollable grief pouring forth from the gaping wound in her soul. It was something which would fester over time if Brighton wasn't careful, but as she sat with Cain's sweater draped over her broken body—grief was all Brighton had.

She'd managed to pick herself up off the floor when the well of tears ran dry—surely to be replenished again before the day was through—resigning herself to pacing back and forth through the kitchen, desperate for something to ease her pain.

It wasn't as simple as swallowing down medication to dull it away or taking a hit of something stronger to blur the edges of reality. What was Brighton supposed to take for something which had no cure?

She managed to turn on the kettle and look at her phone long enough to read a text from her dad.

Checking in. We're worried about you. Spoke to Carrie, and we think it's a good idea if you go to London. I can go with you so you're not alone . . . I think you'll regret it if you don't.

Brighton's chin trembled as she shakily typed out a reply on the cracked screen, worried if she didn't, eventually, her father would show up on her doorstep.

Okay.

Waiting for the kettle to come to a boil, Brighton eyed the parcel with Cain's things inside. With an anxious swallow, she peeled open the seam at the top.

Before she'd left the hospital, they'd handed her a paper

bag of his worldly goods—as if she was lucky to have so much leftover. Merely a handful of little things, they weighed her down like a house on a wicked witch.

First, she pulled free his watch. Without a second thought, Brighton wrapped it around her wrist, reveling in the weight of it and the way the face took up all the space on her arm. With her free hand, she slowly circled the crown, allowing herself to smile as she remembered how often he'd worn it . . . and the morning she'd given it to him.

Brighton fished around in the bag again, finding the shattered remains of his cellphone and his car keys—obsolete now his Range Rover had been completely obliterated—before pulling out his thin, leather wallet.

Splitting it open with her trembling hands, Brighton let out a quiet sigh when she looked over Cain's face on his driver's license—cross, but handsome as ever—and name stamped on every plastic card. In her hands, she literally held his identity. She wore his clothes and slept in his bed. His shoes laid by the door, and laundry sat unwashed in the hamper.

With so much of him left behind, how could it be that he was really, truly gone?

The idea was unfathomable, and the reminder of it came in the sharpest waves when Brighton thought for sure she'd been feeling better.

Brighton cocked her head as she opened the long edge of the billfold, brows puckering with a tug on a small photograph from inside.

A worn crease ran down the middle like it had been folded and unfolded five hundred times. The edges were soft to the touch as she opened it, letting out a quiet, disbelieving huff when she saw her own face inside.

It had been the stupidest thing, something so silly and trivial she thought for sure Cain would never have kept it, not in a million years. Still, the evidence in her hands suggested, not only did he keep it—he *treasured* and looked upon it often.

The photograph tumbled from her hand as she let out a stuttering sob, fluttering to the floor at her feet. Brighton's balance wavered until she stilled herself by laying her palms on the countertop's cool stone.

With a few, deep breaths, Brighton centered herself in the steady sound of her breathing—like Cain taught her. It was something she could control when the rest of her world fell to pieces, drifting away like sand in the desert.

Eyes closed, Brighton slowly counted each one, carrying herself on the calming wave it brought—until she opened her eyes and saw the glittering, emerald cut diamond on her left hand.

Part of her forgot it was there. Now she despised the damned thing. It was beautiful, true—and fit perfectly to boot —but only served as a reminder of what was, what could have been, and what was stolen from them . . . and the reason for his demise.

Brighton thought back to their last conversation with a sob, remembering the look of thrilling hope on Cain's face in the instant before their entire world turned upside down.

He wanted to marry her.

It would be a lie to say Brighton didn't want the same thing and didn't dream of the most heartbreaking moment—with her in a pale-silver dress and Cain waiting at the end of an aisle. Still, the more she thought about it, the more guilt consumed her for what ultimately happened.

Others would tell her it wasn't her fault. Maybe it wasn't . . . but the ring. *The fucking ring.* If Cain left it in his pocket and waited until they got home . . . what would be different? Would he be standing next to her, sipping a cup of coffee as she steeped her tea? Would he be walking through the door, loosening his tie after an exhaustive day, ready to relax on the couch with his best friend—*his soulmate?*

With a yell, Brighton tore the delicate jewelry from her finger and hurled it across the room. It landed with a quiet *thunk* as it connected with the drywall on the other side of the sofa.

As soon as it left her hand, Brighton was consumed with regret, crying out as she lunged into the other room. She sank to her knees to gather the ring up off the floor, slipping it back onto her finger.

Brighton traced the brand-new, ring-sized scar on the wall with a trembling hand . . . the one she put there with such a precious piece of *them.*

She sank onto the couch, crossing her legs with a sniff, looking at the damage she'd done. Even though it was small and surely insignificant to anyone else, the dent in the wall was more like the wound in her heart—the permanent one he'd put there, one she was sure would linger for as long as she lived, and so much longer after that.

The Grey had been jarring at first, but Brighton began to adjust to it as time painfully wore on. She wasn't sure she would ever be used to it—or if she wanted to.

Brighton rose to her feet, twisting the ring around her finger as she remembered how lost for words she'd felt when he placed it in her hand.

That was the funny thing about life. Always full of the cruelest surprises, it gave and took away without a second glance. Sometimes—like she and Cain—you'd only realized the gift you'd been given once it was too late.

Brighton did the only thing she could think she was sure would ease the ache—at least, for a little while.

Standing in the doorway of Cain's bedroom, the time ticked away for what felt like hours. All the while, Brighton anchored herself to the frame as she nervously lingered on the edge.

Brighton rolled the seam of Cain's oversized sweater between her fingers, letting out a quiet sob when another wash of grief tumbled over her. It stole her breath in an instant as she struggled to break free of the suffocating feeling.

It was exactly how Cain left it—eerily similar to the last time she'd hovered in his doorway. The memory of their first fight oozed down to her fingers, making noxious friends with her grief. Brighton *needed* him more than ever, craving the weight of his arms around her to heal invisible hurt.

Both times, Brighton felt desperate to go in and feel his presence even though he was gone. Her wish in February came true in the shape of Cain wrapped around her as she cried in his bed. That was then. That was *before*. Now she was alone.

I'll always be around, Colour Girl. No matter what.

Brighton wet her lips with a broken, dry sob, slipping her toes over the seam in the floor. She ventured inside, hands shaking as she peeled her fingers away from the wooden door-frame. Her chest felt tight with each breath. Brushing her fingers across the grey bedspread, she was finally brave enough to pull back the covers.

Slipping her legs beneath the blanket, Brighton let out a broken cry as she laid her head down upon his pillow. She bathed herself in the smell of him as her eyes fell closed with a fresh wave of her tears.

Was this it? Was this all she would be allowed from now until eternity? Her chin trembled, gathering the blankets to her chest as she tried to hold herself more firmly—holding together the pieces threatening to shake apart with each breath.

Even with her eyes closed, Brighton's head spun. How was it the end when it never felt like goodbye?

Chapter
26

December

$\mathcal{T}$he windshield wipers shrieked in protest with every swipe across the windshield. The world grew colder with each thunderous tick of Cain's watch that never left Brighton's wrist. With Christmas a week away, Chicago winter was already in full swing, smattering her borrowed blue sedan with fine flecks of snow.

Brighton was happy for her friends. Their lives were only beginning, and in the shadow of tragedy, the light of a fresh start blossomed.

Why shouldn't they move on with their lives? Why shouldn't they look toward the future when they had each other—when they had their soulmate? Where else was there to go but up when it hadn't happened to *them*?

Brighton tried not to feel bitter, but maybe that's how her heart was, now.

After a long drive through the twists and turns of a surprisingly secluded road so close to the city, Brighton felt the sting of her bitterness fade an inch or two. She turned down a long, winding driveway leading up to a modest, brick house on the edge of a small lake.

Just like home.

A twist of the key in the ignition silenced the motor, but Brighton's dread kept her firmly planted in the driver's seat. She wished she'd felt better, she wished she'd be excited to celebrate with Andi and Eli, but Brighton still hadn't pulled herself from the fog.

Brighton trained her gaze on the quiver of the second hand on Cain's watch, reminded all over again how staggeringly slow each minute without him had been.

Tick-tick-tick.

Six months. Six months since Cain had gone. Since she'd returned to their apartment without him. Since she'd found herself back at an airport bar in New York City, sitting in the same stool, as she waited for a London-bound flight to board, with only the ghost of his memory to keep her company.

Six months since she'd donned a black wool coat and netted fascinator and Andi gave her an encouraging smile to say, "You're beautiful. He'd love how British you look, babe."

Six months since she watched six strong men reverently heave a wooden casket onto their shoulders—one she followed up an aisle of a London church with his family. The ticking of Cain's watch marked the bounce of pale roses with every step of the pallbearers—drawing them closer to a final goodbye.

For a blissful, heartbreaking moment, as she lifted her eyes to stone arches and stained glass, Brighton let herself see things a little differently in the stately halls of Holy Trinity Church.

Instead of black, she wore starlight-hued silver. She held roses in her hands as—with a flutter of her heart—she met Cain's eyes at the end of the aisle.

Tick-tick-tick.

Six months since she stared at the closed top of his casket

and idly wondered what he looked like inside. She gripped the program in her fist, unable to look at his handsome face on the cover. She even sang along with dreary hymns and listened to a vicar say a prayer for Cain's soul.

Would praying have helped? Would believing in something more than the unshakable conviction she'd find her soulmate have brought him to her sooner? Would it have made her notice? Would their love have been enough, then?

No, if love had been enough, he would be there, he would be alive . . . and *God*—to hell with him or whoever had decided it was 'his time.'

Brighton's resentment bloomed as each second of the funeral waged on, and the processional followed the rose-swathed casket—spilling back out into the London drizzle. In a wave, the sea of black umbrellas burst open, and the air around her was punctuated by the *pitter-patter* of rain on taut nylon.

Tick-tick-tick.

Six months since Brighton sat with her hands around a glass, staring down into the swirls of liquid inside. She knew well enough by the shades of grey there was a difference between the whiskey and the fragile vessel holding it. The longer she stared, lost in the din of the voices surrounding her, the more she silently willed for it to shift and bloom into the warm amber she knew it to be.

Six months since listening to Cain's classmates trade stories about him in the muted darkness of a London pub.

Brighton wasn't surprised when—over and over—Cain proved as remarkable a man to everyone else she'd always known him to be. His old classmates from childhood and beyond told stories of playing rugby in the rain and football at boarding school, and losing track of him repeatedly in a library —only to find him with his nose deep in the oldest volume of Tolkien he could find.

She kept it together through every word, losing herself to

the words of Samwise Gamgee as she absentmindedly traced her fingertip over the round face of Cain's watch. All the while, Brighton stared at a photograph atop the bar, praying for it to come to life and for Cain to give her one last collectible smile.

Over, and over, and over. *Tick-tick-tick.*

The same as the beat of Brighton's heart on the monitor at the hospital or Cain's pulse beneath her fingertips in the car— each measured beat was proof of life.

Hers, anyway.

Tick-tick-tick.

Six months since Brighton returned home and was expected to go back to her life like nothing had happened.

All the books she'd been given told her how to 'overcome' her grief. They gave the steps Brighton was supposed to follow, and once she reached the end—she'd be fixed.

Repaired. Herself once more.

Brighton's grief felt more like a disease with no cure. The longer she spent in it, the more she tried to *cure* the incurable, the sicker she felt. She *was* sick. After all, there were symptoms to it. It wasn't the sort of thing she saw in the movies. It was more than tears or being *sad.*

Brighton felt her grief down to her bones, a physical pain which wouldn't go away—no matter how much she slept or tried to numb it away with a shot or swill of tequila.

Her grief manifested itself in her reflection. Even though her world was grey, Brighton could see the effect of it in the reflection of her gaze, the brightness of her skin, and sallow shadows beneath her eyes.

Thomas told her she needed to sleep. Brighton was more tired than she'd ever been, but no matter how much time she spent wrapped up in his bed—finding herself *rested* was never an eventuality Brighton could achieve.

Tick-tick-tick.

With a staggered quiver of the second hand, Cain's watch

reminded Brighton that she couldn't linger in Andi and Eli's driveway forever. Eventually, one of them would notice her loitering and beckon her inside.

She leaned over the steering wheel into the warm porch light spilling onto the dash. It told her there was good waiting for her inside—but Brighton knew it was a lie. It was a chore, wearing the mask that everything was fine—that she was herself, again.

Scrubbing her palms on her knees, Brighton sucked in a quaking breath before pushing open the door to step outside. Snow crunched under her boots, and wind tugged and snapped at the loose edges of her favorite, once-crimson coat. She lifted her face toward the sky, allowing herself a single solitary moment to enjoy the way the snowflakes freckled her face.

Andi opened the door before Brighton had a chance to walk up to the stoop, wrapping her up in a warm embrace she couldn't help but return.

Eli followed quickly behind, enveloping the pair in his long arms, practically lifting them from the concrete before letting out a loud laugh and shuttling them inside—insisting they were letting out all the hot air.

"How very midwestern of you, babe." Andi rolled her eyes, taking Brighton's coat to hang on a hook by the door.

"I'm learning. However—" Eli grinned, crossing his arms. "Americanize me all you want, but you can't take my tea from me."

"Not for lack of trying on my part. You'll give into my way of thinking, one day," Andi argued, walking through the cozy foyer into an open kitchen and dining room.

Brighton closed her eyes with the ghost of a smile, inhaling the delicious smells coming from the oven as she slid onto a stool at the island.

"Alexandria," Eli slid on a pair of oven mitts as he waved his hands to drive his point home. "The way you drink coffee is horrible, so give it up, babe. It'll never happen."

"It is *not* that bad."

"Is so, and you ought to cut back. Hell, you need to be drinking decaf." Eli pointed with one of his mitt-covered hands.

Andi gave him a look before quickly changing the subject. "I hope you're hungry, Bee. I've been slaving away over this dinner for *ages*."

"By 'ages' Alexandria means she sat where you are and let me do all the work," Eli teased, wrapping his arms around his wife as he peppered her neck with quick kisses until Andi relented with a giggle.

"Okay, fine, I was moral support!" Andi peeled herself away, laughter dying away when her eyes landed on Brighton, sitting quietly on the other side of the granite countertop. "So, how 'bout it? Pot roast?"

"Pot roast sounds fine, thank you." Brighton nodded, glancing at Cain's watch on her wrist, counting the *tick-tick-tick* serving as the constant reminder of what was . . . especially when she looked up and saw a reflection of what could have been.

Andi and Eli were gracious hosts, asking her all the right questions while avoiding the wrong ones—any about Cain.

Still, it was obvious how the subject simmered beneath the surface, especially when it came to Andi. She was never one to shy away from *any* matter, let alone with her oldest friend.

The brunette watched Brighton's every move and thoughtfully listened to each answer she gave when it came to work, how the traffic was on the drive, the Cubs postseason, and the predictions for how bad the winter would be.

All of it was a struggle. Every second, every *tick* of Cain's watch was slower than the last as Brighton trudged her way through the act Andi and Eli could see straight through.

Brighton leaned back in her chair, offering a tempered

smile to Eli by way of thanks when he topped off her wine from across the table. She swirled around the fragrant liquid, glancing down into the bell of her glass before taking a sniff and meeting Andi's expectant gaze.

"What is it?" Brighton set her glass down harder than she meant.

Andi opened her mouth to speak, hesitating when Eli laid his hand across hers with a subtle shake of his head. She took a breath and emotionally backed away, but Brighton couldn't leave well enough alone.

"No, I'm serious. What is it?"

The couple exchanged a quick glance. Eli pursed his lips and shook his head, leaning his jaw against his knuckles when Andi stubbornly forged ahead. "We're worried about you."

Brighton scoffed. "You and everyone else."

"Can you blame us? *We love you.*" Andi reached for her hand across the table. Brighton instantly drew away, staring at a red splotch on the tablecloth.

"H-how have you been holding up?" Eli asked, giving her a kind smile she knew came from a good place, but accepting it was a task unto itself.

"Fine." Brighton's jaw clenched with a quaking breath, eyes glued to the wine in the bottom of the glass.

"Have you been seeing anyone?" Cain's old flat mate bravely pressed on, an impossible shining light of positivity that couldn't penetrate the armor of Brighton's sublime detachment. "... read any books, perhaps?"

"The hospital sent me home with a couple." Brighton shrugged, lifting her glass to take another long drink of her wine. "I don't know what a book is supposed to do. They all want to 'fix' me, but there isn't any fixing this. I can't tear out one of those bullshit pages and tape it over what happened like a band-aid."

"A support group, maybe?" Eli suggested, uncorking the bottle, but Andi stopped him with a single look.

"Why? I'm sad enough on my own, Elijah. I don't need to sit in a circle full of other sad people so I can . . . what . . . feel *sadder*?"

"Talk to *me*, then." Andi reached for her again; eyes like Cain's pleaded with Brighton to *let her*.

"I can't . . ." Brighton curled her fingers into her palm with a trembling breath, watching the same, steady tick of Cain's watch. The tension in the room bubbled to new heights with every forward motion of the second hand.

Brighton knew they'd convinced themselves that, if she would talk about it, she'd feel better. In reality, though, she felt like—on top of the suffocating feeling of her grief—she was bound to drown in their expectations, too, dragged to the depths by every way she disappointed them by not keeping on and carrying on.

"I want my best friend back." Andi's voice quaked, hands curling into fists on the table's surface. "We lost him, too. Loved him, too. We know the pain you feel."

Brighton dared meet Andi's gaze as her numb bitterness twisted into something darker, something angrier than she'd felt before.

"*No*. You don't have any idea the *scope* of what I feel, Alexandria." Brighton held out her hand, brows puckered together as her chin trembled. "Hand me half your heart; then you might get an inkling of what's happened to me. You've seen things for a couple years. I had *my entire life* of *seeing* but not knowing. My whole life, I had *The Glimpse*, now *nothing*. I needed it. I needed *him*, and now *all of it* is gone. Everything is different, and I am *stuck here* while everyone else moves on and forgets he even existed."

Silent tears slipped down Andi's cheeks. "What if *I* need you, Brighton? Did you ever stop to think—maybe—you can have different *kinds* of soulmates? Maybe, it isn't as fucking simple as color and shades of grey? How can *you*, of all people, be so narrow-minded?"

"You don't need me." Brighton shook her head, absent-mindedly tracing her fingertip around the diamond on her left hand. "You haven't in a long time . . . not since Eli."

"*I'm pregnant*, Brighton."

Brighton weaved in her seat, and eyes fluttered closed. Her mind flooded with fleeting, painful pictures she found in her dreams—the ones of a family she'd never get to have with Cain.

Swallowing hard, she opened them again and looked across the table with a slow, downward tilt of her chin as she tried to will away the clenching, heavy weight in the pit of her stomach. "*Oh.*"

"We . . . weren't going to tell you, Bee. Not yet, anyway." Andi dashed away her tears, leaning into Eli as he hugged the curve of her shoulder.

"I—I'm happy for you," Brighton choked out. The words felt like acid on her tongue, and while they were mostly true, they still tasted like a bitter lie.

"It's okay if you're not." Andi wore a wavering smile. "But I hope you will, one day. I need you, Bee. I need my *sister*, and— you might not know it yet—but this baby is going to need you, too."

Brighton glanced down at her hands, watching the way they trembled before rolling them over to run a fingertip around the crown of Cain's watch. *Tick-tick-tick.* Forever reminding her of how life was carrying on around her—carrying on without him.

"I should go." Brighton rose to her feet, pushing back her chair with a squeal of wood against tile.

"No, Brighton, stay." Andi mirrored her, following her to the foyer. "The snow is getting bad outside. We have plenty of room."

The thought alone stirred a panic deep inside Brighton, heart beating faster as she frantically searched for a reason to make them let her leave.

Home. Home was where she needed to be, no matter how well-meaning Andi was trying to be.

"I'm good, I promise." Brighton forced a wavering smile, finally extending a hand to squeeze Andi's before grabbing her coat. "I have an early morning."

Eli gave her a puzzled look. "It's Friday."

"Yoga," she blurted, hoping they couldn't see the sting of her lie when she reinforced it with another. "Trying a new thing. *I'm trying.* I can do this on my own. Just . . . be patient with me, okay?"

Andi's brows scrunched together with a shallow shake of her head. "Drive safe, okay? Text me when you get home, and wear your—"

Brighton nodded, slipping her arms through her coat. "Seatbelt. I know." She offered them another tempered smile, wrapping her fingers around the door handle to pull it open.

A *whoosh* of biting wind fluttered the hair around her face and stung her cheeks, bringing with it a furious flurry of snowflakes dancing around the small entryway and stuck to her coat. Brighton offered one last look over her shoulder and a wave before stepping out into the blustery weather.

The Chicago winter pummeled the lakeside city and its surrounding communities with a frigid, wet wind—blooming into a storm of such ferocity, Brighton wished she wore a warmer coat.

The wipers on her borrowed car worked furiously, swiping a fresh layer of snow from the windshield with each shiver of the second hand.

Brighton held firmly to the steering wheel, leaning closer to the glass as it fogged at the edges. In the light of her headlights, the snow whipped in a storm of silver, something more akin to

Star Wars than everyday life. She pushed forward through the darkness, going around each twist and turn as her heart hammered away.

The tires slid across the road, lurching the car to the side. Adrenaline flooded Brighton's senses, stealing her breath as she kept a white-knuckle grip on the steering wheel.

Fine. Everything was fine. She'd driven in the snow a hundred times before. This wasn't any different.

When the car shifted on its wheels again, Brighton blinked, seized by the memory of her body floating upside down in a Range Rover.

The snow stretched over the dashboard, fueling her rapid heartbeat as she tried to blink away the thought of their mangled car from her mind, the flash of red and blue in the cab, and Cain's blood on her hands.

This isn't the same. You'll get out of the spin.

Brighton's fingers trembled as she wiped the tears streaming from her eyes, sucking in a trembling breath as her traumatic memories came one after the other.

Her arms struggled to grip the wheel and steady the car. Ears ringing, heart thumping, Brighton couldn't quell her panic—not even with a glance at the steady ticking of Cain's watch.

Tick-tick-tick.

Ice. A swerve. The thick trunk of a tree illuminated by her headlights.

Tick-tick-tick.

The screech of metal against wood. Shattering glass. A breath—painful and burning.

Brighton opened her eyes and surveyed the damage around her.

Broken glass. Ringing in her ears. Headlights shining into a snow-covered tree line.

Tick-tick-tick.

Brighton thought for sure there had to be more. More pain. More jarring sounds—the shriek of steel against asphalt.

It was different than before when Brighton had been so painfully aware of every infinitesimal moment as it unfolded in all its horrific glory. This time, it happened so quickly, she couldn't be sure what was real and what wasn't.

A slow lick of her lips brought the sour, copper taste of blood across her tongue. Her hands gripped the wheel, even as the sedan wheezed its last breaths from under the hood. Thomas's car. Snow. Her behind the wheel. *Alone.*

It was real. Painfully, so.

Brighton sucked in a stuttering breath of cramped air, letting out a choked moan when a sharp pain bloomed in her side.

Spots clouded the edges of her vision—or was it fog on the windshield?

Brighton blinked through what was left of the mangled glass, letting out a quiet groan when she watched the snow pile on inch after inch.

Tick-tick-tick.

Lifting her shaking hands to her pounding head, Brighton brushed her fingertips against her temples, letting out a quiet, stuttering breath of resigned acceptance when they came back covered in blood.

Just like Cain. Leaning her head back against the headrest, she blinked up at the snow-covered windshield. Her eyes blurred, hovering on the edge of consciousness. She wondered if she could close her eyes, fall asleep, and *leave.* Could it be that simple?

It seemed easy enough when Cain slipped away beneath her fingertips, gone in the blink of an eye—why couldn't she?

Brighton let her shoulders relax and put the pain from her mind, closing her eyes as a slow smile bloomed across her face. Ready. Waiting. Willing to go home.

Tick ... tick ... tick ...

The sound of Cain's watch was the only thing left, welcoming the darkness and whatever waited for her on the other side while the rhythm grew slower and slower.

"Brighton ..."

A warm wind fluttered the hair around her face, carrying away the cold and snow. She felt herself smile as she opened her eyes. Sure it worked—Brighton gasped as she looked across the faint golden glow of a setting sun stretching its arms into vast, inky blue, lighting the surface of the lake like a mirror in firelight.

She could see.

"Brighton, darling . . . *look at me* . . ." The voice called her again, followed by the warmth of a familiar touch on her face, drawing her gaze to a figure standing next to her and a pair of blue eyes that felt like home.

Cain's thumb skimmed against her cheek, meeting her with a smile as his eyes darted across her face.

Brighton held her breath, blinking back fresh tears as she closed her eyes again. She let out a quiet sob as her mind tried to convince her—like before—the images of Cain were merely a symptom of an injury. When she opened them again, he was still there—as real and warm and *right* as he had always been.

"Fancy meeting you here." Cain's smile wavered, holding her firmly in the palm of his hands as her heart beat wildly in her ears.

"Where are we?" Brighton breathed, slowly licking her lips as more tears of relief spilled down her cheeks, looking over his shoulder at the wheathered hillside. Every edge was blurred— every fleck of fading sunlight, every tree, and every leaf— like she was the subject in a Monet. The only thing that was clear was him. "Did it ... *am I?*"

Cain shook his head. "No, darling. You're not."

"Why? I don't ... I don't want to be here anymore," Brighton whispered, letting out a sob when she traced her fingers through his dark curls—finding them as achingly soft as she remembered. "I want to stay here with you."

"That's your choice. But—" Cain's eyes were haunted, filled with every missed opportunity and stolen moment.

"*But?*" Brighton's voice cracked, leaning into his touch as he tucked a stray ribbon of red hair behind her ear

Cain shook his head. "It's not your turn."

"*I—I miss you.* I am so tired of being alone."

"You're not alone," he murmured, leaning so close; Brighton was sure she might be able to feel his lips against hers. "You have to look in the right places, Bee. There's so much color waiting for you . . . I know it's hard to see right now, but it's there. I promise. So, *pay attention.*"

"Can't I . . . *please?* I want to be with you." Brighton could barely breathe. The choice felt easy, to fade away and be with Cain for eternity. But, her mind buzzed, filled with every face who called her home—*to live.*

Tears brimmed in Cain's eyes as he wiped hers away with the pad of his thumb. "I miss you more than I can say, my darling, but you've got *so* much left to do. It'll be our turn again before you know it. Patience, darling. All will be revealed in due time."

"I hate waiting." Brighton laughed through her pain, welcoming the fleeting joy when Cain laughed along with her. It was replaced by a quiet surge of panic when the viridescent color around her began to evaporate around the edges.

"Time's up, Colour Girl." Cain's smile faded. "You have to choose."

Brighton sucked in a quaking breath, blinking away tears as the faraway sounds of sirens permeated her beautiful dream-state.

"I-I know what I want. I know what I should do, but I don't want to leave you. Not yet. I want a little more time." Brighton cried through each gasp for air, knowing they had seconds before she'd have to wait another lifetime to be by his side. "I'm not ready . . . I can't say goodbye, again."

"You can and you will, Brighton." Cain tilted his chin down to give her an encouraging nod before leaning in to press his lips to hers. "Choose to be brave."

Brighton wished she could hang onto Cain and keep him with her longer, wrap her arms around him, and will him back into existence.

Cain's kiss was her torment and salvation all at once. Brighton lingered as long as she could, knowing it would be the last taste she'd have until it was finally her turn.

Cain pulled away first, cradling her face like she was something precious and pure. He gifted her one last, collectible smile as she began to slip from his hands. "I love you, Brighton."

Her hands fell and shoulders quaked as the blessed glimpse of color evaporated as quickly as Cain did, leaving her deliriously alone and in the dark of the mangled car all over again.

She was awake. She was *alive*. And, she'd *be brave*.

The sirens grew closer, going silent as the grumble of diesel engines surrounded the car.

Brighton leaned her head back against the seat, letting out another shaking sigh when footsteps neared the driver's side. She winced in the flash of bright light, turning her head toward a familiar voice. "Hey, there. The worst part is over. The ambulance is here. Let's take a look at you, alright?"

She held up a shaking, bloodied hand to shield her eyes, gasping when—for the briefest of moments—Brighton saw a glimpse of black, curly hair and warm, bronze skin. All of it —*all of him*—was accompanied by a familiar smile like déjà vu.

Pay attention, Cain said.

"Riyan? Mender of sweaters, guy?" Brighton croaked,

blinking as her eyes adjusted and the world shifted back to grey.

His face split into a *real* smile, letting out a quiet chuckle with a shake of his head.

"Brighton, right?" Riyan leaned forward, setting down his flashlight with another grin. "We gotta stop meeting like this, kid."

Chapter 27

*S*o much of it was the same, but *all* of it was different.

The unimaginable ache Cain left behind remained, and Brighton's body hurt in places she didn't know it could after her second major car accident in six months.

Thomas was there, looking older than Brighton ever remembered.

"Hey, kiddo. You gave us a good scare there."

"Dad," she croaked. "I'm so sorry about your car. I didn't mean... I should have..."

Thomas held up his hand. "Not another word. It's just a car, Brighton. I *can't* get another you."

The hospital didn't keep her long. They determined her blip into unconsciousness was a result of a concussion. Most of her injuries were superficial, easily mended with rest and a bit of ibuprofen.

Brighton's déjà vu continued when she signed her discharge paperwork, and her attention was summoned by a knock at the door.

Riyan stood there, so similar to how he'd been before. Effortlessly cool, he leaned against the frame, one foot crossed over the other. He lingered on the edge of the room with a smile. "I feel like we've been here before, Brighton."

She waved him over with a smile. "You get that inkling, too?"

"Weird, huh?"

"A little, yeah." Brighton took in his slight frame—not as tall and broad as Cain, but handsome all the same with black curls brushing his collar and a shadow of a dark beard around an infectious smile.

Riyan stepped forward, stuffing his hands into his pockets. "That's never happened to me before. A repeat patient, I mean. Especially not after changing departments . . . *and states*."

"How did you end up in Chicago?" Brighton crossed her ankles, leaning forward to balance her chin in the palm of her hand.

Riyan shrugged with a smile. "A feeling."

Brighton couldn't help but smile as she fondly remembered Cain saying the same thing. "Can't quite put your finger on it, right?"

"Something like that," he answered, settling into a spot beside her on the narrow hospital bed. "So, I've got a weird request."

"In the span of the things that have happened to me in the last few months, I doubt whatever you've got to say is going to shock me too much, Riyan," Brighton teased.

He shook his head as he pressed on. "So. I know you're going through *it* right now. I know it isn't easy, and it's hard to find someone who understands. Everyone tries, but . . . it's not enough."

Brighton nodded. "I know they are . . . but . . . it's been hard. I've been a bit of an ass about it."

"That's okay. You're allowed. Anger is a big part of it. I was pissed for a long time, I promise you." Riyan laid his hand on her arm. "You don't have to do it alone, though. I wanna give you my number, if it's okay. If you want to tell me to fuck off, I will, but . . . if you feel like meeting this head-on, if you want a hand to pull you out of the darkness, I can help. There's . . . there's a lot of color in the world if you pay attention, you know?"

Pay attention, Cain said.

Things felt different than before.

Maybe seeing Cain's face and hearing his voice—begging her to stay, telling her to be patient, and he'd be there waiting for her when it was her turn—had helped push her forward, giving her the flicker of hope she so desperately needed.

There was still color in her life, she only had to look for it.

⋈

*B*righton's hands shook when she looked up at the old stone church. "I don't think I'm ready to do this."

"Sure you are." Riyan gave her shoulder a reassuring squeeze, bringing his gaze level with hers. "You don't have to say anything if you don't want to. Listen, I realize I don't know you, but I can't help but think that this'll be really good for you. It's important you know you aren't alone in this." He hooked his knuckle beneath her chin to lift her eyes from the muted grey of her once-colorful Converses. "Now you have me."

Riyan twined his fingers through hers, offering one of his infectious smiles before pulling her inside.

She was instantly overwhelmed by the smell—a mix of old books, dust, and incense. Brighton felt like she was on autopilot, with Riyan guiding her every step. She hovered in his shadow as he shook hands with other attendants.

Individuals from every walk of life milled through the church basement, chatting over paper cups of mediocre coffee. She felt strangely optimistic through the veil of her nervousness, like being around people who understood would finally help her move forward.

Brighton nodded and shook hands, offering faint, anxious smiles to meet knowing, weathered faces. They could all read her like a book, a deer in the headlights, still fresh in her grief.

Once the clock rolled over twelve, everyone settled into their seats. Riyan remained firmly planted by her side, holding her hand like a lighthouse calling a ship to moor in a storm. He offered another smile as the meeting was called to order with a recitation of the Serenity Prayer.

Like a song with a steady cadence of words twined together like poetry, she'd it heard before but never imagined herself as someone who'd ever have to call upon the words.

Brighton's nerves never quite settled as different attendees stood to talk at the front of the room, greeted each time with an echo of *welcomes* and *hellos* when they stated their name.

Riyan sat silently beside her, listening thoughtfully as each member who wanted to speak had their chance. He nodded in agreement at times, laughing at others; ever the picture of calm, like he'd done it a thousand times before.

Brighton sucked in a stuttering breath when the urge to speak came over her, palms cold and clammy as she rose to her feet.

Being amongst others like her—those who'd lost a soul-mate—lent a heaviness to her limbs Brighton didn't quite expect. Still, she'd come to listen and to be brave enough to talk about him. She'd let out the words in her heart, seal up the story of *them*, turn the page, and create something new, color-ful, and incredible with his name permanently inscribed on her soul.

"Hi, I'm Brighton—" She paused to feel the weight of the words on her tongue before releasing them out into the world. She'd kept her grief to herself, the fortified walls too steep to allow anyone else in. Brighton let herself believe that no one else would understand, but when she felt Riyan's fingers loop through hers, she remembered his words—so like Cain's—promising she wasn't alone. "And, his name was Cain."

Her cheeks pinked when everyone's eyes turned toward her, offering the same chorus of welcoming words of support.

Brighton lingered, tracing the fingers of her free hand over her lips and the memory of Cain's kiss as she tried to summon the courage Riyan's smile roused in her.

"Being without him wasn't something I ever wanted to do once we found each other. It wasn't something I wanted to do from the moment I sat down next to him by chance at an airport bar. I never could have imagined being here doing this, but . . ."

Brighton paused, fiddling with Cain's watch with a quiet sob as the tears began to well up. She let them fall free, sucking in a trembling breath as she pressed on. ". . . I miss him so much. I miss him more than I could possibly begin to describe. I was so angry for so long. I was angry with everyone. I was angry with the car for crashing . . . I was angry at God for taking him away from me . . . I was angry with *him* for leaving me behind. Most of all . . . I was angry with myself for not seeing it was him sooner. For not trying harder to find him before it was too late. I can't stop wishing for more time.

"There's nothing more I think about as often as what we could have had. Of the time we wasted. Of how much I *love him* . . . and if something's waiting for us in the next life. I'll admit, sometimes, it is *so* hard to believe there is . . . that I'd be given this gift all over again. I swear, if I did . . . I wouldn't waste a second. Not one. Because every second without him has been *excruciating*.

"I promised I'd be brave. So, I'm trying my best to be okay, because I know, if he saw how I've been lately, he wouldn't want that kind of life for me. So, *I'm trying*. I don't want to lose myself to the darkness. I want to keep living my life like I always did when he was still here . . . like I still have a glimpse of him, and bring the color he gave to me, and live like he is still by my side, because . . . even though it sounds crazy . . . I *know* he is."

"He is, sweetheart. Cain is still with you—*always*." A woman's voice called out from a few seats away. Her sentiment was echoed with a gentle squeeze of Riyan's hand, providing an anchor as Brighton drifted back in from the tumultuous sea of her grief. Every soul around her murmured their agreement.

Afterward, once the meeting-goers dispersed, they swarmed her with well-wishes and support. They shed their anonymity, introducing themselves and offering a source of light on her road to recovery.

Once things quieted, Brighton followed Riyan into the blooming afternoon sunshine. The warmth tingled on her skin, and she shivered when the wind swirled around them and ruffled her hair. She looked up at him, turning together, so his height blocked the sun from her eyes.

"So . . . not so bad, huh?" Riyan gave her shoulder a nudge. "You did good."

"It felt good . . . I think." Brighton toed her sneaker on a smudge on the sidewalk. "Can we do this again?"

Riyan's face lit up. "Yeah, kid. We can. I'd love that."

"So." Brighton chewed the inside of her lip. "What now?"

"Now—" He took a step closer with another one of his contagious smiles. "Now, you let me buy you breakfast. We can talk some more if you want, or not. I'm cool with either, as long as there's pancakes."

Brighton laughed. The sound lifted on the wind and took a weight from her shoulders. "I'd like that, too."

The diner was quiet for a Saturday morning, but the tea was hot, and the company was more than a little pleasant.

Brighton and Riyan shuffled through subjects without effort. All the while, the shadow of their lost *Glimpse* remained in their periphery.

"So—" Riyan topped off his coffee. "How have you been?"

Brighton looked into her tea. "I would say I've been fine, but that's a lie."

"It's okay if you aren't. Part of you never will be. I'm still not, but . . ." His smile faded away as he glanced down at his wedding band. "I know how unfair it is to have something so wonderful be out of reach, but it'll get better. And, you get used to *The Grey*."

Brighton circled a finger around the rim of her cup. "There has to be a way to help people like us. You said I wasn't alone. Look at that meeting. I *know* we aren't."

"You're right." Riyan nodded, leaning forward on his elbows.

"Hell." Brighton's stomach began to flutter with excitement as she was seized by the idea. "Most people live a huge part of their lives without being able to see. Some people never find it at all."

Riyan's smile only grew, caught up in the sudden rush of Brighton's effervescent excitement. "What should we do about it, kid? It's on the tip of your tongue."

"I used to help my best friend pick out her clothes. Designers with the sight are hired all the time to help with that sort of thing. People hire personal shoppers. Why—why shouldn't it be free? Then—" Brighton paused, glancing down at the quiver of the second hand on Cain's watch. She was reminded all over again of the time they wasted, and her wish to have found each other sooner. "Maybe I can help people connect with their other halves. They don't have to waste time like I did. What if there was a way to anonymously compare soul marks? A soulmate search and the sight rolled into one thing."

"You could find a *Glimpse* and be a *Glimpse* at the same time." Riyan looked at her with quiet awe that made her heart flip. "Design it."

Brighton was practically buzzing, smiling wider than she had in months. "I think I will."

"*Brighton.*" Riyan's dark eyes widened, and his lips parted with a breathless smile. "Your smile just lit up my world. *Wow.* I don't know why, but I think I've always known you were a redhead."

Brighton held her breath, her smile quavering as she pressed her fingertips to her heart. "Y-you can *see* me? How?"

"A gift. Just for a second." Riyan took her hand in his, lifting Brighton's palm to the sky. With the other, he plucked a flower from a vase tucked between the maple pecan and blueberry syrups and placed it in her hand. "It's like I said. There's color if you know where to look."

Brighton looked down at their hands. Her mind, her breath, her heart—all of it stuttered and quaked when the carnation in her grasp shifted from muted shades of grey. Every ashen shadow bled away, drawing tears from her eyes as it bloomed into the most brilliant red. She thought the vision of color she'd been allowed after her accident had been a fever dream—a symptom of her concussion. But *this*. This wasn't a figment of her imagination. It was real.

She let out a sob, barely able to tear her gaze away to meet Riyan's. "How are you doing this?"

"I'm not." He gave her a knowing look, holding her hand between his. "Cain is. He's still here. He's *everywhere;* he's all around you. You have to pay attention."

Pay attention, Cain said.

While it wasn't what she had expected, Brighton was happy to have what she could of Cain . . . even if it was only a glimpse, because, in her heart of hearts, she knew they weren't finished yet.

With Riyan, a beautiful kind of friendship—and a unique kind of love—blossomed from the depths of their unparalleled type of grief.

Riyan wasn't her soulmate, not when it came to *The Glimpse,* and Brighton wasn't his.

Still—by his side—Brighton understood there was a possibility of more after losing everything.

With him, she could be happy enough until it was her turn.

Chapter
28

ick-tick-tick.

They got married on a Thursday.

A quiet affair at City Hall, it wasn't at all how Brighton pictured it—far, far away from the pale silver gown she'd tried on in a fleeting moment years before. But, it was enough. Riyan was enough.

Together, while they waited, they were *happy enough.*

Brighton continued to wear Cain's watch, focusing on it less and less as time carried on. She lived her life the way he instructed her to the night of her crash when—in the most beautiful solitary glimpse she was gifted in the time since his passing—he appeared to her and begged her to be patient.

Tick-tick-tick.

Cain had told her to pay attention, so she did.

Brighton had lost herself to her melancholy when Andi and Eli had told her they were expecting a baby; too wrapped in the thought of not having a family with Cain, she didn't stop and give any thought to the family she already *had.*

It was growing, just differently than she'd imagined.

Brighton conjured a lifetime with Cain as she watched her nieces and nephews grow, seeing him in every single ordinary moment of their extraordinary life. In the brightest of them, surrounded by her family, she'd picture him there—as real as could be with the wind in his hair and the sun on his face.

Tick-tick-tick.

When she looked in the mirror, Brighton knew her hair wasn't red anymore. She hadn't seen the vividness of the color since *The Glimpse* was lost. Still, as years wore on, she could feel the difference in the texture and noticed the threads of silver through the darker ribbons she'd grown used to.

Riyan, too, had grown grayer with each passing year. Brighton tried not to linger on the thought long enough to notice. She was too busy looking for—and finding—the color in her life.

All the while, Cain was there, giving her the gift of precious flashes of *The Glimpse*.

I'll always be around, Colour Girl.

Brighton didn't allow herself to be suffocated by the lack of color. She'd learned to do without it as time passed by. With the memory of him, she learned to find it in other places.

It was the smell of autumn leaves on the wind and the way it kissed her face and ruffled her hair. It was in the subtle silence as the breeze rushed through the trees, a musical rustling of leaves across the ground, and the distant call of a flock of geese, riding a southern wind to a warmer place to roost for the coming winter.

Amongst it all, Cain was there.

Brighton could feel him when the rain fell from the sky and caressed the freckles on her face. He was there in the brilliant diamond glint on February snow. His embrace came with the wind, swirling softly around her to make her feel his love amongst the dazzling, uplifting rush of the vermillion leaves circling through the sky in quiet flight.

At night, the ones when she ached for sleep to carry her away, Brighton would imagine herself at the lake house where she grew up—where they'd met. With an ocean of stars above her, Cain was there too.

Tick-tick-tick.

Time was precious, and as soon as Brighton thought she finally had a handle on the rate it went by, the clock skipped ahead like always.

She was old. Older than she'd ever thought she'd be, smiling up at a collection of young faces she'd watched grow up. Riyan had passed years before, gone home to his soulmate —just like they'd always planned.

Faced with another funeral of the man she loved, Brighton was struck by the stark differences. For Cain, she mourned. For Riyan, she *celebrated*. It was his turn, and hers was coming soon.

Tick-tick-tick.

Color hovered at the edges of her vision as she blinked slower and slower, holding firmly to a hand belonging to her oldest friend, Andi. Her heart had grown weak over time, and was slowly, *finally*, beginning to give out.

Tick-tick...

Her family had come to say goodbye to 'Auntie Bee,' tearfully wrapping their arms around her frail, tired body the best they could, placing sweet kisses in the palm of her worn hands as she tutted, "Don't you worry. I'll be alright. I'm going *home*."

... tick ... tick ...

As she waited to be carried away, Brighton's entire life flashed through her mind on a colorful carousel. Every thought, every happy memory, every ounce of color she found, and the love she held in her heart replayed behind her eyes as she started to drift.

... tick ...

When Brighton opened them again, the light was different than she remembered. Gone were the walls of her hospital room—replaced by the butter-yellow of a familiar bedroom. Warmed by sunshine, they were freckled by photos of familiar faces, colorful ribbons tacked to a pinboard, bright blue Cubs pennant, and faded poster of Orlando Bloom on the back of the door.

Rolling to her side, Brighton pulled the rainbow-hued blanket to her chin, and found something precious tucked into her palm.

She lifted her hands—ones belonging to a younger woman—and looked upon the face of a watch. In life, Brighton depended on it, counting the tiniest, infinitesimal movements of a second hand which had finally gone still.

Brighton set Cain's Breitling on the bedspread beside her, smiling in the pink glow of early morning summer light. The warmth of the breeze fluttering the pale blue curtains through an open window curled around her hair, spurring her to further explore.

The room was familiar to her, tugging at the faintest memories in her mind as she placed her bare feet on the floor. Her fingers danced over the walls as she followed the golden streams of sunlight and the sounds of water on a rocky shore.

Brighton let out a quiet sigh when she stepped out the back door and let the wind kiss her face and ruffle the hem of her sage-green dress. It carried the ribbons of auburn hair around her freckled shoulders.

The glow settled, and everything became a little clearer as she followed a dirt path down a staircase carved into the side of a hill—and an all-too-familiar lake came into view.

She was home.

Brighton drew closer to the image of the lake she grew up on, her steps slowing ever so slightly when she saw the silhouette of a man standing on the end of the dock.

Her heart hammered in her chest as he slowly turned around. Their eyes met as his face split into a broad smile, and Brighton's heart stopped all over again. After a lifetime of saving them, it was perhaps the most collectible one of them all.

Brighton's feet couldn't move fast enough. She took the stairs two at a time, leaping over boulders and flowerbeds . . . every second away from him too long now she'd made it home.

Cain, too, bolted from the end of the dock, erasing the distance between them with every long, loping stride.

Brighton slid to a halt, breathless and reeling, when he stopped just inches away. Was it real? Had her patience finally been rewarded, or was it just another glimpse?

No. Cain was there, as she had always imagined him to be . . . waiting for her at the place where they'd first discovered *The Glimpse*.

"Fancy meeting you here, darling."

"*Cain.*" Brighton let out a sob when he lifted a wide palm out to her in the early morning light. She could scarcely believe it—until she slid her fingers into his hand as easily as she'd done in a Chicago movie theater, and felt the same warm feeling rush over her.

He was here, and she was *home*.

Cain pulled her to him, circling his arms around her to nuzzle his nose in her hair.

"I've missed you," he rumbled, the sound of it sweeter to her than anything she'd ever heard.

Brighton burrowed her cheek against the warmth of his chest with a whisper, "I'm sorry I'm late . . ."

Cain pulled his arms from around her waist, lovingly tucking his fingers into her hair to lift her gaze to meet his. "You're right on time, Bee. I would have waited longer if I needed to."

With the brush of his thumb, Cain leaned down and gently pressed his lips against hers.

Brighton pulled away with a shaky, shallow breath, her dark eyes shining with unshed tears before twisting her fingers in his curls—pulling him down into another searing kiss. It was everything words could never be, full of a lifetime of love and comforting in ways Brighton couldn't describe.

Cain pulled her to his chest and wrapped his arms around her. "We don't have long, darling."

Brighton lifted her chin, letting her tears slip free with a tremble of her chin. "So soon? I—I only just arrived."

"Time passes differently here. I can't explain it." Cain brushed his lips against her forehead as she felt a tingle at the tips of her fingers.

"Cain, I—" Brighton gasped as he started to fade away with a smile.

"Don't worry. I'll see you again, soon . . . I promise. We have all of eternity to be together, and finding each other is half the adventure."

Brighton scrambled for something to say, smiling through her tears as she called out, "I love you!"

Cain grinned, giving her one last glimpse of his collectible smile as he answered, "I love you, too, Colour Girl."

Epilogue

2703

The *USS Chicago*, a Sovereign-class heavy cruiser—the first of its kind—sat ready and waiting to go on her maiden voyage, setting off to the stars to explore further than any Galactic Alliance Navy ship had ever gone before.

Brighton Evans—*Lieutenant Brighton Evans*—knew every inch of her by heart.

A matte black, convex saucer made up the widest part of her berth, making a home for the thousands of crew members already walking her corridors who expertly ran every infinitesimal system to keep it up and running.

She had a trio of sleek, pointed warp nacelles on the astern, each one equipped with top of the line propulsion systems, which made her the fastest in the entire fleet.

Brighton wished she could press her nose up against the glass and breathe in the sight of her, idly wondering if the buzz thrumming through her fingertips when she looked upon the ship felt anything like *The Glimpse* did for everyone else.

If it did, she might be in love with her future.

A ping on her wristcom told her time was wasting, and she

—helmsman of the *USS Chicago*—needed to report to the bridge.

Breathless with excitement, Brighton told herself to keep her chin up and *not* make a run for the propulsion lift that'd carry her to the docking level to get on board—where Lieutenant Evans would cross the long, windowed gangplank aboard the Sovereign-class vessel.

Brighton sucked in a deep breath as she strode through Engineering, buzzing with excited energy as she looked over her fellow uniformed personnel.

They were busy preparing for their maiden voyage, checking comms and radiation levels at every terminal.

As Brighton made her way to the central lift to take her to the command bridge, it took every ounce of self-control to keep the smile from her face, ever the image of a measured, confident officer of the G.A.N.

In the silence of the elevator, Brighton spared herself a breathless glance in the shining, metal-plated walls. She gave a quick tug on the hem of her ash grey coat, brushing her palms over the crisp lines of pale fabric covering her shoulders. She pressed a hand against the thick twining of braids at the base of her neck, just *barely* brushing over the straight, open collar.

Giving her reflection a smile as quick as lighting, the eager lieutenant jumped back when the lift slowed and doors opened with a hiss.

Brighton stared down at her boots as a man stepped inside, glancing up in time to see a set of impossibly square shoulders in front of her—decorated with a pair of epaulettes *much* more intricate than hers.

"Afternoon," he stated, giving his own uniform a slight tug as he stood a little taller.

He was *big* and towered over her without effort.

Brighton couldn't help but notice the confident way he held himself—or how the weave of his jacket stretched across his broad back. Her mind wandered for a split second, painting a picture of what laid *beneath* . . . and how the hard planes of corded muscle would feel beneath her fingertips.

Brighton caught herself in an instant, cheeks flushed as she cleared her throat.

"Sir," she answered, sparing a quick glance past him to his reflection on the wall. The shadow of a dark beard covered a square jaw, accompanied by a prominent brow bent into a stern scowl.

Part of her wondered if he could help it, or if it was the nature of his job, but she found herself buzzing with a different feeling altogether when he spoke again, more playfully than before.

"Fancy meeting you here. Looks like lovely weather for sailing, doesn't it?" He pulled on the ends of his sleeves before brushing his fingertips through a thatch of neatly combed curls.

"It certainly does, sir." Brighton found herself smiling along with him as she watched his reflection.

He was oddly familiar, but in a way she couldn't place. The air in the lift was delightfully charged, and it only intensified when he lifted his gaze to look upon her reflection.

Brighton gasped when his face went slack, brows knit in quiet confusion as he stared back at her. "Who are you?"

"Evans. Lieutenant Evans, sir," she answered, her voice trembling as he slowly shifted on his boots, holding her reflection until his head snapped around and looked at her for real.

As soon as their eyes met, Brighton's world shifted on its axis and left her reeling as the world washed in a brilliant array of color.

Brighton brought her hand to her forehead as flashes came to her one after another. She wavered, swaying like a reed in the wind. Her breath hitched when she saw him standing beside her on white cliffs, wrapped up in colorful tartans as the wind tugged and snapped at the hem of a woolen dress.

Things shifted again. Brighton felt blinded by the brilliant shards of gold-hued sunlight. He was there, too. Smirking down at her with a cigar perched in his mouth and a sable stallion standing between them.

She felt dizzy with it, unable to keep up as the glimpses of each life came one after the other. There was the glimmer of his collectible smile at the base of a grand staircase of a magnificent ship on her maiden voyage. Flashes of a stone house on an emerald moor. And a little girl at a lakeside house, offering a tearful smile when a boy helped her snag a plateful of petit-fours.

Brighton heard her ragged breathing and rapid beating of her heart. She stepped forward, lips parting as she looked into the face of a man she knew by heart—someone she never believed existed before, but—with centuries of memories flooding her mind—she couldn't be more sure.

Eyes like cornflower and folded steel looked back at her—so sure and *so right*—flickering back and forth between hers as she brought a shaking hand to trail a ribbon of his dark hair between her fingers.

He curled his hand around her wrist, holding her firmly as he murmured, "You know me?"

His voice. His face. All so familiar to her, Brighton still couldn't quite place it—not until an echo of memory flickered through her mind.

I would know your face whether it was my second life or my hundredth. No matter where I am. Where we are. What we are doing. I'd know.

Brighton let out a stuttering sob as the realization washed over her, somewhere between an unrealized grief and the purest, unadulterated relief as she pressed her palm to his cheek. He leaned into her touch with a crinkle around his blue eyes and the smallest smile so sweet, it sent a rush of memories of precious smiles she'd collected over a lifetime. It only grew as she whispered—

"*Cain?*" Brighton's breaths came in sharp waves as the lift came to a halt and the doors split open at the end of an access corridor. "I remember *all* of it."

"It's our turn, again," he murmured, holding her face in his hands. Cain's eyes darted over every inch of her face, drinking her in as the seconds ticked by. "I've missed you so much. You're a sight for sore eyes, Brighton."

Cain lifted her chin, brushing his thumbs across her flushed, freckled cheeks as he leaned down—eyes flickering to her lips and back.

Brighton shook her head. "We can't. It's fraternization."

"I don't give a flying fuck what it is, Lieutenant," Cain growled as he blindly closed the doors with the press of a button. "I just found my soulmate after *centuries* of waiting. I made the mistake of not kissing her enough in my previous life, and was taken away from her before we ever had the chance to truly live. Now I have her, and I am going to *kiss her* every chance I can get. We'll make the rest of it a discussion for later."

"I-Is that an order, sir?" Brighton teased with a sigh, letting him guide her steps to the back wall of the elevator.

"No." Cain shook his head, working his jaw with a trembling breath of his own as he leaned down, waiting on the edge for her to make the last move.

Unable to resist any longer, Brighton bent up on the toes of her boots and brushed her lips against his.

It wasn't innocent like most first kisses were. Instead, it was steeped in a century's worth of passion, filled to the brim with every moment stolen from them in their last life, and demanding as Cain's arms wrapped firmly around her waist and lifted her feet from the floor.

Brighton twisted her fingers in his hair, pulling him closer as she deepened the kiss—knowing they didn't have much time. They settled into a rhythm all their own as their bodies spoke a language known only to them.

Brighton wanted to linger. She *needed* to bask in the taste of his kiss that comforted her in ways words couldn't begin to describe.

"Bridge to Captain Whitaker."

Cain broke their kiss with a low growl and a clench of his square jaw as he tapped the Galactic Alliance Navy insignia on his chest. "Captain speaking."

"The preliminary checks have finished, sir. Engineering reports ready for launch. We're awaiting the arrival of yourself and the helmsman. Prepped and ready to be underway."

"Don't worry. I found her." Cain gave her the smallest smile with an exasperated shake of his head.

"Aye, sir."

Cain tucked a loose strand of Brighton's hair behind her ear, leaning down to press his forehead against hers.

"Brighton . . ." He prolonged each letter like he was savoring the taste of it on his lips. Before then, Brighton wasn't sure if her name had ever sounded so sweet.

"Duty calls, *Captain*." She smiled up at him, fixing a fallen curl. "We'll make the rest a discussion for later, remember?"

Cain grinned down at her, pressing one more, breathlessly quick kiss to her lips before turning around, squaring his shoulders, and opening the door.

Brighton hovered in his periphery, holding her chin high as she watched her captain—*her soulmate*—stride onto the bridge.

"Captain on deck," the first officer called as the pair of them split off in different directions.

Brighton had been on the command bridge of other ships —each one more technologically advanced than the last. Still, nothing quite took her breath away like the brilliant shades of blue and gold shining from every surface in front of her—and the blanket of stars awaiting them beyond the viewfinder.

The eager lieutenant settled into the seat at her station, busying her fingers with a rapid list of tasks to prepare the ship to leave her docking station. Brighton was ready to see the stars stretch out before them and set off on a five-year-long adventure—at her captain's order.

Brighton practically buzzed at the anticipation of their voyage, smiling to herself when she heard Cain—*Captain Whitaker*—speak to the team at his command.

"Ladies and gentlemen, I'm not really one for long speeches. Let's buckle in and show them what the G.A.C.'s newest flagship is all about, shall we?"

The command bridge flurried with quietly confident activity as each officer did their duty, meeting every unspoken order they'd trained years to do.

"All decks, this is Captain Whitaker speaking. Prepare to go underway. Helm—thrusters."

"Thrusters fired, sir," Brighton answered as her hands flew over the digital systems beneath her fingertips, sucking in a self-assured breath as she guided the *USS Chicago* from her docking and navigated it away from Fortuna Terminal. "Successfully separated from docking station, sir."

"Good work, Lieutenant," Cain replied. Brighton swore she could hear the smile in his voice as he pressed on, "Set course for The Tiesar System."

"Aye, Captain." Brighton followed his every order to the letter, sparing a quick glance and secret smile over her shoulder. "Course laid in. Ready for warp, sir."

Brighton began her day feeling like she was on the edge of something monumental, breathlessly awaiting the adventure of a lifetime. As she glanced back at Cain once more—met with a collectible smile and a wink—it was clear to her the enterprise beginning didn't have anything to do with a starship or the exploration of unknown worlds.

It was him.

Cain gave her a nod, setting every inch of her ablaze in the span of a single look. "Punch it."

Turning her eyes to the vast unknown ahead of them, Brighton pushed forward on the thrusters and sent the stars stretching over the hull of the ship, sending them into their future in the blink of an eye.

THE END

If you enjoyed this book, please consider leaving a review on Amazon and Goodreads.

SNEAK PEEK OF...

Travel the journey from a different road with Cain, from now through the hereafter. Read on for a sneak peek of . . .

A Hundred Times Before

Cain Whitaker was a dead man.

It wasn't his first choice. So many things in his life weren't; merely a series of compromises regarding wishes coming true —all of them of the 'almost' variety. Until the moment his Range Rover careened over a river of black asphalt.

Cain's first thought as Brighton's brilliant red hair floated around her like a halo was simple.

Take me. Save her.

He was allowed a few blessed moments before the end. He thought there'd be more pain, but that came later.

Instead, he kissed Brighton one final time, taking one last glimpse of his *Glimpse* before falling away to deliver on his bargain.

The vision of her, amber eyes shining amongst a flicker of

red and blue, fading further with each blink until all Cain had was the sound of her voice breathlessly calling his name.

I'm so sorry, darling. We'll say hello again. I promise.

Cain didn't know where he was or what came after. Maybe it was a daydream, a delirious nightmare playing his memories on a loop.

They came one after the other. Each one as beautiful as the last. At the center of them, all was Brighton.

The moment he first laid eyes on her lit up Cain's world. Dream Brighton was just as colorful as he remembered, a walking rainbow and the treasure at the end all rolled into one person.

Oh yeah? Who am I gonna find to marry me?

Cain could have drowned in the sweetness of her voice at the first and only syllable she ever said to him. From the moment Brighton said '*no*' into a coupe glass, Cain Whitaker was a goner.

He blinked, and the image shifted to another brilliant wash of color in a Chicago movie theater, when Cain leaned in his seat and saw something too good to be true.

Take me away, I beg you.

There, in the feverish daydream of his memory, Cain did what he wished he'd done in life, taking Brighton in his arms the way he imagined a hundred thousand times and sealing Fate's promise with a kiss.

Cain's vision swam when the image of Brighton morphed once more, and he found himself in the golden-hued sunshine of a Chicago afternoon. The day was like any other, and the lunch hour too short . . . until he spotted a familiar head of fiery red hair and an ensemble more colorful than he'd ever seen.

Brighton was an anomaly, a vision unlike anything Cain had ever seen—one that took his breath away without effort. She always wore the most eye-catching combination of colors. That day it was a flouncing, fluffy red skirt, a bright cerulean jumper, and a coordinating pair of heels that made it *impossible* not to stare.

That was the thing, though. Cain saw past all of it. Hell, Brighton could have dressed in muted shades of grey or a burlap sack, and he'd still be able to *see* his Colour Girl.

Brighton's smile staggered his heart's rhythm, leaving him reeling when she laughed and said—

Fancy meeting you here, Kal El. You come here often?

The rose-colored memories came one after the other— flashes of the life they built together without ever knowing what they really were.

Like pictures on a reel, the image changed again.

Cain sat at El Deseo del Corazón, swirling around a whiskey, neat with a permanent smile. Even in the shadow of his and Brighton's fight, he hadn't been able to shake it. Not with the feeling of waking up with her in his arms wearing only his favorite navy jumper still fresh in his mind. Especially not after his phone pinged with a text from Andi—with a heart-stoppingly beautiful photo of Brighton as a bride.

The image sent a sheet of goosebumps down his arms and conjured another wish; one Cain couldn't banish if he tried with him at the end of an aisle and Brighton at the other. One look and everything he'd ever wondered about fell into place. One look, and Cain was *sure* all the feelings that ever buzzed in the back of his mind were *true*.

Cain didn't understand. His mind buzzed. Why show him all this at the end? What kind of reminder, what kind of lesson was it supposed to be? Was his life flashing before his eyes? Was it a gift to relive all the best bits, a chance to say goodbye before he'd never be allowed to see her again?

Maybe it was a punishment for the time they wasted. Perhaps Gandalf the Grey would stride around the corner at any moment, stroke his beard, and offer poetic advice about the things Cain couldn't change.

The image changed again, shuffling like an old-fashioned movie until it settled once more.

Only, Cain's mind didn't have him reliving moments with Brighton or show him how he wished things had gone. He wasn't allowed to stay amongst what-ifs and second chances. Instead, it gave him a glimpse of what could have been—a family painted in glorious, heartbreaking technicolor.

A little girl, with freckled cheeks and curls, spun with warm, Titian gold, toddled down a grassy, lakeside knoll. She stretched up with tiny, wriggling hands and a crinkle of her blue eyes—eyes like Cain's.

"Daddy, up?"

Cain didn't think, sweeping the toddler from her feet like he'd done it a thousand times before. She giggled—a delicate chime, like birds on a spring morning, and threw her arms around his neck.

A hundred thoughts ran through Cain's mind as he swallowed the urge to cry. Was this it? Could he stay here forever? Could this be what came after?

No, he wasn't that lucky. Any version of forever would be incomplete without Bee—even if a tiny version of her leaned back in his arms and brushed the softness of her fingers against his cheek.

Worry filled her lovely, angelic face.

"What is it, darling?" Cain brushed the copper curls from her eyes.

The little girl's smile faded further. She cast her gaze toward the tree line. Cain followed it, heart stuttering, when he spied a figure venturing up a staircase carved into the side of a hill—one he'd recognize blindfolded.

"Colour Girl?" Cain choked out, a cold sense of dread gripping his every atom. She couldn't be here; he wouldn't allow it. Otherwise, what he wished for would have all been in vain.

"*Mama cries.*" Her hands warmed Cain's cheeks. "*She 'bery sad.*"

Cain set her on her feet, unable to keep away his bittersweet smile when her tiny fingers curled around his finger. They ventured away from the quiet rush of water on the lake's edge, chasing the image of Brighton amongst the Beech and Tamarack.

He blinked, and the girl's touch evaporated, taking with it the color at the edges of his vision. It faded further and further, bleeding away the emerald from the tips of the leaves with each stair Cain climbed—until the only vision of color he had was *her*.

A vision she was. Just as in life, just the sight of her did something to Cain, tugging at every part of him until he ached to touch her. There was something different about her, though Cain couldn't put his finger on it.

Her hair shone in the spotlight *The Grey* provided, but she sagged under the weight of what he'd done. Brighton's shoulders shook as Cain had never seen. Her body was wracked with desolate cries, and he couldn't shake the feeling that it was his fault.

Cain brushed his touch over her stomach, reaching for their shared soul mark. Her breath caught, amber eyes wild when she lifted her tear-strewn face to meet his gaze.

He couldn't help but smile, caught up in the sight of her as he took her freckled cheeks—Cain's whole heart—in his hands.

Cain's joy was fleeting, shattered when Brighton choked out another sob. No matter how tightly he held her, there wasn't any preventing the way she fell to pieces.

"Why? Why are you doing this to me? Can't we—can't we go back to before? Try again? Do something differently? I can't do this without you. *I don't want to.*"

Cain opened his mouth to speak, to ease her mind and tell her—just like he promised—she wasn't alone.

Nothing came out.

No matter how Brighton pleaded or how hard she cried, Cain had no comforting words to offer. He was left with only the bitter taste of everything he wanted to say, weighing down his tongue until every ounce of color bled away.

⋈

Cain woke with a start, the remnants of Brighton's grief lingering in every atom. He rubbed his temples, blinking at a foreign ceiling.

The bedroom was unknown to him, a place he'd never seen, but he'd heard plenty of stories—regaled with tales of Andi and Bee's teenaged slumber parties. In them, he'd been told Brighton's bedroom was just as colorful as she was, with yellow walls and a rainbow quilt.

Cain didn't know how or why he ended up in her childhood home—the place he first found her—wrapped up in her memories. What he *did* know was that the walls were yellow.

There were things he'd imagined, from the photographs freckling the walls to the Orlando Bloom poster on the door, but all of it was merely the ghost of Brighton—deprived of every ounce of color with which she filled Cain's life.

The stripes in the rainbow quilt were merely shades of achromatic, ashen grey.

Cain rose to the window, snapped open the curtains, and staggered.

A dream. It had to be a dream. No—*a nightmare.* Something closer to the first circle of Hell than the place Cain ever thought he'd end up.

He was a good person. Kind, even. He couldn't imagine what he'd done to deserve what laid beyond the window.

Brighton—painted in the same, achromatic hue—laid amongst tubes and wires. Her lovely, freckled face was marred with mottled bruises and fine cuts. Her cries echoed like a siren's song, beckoning him into the depths of her pain, her sorrow—her grief.

If only he weren't already dead.

Cain pounded his fists against the pane, calling her name until he was hoarse, praying that, if he shouted loud enough, Brighton might be able to hear him from whatever great divide he found himself. Maybe, then, he might be able to comfort her the way he wanted.

After all, he was the one who did this to her. It was his wish that caused all this.

Guilt shamed him, spurring Cain to beat his knuckles against the window so hard, he thought it might break. Maybe then, he could leap through and wade his way back, take Brighton in his arms, and tell her he was sorry for ever tearing them apart.

"She can't hear you, you know."

The voice had a familiar cadence and tone, her face achingly familiar, and in it—Cain saw bits and pieces of his soulmate.

Though swathed in the muted, ashen tones of his afterlife, he knew her face, having seen it in photos atop Brighton's dresser a hundred times.

Cain swallowed. "Margot Evans? Brighton's mum?"

She smiled, leaning in the doorway. "Sort of."

His brow creased. "What do you mean, 'sort of?' Either you are, or you aren't."

Wordlessly, Margot stepped up to a wall dotted with photos of a teenaged Brighton and Andi. "I'm your guide."

"My guide?" Cain glanced at the vision of Bee in her hospital bed, heart lurching when she let out another sob, squeezing her eyes shut as the sound of the heart monitor relentlessly squawked each measured beat.

"I'm here to take you to what's next in your journey." Margot pointed at the doorway, smiling softly when the edges began to glow with an otherworldly light. It called to him, beckoning him to whatever waited on the other side.

Cain pressed his hand to the glass, gasping a shuddering sigh. "My journey is with her. I'm not going anywhere. I promised she wouldn't be alone."

"Not anymore, it isn't."

His gaze snapped to Margot, who feathered her touch around the edge of a dreamcatcher. "I don't understand."

"This is how it's done, how it's been done for a millennia. It will continue this way—the two of you will live different versions of this life from now until infinity. Until *they* decide you've had enough."

Cain shook his head. "I don't accept that."

Margot shrugged, picking at a thread in Brighton's quilt. "We don't have any choice. *You* don't have a choice. The cycle is unbreakable."

"So—" White-hot fury curled at the edges of Cain's vision. "If I have no choice, if I'm not allowed to stay here with her, what then?"

Margot smiled, an unfeeling death mask that didn't reach her eyes. "You leave. You move on. You let her live until you're called to the next life."

Cain squared his shoulders. "I can't. *I won't.*"

"They won't allow it." She shook her head. "It isn't your turn anymore."

He made a face, shaking his head. "Who's *they?*"

Margot's lovely face darkened and took the room along with it. "Death."

Cain shivered but wouldn't give in. He'd be strong. "Why? What will they do if I stay?"

"Horrible things. *Awful* things."

Cain shrugged. He wasn't afraid. He could be brave; he

would be brave. It's what he asked Brighton to do. "Whatever it is, I can handle it."

Margot's face was pained. "You won't want to. We're not meant to stay. You'll forget her; they'll make you want to forget her."

He brushed his fingers over the image of Brighton in the glass. "I could never."

"You will."

Cain's face hardened. "I won't let them."

"Maybe not now. Maybe not right away, but it *will* happen. You'll beg by the end."

Cain closed his eyes and pictured the millions of faces he'd seen over his short lifetime. None of them felt like home the way Brighton did—none of them came close. Her touch burned into his skin, and if Cain thought hard enough, he still felt the weight of her in his arms.

He'd never forget it. None of it. All of their memories were precious; the good, the bad, their love, the loss. Snowy Sundays and fresh-cut grass at Wrigley Field. The light of Brighton's smile and the taste of her kiss.

How could Cain ever forget that? How could he ever forget her?

Still, the door waited for him, illuminated around the edges. The tired floorboards of Brighton's childhood home called for him to stride over every seam and cross over into oblivion, with only the promise Cain would find her again—*someday*.

Cain wouldn't forget her. He refused. He'd whisper a reminder over and over, a remembrance that Brighton was the one. Day after day. Night after night. She was always the one. There was never anyone else but *her*.

In a hundred lifetimes or a hundred worlds. In any version of reality, I'll be here; waiting for you, loving you.

Cain pounded his chest, the promise fresh in his mind. "She's in here. I can *feel* her. They can't just take that away."

"That's just a trick; one your mind is playing on your heart. You'd be surprised what you can convince yourself of if you think about it hard enough."

"That's a cruel thing to say."

The vision of Margot lifted her chin. "That's how it is."

Cain rubbed his temples, reminded of the distant ache that took him from his Earthly home by Brighton's side. He belonged there, then. He belonged there, now.

He opened his eyes, taking one last look at Brighton through the window—another reminder that it was her, it was *always* her.

His soulmate.

"I'm staying."

"I beg you. Come with me. She'll follow, eventually." Margot drew closer and settled her hand on his shoulder. "You did everything you were supposed to, Cain. You might have loved her more than you ever have in any of the other lives. We commend you for that."

"Why can't I remember any of them?" Cain shrugged away her hand.

She offered a wistful smile. "It wasn't up to me, and it isn't my place to answer . . . it's the cycle. It's always just . . . *been decided*. That's why you need to come with me."

Cain shook his head. "I refuse."

"If you say so." Margot's face fell, the most human she looked in the few moments they had together. She opened the door, bathing the room in luminous, golden light, pausing to look one last time before disappearing on the other side. "I'm sorry."

"I'm not." Cain's jaw ached; his fists, too.

Margot pulled it shut, snuffing out the glow with one final, chilling phrase—

"You will be."

A crackle of thunder split the silence, summoning a frisson

of goosebumps down the length of Cain's arms. The ashen hue shifted, casting a sinister, crimson glow over every photograph.

Cain slid across the worn floorboard, yanking on the bedroom door, desperate for more answers from the ghost of Brighton's mother. He emerged in a hallway—stomach twisting when a musical, familiar voice called his name.

"Fancy meeting you here."

Cain chased the sound, darting through every doorway until he burst outside. A bolt of lightning cut through a blood-red sky, illuminating every shadow that beckoned him deeper.

But none called to Cain like the luminescent glow luring him to the end of a wide dock jutting out into the glassy, black surface of a lake.

He rubbed his eyes, convinced he imagined it. But there was no mistaking it. There was no mistaking *her.*

Cain's heart stuttered, rattling like a runaway train.

Margot spoke about a trick his mind would play on his heart. First, he prayed she was wrong. Then, he prayed she was right—torn between wishing for the beamingly bright vision of Brighton waiting for him at the end of the dock to be real and hoping she was still safe on Earth.

"Colour Girl?" Cain whispered, unable to keep his smile at bay. "Are you really here?"

He held his breath as she turned, gifted with one of her unforgettable smiles—painted in the same, vivid color he remembered.

"I have many names. You can call me anything you want, Kal El." Brighton cocked her head, her smile falling away into a cold smirk. "But first, we need to have a little *chat* about why *you* are here."

ACKNOWLEDGMENTS

One of my favorite author-y people, Neil Gaiman, said, "A book is a dream that you hold in your hand." It really is. One made up of hard-fought battles with myself, late nights, loud music (sorry, eardrums), and a concerning amount of coffee. At no point, ever, was I alone.

This book isn't just a dream, though—it's a love story.

Not between me and em dashes, no (are you shocked?). But one of friends, chosen family, and the people who own my heart. Without them, this would still be a far-off, very hypothetical idea of a thirteen-year-old girl.

Andrea Dryden—I could write an entire book saying how much you mean to me, and it still wouldn't be enough to properly explain how I feel. You're the Alexandria to my Brighton, the highly-caffeinated coffee to my Lorelai Gilmore, the Meredith to my Christina. My twisted sister. My *soul* sister. You were here at the beginning when the idea of writing a book was so far away, so far out of reach; it was an unattainable thing. Our friendship was instantaneous, like one of those lightning bolt moments where you say, "*Oh.* This is a person I've been looking for my entire life." I am honored to be your friend and beyond grateful to call you my biggest cheerleader. There was never a moment you didn't encourage me or push me forward. From brainstorming names, flinging around plot ideas, and sharing so much sad music, the playlist for this is over six hours long, I can honestly say this book wouldn't exist if it weren't for you. I'm not sure if *I* would exist how I am today without you, either. My love and gratitude are immeasurable.

To Brittany Weisrock, my amazing publisher, and everyone at Lake Country Press. Thank you so much for giving me a chance and giving my book a home. The way you believed in this story and believe in me still shakes my world daily. I will never be able to thank you enough for being the most incredible advocate I could ask for. Your hard work and enthusiasm are contagious, and there will never be a time when I've thanked you enough for making the dreams of that thirteen-year-old girl come true.

A huge thank you to Emily of Emily's World of Design for the unbelievably beautiful, amazing, perfect, indescribably wonderful cover. It's not at all what I imagined and everything my literal dreams are made of. My expectations were shattered the moment I saw it, and I haven't been able to stop staring (or crying) since.

To Shannon Basnett, one of my brilliant CPs. My sides still hurt from reading your comments, GIFs, and "edits" (let's not forget the alternate version where Cain sweeps the pizza and beer off the table at the bowling alley and wins Brighton's heart *right then*). Your advice and eye are invaluable. Please consider becoming an editor, because you are *incredible* at this. You shaped this book in so many ways. There's no doubt in my mind that it would not be what it is today without you. Heck, you wouldn't be reading these acknowledgments without your help.

My darling Beka Westrup, the third in our critique partner trio, and my literary sister. You and your scissors are all-knowing and all-seeing. I promise to always return the favor in whispering "*dewit*" when it comes to plot bunnies, but to reel you in when we've got shit to do. Your storytelling ability is beyond measure and breathtakingly beautiful. I look forward to seeing you fly beyond the second star to the right and straight on 'til morning.

A massive thank you so, so much to Sarah Hawley and Rance Denton for (lovingly) kicking my ass and giving me the best advice to make sure I was query-ready.

To Hannah Rastopsoff, Shana Karnes, and the rest of my Helions—you're the reason "camaraderie" is a word and the #1 reason why I advocate for everyone to have "pocket" friends. From the bottom of my heart, thank you for letting me weasel my way into your friend group. From write-ins to sprints—your company, encouragement, advice, and friendship mean the absolute world to me.

Mary Kate Adduce, one of my oldest friends. Thank you so much for putting up with me through the months where this book was the only thing I talked about, and thank you for *still* being an enthusiastic advocate for it once it was finished. It means so much to me to have someone outside of the "writer circle" feel so passionately about this project. I love you so much and wish we could go back and tell those bright-eyed high schoolers where we'd be, now. I think they'd be amazed but mostly *proud as hell.*

To Barbara Blom, Anne Lawless, and *all* English teachers. I'm afraid some of you will never know the impact you have on your students. You encouraged me to reach for my dreams and write to my heart's content. Thank you for teaching me *so* much, for pushing me to be better, and for championing me and my dreams from the very beginning.

To my parents—thank you so much for being my number one fans from the start, allowing me to go to young author retreats with a teacher, and never telling me I had too many books.

For my grandmother, Fay May Grahn, who taught me everything. The summers spent by your side in the kitchen learning the secrets to spaghetti sauce (I swear I'll never tell) and Swedish rye bread were filled with lessons I'll never forget. But none so much as the time we spent foot-to-foot in the warm afternoon light, reading as Grandpa snored in his chair and Cornish pasties baked in the oven.

To Asuna, the best ever corgi companion who always makes sure I take breaks for walks and belly scratches.

For my smallish humans, Richard, Lorelai, and Wyatt. You're getting less and less small by the day. Watching you all learn and grow has been a privilege, and having the ability to help you with your English homework feels like a win (but please continue going to Dad for the math help). It lights me up from the inside out to see you be proud of your mom. It's my greatest hope that, because you've seen how dreams *can* come true, you believe yours can, too.

And lastly, to my husband, Trever. Our meeting was something more like a literary meet-cute than something from real life. Thank you for being patient through late nights of drafting and impossibly early mornings spent editing. Thank you for running interference with our brood and for buying a bottle of champagne to keep on standby the moment I got my first full request. Most of all, thank you for providing the kindling so I could light a fire under me that burned so brightly, I had the power to shoot for the stars and get there. You will never know just how much I love you.

ABOUT THE AUTHOR

Wife. Mom. Wrangler of corgis. Self-declared real-life Poison Ivy. Mediocre crocheter. Avid music listener. Shameless geek. Kirsten spent unforgettable Michigan summers foot-to-foot with her grandmother, reading the day away.

When she isn't spinning stories and jumping genres, Kirsten can be found playfully heckling batters at Mariners games, knocking things over with her lightsaber, and obsessing over Star Wars. She lives in Seattle with her husband, three smallish-humans, and too many plants.

Follow me on Spotify and on social media:

CPSIA information can be obtained
at www.ICGtesting.com
Printed in the USA
LVHW110843130522
718693LV00003B/73